THEIR RUTHLESS SADIST

Office Intrigue, Book 5

D0871660

By Nicole Edwards

The Alluring Indulgence Series
Kaleb
Zane
Travis
Holidays with the Walker Brothers
Ethan
Braydon
Sawyer
Brendon

The Walkers of Coyote Ridge Series
Curtis
Jared
Hard to Hold
Hard to Handle
Beau

The Austin Arrows Series
Rush
Kaufman

The Club Destiny Series
Conviction
Temptation
Addicted
Seduction
Infatuation
Captivated
Devotion
Perception
Entrusted
Adored
Distraction

The Dead Heat Ranch Series
Boots Optional
Betting on Grace
Overnight Love
Jared

The Devil's Bend Series
Chasing Dreams
Vanishing Dreams

By Nicole Edwards (cont.)

The Office Intrigue Series

Office Intrigue
Intrigued Out of the Office
Their Rebellious Submissive
Their Famous Dominant
Their Ruthless Sadist

The Pier 70 Series

Reckless
Fearless
Speechless
Harmless
Clueless

The Sniper 1 Security Series

Wait for Morning
Never Say Never
Tomorrow's Too Late

The Southern Boy Mafia/Devil's Playground Series

Beautifully Brutal
Without Regret
Beautifully Loyal
Without Restraint

Standalone Novels

Unhinged Trilogy
A Million Tiny Pieces
Inked on Paper
Bad Reputation
Bad Business

Naughty Holiday Editions

2015
2016

THEIR RUTHLESS SADIST

Office intrigue, Book 5

NICOLE EDWARDS

Nicole Edwards Limited
PO Box 806
Hutto, Texas 78634

THEIR RUTHLESS SADIST – An Office Intrigue novel is a work of fiction. Names, characters, businesses, places, events and incidents either are the products of the author's imagination or used in a fictitious manner. Any resemblance to actual persons, living or dead, business establishments, events, or locales is entirely coincidental.

Cover Image: © Wander Aguiar | wanderbookclub.com
Cover model: Tug James

Cover Design: © Nicole Edwards Limited
Editing: Blue Otter Editing | blueotterediting.com

ISBN (ebook): 978-1-939786-99-9
ISBN (print): 978-1-939786-97-5

BDSM Ménage Romance
Mature Audiences

DEDICATION

TO TUG JAMES.

YOU ARE MOST DEFINITELY MY ZEKE. ONLY SWEETER.
IT'S A TRUE HONOR TO CALL YOU FRIEND.

PROLOGUE

ZEKE

THIS WAS MY SAFE HAVEN.

This was where I fit in.

This was the one place I could go where I didn't get wary eyes pinning me in place, curious as to whether I was going to do some serious damage.

I was used to those looks, the ones from strangers who weren't sure what to do with the man who didn't buy his clothes off the rack because even the big-and-tall store didn't know how to outfit six foot eight inches, two hundred eighty pounds of solid muscle.

No, here in the club, I was the giant with a sadistic streak a mile wide, a Dominant every masochist hoped would look his or her way. I was the king in this particular realm, the man who wielded all the power.

And just like every other time I was in the club, I gauged the submissive pool, wondering which of these eager fuck toys would become my plaything for the evening. I would bring at least one to tears tonight, of that I had no doubt. It was my mission, my goal in life. I wanted to break them, to hear them beg and plead, tears streaming down their faces as I brutalized them the way they fantasized about.

Some people craved sugar. I craved doling out pain.

While they were prancing around in an attempt to catch my attention, I was trying to figure out which submissive could handle me. Even if only for a few minutes. Which one I wouldn't cause irreparable damage.

I had yet to meet the one who could endure the darkest side of me. I figured one day I would find him, but I wasn't holding my breath.

"Master Zeke?"

I turned to see a sweet little fluff of a girl with wild eyes and glossy lips, weighing in at a buck five soaking wet. I knew without asking what she wanted from me. This one wanted a firm hand, someone to smack her ass and make her beg for mercy while she giggled and pleaded for more. If I had to guess, she'd heard about me, knew the pain I ached to bestow, and she hoped to experience it for herself.

I knew her type. She was too soft, too sweet. No way would she allow me to have my way with her, to treat her like a piece of furniture, to manhandle her before I breached her virgin ass with my nine-inch cock. Hell, her ass wasn't even as big as my fucking hand. I would likely fracture her if I attempted to spank her the way I needed.

She couldn't handle me on her best fucking day.

Those big eyes peered up at me full of hopeful anticipation. She wanted the big, bad Sadist to toss her around a little, then pull her close and shower her with praise and attention.

I was *not* that man.

"Sorry, sweetheart. Not in this lifetime." I shooed her away with a flick of my hand, dashing that hope in an instant. She wasn't my type.

Not only did I want a man, I *needed* a man. One with power and stamina, hide as tough as leather, an ass made to be plowed, a throat strong enough to take the brutal pounding of my cock.

A scene caught my eye and I sauntered over, crossing my arms over my chest as I stared over the heads of the other bystanders. I couldn't see the submissive's face because he was facing away from me, his hands cuffed above his head, legs spread, ankles chained to hooks in the floor. Long limbs, thick muscle, juicy ass.

It was the tattoo blazed across his back that caught my attention. A dragon rose up along his spine, wide body curling over his shoulder blade, the head disappearing on his other side, lying over his chest.

I knew this because it was a tattoo I'd seen before.

Recently, in fact.

I watched as the baby Dom laid the flogger tails across the submissive's broad shoulders, hitting hard enough to thud but not nearly hard enough to leave a mark. The submissive's body was rigid, but not from shock or pain.

"What's your color, sub?" the baby Dom questioned.

Sadist Rule One: Colors are for kindergartners.

"Green, Sir," the submissive said with a bored monotone that would've been obvious to an infant.

"You want more?" the baby Dom asked.

Sadist Rule Two: Don't ask what they want.

"Yes, Sir," he replied, no inflection in his tone.

The baby Dom swung the tails again and again, over the man's ass, the backs of his thighs. There was no power in his swing, no effort to inflict pain whatsoever. It was the equivalent of a fucking massage.

"Tell me when you've had enough," the baby Dom told the submissive.

Who the hell was this asshole and where did he think he was? This submissive wasn't here to play Twenty Questions. Dominants didn't *ask* permission, they set up the structure beforehand, had a plan and an end goal. A good Dominant didn't ask them *what* they wanted. A good Dominant merely gave it to them because that was what they needed.

After a few more swings, the baby Dom turned and I noticed he was covered in sweat. He'd been at this a while from the looks of it. His eyes met mine and I instantly recognized the respect there. I got it everywhere I went. Not because of my size, either. I'd earned it. And I'd come to expect it.

9

"Master Zeke," he said, grabbing a bottle of water while he clearly took a break.

Sadist Rule Three: A submissive should not wear out the Dom.

Yeah. Fine. I just made that one up.

I nodded to the sweaty baby Dom, but my eyes shifted back to the submissive. I could envision myself standing behind him with my whip, applying the stinging burn from the knotted ends that would have him jerking and twitching, his cock so hard he could hardly breathe from the need to come.

That thirty-five-tail deerskin flogger the baby Dom wielded was the equivalent of a feather as far as this particular masochist was concerned. An attentive Dominant would've known that.

I glanced back at the baby Dom, who was clearly out of sorts, unsure what to do to make this submissive beg.

"Hit him harder," I said, the deep rumble of my voice causing several heads to turn my way.

"What?" The baby Dom appeared confused. "I've been at it for thirty minutes. He's not in the right mindset."

Mindset, my ass. That was a Dom's excuse as to how he'd fucked up a scene.

"You're not hittin' him hard enough." I turned my attention back to the restrained man. "He's not a goddamn toddler. Hit him harder."

The baby Dom clearly didn't like that I was correcting him. Not that I gave a fuck. It was a Dominant's responsibility to see to the needs of his submissive. This fucker was failing in every respect.

"Think you can do better?" the baby Dom taunted.

I jerked my gaze over and cocked an eyebrow. This time, his tone lacked any respect whatsoever. Normally, I would shrug it off, but there was something about this situation that didn't sit right with me.

"I don't think I can. I *know.*" The crowd parted as I moved forward. When the baby Dom held out his little toy, I chuckled. "Your five-and-dime toy's useless."

The baby Dom huffed, then turned to walk away.

"Uh-uh," I snarled. "You stay and watch." I leaned in closer to him, keeping my voice low so no one else could hear. "And don't you ever disrespect me again. Understood?"

The baby Dom's eyes widened, but he managed a jerky nod.

"Good." I turned my back to him and focused my attention on the masochist.

Wanting to get a feel for the submissive's state of mind, I walked over and pressed myself against his back, leaning down and putting my mouth close to his ear.

"Tell me what you need, pretty boy."

The pretty boy's head shifted only slightly. "Pain, Zeke. I need pain."

"Do you want me to deliver it? And remember, I don't provide aftercare. I'll ensure you fly, but I won't bring you down after."

"Yes," he said on a breathless moan. "Yes, Zeke. I want you to deliver it."

"Tell me your safe word."

"Red, Zeke."

"I trust you to use it should you need it."

He nodded and I stepped back, allowing my gaze to run the length of his naked form as I retrieved the whip I had attached to my belt.

It was time to show the pussy Dom exactly how to handle a masochist.

And it was time to show this squirrelly pretty boy exactly what it meant to submit to me.

The question was…

Could the pretty boy handle it?

Later that evening…

After spending the past couple of hours keeping an eye on things in the dungeon, I opted for a break. It wasn't that I didn't enjoy watching Ransom Bishop commandeer two wayward submissives and make them beg for mercy. The man was almost as ruthless as I was. *Almost* being the key word. No one was as ruthless as me.

However, I did make it a habit to observe the technique of others. While Ransom had yet to find what he was looking for, his tastes ran alongside mine. He was looking for a male who had a penchant for the darker side of kink and he didn't waste his time with the sissies who were hoping to cuddle. I appreciated that about him.

Unfortunately, after the scene with the pretty boy earlier, I couldn't bring myself to take another submissive tonight. For whatever reason, my needs had grown exponentially as of late and I feared I couldn't slake my lust regardless. No sense wasting precious energy.

So, after passing off my monitor duties to one of the others, I headed to the bar, downed a couple of bottles of water, and kept my eye on the riffraff moving through the club. It didn't surprise me that I grew bored with that quickly.

Of course, now I had to take a piss, so I wandered through the club, up two flights of stairs, nodding my acknowledgment whenever someone greeted me.

Once I made it to the restroom, it didn't take long to relieve my bladder. As I was washing my hands, I heard a noise in the men's showers.

An interesting noise.

One that consisted of several deep groans followed by a couple of gasps, somewhat masked by the sound of running water echoing in the small stall.

Figuring some asshole had snuck his girl into the men's showers, I decided to take a look. While this was a kink club and there wasn't much they didn't allow, it was against club rules for women to be in the men's locker rooms and vice versa. They had the use of two entire floors; no sense for them to be in here.

As I moved down the rows of tile-walled shower stalls, the sounds grew louder.

"Fuck, yes. Oh, shit. Don't stop."

"Trust me, I don't plan to."

Okay, so neither of those voices were female.

I continued on until I came to the very end. The grunts and groans were coming from the other side of the plastic curtain and it didn't take long to realize there wasn't a female in there. If there was, she was being damn quiet. And based on how verbal they were being, she would be a waste of breath and space. They clearly didn't need a woman to take care of them.

Since there was no rule against men fraternizing in the showers, I started to turn and go.

"Harder, Brax. Fuck me harder. I need ... *more.*"

I stopped midstride, my spine straightening.

There was only one Brax who was a member of this club. Braxton McBride, the masochist I'd come to think of as the cowboy.

"Did he hurt you?" the cowboy asked.

And if that was the cowboy, there was only one other man who would be in there with him. Case Rhinehart. The pretty boy I'd beat on earlier.

"Yes. And it was so fucking good. But I need to come. Fuck, Brax. Make me come."

On the other side of that curtain, the cowboy and the pretty boy were releasing some pent-up energy. And the man who hurt him so fucking good was me. My ego liked that he'd admitted it.

I should've continued walking. It would've made more sense. I had no business fucking with either of them. While I couldn't deny I'd had a few raunchy fantasies about beating on them, I knew better.

But walking away wasn't an option. That wasn't the sort of man I was.

I knew what these two were looking for, and I knew for damn sure they wouldn't find it in each other. I couldn't care less if they fucked each other senseless. Sometimes, it was necessary to take the edge off. In the same sense, they would walk out of that shower still needing what the other wasn't capable of giving.

Slowly walking backward those few steps, I reached for the curtain and yanked it back, the metal rings screeching along the metal bar.

Both men's eyes flew up to me as my brain registered the scene before me: the pretty boy bent over, hands on the wall, while the cowboy stood behind him, his cock lodged to the hilt in the pretty boy's ass, his hands gripping his hips firmly.

I wouldn't be thinking of the pretty boy as Case or the cowboy as Brax. As far as I was concerned, they were fuck toys with no names.

Crossing my arms over my chest, I spread my feet wide, squared off, and stared at them. "Don't stop." I ensured they heard the command in my tone.

Neither man moved.

"Unless you intend to use your safe word? Is that the case, pretty boy?"

"No, Zeke," the pretty boy ground out, his voice edged with lust.

"Cowboy? You gonna pussy out?"

"No, Zeke." Emerald-green eyes remained locked on my face.

"I didn't give you permission to look at me," I barked and both men's eyes instantly shot elsewhere.

"Use your safe word or *fuck* him," I growled.

The cowboy swallowed hard, but he shifted his hips, driving into the pretty boy once more. The pretty boy moaned, his head dropping between his outstretched arms. I could see his cock, thick and long, hard and eager between his legs.

Fuck if that didn't turn me on in a way I didn't expect. A vision of them fucking each other senseless in my living room shot through my brain. I could certainly get used to that.

Truth be told, I'd never considered what it would be like to have more than one fuck toy at a time. Perhaps *that* was what I needed. Maybe two of them could handle one of me. The odds were certainly in my favor.

"Harder," I commanded. "Fuck him like you need him, cowboy."

I noticed the shiver that racked the cowboy's deliciously naked form as he did as I instructed. His muscles flexed, his abs rolling as he leaned over and drilled his boyfriend from behind.

"Oh, fuck," the pretty boy moaned, his hips driving back against his lover.

I didn't move from where I stood. I had no intention of helping them along. Just having me standing here was more than they deserved.

"You better ask permission before you come. *Both* of you."

Those words alone drew long, desperate moans from both of them. I fucking liked that response.

The pretty boy continued to grunt and groan while the cowboy's hips picked up speed. Having me here was intensifying their need, pushing them closer to release. They continued for several minutes and I was rather impressed. They had decent stamina, something that was required to keep up with me. I could work with that.

Hmm. Perhaps there was something to taking them in pairs. And it was clear these two were already acquainted with one another.

"Oh, fuck," the pretty boy yelled. "Oh, fuck ... Zeke ... Fuck. May I come, Zeke?"

Just hearing the plea in his tone made my cock swell.

"No, you may not."

The pretty boy groaned, his disappointment evident. He was so close. I wasn't sure how long he'd be able to hold out, but I was curious to find out.

The cowboy's fingers dug into the pretty boy's muscular hips as he drove forward, retreated, slammed forward again and again. I noticed he was bareback, which meant these two were close. Obviously there was a certain level of trust between them. I liked that, too.

The cowboy was enjoying having his dick buried in the pretty boy's ass if his grunts were any indication.

"Stop!" I bellowed.

The cowboy instantly stopped jerking the pretty boy to him as he filled him one last time.

"Turn and face me. Both of you," I commanded.

After pulling out of the pretty boy's ass, the cowboy turned. He stood tall, his legs shaking, those dark green eyes wild.

"Jack off for me. And you *do* have permission to come. But you've only got fifteen seconds to do it."

They didn't need fifteen seconds. Their hands had barely wrapped around their own shafts when they exploded. I was tempted to make them lick their jizz up off the floor. Had we been at my house, I would have. After all, humiliation was my specialty.

I didn't have to remind them they weren't allowed to look at me. Their eyes remained obediently down on the floor.

"What do you say?" I asked.

They both spoke at once. "Thank you, Zeke."

It was my turn to swallow hard as I stared at them. I'd gotten to know these two a little in recent weeks. I knew for a fact they could fuck each other ten times a day and they'd never find what they were looking for.

The sex alone would never be enough.

I could only hope they could handle what I had in store for them, because for the first time in my life, I was pretty damn sure I'd found exactly what I needed.

Now we would have to see how long it would last.

ONE

ZEKE

One week later
Friday, October 12

I GRINNED AS I LOWERED the dumbbell, my eyes fixed on the shift of my bicep before I raised the weight again. The sudden disappearance of music caused my ears to ring in the silence, but I didn't allow it to derail my attention.

"How can you listen to that angry-man music?" a sweet, chipper voice called from across the room. "It's far too early for so much … *noise*, Zeke."

"Noise, my ass." I chuckled. "The band is Underoath, the song is 'Rapture.' And there's nothing angry about it," I assured my kid sister when she skipped across the room, a huge grin on her wide mouth.

"Whatever you gotta tell yourself, big brother." Jamie nodded toward the weight in my hand. "Pretty soon you'll have to graduate to lifting appliances."

"Well, I won't be doing it while listening to Lifehouse, that's for damn sure."

Jamie giggled. "I happen to prefer Imagine Dragons, thank you very much."

Keeping my focus, I finished my set and placed the dumbbell back on the rack. "Why are you bothering me on a Friday morning?"

My sister rolled her big brown eyes, something she'd gotten eerily good at over the years. "Because I show up *every* Friday morning, goober. You owe me breakfast."

A deep, rumbling laugh came out of me. "*Owe* you? Why would I *owe* you anything?"

I couldn't help but smile at the little girl. Granted, at six foot even, my twenty-four-year-old sister wasn't all that little anymore. However, as far as I was concerned, Jamie would always be that sweet kid with the pigtails and worshipful eyes, who insisted on following me around even when I threatened bodily harm. Not that I ever would've harmed a hair on that kid's head, but she hadn't known that.

"Where's Tank?" she asked, her gaze scanning the basement that I'd set up as my personal play space. To most people, it appeared to be a home gym, but I was privy to the other toys that discreetly filled the space.

"Probably upstairs," I told her.

"He doesn't like the angry-man music either?"

I reached for her, but Jamie danced out of the way, giggling like a little kid.

"Uh-uh. Don't you touch me, you big, sweaty beast." She put another foot between us. "So, where're you taking me for breakfast?"

"Your choice," I told her after grabbing a towel and wiping my face. "Let me shower and we'll head out. You mind feeding Tank?"

"Nope, I don't mind," she said cheerfully before bolting up the stairs.

I found myself smiling as I followed the far-too-chipper-for-six-in-the-morning girl up to the main floor.

Fifty minutes later, I was strolling into the small diner with Jamie on my arm. She waved at the familiar faces as we headed to the booth in the far back. The girl had never met a stranger in her life. Everyone in this little hole-in-the-wall likely knew her life story—something I wasn't exactly happy about. There was something to be said for discretion. However, Jamie was the sort who talked to anyone who would chat with her. A gene I didn't share with her, that was for sure.

My kid sister had somehow wrangled me into treating her to breakfast every Friday. While I offered to take her to any damn restaurant in the city, the girl insisted on this diner. Said they had the best waffles in the world. I'd have to take her word for it. I preferred meat.

After we were seated, the waitress came over to confirm our order, wanting to ensure we hadn't changed it after nearly four years of coming here week in and week out ordering the exact same thing every time. Ever since my breakup with the first and only guy I'd ever truly committed myself to, Jamie had made a point to keep me company even on the days I insisted it wasn't necessary.

"Thanks, Bev," Jamie called out when the waitress shuffled to the next table. My kid sister turned to me. "She likes flirting with you."

I grunted. A lot of women flirted with me. "Who? The waitress?"

Jamie rolled her eyes. "Her name's Beverly and she's been waiting on us for three years, Zeke."

"Names are irrelevant," I told her.

"I know, I know." She sighed. "Less personal that way. Plus, she's not your type."

My baby sister knew I wasn't into women. Never had been, never would be. I didn't make excuses for it. I lived my life how I wanted to live it. I spent time with those I wanted to spend time with. And no one could or would sway me otherwise.

"How's school?" I asked, following the same pattern we'd fallen into for as long as I could remember. I would ask how school was, she would say good, and then we could get on to the real reason she was here. Jamie *always* had a reason.

"Good," she said, smiling up at the waitress when she placed a cup of coffee in front of me and apple juice in front of Jamie.

Rather than shoot me a wide grin and ask some off-the-wall question she'd been pondering for the past week, such as *What do you think of self-actualization?* Or *How does the mind-body connection affect our emotions?*—my kid sister was a psychology major—Jamie turned far too much attention on her apple juice.

"Spit it out, kid."

Those big brown eyes lifted to mine and I knew that whatever was about to come out of her mouth was not going to be good. I wouldn't get lucky enough to debate nature versus nurture with her. I knew her better than she knew herself and that gleam in her eye was the equivalent of a semaphore flag.

Considering our parents died when I was sixteen—Jamie was six—I'd spent more than half my life raising her. Not solely, of course. When our folks went out to celebrate their seventeenth wedding anniversary and never came home thanks to a drunk driver causing a three-car pileup involving his truck, our parents' car, and a semi, Jamie and I had gone to live with our maternal grandfather.

I'd grown up close to Oma and Opa, spending plenty of time there when I was little. Oma had passed away when I was fourteen from complications after a heart attack, leaving the rest of us reeling. Although still mourning the love of his life, Opa had done right by us, taking us in and doing everything a seventy-six-year-old man was capable of doing for a couple of distraught young kids. To thank him for sacrificing so much for us, I had taken care of the man until he died a year and a half ago. I still missed him. Hell, I missed all of them.

But I still had Jamie. We were the only family each of us had and we'd forged a bond over the years.

"I have a favor to ask," Jamie prompted, her eyes still glued to her glass.

I picked up the coffee mug, aware once again that it was the equivalent of a child's teacup in my giant hand. "What favor?"

I leveled my stare on her, waiting for her to reveal whatever devious scheme she had in the works. Admittedly, Jamie was a good kid. During her teenage years, rather than chase boys, she had focused on her classes, keeping her grades up. Every night, she would regale me and Opa with stories of all the shit she'd learned. She'd graduated high school top in her class, then gone on to college with academic scholarships. And now she was working toward her master's degree in psychology of all things. Of course, that wouldn't be enough for Jamie. She had every intention of going on to get her doctoral degree as well.

Jamie stared at her apple juice, wiping the condensation from her glass. "I was thinking maybe I could…"

The girl knew I would do damn near anything for her. The fact she was having a hard time spitting it out bothered me. It was usually the precursor to something I was not going to like.

"What is it, kid?" I used the rough, no-nonsense tone I used with irritating submissives.

She heaved out a breath as she sat up straight. Her words came out in a mad rush. "I was thinking maybe I could go to the club with you. You know, just to check it out. See what it's all about. Maybe—"

Well, hell. That was easier than I'd expected. "No."

She huffed, her breath causing her bangs to flop on her forehead. "Come *on*, Zeke. You didn't even think about it."

"You're right. I'm sorry." I took a sip of my coffee and pretended to consider it. "Still no."

Absolutely no way in hell was I letting that kid in a kink club.

She flopped back and fiddled with her spoon while trying to kill me with a glare. "Why not?"

I lowered my voice and leaned forward. "Because I'm a misogynistic, hypocritical asshole who thinks you have absolutely no business in a BDSM club."

Jamie rolled her eyes "Pfft. Nice try. I know you better than that."

I shrugged. "Not gonna happen, kid."

Her eyes narrowed and she mirrored my position, sitting up straight and cocking her angled chin up. "You know I don't actually have to *ask* your permission, right?"

I didn't respond, swallowing half of my lukewarm coffee.

"I'm twenty-four years old, Zeke. I can go to any club I want."

I took a sip and glanced out the window, pretending to be ignoring her.

"There's another club right down—"

I slammed my coffee cup on the table and leaned forward again. "Don't you dare go to that club, Jamie."

"Why *not*?" She had an extra amount of whine in her tone that time. "If you won't let me in Dichotomy, I have to go somewhere. Razor Wire's as good a place as any."

A strange sensation filled my chest. Disbelief mixed with anger. How could she be so damn naive?

"It may not be as nice, Zeke, but—"

"They had two women file *rape* charges against the owner, Jamie," I stated firmly, trying to keep my anger in check. "Don't you go anywhere near that fucking shit hole."

The waitress appeared and I sat up slowly, never taking my eyes off my sister. I could see her brain working, knew she was trying to come up with an argument.

I waited until our food was in front of us and the waitress had refilled my coffee cup before I leaned close to my baby sister again.

"You have *no* idea what goes on in those clubs."

She huffed a laugh but there was no humor in it. "Trust me, I know. That's why I want to go." She narrowed her eyes. "So I can find out."

"No you don't." This was a stupid conversation. I couldn't believe I'd allowed her to drag me into it.

She frowned. "So, why's it okay for you but not me, huh?" It was obvious she was pissed. "Have you ever thought that maybe I have the same cravings you do?"

I shook my head, thoroughly dislodging every one of those words before they could take root. My kid sister wasn't allowed to have sexual cravings. Not now. Not ever. And certainly not like mine.

"It's not like I'm a virgin, Zeke."

I slammed my hand down on the table, causing the silverware to bounce and drawing attention from several people sitting around us. One man cast a concerned glance my way. I didn't necessarily blame him. While Jamie might've gotten some of the height genes from our father's side of the family, I still towered over her, dwarfing her with my bulk.

"We're not talking about this, Jamie. The answer's no. And don't you dare go to that … that *brothel* down the road."

My sister watched me and I knew without a doubt she was considering doing something stupid.

"I mean it, Jamie."

"Fine," she said, grabbing her fork. "Now eat your breakfast before it gets cold."

After thinking about my kid sister in a kink club, I wasn't sure I could ever eat again.

Brax
(The cowboy)

MOVING SUCKED. LIKE, SERIOUSLY FUCKING sucked.

It was made all the worse when you were moving damn near across the country. Granted, this wasn't the first time I'd been uprooted only to move several states away from the place I'd called home. My parents had left North Carolina when I was twelve. I never understood why they opted for the blistering heat of Texas but that was where we ended up and I hadn't had a say in the matter back then.

This move was different. For one, I got to make the decision. Well, not only me, but Case hadn't put up a fight when we received the offer to relocate our lives from Texas to Illinois.

Did you know that the driving distance from Dallas to Chicago was roughly nine hundred sixty miles? Well, it was. And of those miles, I'd just driven all of them.

Yes.

All.

Of.

Them.

Because Case was a diva, and somewhere during our years of friendship and routine sexual encounters, the diva had come to the conclusion that I was his chauffeur. And his chef, and his maid. And his… Well, you get the idea. Having spent the past twenty-six months with Case, in the most passionate relationship of my entire life, I'd gotten used to doing things for him. And yes, he returned the favor because that was how we made it work.

Not that I minded driving. I'd seen Case's skills behind the wheel, or lack thereof. Unless you were a NASCAR fan or one of those people who drove the Autobahn on a daily basis, I didn't recommend it. Since my desire to actually *make it* to the Windy City was rather great, I hadn't argued too much.

"How much longer?" Case grumbled from the passenger seat as he wiped his eyes and peered up through the window, his thick neck straining to hold his head up.

And *why* couldn't he sleep for the last ten miles of the trip?

"Depends," I told him as I set my now cold coffee in the cup holder.

He frowned, his dark eyebrows darting down toward his nose. "On?"

All right. I had to admit the man was ridiculously appealing to the human eye. All those sleek muscles and the enormous dragon tattoo that somehow defined the beautiful planes and angles were definitely my cup of tea. I'd spent my fair share of time trying to memorize every inch of his six-foot-three-inch frame with my tongue.

And perhaps the reason I tolerated his inner diva was because I happened to be in love with the guy.

Love or not, he still irritated the shit out of me at times. Especially after I'd spent the better part of the past two days sealed in a car with him.

"Whether or not I kick your ass out and make you walk the rest of the way," I told him, my drawl thicker than usual due to my exhausted state.

His head jerked toward me and I could see the concern there. He was trying to determine how close to the rocky edge of sanity I was hovering.

I could admit it. I was cranky. I was tired. And I was damn sick of being in this damn car. I needed to stretch my legs and more coffee certainly wouldn't hurt.

Case chuckled as he pressed the button to lift his seat. "Well, we can't have that, now can we?" His hand slid over and patted my thigh. "I'll keep you company the rest of the way."

If you knew Case, you'd understand the threat those words implied.

"It's twelve thirty," he noted. "I thought you said we'd be there by now."

I cast a quick look his way. His dark hair was as pristine as it always was. No bedhead for him. Then again, Case didn't have any hair to muss because he kept it military short for whatever reason. His iridescent green eyes were filled with amusement, as always.

"You know, if it weren't for the exquisite blow jobs, I would've kicked your ass to the curb a long time ago," I huffed even as I grinned. His blow jobs *were* exquisite and the rest of him wasn't too bad, either.

He leaned his head back and turned it my direction, those hooded eyes fixed on me. "I do give good blow jobs, huh?"

My cock certainly thought so, proven by the way it was hardening in my jeans. "Don't let it go to your head."

"Or yours?" He slid his hand up my thigh, his fingers brushing my cock through the denim. "Never mind." He chuckled. "Too late."

I instantly thought of the ruthless Sadist who had become a fixture in my head for the past … month? Two? Ever since that damn flight from Dallas to Chicago when Zeke Lautner commanded us to strip and kneel before him, I hadn't been able to get him out of my head. He was taking up too damn much space, taunting me with that evil smirk and those *Prince of Darkness* black eyes.

Perhaps some people might consider my fascination with the six-foot-eight-inch beast of a man a form of cheating. Technically Case and I were in an exclusive relationship, so I could understand how it appeared from someone else's viewpoint.

However, I wasn't cheating. Nor was my brain.

Did I mention my boyfriend was quite taken by the giant Sadist as well? Well, he was. As much as I was, in fact. And neither of us was jealous, because there was nothing to be jealous of. Zeke Lautner was a man who could give Case and me something we couldn't give each other. He was also one of the reasons we were eager to get to Chicago.

"When's the moving truck gonna be here?" Case asked, arching his back as he stretched that damn T-shirt in a manner that had my cock stirring again.

"Not till next Thursday. Hope you brought your toothbrush."

Case scrubbed a hand over his face, the rasp of his stubble loud in the car. "I only used yours because I couldn't find mine. I told you, it's in my bag somewhere. But I didn't pack a razor." He glanced my way again. "Gonna need to go to the store."

"Not until we're in the apartment. You can go wherever you need to after that."

As for me, I was going to sleep for a couple of days. Screw shaving.

Our belongings were being brought via the boys with the big trucks. They had everything we owned, including Case's Ford F250. It had taken some finagling, but I'd finally convinced him we couldn't drive the gas guzzler across the country. He didn't like that I was right, but he'd finally accepted it.

At that point, Case and I had packed up the necessities, loaded everything into my Chevy Traverse, and hit the open road. After one night in a cheap motel with a crappy mattress and an equally crappy continental breakfast of stale biscuits, overcooked bacon, and green bananas, we were on the final leg of this journey. I could see the Chicago skyline in the distance.

"I really don't want to live in a damn apartment," Case griped, not for the first time. "When we checked it out, I felt like the walls were closing in."

"Not much of a choice. They offered us free rent." Who could pass that up? More importantly, who *would* pass that up?

"I know. But I'm claustrophobic, Brax. I need air."

He always did have a flair for the dramatic.

"There's air in an apartment. And you are *not* claustrophobic."

"Stale air, maybe. And I've got an aversion to concrete. I'll lose my shit living in the city."

"Which is it? You can't have both."

"Sure I can," he said firmly. "I hate the city."

I sighed heavily, gripping the wheel with both hands as we slowed to a snail's pace in the thick traffic.

We'd had this conversation a dozen times since we were offered this opportunity. Honestly, I'd thought being Trent Ramsey's personal chef was quite an accomplishment. Cooking for an A-list actor wasn't exactly my dream job, but I didn't have any complaints. The guy paid me handsomely, and he was easy to work for, not to mention easy on the eyes. On top of that, he valued what I had to offer him. He wasn't the bologna-and-cheese kind of guy, that was for damn sure. And because of all the time I'd spent with him, he'd become a good friend to both Case and me over the years.

Needless to say, it had come as quite a shock when the partners of Chatter PR Global informed me they wanted me to be the head chef at a new restaurant they were opening. Apparently, owning one of the biggest public relations firms in the world wasn't enough for these guys. They were venturing off in many different directions, and somewhere along the way, they'd come up with the idea of opening a restaurant in downtown Chicago, cuisine to be determined by me.

Who the fuck would turn *that* down? This was what I'd spent most of my adult life dreaming about. A restaurant of my own.

And to sweeten the pot, they'd offered Case—who happened to be Trent Ramsey's personal trainer/nutritionist—a job managing the gym they were installing on the second and third floors, in the same building where Chatter PR Global resided. It was supposed to be some fancy place that served protein smoothies to go along with bicep curls, sprinting on the treadmill, and pruning in the sauna. They would be open to the public and the hundreds of residents of that building would get free memberships.

Of course, accepting a couple of dream jobs had been easier considering Trent was the one who set it all up in the first place. With Trent officially bringing his latest business venture—his own talent agency—to Chi-Town, the man wouldn't be far away. I seriously doubted the partners would've pilfered us otherwise. While Trent insisted we'd gotten the opportunities based on our own merit, I knew it didn't hurt that Trent had gone into business with the firm.

And until the day the restaurant opened, I would continue my role as Trent's personal chef while I gave my two cents on what needed to go into the elaborate kitchen of the new restaurant.

Just the thought made some of the exhaustion evaporate, filling me with a sense of genuine excitement. I was ready for the next phase of our lives. I looked forward to the idea of exploring a new city with the man I loved.

And maybe, if we were lucky, we'd get to explore a few other things as well.

TWO

ZEKE

"TELL ME WHAT IT IS you're looking for," I said around the frustration coming to a rapid boil in my gut.

"That's not my department," Everett Knowles the Third—*who the fuck introduces himself like that?*—said, his snooty tone wearing on me. "I'm merely passing on the information. I was told we need to enhance our firewalls. I found you through a Google search."

Great. The guy knew how to use the Internet at least. I wanted to ask the smug bastard to explain to me what he thought a firewall was. Fortunately for him, I didn't have the patience for it today.

With a deep sigh, I sat up straight in my chair and tapped on the keyboard. "I can get by there in a couple of weeks. My schedule's booked next week, but the week after looks good. Probably Wednesday or Thursday afternoon."

"Probably?" He sounded skeptical.

Did I stutter? Was I slurring my words?

I didn't respond because it would've ended badly.

"I'm an executive here," the snooty man said, his tone translating to: *I am God in a cheap brown suit.* "I don't have time for *probably.*"

"How about never?" I suggested, tired of this pissing match. It was obvious the *executive* at the five-person temp agency thought far too highly of himself.

There was a brief pause followed by, "Okay. Wednesday it is. I'll let the boys know you're coming."

"Should I ask for you?" *God, tell me I won't be working with this jackass.*

"Oh, heavens no. Like I said, I'm busy."

Yep, busy keeping your chair warm with your lazy ass.

"Ask for Peter Jones," he said. "He's the one who asked me to call."

I had to wonder whether or not Peter Jones knew how to use a phone. We could've accomplished a hell of a lot more if he did.

I jotted down the name on my notepad. "What's his number? I'll call him beforehand to ensure I'm not wasting my time."

The man cleared his throat as though I couldn't possibly have said that. They didn't pay me the big bucks to be some wannabe bigwig's pansy-assed bitch. If I was going to put forth the effort, I would ensure they knew who was in charge.

"If this isn't something you're equipped to handle, Mr. Lautner, perhaps I should speak to your supervisor."

"I *am* my supervisor," I said, keeping my tone firm, the rough edge noticeable. "But if you'd rather call someone else, I've got plenty of shit to do. You were the one who called *me*, remember?"

I could tell you, Chatter PR Global did not hire me for my customer service skills. I was good at what I did—cybersecurity—and the companies I'd already brought on board in the short time I'd been here knew that. However, they learned quickly that I didn't waste time with the political bullshit. Ask for my supervisor and you'd get my size-sixteen boot right up your ass.

Thankfully, the man wised up and rattled off the knowledgeable one's number.

"Great. I'll call him and set something up."

"Fine."

I didn't bother with the social niceties, either, which was why I hung up the phone and leaned back in my chair.

"Tank, I think I'm gonna need some stress relief tonight, boy. Dichotomy's calling my name. You're gonna be home by yourself for a bit. Hope you don't mind."

My four-year-old yellow Labrador retriever lifted his head from where it rested on the couch cushion.

I thought back to my breakfast conversation with Jamie that morning. I'd reiterated my point several more times before we parted ways, but I got the feeling she was going to defy me. Perhaps I should lock her in the house with Tank. They could keep each other company.

Tank's nose twitched as though he could read my thoughts.

"Don't worry, I'll make sure you get dinner first," I told him.

His big head flopped back onto the cushion. Provided I fed him and spent at least two hours a day throwing the ball, Tank didn't usually complain.

"That's what I thought." I picked up my pen and spun it between my fingers.

I spent a lot of time talking to my dog and I didn't apologize for it. Tank had come into my life when he was little more than a sack of fur and fumbling paws. I hadn't been in the market for a dog when my kid sister showed up on my doorstep cuddling him close. According to Jamie, she'd found him wandering our grandfather's neighborhood during one of her weekend trips home from college. I found it damn near impossible to tell the girl no, so I had told the then twenty-year-old that I would allow Tank to be my best friend.

That was how Tank and I came about.

Turned out, Jamie hadn't found Tank anywhere. She'd gone in search of him specifically for me after my shitty breakup, hoping Tank could fill the void no one else could. Since she knew me well, she'd concocted the story to appeal to my softer side—she insisted I had one no matter how much argument I gave her. By the time I learned of her evil, *evil* ways, Tank and I had been together for two years and already bonded.

Now, I wouldn't know what to do without him.

A knock sounded on my door and I looked up to see Benjamin Snowden—one of the partners in the company—standing in the doorway.

"What's up?" I asked, spinning around to face him.

He stepped inside and passed over a sheet of paper. "I've got a new client who's interested in talking to you."

"Please tell me it's not the self-appointed CEO," I grumbled as he set the paper down.

His dark eyebrows shot downward, his forehead creasing. "No. Why?"

I smirked. "No offense, but I prefer to talk to those who know what they're doing."

Ben chuckled. "I assure you, the CEO—and he's not self-appointed—knows what he's doing. However, he also knows that he pays people to handle this sort of thing." He motioned toward the paper. "That's the head of their cybersecurity division. They had an incident recently and they'd like a second opinion."

Fuck. I really needed to hire some people to handle this shit for me. I'd been given the go-ahead by the big dogs, but I hadn't yet found the time. Plus, I didn't care for people all that much and hiring a few would mean I'd have to deal with them.

"He local?" I asked, glancing down at the chicken scratch scrawled across the paper.

"Valparaiso, Indiana," Ben said as he squatted down to pat Tank, who had ambled over to see who I was talking to. As he rubbed Tank's wide head, Ben's eerie gold eyes shot up to my face. "I heard Addison's been sneaking him treats."

I laughed. "Yep. She's bribing him. I told her it wouldn't work."

"I wouldn't bet money on that," Ben said as he got to his feet. "She's quite gifted at getting what she wants."

Most submissives were, I'd learned.

"You gonna be here this afternoon?" he asked.

"Planned on it. Why?"

"We've got a contractor coming by for the restaurant. I've got a meeting at three, Mr. Parker's out of town until tomorrow, and Langston and Landon are cutting out at lunch. Need someone to meet with them."

"Yeah. Sure. What do you need me to do?"

"Probably nothing. Brax should be here by then, but I'll need someone to keep them in line. While we've given Brax carte blanche, I need a level head there to ensure he doesn't go overboard."

I nodded my head even as my cock jumped to attention at the mere mention of the cowboy's name.

"He in town again?" I asked casually.

"This time for good," Ben confirmed. "They're driving in today." He glanced at his watch. "Should be stopping by to get the keys to the apartment any minute now. Speaking of," he said as he reached into his pocket. "Think you could pass these over to them when they get here?"

He held out a key ring that had two gold keys dangling from it.

"I promised Addison I'd take her to lunch. She tends to get antsy when Mr. Parker's out of the office."

I wasn't sure Addison was the only submissive who got antsy when their Master was away. Ben wasn't as good at hiding it as he thought he was. The switch had a soft spot for both his Dom and his submissive.

"Yep." I reached for the keys, letting the ring slide down my finger before twirling them. "I'll make sure they get them."

Ben's golden gaze met mine. "Be nice to them, Zeke."

A wicked smirk pulled at my lips before I could hold it back. "You've got my word. I won't give 'em anything they don't deserve."

Ben rolled his eyes and chuckled. "Sometimes I wonder if they knew what they were in for taking these jobs."

Oh, they knew, all right. Because I'd mentioned it last Monday, when they were here to scope out the apartment Chatter had so graciously offered them. I was oddly intrigued that they'd actually accepted the offers. That meant they would be here indefinitely.

My body hardened when I thought about that day.

Holding Tank's leash with a firm grip, I waited until the elevator emptied before I stepped on and punched the button to get me up to the thirty-second floor. Just as the doors were closing, I heard someone yell for me to hold it.

I didn't. No one had ever accused me of being chivalrous. They could wait for the next one.

Before the doors could completely shut, a hand reached in to stop them.

After briefly considering breaking those interrupting fingers, I sighed as I took a step to the side, offering some room. It didn't make much difference. My frame filled the majority of the small, cramped space no matter where I stood.

The two men who appeared when the doors fully retracted had my entire body humming with approval. I wasn't sure what it was about the cowboy and the pretty boy that heated my blood and made me want to do wickedly dirty things to them, but there was something. I'd felt it since the day I encountered them on Trent Ramsey's private jet. The two masochists had somehow wriggled into my subconscious and it'd been hell not thinking about them since.

"Zeke," the pretty boy said as he stepped on and moved to the opposite side of the elevator.

I didn't respond.

The cowboy wasn't quite as chatty. After he punched the button for the thirty-third floor, his emerald-green eyes lifted to my face but instantly dropped. I had to wonder if he was thinking about what happened on Friday night, when I'd caught them fucking in the shower at the club.

The doors finally closed, sealing the three of us inside. Tank whimpered and I glanced down to see his tail wagging so hard his ass was bouncing back and forth.

"Greet them, boy," I ordered the dog.

Tank was instantly on his feet as he moved closer. I watched as both men smiled widely before showering my dog with stupid greetings and full-body pats. It would've helped if they hadn't taken to my dog. I didn't need a reason to like them and the fact they liked Tank didn't help.

"Enough," I barked a few seconds later.

Following my command, Tank backed up until he was heeling at my feet while the cowboy and the pretty boy stood stone-still, their eyes dropping to the floor.

Good to know that command worked on more than my dog.

"What're you here for?" I asked, wondering which of them would be brave enough to speak.

The pretty boy was the one to lift his head. "Justin asked us to look at a couple of apartments."

I allowed my gaze to trail over the dragon peeking out from beneath the neck of his tight T-shirt. "For?"

"Temporary residence," he said, although it sounded more like a question. "We've accepted the job offers and we're moving here at the end of the week."

"What does Trent think of you abandoning him?" I questioned.

The pretty boy grinned. "We're still employed by him. Will be until everything's up and running. It'll probably be a year before we're needed in our new roles."

"A year, huh? And you'll be here in Chicago?"

"Yes," the pretty boy said, his eyes heating. He evidently knew the route my brain had taken.

"Good. I can think of a few things to keep you busy."

"Really?" The pretty boy looked far too hopeful.

"Provided you don't mind being naked and on all fours for a majority of the time. I can think of at least a few dozen ways to use you for my own benefit."

They'd lucked out that day. I didn't require either of them to give me an answer or to crawl around on all fours to interview for the position because the elevators had opened on my floor and I'd stepped out without a word, leaving them to take care of their business.

What I'd wanted to do was have them come into my office so I could pick up where we'd left off at the club the Friday before.

Looked as though I was going to get the opportunity to do so now.

I let my eyes stray to the floor-to-ceiling windows and the building that was directly across from me. I wondered what those old boys across the way would think if they saw a couple of naked masochists posing as furniture in my office.

I glanced at the keys and smiled.

Yeah. This might end up being a good day after all.

Case
(The pretty boy)

"AH, CHRIST! THERE'S CONCRETE EVERYWHERE, Brax. I'm gonna lose my mind." I gripped my head dramatically because what else was I going to do? Somehow I had to make Brax feel my pain.

"We're in a parking garage," he stated, not giving in to my drama.

"It's not any better on the street," I said as I pulled my sunglasses over my eyes when we stepped out of the shaded parking area. It didn't make much of a difference because the brilliant Chicago sun was blocked out by all the surrounding concrete.

I should've felt bad for giving him shit, but I didn't. I knew Brax was exhausted after that hellacious road trip. So was I and I'd taken plenty of naps throughout. In my defense, I wasn't a huge Florida Georgia Line fan (I preferred Brantley Gilbert), but the man I'd fallen in love with was. So, in an effort to save myself from wanting to jump out of a moving vehicle, I'd feigned sleep until it finally caught on.

"Who has the key to the apartment?" I asked Brax as we stepped into the building. We were surrounded by marble and chrome, straight lines and stale air.

I am officially in big city hell.

"Ben said he'd have it."

"Mind if we stop at the restroom before we head up?" I motioned toward the back of the building, past all the gleaming black marble, fancy fixtures, and suits wandering around aimlessly.

Brax sighed as though he was put out. "Fine."

The man had been downing coffee like it was nearing extinction, so I didn't buy for a minute that he wasn't in need of the facilities.

A few minutes later, feeling ten pounds lighter, I emerged from the restroom and waited for Brax to finish with his pretty-boy routine.

I grinned to myself. I found it ironic that Zeke had taken to calling me pretty boy instead of Brax. Granted, there was a hint of condescension in his tone when he did it, so I wasn't mistaking it for a compliment. Still, it amused me to no end.

I'd never been called pretty in my life, and believe it or not, I wasn't the sort to prance around in hopes someone would check me out. That came naturally and it had nothing to do with ego. At six foot three, two-hundred twenty pounds of solid muscle, I got the stares without even trying. I was a big man and I worked damn hard to keep it that way. The single dragon tattoo that adorned the upper half of my body garnered some attention as well.

But I was no pretty boy. However, there was something erotic about the way Zeke said it, so I wasn't complaining.

The truth was, Brax was the pretty one in the relationship. With his perfectly mussed golden-brown hair, those emerald-green eyes, and the baby face, he looked roughly ten years younger than he was. Which was saying something considering he was all of twenty-seven. Most people figured him for a teenager.

He damn sure wasn't a teenager. I could vouch for that.

The men's room door opened and Brax stepped out, pressing his Stetson firmly on his head while those curious eyes scanned the space around him.

Fine. With the cowboy hat and those sexy-as-fuck Wrangler jeans and boots, he didn't look like a teenager. He looked like a man you wanted to strip naked and engage in some wild and kinky sex. For the record, I'd done that plenty of times.

"You ready?" I asked, pretending I was tired of standing around waiting for him.

He turned to me, a serious expression on his face. "You have to be on your best behavior, Case."

I frowned. "Me? Why wouldn't I be?"

"Because the last time we were here, you got Addison in trouble. That girl doesn't need any more trouble."

I chuckled. "No, that girl *lives* for trouble. I didn't do anything. She used me as an excuse to get her ass paddled by her Doms."

"You locked her out of her office," he declared.

"No I didn't. She did. I merely engaged the lock. She was the one who shut the door."

Brax rolled his eyes, then pivoted toward the elevator.

"You think Zeke's here?" I didn't want to voice the question, but I had to get it out there. That damn Sadist was all I could think about these days.

"Not if we're lucky," Brax said, his voice pitched low.

I knew Brax was looking forward to seeing Zeke every bit as much as I was. Perhaps more. Okay, maybe not more. Ever since that damn scene at Dichotomy, when Zeke had whipped me right into subspace, my dick had been perpetually hard. No matter how often I came—by my own hand or Brax's phenomenal ass or mouth—it didn't seem to help. I wanted what Zeke Lautner could give me. *Us.*

Since the day I met Brax, I had never questioned what I found so appealing about another submissive. He was one of the greatest men I'd ever met. Wicked smart, eerily attentive. ridiculously attractive, and damn good in the sack. Those were all qualities that appealed to me. However, he was a masochist like me. He wanted someone to give him pain, not to offer it.

Insert Zeke Lautner. Big, brooding, and brutal. All the things I longed for in a Sadist. Brax and I agreed that Zeke was the only man who could give us what we needed. While I was content with the status of my relationship with Brax—I loved the man, for fuck's sake—we both knew we needed more than what we could give each other.

See, we were both masochists, and while we longed for pain and humiliation, neither of us was equipped to dish it out. We took care of each other and we sated those basic biological functions, but there was still that underlying need, the ache to be manhandled, beaten, fucked within an inch of our lives.

Hence the reason we went to Dichotomy as often as possible. It was our attempt to find a Dom with a heavy hand, one who might strip us of our control by beating us down in an effort to build us back up.

I'd been to plenty of clubs in my day, including those that were glammed up on the outside but filled to capacity with men and women who were mere caricatures of the roles they attempted to play. Fortunately, I'd found Dichotomy in Dallas and had since managed to at least find one or two Doms who could give me a little of what I so desperately needed. However, no one had ever delivered it the way Zeke had.

Believe it or not, the truly sadistic Doms weren't easy to find. While safe, sane, and consensual was the unspoken rule in the kink world, in my experience, most Doms were so caught up in it they couldn't be effective. Always asking if I was okay, wanting to know my color, fearful they were going to make one wrong move and cause more pain than I could handle when, in reality, they rarely even registered on the low end of my pain threshold.

And that was the main reason I'd developed some sort of strange fascination with Zeke Lautner. I'd never met a man like him before. He didn't ask questions like, "Color, sub?" or "Do you want it harder?" or "Are you ready to come?"

Nope. Zeke didn't ask questions because he didn't give a shit what my color was or if I needed to be hit harder or even if I wanted to come. Whenever I was in his presence, there was no question as to who was in charge. And I wasn't sure how, but he seemed to know what I needed. I'd experienced his personal brand of Sadism only once, but it was an experience I would never forget.

"Tell me you're really not hoping he's here," I taunted Brax when the elevator doors closed, sealing us into the small box. I fucking hated confined spaces. I imagined the higher we went, the thinner the air got, my chest squeezing for fear I wouldn't be able to breathe.

"I'm really not."

"Liar."

A smile pulled at Brax's mouth. I knew it. He was lying.

When the elevator stopped on the thirty-third floor, I waited for Brax to exit before I stumbled out, hoping no one noticed my misstep.

"Well, well, well," Dale Cooper said as he pushed to his feet. "Look what the cat dragged in." He moved around the reception desk and grinned. "Glad you made it all right. Long drive?"

"That's an understatement," Brax said, shaking Dale's hand. He nodded toward me. "Not that he'd know. He slept the entire trip."

I shook Dale's hand. "Only because his singin' makes me wanna stab out my own eardrums."

"Fuck off," Brax said on a laugh, that sexy grin of his heating my blood. The man had a way of derailing me from all good intentions.

Brax turned back to Dale. "We're here to get the apartment key. Ben said he'd have it."

"Ben took Addison to lunch."

Well, fuck. I'd been looking forward to a shower.

Dale smirked. "However, I heard a rumor that Zeke has your keys."

My back straightened and my cock made certain my brain was aware he was there.

"Hold up a sec." Dale marched back around his desk and grabbed the telephone receiver. He punched a couple of buttons. "Mr. Lautner, I've got Brax and Case here. They stopped by to get the keys to their apartment."

While I couldn't make out what was being said, I did hear the distinct rumble of Zeke's rough baritone. I noticed the way Dale's eyes flared slightly before he quickly masked it.

"Yes, Sir. I'll let them know"

Although my brain was screaming, "Oh, shit," my body was having an entirely different reaction to this curious turn of events.

THREE

ZEKE

"PATIENCE IS A VIRTUE, DALE. They can wait," I told the receptionist when he delivered the news that the pretty boy and the cowboy had arrived.

"Yes, Sir. I'll let them know."

Disconnecting the phone, I glanced out the window. The sun had slipped behind the clouds, darkening my office.

What the fuck was I doing? Was I really contemplating the idea of fucking with these boys? It would make more sense if I simply pretended they didn't exist. It wasn't like me to play with the same submissive more than once. I'd done it before and it had gotten me absolutely nowhere. Since I wasn't a glutton for punishment, I should take a page from my history book and leave these two alone. Even if I was entertained for a short period of time, nothing good could come of it in the long run.

Still, I was thinking about them even as they sat one floor up in the reception area. I remembered that day on Trent's jet. The day I learned one of my good friends had set me up. I'd been relaxing with Ransom while the pretty boy sat across from me, his gaze frequently straying my way. The moment the cowboy came into the room, I found myself unable to resist fucking with them.

"Trent wants these boys to meet with Justin," I told Ransom.

"Why?"

"Hell if I know." I smirked. "Maybe he's looking to add some decoration to the office."

Ransom's gaze strayed to the pretty boy. "Well, that'd do it."

I peered over at my friend once again, gauging his interest in the two. If Ransom wanted these two for himself, I'd certainly hand them over on a silver platter. I didn't need the fucking headache.

Unfortunately, Ransom's appreciation was only skin deep. He wasn't interested in the pretty boy or the cowboy.

"String 'em up naked," Ransom said. "Maybe in the lobby so everyone can watch."

Yep, the man was as sadistic as I was.

But he was right. These two would make nice office decor. I could admit I wouldn't mind seeing the pretty boy tied up and at my mercy. Perhaps trussed up beneath my desk while I worked. I could use the other for a footstool.

Speaking of other…

The cowboy appeared in the doorway, his green eyes instantly landing on his friend.

"Sit," I commanded, pointing toward the spot beside the pretty boy. "Better yet, both of you kneel."

Without a word, the pretty boy inched off the edge of the seat and right onto the floor. His actions didn't surprise me one bit. He was eager to please. I'd seen it in his eyes when ours met earlier. The cowboy followed suit, moving close.

"I've seen you both before," I said.

Neither of them spoke.

They were good boys.

Exactly how I liked them.

"How old are you, pretty boy?"

The pretty boy's mouth moved, but the rest of him remained still. "Twenty-eight, Sir."

"And you, cowboy?"

A small smile curved the cowboy's lips. "Twenty-seven, Sir."

"You two like to play?" I asked.

Neither spoke, but I hadn't addressed one or the other, so it made sense.

"Pretty boy," I called out. "Answer me."

The pretty boy nodded his head. "Yes, Sir."

"Are you collared, pretty boy?" They weren't wearing collars, but being this was a business trip, it was possible they'd simply left them at home.

"No, Sir."

"What about you, cowboy?"

"No, Sir."

"Zeke," I clarified. "I don't like Sir. When you speak to me, refer to me as Zeke."

"No, Zeke," the cowboy corrected. "I'm not collared."

"If I insist you strip right here, what would be your answer, cowboy?"

"I would oblige, Zeke," he said, his voice raspy.

I peered over at Ransom. He offered a shrug as he grabbed a magazine and moved to one of the chairs farther away from me.

He was giving me free rein and who was I to pass up the opportunity?

"Stand," I insisted. "From here on out, I'm speaking to both of you."

Both men stood slowly, their eyes remaining glued to the floor.

I took a moment to look them over from head to toe. I definitely liked what I saw. I liked my submissives strong but compliant. And I could tell by the bulges behind their zippers that they were enjoying the fuck out of this.

I decided to call the cowboy's bluff.

"Strip," I demanded. "Right now."

While I hadn't touched them that day, I had admired the view. Forcing them to kneel while their cocks stood proud and eager had been a rather pleasant way to pass the time.

Regardless of my past, I hadn't had a submissive draw my attention quite the way they had. Not in a long damn time, anyway. That didn't mean this was a smart move on my part. I tended to overwhelm people. Anyone who knew me would say I wasn't normal. Not in any sense of the word.

Of course, I dealt with a myriad of stereotypes from all walks of life. People who didn't understand my lifestyle and those who confused my desires with something else.

The bottom line was, I was a Sadist.

By definition, a Sadist was a person who received sexual gratification from causing pain and degradation to another. Yes. That was me to a T. I didn't hide it, either. I only played with those who understood what it meant and who were willing to indulge those desires.

However, people were often trying to tie it to some psychological defect. Some went so far as to say Sadism had something to do with anger, a need to punish or to overcome some trauma from their childhood.

First of all, I wasn't an angry man. Not by a long shot. I had a great life, good friends, people I depended on, and those I would lay my life down for. I didn't walk around in a rage, wanting to beat on someone for the hell of it. And despite what my baby sister said, I didn't listen to angry-man music. It was merely music to me. It suited me.

Secondly, I'd experienced trauma like a lot of other people. Losing my parents had been horrific. I wouldn't deny it. I'd spent time talking to counselors, grieving, mourning the loss of two incredible people. I had learned to deal and moved on. The pain was still there, but it didn't haunt me the way it had initially. I wasn't looking to punish other people for my loss. What fucking good would that do?

Of course, some people believed Sadists lacked empathy. Not true. If they did, it likely had nothing to do with their sadistic streak. There were plenty of people who lacked empathy. That didn't mean they had the desire to cause physical pain to another person. Personally, I cared about plenty of people. Namely, my baby sister. Also, the friends I'd made over the years. And fine, perhaps by referring to people by nicknames rather than their given name allowed me to keep my distance. That didn't mean I lacked the ability to associate with them. I merely wanted to keep them on the periphery of my world. It was my preference.

What I *did* have was a deep desire to cause pain, but only to those who wanted it. And a masochist wanted it. They were fueled by dark urges the way I was. There was no reason to make a million excuses or try and explain it away as some psychological malfunction. It was what it was.

Ask any of the submissives at Dichotomy and they'd have a varied tale of who they believed I was. I'd heard plenty of adjectives whispered about me. Mean, cruel, distant. People dissected me in varied ways, but I could say the majority of them didn't understand me even on a base level.

I didn't make small talk with every Suzy Whatsit who wanted to chat about how she hoped to get fucked by the big, mean man. I wasn't interested in pussy.

Nor did I entertain those I knew I wouldn't have anything in common with. I didn't go to the club with the intention of slapping around some eager-eyed submissive who wanted to believe I would get off by smacking their ass. What I wanted surpassed that shit by a country mile.

I was primal in nature, a beast to the core. I had a deep desire to destroy, but not out of anger. My deviously kinky brain should come with a warning label, something to let trespassers know I would gladly shatter them and walk away, leaving them for someone else to put back together.

I was a loner. I didn't need the company of others to feel complete. I wasn't looking for companionship or love. I didn't want a relationship, I wanted to fuck. I wanted to expel the urge, then allow it to build again. I wasn't interested in having some little fuck toy wake up in my arms, believing there would be rainbows and unicorns coming out of my ass when I walked away.

I preferred the mind fuck. I craved it. Watching a submissive mentally writhe while desire filled them until they couldn't breathe. No one but me truly knew what I was capable of. And I liked it that way.

But for whatever reason, I felt a connection with the pretty boy and the cowboy. Nothing deep, mind you. I didn't experience that giddy, lovestruck feeling. I might've been born with that gene, but it had long since disappeared, consumed by the overwhelming urge to dominate and destroy.

However, when it came to the pretty boy and the cowboy, there was a physical attraction that was undeniable. They definitely made my dick hard. And the thought of beating on one or both of them tripped my trigger. I'd seen firsthand what the pretty boy desired. Hell, I'd delivered it. And I'd thought about it every day since.

I peered over at Tank. "How long should I make them wait, boy? Think I should put them out of their misery? Long drive from Texas to here."

Of course, Tank didn't acknowledge me. He didn't care what I did as long as he could tag along.

Grabbing my phone, I decided it was time to get this underway. After all, I still needed to figure out if this really was something I was willing to pursue.

Of it was merely a passing fancy.

Brax
(The cowboy)

I DIDN'T MIND WAITING. NOT usually.

At the doctor's office, a good restaurant, at an amusement park. As a society, we'd come to expect it. Patience was a virtue.

However, waiting twenty minutes for Zeke to be available hadn't been on my agenda for the day. I'd hoped to stop in, grab the keys, head up to the apartment, and sleep for a while. At the very least, get a shower and wash off some of the travel grime.

Then again, I doubted Zeke gave a shit about my agenda or whether or not I shuddered anytime I thought about those sheets I'd slept on last night. The shower I'd taken in the hotel room had done nothing to dispel that itchy feeling. Had we planned ahead, Case and I could've slept in a four-star hotel. Instead, we'd stopped at the first place we came to when it became damn near impossible to keep my eyes open. Lesson learned.

And now I should've been minutes away from a nap. Instead, I was sitting on the leather sofa in the fancy reception area waiting for Zeke to stop fucking with us. Any other day, perhaps I would've been impressed by the power play. Today was not that day.

The phone on Dale's desk rang, and based on the way he answered, the call had come from inside the office. He hung up and glanced over. "Zeke will see you now. His office is downstairs." He motioned toward the hallway.

"Thanks," I offered as I pushed to my feet, my back cramping. I needed to be horizontal for a while.

"Good luck," Dale said with a smirk as we passed by.

I allowed Case to lead the way, following him down the wide hallway that opened up to the offices belonging to Landon, Langston, and Luci.

While I desperately wanted to play it cool, I wasn't sure that was possible as Case and I headed down the stairs leading to Zeke's office. My exhaustion disappeared as did the pain in my back. There was a strange buzzing in my head, as though I was walking the plank, and any second now, the floor would be ripped out from under me, leaving me at Zeke's mercy.

Strange, huh? Yeah. My brain tended to do shit like that when I was nervous. Conjuring up nonsense.

I glanced around, noticing all the closed doors. The place was a ghost town today. The only warm body we'd encountered had been Dale back in the reception area, and from what I could tell from all the dark rooms, no one else was here.

While my imagination worked overtime to get away from me, I tried to remind myself that we were in an office building. Not a club. I seriously doubted I had anything to worry about with Zeke. Not like he was going to command us to strip naked in his office. Right?

Granted, that hadn't stopped him on Trent's personal jet during our trip from Dallas to Chicago. In fact, Trent had been in the next cabin. Not to mention, Troy, Clarissa, the pilot, and the flight attendant. They'd been on either side of the room where I ended up stripping buck-ass naked and kneeling for the big Sadist.

But this was an office building. A professional place. Nothing kinky should be going on here. Then again, I did recall the time I walked through, serenaded by the cacophony of Luci's squeals while she was getting her ass paddled by one of her Doms. That was just last week sometime. They certainly hadn't cared that anyone had overheard them.

Maybe I should be worried.

Once we made it down the stairs, I took a deep breath and put one foot in front of the other. I'd noticed how Case was breathing a little roughly for someone in such good shape. The guy was built like a Mack truck, but he had the cardiovascular system of a damn runner. Which meant he was getting worked up from the mere prospect of seeing Zeke again.

For some reason, I was no longer worried what Zeke would do, I was worried he would do nothing at all.

I was depraved, no doubt about it.

I felt like a teenager being called to the principal's office for something. I wanted to shove Case in front of me so I could hide behind him as we approached the open door to Zeke's office.

"Hey, Zeke," Case said in a ridiculous attempt to sound casual.

I wanted to laugh because the man nearly choked on his own words. I stifled it by squeezing my lips together.

"Pretty boy," Zeke acknowledged from where he sat behind that massive desk.

I stepped around Case and took a good long look at the Sadist who plagued my thoughts. His bald head gleamed in the fluorescent lights above him, his dark eyebrows shadowed those piercing black eyes, and his thick beard framed the lips I'd fantasized about. Yep. I was a fucking mess because this man, who wasn't attractive in the traditional sense—he was too aggressive-looking for that—made every cell in my body come alive.

"Cowboy," Zeke smirked. "Nice hat."

"Thanks."

"You ever ride a horse, cowboy?"

"Yes, Sir." I swallowed. "I mean, Zeke."

"Ever ride a bull?"

For fuck's sake. I actually started to sweat from that simple question.

He raised an eyebrow.

"Actually, yes. I have." However, I got the feeling Zeke wasn't referring to the four-legged version.

Tank chose that moment to wander over and sniff my hand. I couldn't resist petting the dog, even as I wondered how a beast like Zeke had ended up with the cutest damn dog I'd ever seen.

"Hey, Tank," I greeted softly, letting my gaze naturally shift to the floor.

"We came by for the keys to the apartment," Case said, his voice stronger than before.

I was impressed.

"Did you now?"

"Yes, Zeke," he said obediently, a slight tremble making an appearance.

I'd bet money Case's cock was as hard as a steel pipe right about now. Mine was, which was weird because I was still petting the dog.

Stop petting the dog, you dumb ass.

Standing up straight, I glanced over and noticed two keys sitting on the top of Zeke's desk. Were those ours? Was he wanting us to grab them and turn around? This could've been a simple in and out, but Zeke made no move to get them.

"What's in it for me?" Zeke asked, steepling his hands as he leaned back in his chair. It was a wonder the damn thing didn't snap in two from the sheer weight of him alone. I'd venture to guess the man weighed somewhere between two sixty and two eighty. At six eight, he was a monster. Which had me curious as to the size of his dick.

No. Nix that. I *wasn't* curious. I was here to get the keys. Then, if I couldn't catch some Z's, maybe I'd find some coffee and I could get on with my day.

"What would you like?" Case asked.

Christ Almighty. That was not a question you asked Zeke Lautner. The gleam in his eyes alone said he was thinking all sorts of things and I doubted a single one of them didn't involve some sort of humiliation.

Strangely, that made my cock harder.

Zeke motioned across the room. "Have a seat."

It wasn't a request, it was a command. One that had Case and me moving across the room even as I wondered why the rush.

I'd long ago stopped questioning the perversion I had when it came to Domination and submission. It wasn't something I'd experienced until after I came to work for Trent. Oh, sure, I'd gotten off a few times to an ex-boyfriend wanting to pull my hair or nail me to the wall. Aggressive sex had always turned me on. But it wasn't until I'd witnessed a scene at Dichotomy between a Sadist and a masochist that I'd truly understood some of the darkness that fueled me. It was then that I'd realized I hadn't even scratched the surface of the true depth of my depravity.

However, my desire to explore Zeke's particular brand of Sadism had been cemented the night I watched as Zeke took over a scene with Case. Another Dom had offered to flog Case in an effort to get him off. It was the very reason we went to Dichotomy. We sought the release that came with scenes of that nature.

Case and I had come to the understanding back in the beginning that we needed to experiment to see how to sate some of the deeper urges we had. And we'd agreed to do it together. So, as long as we were at the club, we rode the wave where it took us. We'd scened numerous times with various Doms, and our limits were minimal. The only rule we had was that we discussed the scenes afterward, in depth. It was important to us that we kept each other in the loop as to which direction our desires were headed.

I'd known from the beginning that I could never give Case everything he truly needed when it came to sex. While my kink leaned toward the humiliation department, Case was into serious pain. The sort I couldn't inflict even on my worst day. I was sure a therapist would've had a field day outlining the cause of Case's obsession. Surely there was something in his past—abusive parents, neglectful family, inappropriate contact with someone in his life— that had molded him into what he was today.

While I got the feeling *something* had caused Case to seek the pain, he insisted otherwise. Aside from having sex at an early age—he'd lost his virginity at the ripe young age of fifteen—Case insisted he'd had a normal upbringing. Nothing that would trigger a need to be beaten. I knew in my soul that when Case told me he was mentally intact that he wasn't lying. His parents were still married and we'd spent quite a bit of time with them over the course of our relationship. They didn't have an issue with Case being gay or even that he had a fondness for kink clubs. They were actually more tolerant than most people I knew.

Sometimes, people just needed things they couldn't explain.

I agreed with that sentiment; however, I still believed there was something in Case's past that had him seeking someone to deliver pain that most people purposely ran from.

After we had taken a seat on the couch, Zeke continued to stare at us without saying a word. I didn't look him in the eye, even as I admired the hard lines of his face, the angle of his nose, the aggressive slant of his eyebrows. The man scared me, had from the moment I met him. But it was the sort of fear that made me feel alive, made me crave the darkness I could see in his aura.

"I can only assume I didn't scare you off completely," he finally said, pivoting his chair so that he was facing us.

The office was large, with a wall of windows that offered a shitty view of another building. Granted, it allowed sunlight to filter in, which was a good thing. Aside from the monstrous desk, there was the black leather couch we were currently seated on, two chairs facing Zeke's desk, a four-drawer black metal file cabinet, and an overstuffed, navy-blue dog bed in the far corner, where Tank had retreated. There weren't any pictures on the wall, no diplomas or other certificates. Nothing personal, either. On the desk was a laptop computer, a banker's lamp and the keys I assumed were for our apartment.

In a word, the office was bare. Almost minimalistic in nature. As though Zeke didn't spend any time in here and when he did, it was simply to work and nothing else.

"You didn't scare us off, Zeke," I said when it was obvious Case wasn't going to respond.

"Yet." He sounded as though he truly believed we might be gone on the next strong breeze. In fact, I got the feeling Zeke did his best to get people to run far and fast away from him.

Despite my curiosity about the man, I hadn't asked around the club for fear word would get back to him. I couldn't imagine it would go over well if Zeke found out we were trying to get the lowdown on him. When most people said his name, it was either in awe or pure terror.

Personally, I felt a significant amount of both when I was this close to him.

Yet I couldn't even fathom walking away.

FOUR

ZEKE

I SHOULD'VE TOSSED THEM THE keys when they appeared in the doorway. In mere seconds, they could've been on their way and I could get back to doing the shit I needed to be doing. It would've been the smart thing to do.

Despite my college degree and my rather high IQ, no one had ever accused me of being smart. Most of the adjectives associated with me were in line with enormous, mean, sadistic, and intolerant.

Enormous and sadistic, sure. I would admit to those. Mean and intolerant ... no. I didn't see it. Nor was I a glutton for punishment.

Which begged the question: what the hell was I doing entertaining the notion of fucking these boys' lives up by getting involved with them?

Unfortunately for all three of us, I didn't have an answer.

I could only think it had everything to do with that scene I'd interrupted at Dichotomy. When I'd whipped the pretty boy until he was flying so fucking high I feared for a moment he would never come back down, a strange obsession had followed. Watching him mutter and moan as the tails did all but split his skin wide open had fueled me in a way I hadn't experienced in quite some time. Seeing my stripes on his back had stirred the beast within and now he was taking over.

I'd dreamed about it since. Strapping the pretty boy's beautiful naked ass up and beating him black and blue, pushing him harder until he whimpered and cried, pleading for me to stop. Only then would I give him enough to send him over the edge. Admittedly, I'd been surprised by his pain threshold. Once I'd witnessed it for myself, I had wondered whether anyone before me had ever given him what he needed.

As for the cowboy … I'd had some rather interesting thoughts about him, too. Most of them consisted of me laying him out, burying my fingers in his ass, and fucking him so goddamn hard he was crying out with the need to come. My cock always followed my fingers as I chased my release, brutally nailing him as hard and as deep as I could. And every damn time, they were both begging me to never stop.

It wasn't until I'd found them fucking in the shower that I realized the two of them had a relationship. Not that I cared. As long as they were willing, I didn't give a fuck what they did in their spare time. I didn't give a shit who their parents were, whether they had a good relationship with their siblings. It didn't matter to me if they'd graduated from high school with honors or by the skin of their teeth. I couldn't care less if they called their mommas every damn day or hadn't spoken in ten years. I didn't need to know anything about them personally and that was the way I liked it.

Entertaining the idea of dominating them made sense. I needed it. They needed it. Being on a first-name basis with them was not on the table.

I could see the fear in their eyes, the terror warring with excitement. I knew they wanted the unique brand of pain I could give them, which had me curious as to how two masochists—one with a ridiculously high threshold for pain—had ended up together. It was a question I would ponder but never ask. I had no desire to get to know them. I wasn't here to be their friend or their lover.

I could offer only one thing: to make their deepest, darkest fantasies come true. In return, they would offer me one thing: complete and total surrender.

"I can practically hear you thinking," I said when the silence had beat on for a few minutes. "The wheels in your heads are spinning. You're curious as to why you're sitting there silently while

I stare at you. It doesn't make sense, does it? This strange hold I have over you?"

Two sets of green eyes—one light, one dark—leveled on my face.

"You're wondering what I want to do to you, whether or not I'll give in to those impulses, the urge to beat you down until you're shattered and broken."

Neither man moved.

"I can see it in your eyes. You would do anything I told you to do. No matter how perverted or depraved it may seem. In fact, you're eager for me to hurt and humiliate you the way I did before, only this time, you're thinking no holds barred. You want me to unleash on you, to show you a world of agony you've never experienced, to help you come to terms with why you are the way you are."

I watched them for a moment, enjoying the fear I could see. The way their chests expanded rapidly, their throats working as they swallowed the fear back. I fed off that trepidation. It made me invincible. Especially when dealing with two large males who likely didn't submit to anyone other than the Dominant who could give them what they craved.

"Trust me," I told them. "I've considered it."

That was hope glittering in their eyes, and I had the need to quash it before it grew wings and took flight. It was true, these two were quite possibly stronger than any masochist I'd dealt with before, but I knew they could never handle me. They were all looking for the same thing. A sadistic bastard who would beat on them, then cuddle them close and shower them with praise. I wasn't that man.

I would *never* be that man.

I locked eyes with the pretty boy. "I've played with you. I know what you need. Pain, hot and fresh, searing your flesh until your fucking cock's so goddamn hard you're blinded with the need to come. But you don't know what true pain is. It's not only physical, pretty boy. The mental aspect will wear you down. The wrath I would inflict on you would have you cowering in a corner, begging for mercy. I'd give you two days tops."

"You're wrong," he said, his tone firm, far too self-assured for his own good.

"Am I?"

"Yes, Zeke."

"And how can you be so sure?"

He didn't so much as flinch before he answered. "Because no one has come close to scratching the itch. You got me off. Sure. And I suffered greatly in a way I'd only dreamed about. But it wasn't nearly enough."

I was surprised by his admission and not at all disappointed.

"And you, cowboy? What in the ever-loving fuck would you want from me?"

He swallowed hard but didn't look away. "Whatever you're willing to give me, Zeke."

"No matter how filthy? How disgusting? Because, little boy, my mind knows no bounds. My fantasies scare the devil himself."

The cowboy's chin tilted up slightly. "I would give you everything that I am, Zeke."

I glanced over at the pretty boy. "Do you like hearing that? Knowing your boyfriend's willing to bend over and let me fuck him rough and hard while you watch? Does it turn you on?"

"It does. Yes." The hard ridge behind his zipper said he wasn't lying.

I leaned back and regarded them. That had been a test. One I was surprised they passed. Most submissives started to cower, then beg. Only once had I found a submissive who had the balls to stand up to me. But he and I didn't see eye to eye. Apparently, I wasn't the man he needed.

I picked up the keys and tossed them to the pretty boy.

"Get settled in. We'll meet at three to walk through the restaurant with the contractor. Tonight, you'll meet me at Dichotomy so we can discuss this some more. At that point, if I think you're worth my time, I'll let you know."

I motioned toward the door.

"You're dismissed."

"Thank you, Zeke," they both said at the same time before getting to their feet and heading for the door.

I stared at the space they'd vacated for a long time afterward, wondering just how far they would let me go before they decided I wasn't worth even the most wicked orgasm.

That time would come.

It always did.

Case
(The pretty boy)

ONCE WE GOT THE KEYS, Brax and I went back down to the car to grab the things we'd brought with us. Nothing more than a couple of bags with necessities, two suitcases full of clothes, and pillows. We still needed to buy a blow-up mattress so we weren't obligated to sleep on the floor until our things arrived next Thursday.

During the entire round trip to the garage and then back up to the apartment, neither of us said anything.

Not a single word.

Although, the silence spoke volumes.

My head was spinning from the unexpected conversation with Zeke. The fear he'd instilled in me was liquid fire in my veins, fueling a desire I'd done my best to repress for so long now. I wanted what that man could offer me, and I was willing to do damn near anything to get it.

It wasn't until we stepped inside the apartment that all thoughts of that conversation fled and I was once again filled with that absurd feeling of being trapped inside a box. I'd felt it last week when we came to look at the apartment, but I had shrugged it off. Mostly. It was now back with a vengeance, making it difficult to breathe. The walls felt as though they were closing in, pushing all the air out.

Which was strange when I thought about it. I didn't have an issue with restraints of any kind. Chains, cuffs, suspension, stockade. In the clubs, I'd done it all and not once had I ever panicked, nor had I ever felt too restricted, confined. I'd go so far as to say the restraints heightened the sensation for me. The fear they instilled was welcome.

This—being inside a box within a box high up in the sky— made me desperate for air, as though my lungs couldn't fill fast enough. I couldn't stand to see so many walls and not nearly enough windows, no doors to the outside, no way to break free if necessary.

Back in Dallas, Brax and I had lived in a house. Nothing fancy. Three bedrooms, one bathroom, postage-stamp-sized yard. But when I stepped out the door, I was instantly greeted with fresh air. Here, I ended up in a hallway that led to an elevator, a maze I had to overcome before I ever broke free.

I wasn't sure I could go through with this.

"Hey." Brax's concerned tone had me turning to face him as I dumped my bag on the kitchen counter. "You okay?"

"Nope," I admitted. "Not even a little bit."

He must've realized I was serious, because the next thing I knew, Brax was up in my face, his big, warm hands curled around my neck, gently kneading the muscles there. He was frowning, his warm gaze scanning every inch as though the answer might possibly be written somewhere on my face.

"Case. Look at me," he insisted. "Take a deep breath."

I tried, but I couldn't focus. My lungs were racing to fill, but nothing seemed to be coming in. My hands were numb and my body felt heavy. Too heavy. My gaze darted to the bedroom door behind him and more trepidation filled me.

"Breathe, babe," Brax stated firmly. "You're gonna be fine."

I shook my head, gripping his shirt in my hand. "I'm not." I was fucking gasping for air, and though I knew it was ridiculous, I couldn't seem to stop.

"You are." He didn't sound convinced. "I promise. Just breathe. Slowly."

"I…" I swallowed hard, the air somehow suffocating even as it moved through my lungs. "I need to go outside."

"All right," he said quickly, taking my hand. "Let's go outside. We'll take a walk."

I nodded and allowed him to lead me out of the apartment. He locked the door, then steered me to the elevator. Minutes felt like days but then we were finally outside. I stumbled over to a rock wall and perched my ass on the edge. I inhaled deeply, exhaled slowly. People passing by glanced my way, a few seemingly concerned although no one stopped. Damn big city.

My hands were shaking, but at least the air didn't seem so scarce out here. It wasn't much better, but it wasn't worse, either. I hated the concrete jungle that was the city. I wanted to see grass and trees, not parking meters and storefronts on every side of the road. Car emissions made me feel as though I was choking.

Brax stood beside me, his warm hand on my back. I could tell he wanted to do something but he likely didn't know what. Hell, I didn't know, either.

Cars passed, horns blaring, people shouting. There was so much traffic, so many people. Why had we thought this was a good idea? I would've given anything to go back to Texas, to drive down a winding country road, the windows rolled down, wind in my face. Here I had to settle for a chilly breeze that smelled like gasoline and concrete and did nothing to cool me down.

"Let's take a walk," Brax said as he motioned me toward the sidewalk.

"Yeah. Okay." I pushed to my feet and straightened my spine. I took a few steps, then a few more, allowing Brax to steer me where he wanted me to go.

"There's a coffee shop around the corner," he told me, glancing at his watch. "We've got half an hour before we have to meet Zeke at the restaurant. We can get some coffee and relax for a few minutes."

I didn't drink coffee but Brax knew that. He drank it, though. By the gallons. I liked to give him shit about it because I could. It was one of his few vices.

We turned the corner and I inhaled deeply, finally feeling the sun shining down on me, warming the air as it peeked through the horde of buildings and the thick, gloomy clouds. I wasn't watching where I was going, making sure my feet were moving, trusting Brax to lead me safely, so I came up short when I slammed into his back.

"What's wr—" I cut myself off when I looked up to see Zeke standing in front of us.

He was frowning, his black eyes scanning my face.

"What's wrong with you, pretty boy?" I was almost certain there was a hint of concern in his tone.

"He just needed some air," Brax explained, his apprehensive gaze bouncing back and forth between me and Zeke.

The dark slashes of Zeke's brows didn't shift. Clearly he wasn't convinced.

I pointed toward the sky. "I've got an issue with apartments," I admitted. "Gonna take some getting used to."

"What kind of issue?" His words came out slowly, as though he was still wrapping his head around the term.

I shrugged and Zeke looked at Brax.

"He has an issue with confined spaces. Apartments to be very specific. As we just learned."

"You claustrophobic?"

I shook my head. "No, actually. Well, I hadn't thought so. It's the idea of being locked in a box with no means of escape." It sounded stupid even as I tried to explain it, although deep in my soul I knew I was admitting something I'd never admitted to anyone before.

"There's an elevator and stairs," Zeke stated, as though I hadn't already thought of that.

"I know." I shrugged again. "I'm sure it'll pass once I get used to it."

"You ever live in an apartment before?"

I shook my head. "No."

"Visited one?" he questioned.

"Well, yeah. But most apartments in Texas have exterior doors." And stairs that led down to grass.

"You've lived in Texas your whole life?"

"Nope." I did the math in my head. I was twenty-eight. We moved there when I was fourteen. I smiled. "Just half my life."

Whether Zeke was buying my excuse or not, I couldn't tell. However, he did glance at Brax, who held up his phone. "I was going to get coffee."

Zeke nodded. "There's a dog park around the corner. Meet us over there when you're done."

Brax glanced at me. I nodded, not sure what else to do.

"Sure. Can I get you anything?" he offered.

"I'm good. Get the pretty boy some water."

"Will do."

Zeke's eyes narrowed and Brax must've realized how he sounded because he quickly amended his response with a "Yes, Zeke." Without looking back at me, he took off down the street.

I didn't know what to do or why Zeke felt it was necessary to split us up, but I was still focused on taking deep, cleansing breaths. My chest was looser than before, the panic abated, and my hands had stopped trembling. I considered that a good sign.

"Were you coming back?" I asked. It made sense because Zeke had been walking toward us.

"It doesn't matter. Walk," Zeke commanded and I did. "How long've you had this problem?"

"Just today," I told him. "Seriously. It's only this building. I'm not big on the city, and I guess it closed in around me." I was sure I was being overly dramatic. Then again, I hadn't faked the panic attack. "I probably just need some sleep. It's been a long couple of days."

"Interesting. I would've pegged the cowboy to have issues with the city."

Yeah. Me, too. After all, Brax's family did live on a small farm, complete with goats and pigs and a couple of horses. I loved spending time at his parents' house, helping with the animals. I hadn't grown up like that, but the suburbs always felt like home for me. Less people.

We made it half a block before things opened up. The buildings gave way to trees, concrete morphing into an abundance of grass. I finally managed to relax, the tension in my shoulders easing.

What the hell was I going to do? How the fuck was I supposed to live here if I couldn't even go inside the apartment? I knew Brax was only doing it because it was free rent, and until we got a feel for the area, he didn't want to find a more permanent residence. Not that I blamed him.

Brax was the rational one in our relationship. He managed our money with the skill of an accountant, investing when necessary, saving as much as he could while still allowing us to live a comfortable life where we enjoyed being able to do things.

"Sit," Zeke commanded.

I did and it was about the time my ass hit the park bench that I realized he had been talking to Tank, not me.

"Obedient." He chuckled.

Yeah. It appeared I was.

FIVE

ZEKE

SEEING THE PRETTY BOY'S PANIC-STRICKEN face brought back memories of my mother. The first time I recalled her having a claustrophobia-induced panic attack had been when I was twelve. My baby sister—two at the time—had been sick with a weird, almost strangling cough. Croup, I think they'd called it. My mother had asked me to go to the doctor with them to help out. I was big at twelve and carried Jamie around almost everywhere we went.

It was a regular trip, nothing out of the ordinary. We piled into my mother's Ford Taurus. Although she was worried about Jamie, she was in good spirits, chattering on about nothing, a smile on her face. Right up until we walked into the building and approached the elevator. I'd known immediately that my mother wasn't eager to get in. Perhaps it had been a premonition, but a few minutes later, we got inside, the doors closing securely behind us.

About thirty seconds into the ride up, there was an abrupt jerk and the elevator stopped suddenly, the lights flickering, then going out before some sort of backup light clicked on. My mother had let out a panicked gasp. I thought nothing of it, moving to the buttons, wondering whether or not it would start if I simply pressed the one for our floor again. It didn't. I punched it several more times with the same result. Nothing.

Jamie had fallen asleep on my shoulder at that point, clinging to my neck, her body—warm with fever—making me sweat. Still, I remained calm, trying to figure out how to fix the situation. My mother, on the other hand, wasn't faring so well. I looked over to see her pressed up against one of the walls, her fingers curled around the thin metal bar behind her. When she started gasping for breath, I knew something was wrong.

"Distract me, baby," she had pleaded. "Please, Zeke."

To this day, I could still hear the terror in her usually sweet tone.

Not sure what she wanted me to do, I had walked over and stood in front of her. "Count backwards from ten, Momma."

She had. Twice.

"Now the alphabet," I had suggested. "Starting with J."

That had been one of the toughest days in my childhood. Watching my mother, the fear in her eyes, her voice trembling. A man's voice had come over the speaker advising they were aware of the issue and looking into it immediately. I'd wanted to tell him to hurry, but I knew to remain calm.

Someone had to.

Luckily, the elevator had kicked a few minutes later, then began its ascent to the higher floors. A short time later, my mother was stumbling out of the elevator, her face pale, hands trembling. It had taken another fifteen minutes before she was able to breathe regularly and the tremors in her fingers stopped.

From that day forward, my mother never took an elevator again.

Seeing the pretty boy's face as he stumbled along behind the cowboy had stirred something inside me. A strange urge to protect him from whatever had put that terror-filled look in his eyes. At the same time, I wondered how he would fare in the cage beneath my bed. I'd purchased it with the intention of utilizing the confinement but hadn't yet had the chance. However, in recent days, I'd entertained the notion of putting the pretty boy and the cowboy in there, keeping them safe while I slept.

Now, as we strolled into the dog park—the same one Tank and I had left only a few minutes earlier—I wondered why the fuck I'd bothered to get involved. This wasn't like me. I wasn't prone to worrying about anyone who wasn't Jamie.

Good news was the pretty boy was getting some of his color back. Now that he was sitting, I didn't have to worry that he would fall over.

"You stay there," I told him. "Tank, looks like it's your lucky day. Let's play ball."

That word *ball* had Tank's ears perking up.

As I strolled across the park, I didn't look back, refused to be concerned for the pretty boy. He wasn't my problem. The last thing I needed to do was concern myself with his well-being. It would ruin everything. No way could I play with those boys if they thought I gave a shit about them. That was only asking for trouble. I'd been down that road before. Submissives who thought I was denying my feelings when, in actuality, I didn't have any. Not for them.

However, I still had an overwhelming urge to give them exactly what they needed. Something they were missing from the sweet little love fest they'd built for themselves.

Now, I simply needed to figure out whether or not I could get in that pretty boy's head and chase out all those nonexistent demons so I could fill the space with only one demon.

Me.

Brax
(The cowboy)

AFTER ORDERING A LARGE BLACK coffee and a bottle of water, I headed in the direction Zeke had told me to go. It took a little longer than it should have because, while I dodged the people walking toward me, I was busy searching my phone for potential rentals in the area. A house, to be specific.

Ever since Case learned we would be staying in an apartment once we moved here, he'd been giving me shit. Since he gave me shit about a lot of things, I hadn't put any stock in it. I thought it was his way of bitching and moaning just to get a rise out of me. He was good at that.

I honestly thought he would get used to living in the same building where he would be working. Convenience was a big thing for Case. That was one of the reasons we'd lived relatively close to Trent Ramsey's Dallas home. Most of our time had been spent there unless Trent was traveling. At that point, Trent generally had a place for us. If not, hotels were the norm, and Case was usually the one who picked those out. Like I'd said, Case was the diva in our relationship, yet it worked for us.

The image of his face, so pale and drawn, popped in my head again. I'd never seen him look like that in all the time I'd known him. Not much scared the man I loved. But the second I'd realized how labored his breaths had become, it had dawned on me that he wasn't fucking around. For whatever reason, that apartment sent him into a tailspin. It had scared the shit out of me, and free rent or not, no place was worth seeing him like that.

So, I was on a mission to find something we could move into that would allow him the space he needed to breathe. Preferably before our belongings arrived in the truck next Thursday. There were a ton of options, but I had no idea where they were—good area or not. Maybe it was time I found a Realtor, someone who could navigate the city for us.

I kept walking until the dog park appeared in front of me. I saw Zeke first. He was on the far side of the park, throwing a ball while Tank hauled ass to retrieve it only to dutifully return and drop it at his feet before sitting and waiting for another round.

I found Case sitting on a bench in the sun, elbows on his knees with his head in his hands.

"Hey, babe. You okay?" I took a seat beside him and passed over the water bottle.

He glanced over at me and smiled. "Much better." He took the water but didn't open it. "Sorry about that. I'm not sure what came over me."

"Don't be sorry."

I should've seen this coming. Somehow.

I nodded toward Zeke. "He say anything?"

"Nope. Probably tryin' to figure out how to let me down easy. Who wants a masochist who's claustrophobic?"

"For one, Zeke doesn't let anyone down easy. And two, I'm not sure this is claustrophobia." Although, I wasn't sure what else it could be called.

Truth was, as far as I knew, Case had never had this sort of reaction to anything. While I had waited in line at the coffee shop, I'd thought about all the scenes he had done at the club. A time or two, a Dom would find it amusing to put Case in a cage. Not once had I seen him panic, even when a heavy padlock kept him from escaping.

So what was it about the apartment?

"What are you doing?" Case nodded toward my phone.

"Trying to find us another place to live."

His back went ramrod straight and he dropped the water bottle. "No. Don't do that. I just need some time to get used to it. I'm sure I'll be fine after a while."

"Nothing about that situation was fine," I told him, picking up water bottle and passing it back. "And I'm not about to let you suffer, so just sit there and breathe."

I could tell he wanted to argue, but thankfully he didn't. His attention shifted to Zeke and Tank.

I continued to skim through my phone, glancing at rentals. Nothing even remotely caught my attention. It wasn't that money was an issue, because between the two of us, we made a decent living, and over the last year or so, I'd managed to save quite a bit. Working for Trent Ramsey had afforded us a comfortable lifestyle. I'd prefer to own a place, but not knowing the area, I wasn't sure that was feasible at the moment. Even if that was the route we took, we would have to stay somewhere in the interim.

However, I also wasn't sure I could take Case back up to the apartment and watch him fall apart again. Masochist or not, no one should suffer like that.

Half an hour later, we were back at the Chatter building, wandering through what would soon become the upscale restaurant. As of right now, it was laid out for the bank that had once inhabited the space. Tiled lobby area, counter where the tellers had worked, even the cheap carpet where the cubicles were, desks still there but empty. It looked nothing like it would once the conversion was complete; however, I could see the potential everywhere I looked.

As soon as I stepped into the space, I felt a strange sense of peace. As though this was where I belonged. I could imagine people filling the dining room while I worked away in the kitchen, producing the meals they would be consuming. Damn, I longed for that day. When people would come here because I was here. I envisioned them telling their family and friends to check it out because it was amazing.

I'd never imagined myself becoming an Emeril or Gordon Ramsay or even Bobby Flay. I simply wanted people to eat what I prepared because they enjoyed it. I wanted my restaurant to be on their list of top three. The place they wanted to go on a Friday or Saturday night for a romantic, elegant escape from their everyday. And yes, perhaps I wanted to hear my name on their lips when they mentioned the reason they came.

This was what I'd spent my life dreaming about. Ever since I was a kid in my mother's kitchen, working alongside her to prepare the family meal. I'd started cooking at a young age. Due to the size of my family, the kids—eight total, including me—had been required to pitch in for everything. Cooking, cleaning, mowing the lawn. I had grown up knowing it was my responsibility to help out. Any arguing would've earned us a nice wallop with my dad's belt. It only took a couple of times before I realized that wasn't the route I wanted to take.

I had spent a lot of time in the kitchen with my mother. She loved everything to do with the kitchen. Cooking, baking, casseroles to cookies, it didn't matter. She could make a meal for twenty and have a variety of pies to go along with it, never breaking a sweat. Thanksgiving and Christmas dinners were always held at her house—to this day—and she never asked for help, although I insisted on being there to offer my services. While I pitched in with the cooking, my sister—who owned a bakery—helped on the baking front.

"I've come up with a timeline," the contractor stated as he followed close behind me. "It's not locked down at this point, but I think it'll give you a good idea of what to anticipate."

The man passed over his iPad and I scanned the screen although I had absolutely no idea what I was looking at. It outlined what I assumed were the steps. Demolition, electrical, plumbing, plus names of people I assumed he had hired to handle it.

Truth was, I was a chef, not a building inspector. I didn't give a flying fuck about drywall or electrical panels or any of the things necessary to construct the space. I simply wanted to have input on the design as well as full control of the kitchen. I sincerely hoped Ben and Justin weren't looking for me to provide input on how to get from here to finished product. Not only because I didn't want to but also because I was bound to fuck it up somehow.

Once I'd given the document a good once-over, I passed it back.

"Honestly," I told him, "we're gonna look to you to keep things on track. As much as I wanna help you there, it's not my area of expertise. However, I will have a say in the kitchen. That's my domain and I have something specific in mind. I'll do my best to help out in the interim, but like I said, it's not really my thing."

"I was told you'll be the one signing off on everything," he stated, his confusion evident.

I frowned. "Who told you that?" I damn sure didn't want to be responsible. Not for everything.

"He won't be signing off."

My head snapped over and I saw Zeke standing in the doorway, his eyes trailing over me briefly.

The man—Jay or Jeff or something—didn't look happy about that. "I was told—"

"Don't. Argue," Zeke snapped, his eyes going cold as he stared the contractor down.

I almost felt bad for the guy. Zeke was a very intimidating man. And the thing was, I didn't think it was necessarily intentional. He simply came across as the alpha and the omega, the be all, end all.

I had the sudden urge to drop to my knees in front of him.

Not that I would.

Not here.

And certainly not unless he told me to.

"I'm gonna…" I motioned toward the door.

I didn't know what I was going to do but standing here wasn't serving any purpose.

SIX

ZEKE

IT TOOK NEARLY HALF AN hour to get the contractor to finally shut up and listen. While he was making my ears bleed with his incessant chatter, I made a mental note to never agree to fill in for Ben again. Not when it came to shit like this. It might've helped if I had cared even a little about this endeavor of theirs, but I didn't. I wasn't an uptight hipster foodie. I tended to cook at home and from time to time I would splurge on pizza or a good burger. Sautéing up sauces and herbs that appealed to the palate was lost on me.

Fortunately for everyone involved, the contractor finally took the hint, although it was obvious he wasn't happy with me. No, I didn't know where they wanted the dining room or what the layout of the kitchen should be. I didn't give a flying fuck where the water or gas lines came into the building and I had told him so repeatedly. In fact, we had accomplished exactly nothing by being there.

I'd wanted to give the contractor a piece of my mind. To let him know that it was rude to waste other people's time. He'd had no real purpose for this visit and that irritated the shit out of me. I did not like wasting time. It was too precious to begin with.

"If I'm not working with Mr. McBride, who will be my point of contact?" the contractor asked. "Will you be running point?"

"Fuck no," I mumbled. "I think it's best you contact Ben. He'll be able to give you more direction. I'm merely filling in for him."

The man nodded while his eyes were glued to me. In fact, I wasn't sure he'd looked away once since I interrupted his conversation with the cowboy. I could practically smell his fear, and while it usually amused me, I was growing more irritated by the second.

"Well, then. I guess that's all for now. I'll call Ben."

"Good idea." To ensure Ben was aware, I pulled out my phone and shot him a quick text. I didn't go into detail, simply let him know he should expect a call.

Once the contractor finally left, I locked the door behind me and went in search of the cowboy and the pretty boy. I'd asked that they take Tank and wait in the lobby.

I found them sitting against the wall, the cowboy on one of the cherrywood benches while the pretty boy was on the marble floor, back to the wall with Tank between his spread legs. He was absently rubbing Tank's fur while staring off into space.

The scene had me pausing in my tracks. The pretty boy looked quite content to be sitting with my dog. All three of them were silent while the cowboy was skimming something on his phone.

Tank heard me first, because his head turned, a wide smile forming on his face. And yes, dogs fucking smiled. Mine did.

When I approached, the pretty boy pushed to his feet, then passed Tank's leash over to me.

"I'm sorry about that, Zeke," the cowboy said when he stood. "I wasn't sure what it was he needed from me."

"I don't think *he* knew," I assured him. "I told him to get with Ben."

I turned my attention back to the pretty boy. "You good?"

"Yep. Much better now."

He was lying, I could tell.

I should've turned and walked out of the building, but something kept me rooted there. Ever since I saw the pretty boy's pale face outside the building a short time ago, I'd been worried about him. Not that I was prone to worrying. Nor was I condoning my behavior. Whatever he was dealing with wasn't my business.

"What's the plan?" I asked.

The cowboy tucked his phone into his pocket and sighed. "I don't know yet."

"We're going back up to the apartment," the pretty boy stated, as though it was obvious. "I'll be fine. I just have to—"

I cut him off by motioning toward the elevator. "Come on then."

Neither of them moved.

"It wasn't a request," I said, casting my voice lower than before.

The pretty boy's eyes widened, but his legs started working. If nothing else, he was relatively good at following instruction.

"Where are we going?" the cowboy asked as he fell into step with me.

"Up to the apartment." I wanted to see the pretty boy's reaction for myself.

"I'm not sure that's a good idea. Case needs—"

"I didn't ask for your input," I told him, catching and holding his stare. "Now, let's go."

The cowboy was obviously confused, perhaps even a little pissed—it was written all over his face—but when the pretty boy started walking, we followed.

It wasn't like I was going to toss them in the apartment and force the pretty boy to suffer. I had an idea, something that would potentially take the pretty boy's mind off whatever had triggered his panic attack. Not only would it benefit him if I could get him distracted, it would benefit me. I needed to assess this situation. Considering what I had in store for these two, it was imperative that I knew what I was up against.

I needed to determine whether or not the pretty boy was capable of scening with me or not. I'd seen him restrained before, and at the time, I hadn't gotten any indication that he had a problem with it. So, perhaps the restraints weren't the issue. However, the idea of being boxed in could be, as well as the amount of space he had around him. I wouldn't know until I saw it for myself.

Once inside the elevator, I kept an eye on the pretty boy as he leaned against the wall. He was trying to appear unaffected, but the color was already draining from his face.

"Do you have an issue with elevators?" I asked.

"Not a huge fan, no."

"The confinement?"

He shook his head. "More so the lack of air."

I glanced up at the ceiling. There was plenty of air, but I understood what he meant. His brain wasn't registering the ventilation.

When we stepped out of the elevator, he stumbled once but managed to catch himself. With Tank beside me, we followed them down the hallway. The cowboy unlocked their door and then stepped inside. I was right behind them.

The door shut and the pretty boy flinched.

"Go open all the blinds, cowboy."

The cowboy nodded and headed toward the windows. It was a nice-sized apartment. One bedroom, probably nine hundred square feet. Plenty of space, although, thanks to all the window coverings, it was rather dark. Considering the clouds were choking out the sun, there wasn't a whole lot of light to begin with.

I unhooked Tank's leash from his collar so he could sniff at his leisure, then turned to stand directly in front of the pretty boy.

"Look at me," I demanded.

Light green eyes snapped up to mine. His chest was expanding rapidly, his eyes a little wild.

"Breathe. Slowly in. Then out. Focus on that." I watched him. "In." I paused. "Out. Now I want you to repeat after me. Eight, four, two, nine, seven."

Confusion contorted his features but he managed to repeat the numbers.

"Again."

Once more, he ran through them.

"Now backward."

I wasn't a therapist, and I didn't know whether or not the method would work for his situation, but it had worked for my mother that day. I'd done it a time or two in the club since then. When an overeager submissive found themselves in a compromising position, it wasn't all that uncommon for them to panic. Being a Dom, it was my responsibility to guide them through it, to ensure their wellbeing, whether I played with them or not.

Some people accused me of lacking empathy, but that was simply their way of trying to explain away my sadistic tendencies. The fact that I took extreme pleasure in a masochist's pain had to be wrong in some way because it didn't make sense to everyone. Why in the hell would someone want you to spank them, pull their hair, whip them, chain them up, lock them in a cage, or hold them down while you fucked them? More importantly, why would someone want to *do* those things to someone else? It was barbaric.

Yeah. I'd heard it all. After all, ignorance made for the best tirades.

I'd long ago stopped making excuses for my desires. I didn't give a fuck what anyone thought about me or those I chose to engage with. As long as the submissive was willing and truthful, I didn't give a shit about the condemnation that came from the outside.

"Come here, cowboy."

He strolled over after he'd opened all the blinds in the apartment. It wasn't a big difference, but it allowed the outside in just a little. I removed the hat from his head and set it on the counter. He ran a hand through his golden-brown hair. I briefly imagined myself pulling it while I fucked him hard.

I took a deep breath and composed myself. I needed to focus.

"I want you to stand behind this *pretty boy.*" I purposely used more condescension on the term than normal.

The cowboy got into position.

"Take off his shirt."

The cowboy lifted the hem and the pretty boy raised his arms, allowing him to remove it. I watched the pretty boy's face for any sign of displeasure but I didn't find anything except genuine curiosity. He wanted to know what I was up to.

"Now your shirt."

The cowboy stripped his shirt over his head and tossed it onto the counter with the other.

"Now place your arms under his. Curl them over his shoulders like you're restraining him."

He did.

"Pull his arms back wide." I kept my eyes locked with the pretty boy's while I gave the cowboy instructions. "Not enough to hurt. Just enough to open his chest. And you, pretty boy, I want you focused on my face and my voice. Nothing else. Understand me?"

"Yes, Zeke." Those bright green eyes glittered, but his breaths were still choppy, labored.

"What are you feeling right now?"

"Like it's hard to breathe."

"Pull back on his arms a little more. Take a deep breath, *pretty boy.* Your airway's open. You're not suffocating."

He gave a jerky nod.

"The only thing you're allowed to think about is me. Think about what I could do to you right now in this vulnerable state. How I could pinch your nipples until you squirmed, until you begged me to release you."

This time when he inhaled, it was labored but the panic was starting to ease. He was imagining me touching him, hurting him.

"You like the idea. What if I bit your nipple? Does the idea of that make your dick hard, pretty boy?"

"Yes, Zeke."

I allowed my gaze to lower. Slowly, so he could see my appreciation.

"You ever wear a cage on your cock?"

"Yes, Zeke."

"By choice or a demand from a Dom?"

"Choice."

"How many Sadists have you played with?"

"A few. Over the years. But never consistent."

That was the problem. He was seeking something but attempting to find it with varied partners. I figured he had never been completely satisfied. In all fairness, a Dom needed more than one session to get to know a submissive. They had to take the time to learn what fueled them, what turned them on, what brought them pleasure. While I didn't practice what I preached, I did observe the club submissives. I paid attention to them during other scenes so I could get a feel for what it was they wanted. That way, in the event I did play with them, I had a better understanding.

My phone buzzed in my pocket but I ignored it. I had somewhere I needed to be before I headed to the club and that was likely my reminder.

I took a step closer. Close enough the pretty boy was forced to look up to maintain eye contact. With a firm hand, I gripped his jaws and squeezed. Hard enough to keep his attention.

"Do you wish to please me?"

"Yes, Zeke," he forced out.

"Then I expect you to do exactly as I say."

He tried to nod, but I held his face firmly.

"When I leave, I want you and the cowboy to strip. Completely naked. For the rest of the time you're here in this apartment this afternoon, you will be naked. Under no circumstance are you allowed to touch the cowboy's cock and he is not to touch yours. The only time you're permitted to touch your own is when you shower. And only to wash. Understand?"

"Yes, Zeke."

"I want you to shower together. I want you to wash each other. Again, you are not permitted to touch his cock and vice versa. Do not breach his ass and do not allow him to breach yours, because tonight, your dicks and your asses belong to me and only me. I am the only one allowed to touch you intimately. Understand?"

"Yes, Zeke."

"I want you both to dress right before you leave the apartment. Jeans and T-shirts only. You are to be at Dichotomy at exactly nine o'clock. At the club you will not be permitted to wear shirts, shoes, or socks. No underwear either. Understand?"

The pretty boy's voice cracked slightly when he said, "Yes, Zeke."

It was a start.

"You might as well bring all your shit, because once you leave the apartment tonight, I do not anticipate you'll be coming back."

He tried to speak, but I squeezed his jaw tighter, cutting him off.

"Once you arrive at the club, you have fifteen minutes to dress as I've stated and to meet me in the dungeon. If you're even one minute late, everything's off. Understand?"

"Yes, Zeke."

"When you find me, you will kneel appropriately in the nearest corner, facing me, and you will not move until I tell you to. Under absolutely no circumstance do either of you have my permission to move. Understand?"

"Yes, Zeke."

I narrowed my eyes, holding his gaze. "Tonight, you will learn what it is I want, what I expect from you, and what you'll receive in return. Should you be inclined to accept my proposition, you will be going home with me. Both of you. This isn't an either/or offer. It's both of you or neither." I squeezed again to reiterate my next statement. "This is only temporary. I don't do permanent, and I don't do long term. You better consider that before you make a decision, because that's my one main rule. I'm not in it for a relationship, I'm not looking for love, and I damn sure don't intend to give either of you a commitment. Understand?"

He didn't sound quite so confident when he said, "Yes, Zeke."

Releasing his face, I took a step back and whistled. A second later, Tank was at my side. I glanced at the cowboy, ensuring we made eye contact. While I'd directed everything to the pretty boy, that had been a distraction, something to keep his mind off where he was and the panic that threatened.

"Do not be late. If you are … well, it was nice knowing you."

With that, I turned and walked out of the apartment without a backward glance.

After leaving the apartment, I headed out for the errand I needed to run before I headed over to Dichotomy. I knew the club wasn't open yet, but since this wasn't a social call, that wasn't necessarily important. Certainly not to me.

Stepping up to the oversized metal warehouse building, I pounded my fist on the door and waited. Someone was here. The cars in the parking lot were proof of that.

"We're not open for another hour!" a disgruntled male voice yelled from inside.

"Open the goddamn door," I grumbled, pounding on it again.

The clank of a latch being unhooked sounded before it squeaked open an inch.

"What do you want?"

"A word with the owner," I told the sleazy fucker who stuck his head out. I pressed one big hand on the door and pushed, effectively gaining entrance.

"What the fuck, man? You can't just barge in here."

"Too late for that," I told him, slamming the door. "Where's the owner?"

The grungy guy studied me for a moment, as though weighing what answer he felt appropriate. "Razor's a busy guy, man. He doesn't allow walk-ins to meet with him. Plus, I'm not even sure he's here."

I peered down at the man, cocking one eyebrow so he could see my skepticism. "He's here. Now where is he?"

He slid a hand through his greasy hair, forcing it back. I hoped like hell the fool showered before he played because he looked as though he'd been rolling around in a vat of grease all morning.

"Fine," he said with a huff. "He's at the bar."

I pushed by him toward the interior of the club. I'd never been to Razor Wire, but the club had a reputation in the kink community. Not a good one, either. A lot of shady shit went down in this place. Drugs, prostitution, numerous reports of sexual assault, some against the owner himself. They'd been accused of plenty of illegal activities but none had been proven. Yet.

"What's up, bro?" Tom "Razor" Miller looked cool and calm as I approached the bar.

"I'm not your bro."

He snorted, but I noticed the concern in his dark gaze. "Hey, aren't you Zeke? I've heard about you." His smile was feral. "You interested in hanging out here? I'll need you to fill out an application and pay the fee."

"First of all, you don't take applications and you don't charge fees. And no, I'm not interested in *hanging out here*. I came to deliver a warning."

He smirked. "You came to warn *me*? Do you even know who I am?"

"Yeah. And I don't care."

That didn't seem to please him. His shoulders bunched and he turned to face me, finally acknowledging I was a real threat. "Fine. What do I need to be warned about?"

"My sister," I stated bluntly.

His eyes widened. "Dude, I didn't know she was your sister. And I swear to God, she said she was cool with it."

My hands clenched into fists. I'd be doing the city a favor if I fucked up his face a little more than it already was.

"You fucking moron. You don't *know* my sister."

"Oh." He grimaced, all his confidence from before deserting him. "Then what the hell do you want?"

"Should she come sniffing around this place and you even let her in that front door, I'll be paying you a visit again. And when I do, I'll call the ambulance ahead of time because you'll need it."

Footsteps echoing off the concrete floors had me turning, assessing the situation.

"Hey," the new arrival said. "I know you." His eyes shot to the owner. "Why's he here?"

For fuck's sake. It was that stupid twit I'd taken care of a few months back. He'd been tossed out of Dichotomy after he'd physically abused his girlfriend in the club. I hadn't been there that night, but I'd heard all about it. So, when Justin asked that I pay the fucker a little visit, I had.

"I see you're outta the hospital," I told him, ensuring he heard the venom in my tone.

He held up his hands. "Man, I haven't messed with her. I've stayed away from Addison. Just like you said."

Since I hadn't heard anything from Justin on the matter, I had to assume he was telling the truth. But my beef wasn't with him anyway. Turning my attention back to the owner, I narrowed my eyes on his face. "Do we have an understanding?"

He shrugged. "I don't even know who your sister is."

"Last name's Lautner. Let her in and you can ask your *bro* here what's in store for you. Understood?"

I took a step closer, the bar keeping him safely out of my reach. Lucky for him. Granted, he still took a step back, as though I could crash through the warped wood.

"Yeah. Sure. Whatever. I won't let her in."

"I don't play games," I informed him. "And trust me, I will find out."

With that, I turned to go, content for the moment. While I'd made two stops at other clubs, intimidation tactics hadn't been necessary. There were plenty of kink club owners who ran a top-notch place, but I still didn't want my sister stepping foot inside one. However, I'd received the owners' assurances they would put her name on a block list merely out of respect for me.

This was not one of those places.

As I passed the guy manning the door, I thought of a dozen ways I could inflict pain on the three of them if they disobeyed.

God forbid that happened. I was a relatively sane man, but if some low-life piece of shit tried anything on my baby sister, I'd break every bone in their fucking body.

Twice.

☯

Case
(The pretty boy)

"SHIT," I GROANED. "DO WE really have to get up?" I stretched my back muscles. The damn things were spasming after having slept on the floor.

"Unless you're willin' to forego any future opportunities with the big guy," Brax said sleepily, "we have to shower."

"Yeah, we do." I couldn't resist sliding my hand over Brax's warm skin. I was still spooned against him, my rigid cock pressed against his ass.

Because Zeke insisted I could not touch my dick, that was the only thing I could think about. The unruly appendage ached like a bad tooth, a consistent reminder that it was there and it was needy.

But a command was a command, so I refrained.

For four hours I'd managed to remain in that apartment. Half an hour was spent trying to find a place to sleep. The instant I walked into the bedroom, I'd balked, spinning around and escaping as fast as I'd entered. The next three hours were spent sleeping. I hadn't wanted to, but I knew Brax needed it. So, I'd convinced him to curl up with me on the carpeted floor in the hallway with the pillows we'd brought with us. I spooned him from behind, and a short time later, we'd both passed out.

Thankfully, Brax had set his phone alarm or we probably would've slept through the night.

"Come on," Brax groaned as he pushed up to his knees. "I'll start the water."

"Fine."

We had just enough time to shower before we needed to head out. Being that we did so together should've saved some time, but that wasn't the case. Once Brax was under the water, I was compelled to touch him as often as possible.

"Keep your hands off my dick," he moaned when I kissed his neck.

"I promise," I told him, cupping his face and pressing my lips to his. "I just want to kiss you."

"Damn, babe." He moaned softly as he pulled me into him, his hands sliding over my back. "You don't know how badly I want to fuck you right now."

Oh, I knew, all right. I wanted the same damn thing.

A few minutes passed while we kissed and groped before Brax managed to extricate himself from my grip. "We have to hurry."

"Fine." I grabbed the body wash and smiled back at him. "You first."

I proceeded to wash him from head to toe. Of course, I never once touched his cock, nor did I attempt to breach his ass. However, there wasn't anything innocent about it.

When that was through—my dick in even more despair—I dug a pair of clean jeans and a T-shirt out of my bag before shoving everything else back in. Zeke insisted we bring our stuff with us, but I wasn't sure it was necessary. I didn't want him taking pity on me because I'd had a panic attack. I'd felt a hell of a lot better after he left. So much so, I had been able to sleep. However, I wasn't going to defy an order from Zeke. Not until I knew what he had in mind for us.

So, after grabbing everything we'd brought with us, I followed Brax back down to the car.

"What do you think he has in mind?" I asked Brax as he drove us to the club a short time later.

"No idea."

I sighed. "I really don't want his pity."

Brax barked a laugh. "Zeke? Pity? Have you *met* the guy?"

Fine. He had a point. Zeke didn't seem like the type who gave a shit whether I endured a panic attack or not. The only reason it would concern him would be in regard to a scene. He was probably invested for as long as it would take to determine whether I was in the right headspace or not.

Now that we were out of the apartment for the foreseeable future, I was fine.

"I'm curious," Brax said.

"About?"

"How is it you've never had a breakdown when we've stayed in hotel rooms? I mean, you know. The ones like the apartment. With hallways and elevators. It's just … I've never seen you panic like that before, and I'm tryin' to make sense of it all."

That got me thinking because it was a damn good question. We'd stayed in plenty of hotel rooms over the years, a lot of them set up in buildings similar to the Chatter PR building. Vegas, for example. I never had issues there. Perhaps it was because it was temporary or whatever had been going on was enough of a distraction to keep me from focusing on it.

Or—something I wasn't going to tell anyone—it was the apartment specifically. It brought back memories. Memories I'd spent my entire life trying to repress.

"Hell if I know. But you're right. It's never happened to me before." I glanced over at Brax. "Maybe it was the long drive and the crappy night's sleep?"

It sounded good, anyway.

"Maybe there were more windows," Brax mused.

I reached over and took his hand. "Look, I'm really sorry."

He squeezed my fingers. "What? No. I don't want you to be sorry. I'm just tryin' to figure out how to fix this. We can find a place, but it's probably gonna take a little time. At least a week or two. If we wanna buy something, it'll be thirty days minimum. We have to live somewhere in the meantime."

And he was thinking the same thing I was: our time with Zeke was extremely limited. Perhaps a night or two, max.

"Are you worried about what Zeke's gonna want from us?" It'd been on my mind a time or ten, so I could only imagine Brax was thinking about it. "He did say we weren't goin' back to the apartment. I assume that means we'll be stayin' with him?"

"That's what I got from it. Which we both know is temporary. Maybe until our things get here?" Brax's forehead wrinkled. "Which means we'll have to have a place to go when he kicks us out. And yeah. I'm a little worried. It's overwhelming. I hadn't expected it. Maybe he'll outline it for us. Like a timeline or somethin'."

He was clearly relaying his thoughts aloud while I was stuck on one particular point. "You said you were worried. About us? Me and you?"

He shrugged and I felt my heart lunge into my throat. I shifted to face him, wanting to hash this out now, before we got to the club.

"Are you serious, Brax? 'Cause I'd just as soon forget the whole thing if it means we're gonna have issues."

He came to a stop at a red light. "I honestly don't know. There's no way to tell how things'll turn out." Brax sighed. "But this is what we wanted, right? To experiment? To see what it'll take to assuage these urges. You know I can't hit you. That's not who I am. And I know you can't, either. It's … Zeke seems like the perfect opportunity to explore this further."

He didn't have to say *because he was temporary*. That was implied.

Brax was right, but we'd known that from the beginning. Ever since we agreed to pursue our masochistic sides while still engaging in a permanent relationship, I'd wondered how we could sustain both.

I sighed and flopped back against the seat. "This is so fucked up. Why do we have to be so fucked up?"

Brax laughed. "Because that's the nature of the beast. We want what we want. We've been up-front about that all along."

Yes, *I* had known it since the beginning. I wasn't sure it had always been the case for Brax. He wasn't even in the lifestyle when I met him. I was the one who introduced him to kink clubs and BDSM. Things progressed from there. We were friends in the beginning and that developed into a sexual relationship, which then turned into something more until I found myself in love with the guy. I didn't think about how it came about, but I damn sure couldn't *not* think about it falling apart.

What if he figured out he didn't need the same things I did? I mean, I knew he was into rough sex, enjoyed humiliation. I'd seen him flogged a few times, and from the outside looking in, he appeared to enjoy it. But what if he was doing it all for me?

I glanced over at him and studied his profile.

He must've felt me looking, because his eyes cut to mine before returning to the road. "What?"

"I love you." I needed him to know that.

He squeezed my hand. "I love you, too. With everything that I am."

Those words triggered the memory of our conversation with Zeke in his office. When the big man had been questioning Brax. He'd said something similar then.

"And you, cowboy? What in the ever-loving fuck would you want from me?"

"Whatever you're willing to give me, Zeke."

"No matter how filthy? How disgusting? Because, little boy, my mind knows no bounds. My fantasies scare the devil himself."

"I would give you everything that I am, Zeke."

I'd never been prone to self-doubts or irrational fears. I moved through life believing that I was exactly where I was supposed to be when I was supposed to be there. However, as I looked at the man who owned my heart and I thought about the man who could own my body, I had to wonder if I would find myself in over my head. What if Brax and I weren't strong enough to survive this?

Was I willing to risk it because, no matter how much I loved Brax, I still didn't feel complete? While I could repress the darker side of myself, would I end up regretting that in the long run? And what about Brax? What if I found what I needed in Zeke and it changed me? Would he be able to handle me then? Would he even *want* me then?

As we pulled into Dichotomy's parking garage, acid began churning in my gut.

I was no longer sure this was the right thing and that scared me more than the thought of Zeke Lautner beating on me.

SEVEN

ZEKE

WHEN I ARRIVED AT DICHOTOMY a little before nine, I found Ransom and Greg already there. They were sitting in the third-floor Masters' lounge, feet propped up, television on but muted.

"What're you here so early for?" Greg asked. "Not used to you showing up until the hard-core set arrives."

I sighed as I dropped onto the sofa across from the two men. "Had to take care of a few errands. Didn't want to go back home."

"Yeah?" Ransom chuckled. "Like paying a visit to a couple of clubs?"

"How'd you hear?"

"Can't reveal all my secrets," he said with a grin. "But let's just say you make quite the impression on people."

"What's going on?" Greg asked, his eyes darting back and forth between me and Ransom. "What clubs?"

I figured I might as well get it off my chest. "My sister decided she wants to visit a kink club. She asked about here and I told her no. Then she told me she would just go somewhere else. I had to ensure no one would let her in the door."

Greg laughed, but there was no humor in it. "You are one brave soul. Jamie's going to have your ass when she finds out what you did."

"Yeah. Well. There are worse things." Such as some bastard putting his greasy fucking hands on her. *Fuck.* I couldn't even think about it.

"Never figured you for a hypocrite, Zeke." Ransom's tone held only a small amount of disappointment.

Propping my elbows on my knees, I stared at my closest friend. "And what do you suggest I do? You want some asshole beating on your kid sister?"

Greg was the one to answer. "Not all Doms are assholes."

"Maybe not. But it's not like I can handpick someone to give her a glimpse into the lifestyle." The thought was absurd. There were only a handful of people I trusted, but I wasn't sure I trusted them with my kid sister.

"What if you could?" Ransom asked, his tone suspicious.

My fists clenched as I pinned my meanest glare on my friend. "You are *not* touching my sister. I've seen the destruction you leave in your wake."

"Never anything they didn't ask for." He laughed, a deep, rumbling sound. "Plus, you know she's not my type, Zeke."

True. For one, she was female. "Then who?" I grimaced. "And be careful. You might be signing some Dom's death warrant."

Ransom's grin widened, his eyes cutting over to Greg. "Why not Edge? He's the resident Dom here and he runs the submissive training classes. Who better to introduce a newbie into the lifestyle?"

Greg sat up straight and glared at Ransom. "Are you fucking crazy?" His gaze shot to me. "I swear, Zeke, I would never touch that girl. I don't care—"

"It's not a bad idea, actually," I said, surprising even myself.

"Okay." Greg held up his hands. "You two are not allowed to drink before you come to the club. You know that."

I laughed. I rarely drank at all, and on nights I had scenes prepared, I didn't touch alcohol. So, he couldn't blame the irrational thoughts on that. And they *were* irrational, even if they made sense.

"You don't find her attractive?" I teased my friend.

Greg's entire face fell, and for a second, I had to think about anytime the man had been around my kid sister. Sure, he knew her. Everyone knew her because I'd brought her to events outside the club. Weddings, birthday parties. That sort of shit. Never had I seen anyone talking to her, though. Not without me being present, anyway.

"Zeke, you can't be serious." Greg looked sincerely confused. "I can't... I don't..." He shot to his feet. "You know what? This conversation is ridiculous. I've got things to do."

Don't ask me why I felt compelled to convince one of my closest friends to do this. However, I trusted Gregory Edge. He was one of the good ones. Sure, he could be hard-core and he had the ability to scare some of the submissives, but he was still a good man. I would trust him with Jamie.

Perhaps I was having a mental breakdown.

"I went down to Razor Wire," I explained, "to tell them not to let her in the club. It wasn't until I walked in there that I truly thought what might happen if Jamie decides to explore kink on her own. I can't stand the idea of her being inside that place."

Greg shook his head, facing away from me. "I would kill one of those fuckers."

"I know. That's exactly how I felt. Then I saw that asshole who hurt Addison. He's a member down there."

Greg spun back around, his expression grim. "Why would Jamie go there?"

"I'm not saying she will." However, I knew my baby sister. She was hardheaded. The simple fact that I'd told her not to was enough fuel to have her stubborn streak coming out. She would likely go simply to defy me, then convince me it was all on the up-and-up and I had nothing to worry about.

That thought made the idea of having Greg show her the ropes—not literally, of course—the lesser of two evils.

"What if she came here for one night?" I suggested, then thought it through a little more. "You know, on a night when I'm not fucking here because *no* fucking way am I gonna witness that."

Greg stared at me like I had an arm sprouting out of my head.

What I really hoped was that this was a bad fucking dream and I was going to wake up to find out I was not attempting to convince one of my closest friends to top my sister.

For fuck's sake.

Brax
(The cowboy)

DICHOTOMY IN CHICAGO WAS FAR busier than the sister club in Dallas on any given night. I'd learned that during my recent trips here. And it seemed all the freak flags were flying on Friday night. They were packed. Not quite like it had been on the night of Trent's surprise collaring ceremony but pretty close.

Not that I had time to even say hello to anyone I knew. Case and I blew right past a couple of submissives we'd befriended during recent trips. While I would've been the first to offer apologies for our rudeness, fifteen minutes didn't allow me to so much as take a piss, much less chat it up with anyone. So I followed Case up to the men's changing room and went right for our locker.

I could tell something was bothering Case even as we ripped our T-shirts off, tossing them, along with our shoes and socks into our locker. The deep discussion we'd had in the car probably hadn't been the best idea for pre-kink club conversation. Certainly not before we were to scene with Zeke.

Before Case could dart back out, I grabbed his arm and forced him to look at me.

"Are we cool?"

His eyes softened. "Always."

I nodded as relief swelled inside me. I wanted to talk it out, but unfortunately, we didn't have time to dwell on it.

We made it down to the dungeon at 9:14 p.m. Twenty seconds later, we had located Zeke, and before my watch hit 9:15, we were kneeling in the corner nearest him. As though his brain was set to an internal alarm, Zeke's eyes immediately shifted to the corner. I dropped my gaze, my heart beating faster than normal.

I had absolutely no idea what Zeke had in store for us tonight, and despite my reservations—the fear that this potentially had the power to come between me and Case—I was excited. Trembling, in fact.

I should've known Zeke didn't have any intention of going easy on us. Rather than come over and acknowledge our presence, he disappeared completely. Figuring some other Dom had been tasked with keeping an eye on us, I didn't move, even as the unforgiving concrete floors bit into my knees.

Minutes passed. A lot of them. Due to the way I'd positioned my hands, I could see my watch. Thirty-two minutes had slipped by while the dungeon and its occupants existed around us. The usual sounds of moans, cries, and impact tools hitting flesh echoed in the large space, but not once did I look up.

When we hit the hour mark, I started to worry Zeke had said to hell with us. I wouldn't put it past him to be off playing with someone else, tormenting them the way I wanted him to torment me. But I wouldn't move, because if I did, Zeke would never return. We would be passing up the opportunity of a lifetime.

The only thing that would get me to move was the signal that the club was closing or the fire alarm.

Otherwise, I was in it for the long haul, bruised knees be damned.

Zeke finally reappeared at 10:47 p.m. A solid hour and a half after my knees first hit the floor. I knew because his big booted feet appeared in my line of sight. At least I hadn't fallen asleep, although it had been touch-and-go there for a while.

His behavior didn't surprise me in the least. I'd played with a couple of Doms who were sticklers for patience, but never had I met anyone who liked to dish it out like Zeke Lautner. The man knew that when he was in this space, he was the sun. Everyone else revolved around him.

The only acknowledgment he offered was a tap to the head. No words came out of his mouth, but it was obvious he wanted us to stand. I got to my feet, remaining beside Case. My heart was racing as though I'd been running a marathon, not chilling in a dark corner for the past ninety-two minutes.

Zeke motioned for us to follow him.

We didn't go far. Only a couple dozen feet to the opposite side of the long, narrow play space. There were no spanking benches or St. Andrew's crosses in this corner. Only large wooden beams across the ceilings, chains dangling from them, and some hooks in the floor.

My brain blazed through dozens of scenes I'd witnessed as I tried to figure out what he had in store for us.

"Both of you naked," Zeke said dismissively.

Naked we got.

Standing in a room full of people with my dick hanging out wasn't my favorite thing in the world, but I'd gotten used to it. Funny, since I'd never even stepped inside a BDSM club before I met Case. Hell, I hadn't even fantasized about it. Before Case, I'd been what the kink community referred to as vanilla. Maybe a little roughing up during sex, hair pulling, biting, that sort of thing. Definitely not being chained to a beam and spread wide for the entire room to see.

Without a word, Zeke came over and took my wrist in his giant hand. He removed my watch, then led me farther into the corner, positioning me the way he wanted before he proceeded to chain me in place. Hands above my head, arms spread wide, wrists wrapped with leather cuffs, my dick on full display to the growing audience and I wasn't going anywhere. He pressed his foot to the inside of my leg, brushing against my ankle. I shifted my stance to accommodate. He squatted down and cuffed my ankles, hooking the restraints to the eye-hooks in the floor.

My dick stirred because … well, because I was in a kink club and Zeke Lautner was kneeling in front of me. While he deftly hooked me in place, I didn't say a word, but my heart raced like a prized thoroughbred after the Kentucky Derby.

Case was the next to be positioned. Again, Zeke never said a word, moving him into position, restraining him the same way he'd restrained me. We were standing beside one another, my right hand almost touching Case's left.

Of course, we'd drawn quite the audience already and the exhibitionist in me—as well as my dick—was rather enticed by all the eyes shifting and searching, taking it all in. That was the nature of a club like this. People gathered around to watch the scenes that appealed to them. And anytime Zeke did a scene, it was always packed.

Still, Zeke never said a word as he went over to the large leather bag he had sitting on a nearby table. He laid out a few things, but from the angle I was at, I couldn't tell what they were. Likely his plan.

Several more minutes passed before Zeke came back around to stand in front of us.

"From this moment on, you are fuck toys and nothing more. Tell me, are you here of your own volition?"

"Yes, Zeke," I said instantly, Case's agreement coming at the same time.

He pointed his hand toward me. "Here in the club, you have a safe word. *Only* because it's required. Tell me your safe word, fuck toy."

The term *fuck toy* was not one I'd had anyone use on me before. Generally, my previous play partners had called me sub or boy. This was interesting, to say the least. A bit of mind fuckery, I figured.

"Red, Zeke."

He did the same to Case, earning the same answer.

"If at any time you need to use it, I expect you to. As for after the scene, everyone knows I don't do aftercare. So, I've enlisted the help of Mistress Jane and Mistress D. They will take care of you. If you have a problem with that, I'll release you now."

"No issue, Zeke," I told him when he pinned those black eyes on me. Case verbalized the same.

I found it interesting that Zeke had selected Dommes to tend to our aftercare. Considering Case and I were not bisexual—which I had to believe Zeke knew—there would be nothing arousing about aftercare with a female. Had he done that on purpose? Or was I merely reading more into it?

Probably the latter.

Zeke stepped forward and gripped my jaw the same way he'd done to Case earlier. His fingers were tight, digging into my skin and pressing along the bones. It was rough and it hurt and my cock thickened as soon as the pain registered.

"You are only to speak when you are spoken to, fuck toy. If I ask you a question, you answer. Otherwise, your mouth should remain shut. I do not want to hear *anything* from you. Fuck toys do not speak. Understood?"

I managed a strained, "Yes, Zeke."

He studied my face momentarily before releasing me and moving over to Case. Once he got that part out of the way, he turned back to his bag.

I'd noticed Zeke never addressed the room when he was doing a scene. Some Doms explained what their intentions were and what they expected from their submissive. Zeke didn't pay attention to anyone else and I knew absolutely no one would make a sound during the scene either.

Otherwise, what we were getting from him would be child's play compared to what he would do to them.

And yes, my dick was still hard.

EIGHT

ZEKE

AFTER CAREFUL CONSIDERATION, I OPTED for something special tonight. A thick plug to go along with a little bit of cock and ball torture to induct my new fuck toys into my world. It wouldn't take long before they understood *exactly* what they could expect from me.

And I'd started thinking of them as mine ever since I left their apartment. I wouldn't be keeping them in the long term, but provided they were still willing once this was over, I would own them for a while. How long was yet to be seen. I tended to avoid putting time limits on my endeavors because one never knew how things would go. Maybe a day, two. Perhaps a week. A month. I doubted they would hold my interest for any longer than that.

They never did.

After walking around them a few more times, I grabbed the bottle of silicone lubricant and a latex glove. I liked silicone because it didn't dry out easily, and since this wasn't going to end quickly, I had to take care of my property.

I stood in front of them as I snapped on the glove. It was all part of the game. The mind fuck. Not knowing what my plan was only built their anticipation. And while I did receive intense pleasure from abusing my toys, it only worked if they got something in return. It was all about the power exchange, the mutual desire—one to top, the other to bottom. Or in this case, two bottoms.

Once I lubed two fingers generously, I walked around behind the cowboy. His legs were spread wide, his cock already thick and heavy, eager for my attention. But it was his ass I was interested in.

I hooked one hand over his shoulder, ensuring he was aware of my presence. Without preamble, I inched one lubed finger into his ass, enjoying the way his sphincter squeezed me. I worked the lube in as deep as I could, then added another finger. I fucked him a few times, enjoying the way his breaths increased. At the point where I knew he was enjoying it, I withdrew my fingers and pushed in a thick plug.

I changed gloves and did the same to the pretty boy.

Neither of them moaned, groaned, or even sighed.

So far, so good.

When they were both plugged, their asses being stretched nicely, I took a moment to admire my work. The quick trip I'd taken to the adult toy store before I came here was well worth it. I'd found a couple of things I looked forward to using on them—the plugs included. However, the more complicated torture devices couldn't be picked up at an adult novelty store. No, the tools in my arsenal were of a much higher quality. Had to be. I was hard on my toys. Especially the human ones.

After disposing of the second glove, I pulled on a fresh one, retrieved the lube, and took my time coating their balls, kneading and pulling firmly. First the cowboy. I wasn't gentle and I was impressed that he didn't so much as hiss although I knew it had to be rather unpleasant. It was also pleasurable, I could tell by the way he was breathing.

The pretty boy handled it equally well, not moving a single one of those deliciously defined muscles even as I roughly squeezed and tugged. In a few minutes, he wouldn't even remember that pain.

Once they were ready, I retrieved the two parachute ball stretchers that I had brought with me. These were devious little torture devices made of a thick, supple adjustable leather that looked like shortened, upside-down funnels. From their positions, my fuck toys wouldn't even know there were roughly twenty stainless steel tacks with five spikes darting out from each on the underside. Those would give just enough sensation to keep their attention where I wanted it. When I added weights to the chains that dangled down, they would get the full effect.

I garnered a sharp inhale from the cowboy when I fastened the leather around the top of his scrotum, ensuring it wasn't too tight. I carefully worked it in place, covering half of his ball sac. It was about causing him pain, not irreversible damage. When satisfied, I moved to the pretty boy. He remained motionless when I put his in position. I could tell immediately that he would require more weight than the cowboy.

But that would come in time.

While I had no intention of asking them whether they were okay or not, I did make a valiant effort to watch their body language. While some Doms preferred a verbal response, some sort of confirmation that they were doing the right thing, I didn't. I wasn't here to get their approval. I didn't care if they were comfortable.

On the other hand, I did care that I wasn't causing unintentional physical damage. I consistently glanced at their hands, which were cuffed high above their heads. I didn't want to cut off any circulation or cause nerve damage. So, while it appeared I didn't give a shit one way or another, I was constantly assessing the scene. Their safety was paramount and just as important to me as their pain.

The key was not letting them know that. It was all about the mind fuck. Getting into their heads, building the fear, the uncertainty, then delivering what would send them into subspace if that was something they could achieve. I got the feeling the cowboy could with little effort. Pretty boy was harder to read. I could tell by his lack of responses that he was used to being let down, not getting what he truly needed.

"Ever worn a parachute harness before, cowboy?"

"No, Zeke."

"Tell me what it feels like."

"Little spikes stabbing my balls." His breaths were coming rapidly, his eyes wide with desire.

I wasn't going to be quite so kind to the pretty boy. I grabbed my crop from the table and moved closer to him.

"You enjoy the spikes." It wasn't a question and he knew that. When he didn't answer, I smacked his cock with the crop. Not for doing anything wrong. Quite the opposite. My fuck toys would know I detested bad behavior, and that I would certainly reward them when they pleased me. As for punishment ... well, let's just say they'd be very aware of the difference.

The only outward sign that the crop had the desired effect was the way the pretty boy's eyes drooped shut, his throat working as he swallowed.

I could feel all the eyes on us, curiosity mixed with concern. Some of them understood who I was, *what* I was, and what I was capable of. They'd been at my hands before. Doms had worn my stripes during training exercises, getting familiar with the tools of the trade. Submissives had felt my wrath, most of the time as a way to assuage their curiosity. Not so much to sate their inner masochist, more because they believed me incapable of being as demanding as my reputation proclaimed I was. I always ensured they understood they were wrong. I was *that* demanding.

Not once had anyone in this place received aftercare from me. That was a line I drew and I wouldn't cross it. There was only one man in existence who had ever seen my softer side. I learned a little too late that that wasn't a side of me he was open to seeing. So, I had tucked it away, refusing to let it out to play.

Which was why the human toys I played with were someone else's responsibility when I was finished. I ensured they were in good hands before passing them off and putting them out of my mind. The experiences were what stayed with me. The feelings I got from watching a submissive take the pain I willingly delivered. The faces had all morphed together over time, some not having faces at all.

As I turned, I skimmed the crowd, mentally tallying the number and wondering how many would be left when I was finished.

Because they hadn't seen anything yet.

Case
(The pretty boy)

I HAD TO GIVE IT TO him, Zeke had a way of keeping me focused on him and only him. Not once had I gotten lost in my own head. I didn't have time to worry about anything outside of the walls of this club. Or anyone, for that matter.

Every muscle in my body was hard, my blood pumping fast through my veins, every nerve ending on alert, the endorphins steadily flowing. I couldn't even focus on Brax because Zeke had wrapped an invisible hand around my throat and he kept me inching closer to the promise of release with every breath.

When he had smacked my cock with that crop, I imagined that was what it felt like for a drug user when they got their fix. Pure, raw bliss had shot through my bloodstream. I needed more, but I wouldn't ask for it.

Zeke made his way over to his bag, but I couldn't see what he picked up. When he turned back around, I didn't see anything except for the crop still in his hand. The beast of a man strutted back over, his body blocking my view of everyone and everything. I watched him, eager, anxious. Desperate.

"Do you wish to be my fuck toy, pretty boy?"

The sound of Zeke's voice was fuel to the fire he'd ignited inside me. The more I heard it, the higher I got. "Yes, Zeke."

He moved, bending at the waist in front of me, and I felt the parachute tighten over my balls. He'd added a weight. It caused the spikes to pinch a little more.

"Do you know what it means to be my fuck toy, cowboy?"

"No, Zeke." There was an edge of tension to Brax's tone.

"Yet you want to be my fuck toy, too?"

"Yes, Zeke."

Zeke bent in front of Brax and I assumed he added a weight to him, too.

He slowly stood and turned his attention to me. "And why is that? What is it you think I'll give you, pretty boy?"

"Pleasure, Zeke. In the form of pain."

"Is that what you need, pretty boy?"

"Yes, Zeke."

He bent and added another weight, the pain blooming in brilliant Technicolor. It wasn't quite enough.

"And you're willing to do anything to get it?"

"Yes, Zeke." I'd never felt so strongly about anything in my life, except perhaps my feelings for Brax.

Another weight was added and I swallowed hard, the spikes digging into my balls. They weren't sharp enough to puncture, I could tell by the feel. But they were a constant sensation, that delicious bite of pain I craved.

"As my fuck toys, you will cook for me, clean for me, do any depraved thing I want. Outside the confines of this club, you will have no safe word, no limits. You will belong to me." Zeke stepped up in front of me, his voice lowering. "If I choose to make you sleep in a cage, you will. If I want you to jack off ten times a day, you will. If I tell you to bend over so I can shove my dick in your ass, you will. You're a fuck toy for me to use and abuse, nothing more. Is that what you want?"

"Yes, Zeke."

His crop smacked my dick, and I bit back the moan as the heat registered, the sting in my balls more powerful. I was to make no noise. Fuck toys did not make a sound. I was only allowed to speak if spoken to.

"In return, I will hurt you, humiliate you. It will be my sole desire to break you." He stepped over to Brax. "Is that what you want from me?"

"Yes, Zeke."

Zeke bent again and this time Brax released a soft moan. He was affected by this the same way I was.

Zeke moved around behind me. I could feel his warmth as he stepped in close, something—I assumed the handle of the crop—pressed against the plug in my ass.

"You will be bound to me by an iron-clad contract. You will wear my collar day and night. Is that what you want from me?"

"Yes, Zeke."

The crop handle bounced off the plug and I swallowed a groan as pure pleasure detonated inside me. My cock was rock hard, pre-cum generously pooling at the tip, my balls tight as the spikes pinned them in place.

The warmth of his body moved away.

"The only time you will be out of my sight is when you are obligated to do your job. Otherwise, you will be at my mercy. Day and night. Wherever I want you. I will own you, my word the only one you listen to. You will ask permission for whatever you need. It will be my decision as to whether it will be granted. Can you handle that?"

"Yes, Zeke," Brax ground out.

In my peripheral vision, I saw him jerk, and I assumed Zeke had used the crop on him as well. That did something for me, too. I wasn't sure I was supposed to be turned on by the idea of Zeke hurting Brax, but I was.

The big man reappeared. "If you whine, you will be punished. If you disobey, you will be punished." He stepped up, centered between us, and once again I found my jaw compressed by his big hand. "And if you try to top from the bottom, you'll be out on your ass. Do you understand me?"

"Yes, Zeke."

He released me with a jerk of his hand.

"Ask anyone here, I don't play games. I'm not here to be your friend, your confidant, or your lover. I will fuck you when it suits me. I will deny your orgasm when it suits me. I will beat you when it suits me. My rules, always." He met my eyes. "Can you handle that, fuck toy?"

"Yes, Zeke."

He turned to Brax, who gave him the same answer.

I wasn't sure whether Zeke had come to a final decision or not, but he walked back to his bag and laid the crop down. He picked up something else. This time when he turned around, he didn't attempt to conceal the small ball weights he had. The size was deceiving, I knew. That one ball added to what he already had hanging from the parachute would drag my balls down farther, compressing the spiked leather into my scrotum. My dick surged with anticipation.

His eyes met mine briefly before he bent down and placed the weight on the dangling chain.

I gritted my teeth. Pain—sharp and bright—sizzled through me. That weight was much heavier than the others.

Fuck, fuck, fuck.

I was starting to sweat, unsure whether I could handle much more. I needed him to hit me, to use a whip, a flogger, a crop. I didn't care what torture implement he chose, but I needed it more than I needed the breath filling my lungs.

When Zeke bent to place the other weighted ball on Brax, the man I loved moaned in earnest.

Zeke stood tall, getting right up in Brax's face. "I should not hear you, fuck toy."

It was obvious Zeke was waiting to see if Brax would use his safe word. Although I knew Zeke didn't want us to have one, there was no way around it here in the club. It was a club rule. However, if one of us used it, I got the feeling Zeke would wash his hands of us.

I could see the question in the Sadist's eyes, but he didn't voice it. He wouldn't voice it. Zeke didn't offer an out, he demanded obedience.

Somewhere in the back of my mind, I worried about Brax but I couldn't hold on to the thoughts. My entire being centered around those spikes buried in my balls and the plug filling my ass. With every breath, the pain intensified. God forbid I move. My knees were weak and I gripped the chains above my head, needing something to hold on to.

Zeke's movement caught my eye and I focused on him. He stepped away slowly, then removed his shirt. I heard someone gasp, knew they were thinking the same thing I was. One, Zeke never removed any of his clothing during a scene. And two, he was the most incredible specimen I'd ever laid eyes on. Not an ounce of fat on his oversized body. His wide chest narrowed to lean hips and his thighs stretched the fabric of his jeans.

When he tossed the shirt toward the table, every muscle rippled, the various tattoos covering his chest and arms danced, the mere sight making my dick throb at the same time my balls felt like they were on fire.

His eyes met mine. "That was the easy part, fuck toys." He glanced at Brax. "Now for the fun part."

NINE

ZEKE

AS FAR AS SCENES WENT, this one was setting up nicely. I was rather impressed with how my new fuck toys were handling themselves. I'd figured the cowboy would've caved by now. The weight on their balls alone would cause enough pain most submissives would've screamed out their safe word ten times over.

Not these two.

Granted, they technically didn't have a safe word. I only said as much because we were in the club. If either of them used it, that would be the end of our scene *and* our interactions.

I could tell by the look on the pretty boy's face that he was getting his fix. He could handle more than I'd given him, but this wasn't about a race to the finish line for him or for me. I needed to give them time for the pain to register, for it to sink into their brains. At this point, a submissive would be trying to figure out how to stand to ease some of the ache in their joints from the position of their limbs. But every movement would cause those tiny pricks on the underside of the leather to stab into their balls. Just enough to make them catch their breath.

I enjoyed cock and ball torture because it was a humbling experience for a submissive. Naked and on display, their most sensitive parts being tortured before an audience. They wouldn't have time to feel modesty because they were too busy addressing the pain of having their family jewels pulled away from their bodies.

Admittedly, these two made me feel invincible. They were worthy opponents for sure. It was the very reason I'd removed my shirt, something I wasn't prone to do in the club. It wasn't necessarily a rule of mine, but I generally avoided it. Same as I avoided having sex in the club. I didn't need a bunch of submissives slobbering all over me and that tended to happen. It wasn't ego, either. I had no delusions that I was a handsome man. It was the edge of danger I presented. The bald head, beard, and tattoos exacerbated the danger. Six foot eight inches, two hundred seventy pounds of solid muscle posed an enormous threat.

I could see the appreciation in my fuck toys' eyes as they stared back at me. You could put the pretty boy up against any other man in this building and he looked like a beast. Put him up next to me and I made him small in comparison.

And while I didn't usually seek approval from anyone, I appreciated the admiration I could see staring back at me from both of my new toys. I'd go so far as to say I wanted it.

"Seriously," someone whispered from behind me. "He took his shirt off. I can't believe this."

I pivoted around to find the owner of the voice. There in the front row was a scrawny submissive, his eyes wide as he stared up at me. I took three steps closer and glared down at him. "One more word out of you tonight and you'll become intimately familiar with figging."

The boy's eyebrows raised. "What's that?"

Someone gasped because, yes, with those two words, he had already violated my warning. And I wasn't the sort to let anyone off easy.

"It's when a ginger root is shoved up your ass," I said, being purposely crude. "The ginger oil causes a burning sensation. Starts out mild, but the more you clench on the root, the more intense it gets."

The boy's eyes were wide.

I smirked, then glanced toward the back of the group, locating one of the more revered Dominatrixes. She enjoyed doling out pain almost as much as I did.

"Mistress Cameron, since this submissive doesn't know when to keep his mouth shut, I'd appreciate your help in showing him just what it feels like."

"It'd be my pleasure, Master Zeke." She moved around the group, coming to stand beside the boy.

"Should you choose to safe word out, you will be banned from the club for two months," I informed him. It was one thing to use a safe word when things became overwhelming, another altogether when it was to avoid punishment. "Do you understand?"

"Yes, Master Zeke."

Mistress Cameron raised one hand, her red-tipped talons curling around his bicep. "Right this way, pet. I promise, you will *not* enjoy this."

Once they were heading up the stairs leading out of the dungeon, I scanned the crowd. "Anyone else have anything to say?"

No one spoke. I hadn't expected them to. The Doms in the back row grinned. They were often amused by the amount of control I maintained during a scene. It was imperative that these toys learned how to behave. What was the point in owning one if they didn't do as you wanted?

Pivoting back around, I took in my two fuck toys. I paced in front of them while my eyes raked over them, checking their wrists, their ankles, their balls. So far, so good.

Now it was time to show them what real pain was.

Brax
(The cowboy)

WHEN ZEKE TURNED AROUND TO face us after sending the submissive off to have a ginger root shoved up his ass, I could see the intent in his black gaze. His muscles flexed, as though they were readying themselves for battle. He was getting down to business.

Red!

Red, red, red!

That was the only thing blazing through my brain but no matter how badly I wanted to yell out my safe word, I couldn't. Not because I wasn't physically capable. I was. I could speak if I needed to.

No. It wasn't inability that held me back, it was a deep, dark hunger that willed me forward. I'd never experienced anything quite like this before. The damn plug in my ass, the fucking harness thing on my balls, those brutal weights causing the steel spikes to stab into my scrotum, heat blooming on my skin, a fuzziness forming in my brain. I was high on endorphins. It was too much, but for some reason I wanted more.

And the moment Zeke had stripped his shirt off, I'd thought I would come from the sight alone. I'd seen him play plenty of times, but the giant Sadist wasn't one to remove his clothing in the club. I'd never even seen him without a shirt. And fucking shit, I wasn't sure I was going to survive it now.

I couldn't help but feel a sense of pride. It felt as though Zeke was doing it for us. Possibly without knowing it, he was giving back to us as a reward for what we were giving him.

He was the most incredible thing I'd ever seen. At six three, I wasn't a small man. I always felt relatively small compared to Case because I didn't have the muscle mass that he did. But up against Zeke, I was minuscule in comparison. It caused an odd sense of vulnerability to wash over me.

I breathed in deep, exhaled slowly, allowing the pain to morph into intense pleasure. I was doing relatively decent until Zeke pulled a braided whip from his belt. How I hadn't noticed it earlier, I wasn't sure. But it was long, with multiple tails and knotted ends. Like a flogger on steroids. It was the same one he'd used on Case when he'd overtaken the scene I had observed a week ago.

Zeke turned away from us, then pointed to a submissive standing near him. "You. Unchain his feet," he instructed the submissive as he pointed to me. "And I want him"—he motioned to Case—"released completely. For now."

Oh, fuck. Unchaining my feet meant I would be shifting, which meant the damn torture apparatus on my balls would move and it was possible I would pass out.

The submissive rushed to do as instructed while Zeke stood back and watched. I noticed his eyes continued to look at our hands, our arms. He was assessing the scene, ensuring we weren't enduring any unintentional pain or damage. I wasn't sure I'd ever seen a Dom quite as attentive to that sort of thing as Zeke. Or maybe I just hadn't paid that much attention.

"Move your feet together," he commanded when my ankles were free.

My teeth were going to be chalk by the time this was done. I eased my legs together, grunting as the weight dragged those damn spikes into my balls. It felt as though they'd punctured the skin, but I knew they hadn't. That wasn't the intent of them. The pain was the goal, the constant pin-prick like stabs to my most sensitive area, sure. Not blood.

Standing tall allowed some of the strain on my shoulders to ease. I flexed my hands, then gripped the chains, trying to relieve the tension. Zeke didn't miss the movement, his eyes shooting up to my hands, then down to my face. He must've approved of what he saw, because he turned to Case.

"Move back against the wall. I expect you to watch."

"Yes, Zeke." There was a grunt to follow Case's words as he stepped back out of the way. I could imagine it felt as though he was dragging his balls on the ground.

When the submissive scurried off and Case was out of the strike zone, Zeke gripped the tails of his whip, dragging them through his big fist as he moved closer. His eyes were fixed on me and only me. The intensity I saw there had my breath halting in my lungs.

"Five," he told me. "That's what I expect you to take."

Five licks with that thing? Fuck. That seemed like a million at this point.

When Zeke had played with Case, he'd dished out twelve before Case came. He was going easy on me.

Zeke came to stand directly in front of me. I tilted my head back to look in his eyes.

"Five, cowboy." His voice was low enough I doubted anyone else heard him. "You survive that, you will go home with me and be wearing my collar by the end of the night. Can you do that?"

"Yes, Zeke." My voice trembled because the excruciating pain continued to flood my system. My balls felt as though they were dragging on the floor, seconds away from being ripped from my body. Yet my mind was now on the potential of being collared by this man. A strange feeling filled my chest. As though there was some sort of light on the inside, daring to come out.

"After five, you have my permission to come."

"Yes, Zeke." I wasn't sure that was even possible with the torture apparatus on my balls, but there was no time to contemplate that because he disappeared behind me.

The audience was focused on me, a few shifting, probably to get a better view of those fucking tails licking my skin. I tried to relax, knowing the tension in my muscles would only make it worse. I remembered the first time I'd been flogged. The pain had been minimal compared to what I'd expected.

I doubted that was going to be the case now.

The deep throb of the music warred with the sound of my blood rushing in my ears. I waited, no way to see what Zeke was doing or when he was going to—

"Fuck!" I cried out as those wicked tails snapped against me. It felt as though the skin had been ripped away, the fires of Hell having nothing on the agony that lanced me. I breathed through it, my cock throbbing despite the pain. Or maybe because of it. I didn't know at this point.

I thought I was ready for the next one, but it took me by surprise, coming far sooner than I anticipated. I jerked, my balls swinging, the spikes and the weight making my eyes water.

When the next one came, it wasn't quite as intense. I figured that was due to the shock, the weird feeling that overtook me. Like I was floating above myself. I shifted forward, groaning from the torture. It morphed into one fireball of agony that seemed to bloom over my entire body.

The fourth one caused my arms to weaken, my hands releasing the grip on the chain. And the fifth came right after. My brain registered the number, my cock swelled, my balls drew up tight, and I came in a rush that was so fucking painful I would've fallen to the floor had I not been held up by the cuffs around my wrists.

"Release him!" Zeke yelled, his voice a dull roar in my ears.

The next thing I knew, two submissives—big men I didn't know—came forward. With a strange sense of urgency, they freed me, then bore my weight on their bodies, broad shoulders tucking beneath my arms.

Zeke appeared before me. "You did good, cowboy."

His praise didn't lessen the intense sensations stabbing into me but it was more than I expected.

"Thank you, Zeke."

When Zeke moved away, I was vaguely aware of a submissive wearing rubber gloves rushing forward with a towel and spray bottle filled with some sort of cleaner. The mess I made was quickly cleaned and then Mistress Jane was coming forward, her hand dipping down between my legs. In an instant, my balls were freed and air slammed into my lungs as the pain reversed, only to transform into something equally fierce, the spikes dislodging from my tender skin. Mistress Jane offered a nod behind me before she turned.

With the submissives' help, I put one foot in front of the other. And as they led me into one of the private aftercare rooms, I found that I was smiling, the euphoric feeling taking over.

It was the first time I'd ever experienced a high quite like that. And it had me wondering just what I'd been missing out on.

More importantly, just what I was getting myself into.

TEN

ZEKE

I WATCHED AS JANE'S TWO submissives practically carried the cowboy to an aftercare room. The moment they were out of sight, I turned my attention to the other fuck toy who was waiting for me. I would check on the cowboy later, meet up with Jane to get an overall assessment. I wasn't the sort to offer aftercare because some submissives took it to mean more than it was. I didn't want to give anyone false hope, but I wasn't a monster despite the rumors.

"Back to the chains," I ordered.

His movements slow, the pretty boy managed to get back into position. Since Jane had taken the two biggest submissives available, I opted to reconnect the cuffs myself.

Once the pretty boy was back where I wanted him, I came to stand in front of him. His eyes were glazed, the pain still surging through his body.

I gripped his jaw because I'd noticed how he responded to me when I did. The man wasn't in this to see how much pain he could handle. He knew how much he needed, that was clear. And he was desperate to receive it.

I would be the man to give him that.

"You will take ten," I told him, holding his gaze, those bright green eyes glassy. "You will take all ten graciously and without complaint. If you do, you will go home with me and be wearing my collar by the end of the night."

"Yes, Zeke." His chest rose and fell, his body succumbing to the constant sensation beating on him. Between the plug in his ass and the weights stretching his balls, those tiny steel spikes biting into sensitive flesh, I would be surprised if he made it to five before he was flying.

Still gripping his jaw, I leaned in closer. "I do not expect you to come if you fly, pretty boy. However, should you not hit subspace, you may come after ten. Understand?"

I could see the plea in his eyes. He wanted subspace more than he wanted to come. It didn't surprise me.

Releasing his face, I took a step back. I raked my gaze over his entire form, confirming he was where he should be. The cuffs weren't cutting off the circulation and his balls weren't discolored from the leather binding them. Content that he wasn't suffering unnecessarily, I walked behind him.

While I had only given the cowboy five, I'd known the pretty boy would need more. He was far more experienced with this, far more in tune with his own needs. I appreciated that. It made my job easier. I didn't have to worry that he would take this only to please me. He needed this as much as I did.

Once I was behind him and no one was in danger of getting the ends of my tails, I pulled the whip back and snapped it forward, ensuring the ends did not touch his skin. As I expected, the pretty boy didn't move, his body primed and ready for the blow.

The next time I pulled back, I let go, following through and allowing the nine knotted ends to snap over his back.

The pretty boy moaned, but he didn't move.

I continued, delivering blow after blow, taking several seconds between, sometimes a little longer, prolonging the torture. It wasn't until the seventh that his knees buckled. My eyes shot up to his hands. He wasn't holding on to the chains, merely dangling from the cuffs. He couldn't remain there for long or he'd cut the circulation off in his hands.

I delivered the last three in rapid succession, the pretty boy's deep bellows confirming my suspicion. He was flying high, his mind wrapped up tightly as the pain consumed him and the endorphins offered the escape he sought. It was the relief he wanted, the high he chased, and I'd given that to him.

I tossed the whip to the side and moved forward. I caught Trent's attention and he stepped forward instantly, Ransom moving in beside him. There was no one else nearby capable of bearing the pretty boy's weight, which explained why the two Masters were there to assist.

I turned to face the pretty boy, leaning in close but not touching him. "You did good. I look forward to seeing you wear my collar."

"Thank you, Zeke," he mumbled, his words slurred.

Mistress D stepped forward almost instantly, releasing the parachute from the pretty boy's balls, dragging a long, ragged moan from him. She gave me a nod—her confirmation that she was taking responsibility for him—before turning and leading the way to another aftercare room.

"Master Zeke, may I clean up for you now?" a soft female voice sounded from behind me.

I turned to see one of the submissives who volunteered here at the club. She had asked prior to my scene if she could assist and I'd granted her permission. I appreciated the fact she had asked. "You may."

Without hesitation, she hurried to get the toys from the floor and the cuffs still connected to the chains, bringing them over to me before she grabbed the cleaner and towels. I shoved the used toys into ziplock bags and stowed them in my bag to clean later.

As I tucked them inside, I smiled to myself. I wouldn't have to clean them later. I had two fuck toys who would handle that for me.

The thought made me chuckle even as a foreign sense of anticipation shot through me.

Two hours later—just after one in the morning—I was walking into my house while the cowboy and the pretty boy were pulling into the driveway. It had taken some time for them to come down from the scene. While I had checked in on them both a couple of times, I'd left their care to the others and by the time I told them I was ready to leave, the two masochists were in good spirits, if not exhausted.

I couldn't blame them. I'd put them through hell and enjoyed every second of it. Didn't mean I was done with them tonight.

"What's up, boy?" I greeted Tank when he rushed to the front door, his tail wagging ninety miles a minute. "You wanna go outside?"

It only took the word *outside* to get him darting for the back door. After setting my bag on the counter, I followed. Opening the sliding glass doors, I freed him from his indoor prison. He raced out into the yard and wandered for about thirty seconds before finding a spot to do his business.

I watched, smiling as I did. I had no clue what it was about that dog, but I missed him when I was away. It was one of the reasons I'd insisted that he be allowed to come to work with me before I accepted the position at Chatter PR.

Aware that Tank would sniff around for a good twenty minutes, I left the door open and headed back to the front door in time to see the cowboy and the pretty boy step inside. Their eyes were wide as they peered around.

I knew what they were thinking when they scoped out my living space. It likely didn't suit me based on what everyone knew about me. It wasn't dark and gloomy. There weren't sex toys hanging from the walls. I had some, but I kept those secured in the basement. However, this was home and I was comfortable here.

"Come here," I instructed.

Both men moved toward me, their curiosity morphing to concern as they likely tried to decipher my tone.

"I want you both to kneel. I'll be right back."

Leaving them to do as I asked, I jogged upstairs to my bedroom and over to my dresser. I retrieved the two items I'd ordered a week ago. Perhaps I'd been a little optimistic when it came to them, but it wasn't something I was going to dwell on.

I returned downstairs to find them exactly where I'd asked them to be. That was one thing I greatly appreciated about them. Neither was going to require any special training. They were willingly obedient and that alone was refreshing. Too many times I'd dealt with submissives who thought a Dom wanted to train them to be the perfect little fuck toy. Perhaps some Doms did. I was not one of them.

I stopped directly in front of them both.

"Look up at me, pretty boy." When his light green eyes met mine, I locked my gaze with his. "I'm offering you my collar with the understanding it's to be worn at all times. While it may be temporary, it shows proof of ownership. Do you accept?"

"I do, Zeke."

It only took a second to hook the plain black leather dog collar around his neck, locking it with a titanium padlock. I would wear the key around my neck for as long as he wore the collar.

When I was done, I turned to the cowboy and gave him the same speech. He was far more expressive than the pretty boy, anticipation lighting up his dark eyes. "Do you accept?"

"Yes, I accept, Zeke."

I connected his collar—exactly the same as the pretty boy's—before taking both keys and placing them on the silver chain that I wore around my neck.

"If at any time you remove the collar, I will take that as your decision to void our contract. And when *I* remove the collar, that is confirmation that our contract is null and void as well. Understand?"

"Yes, Zeke," they said in unison.

"Good. You may stand." Once the chain was hooked around my neck, I motioned toward the stairs. "There are two guest rooms upstairs. I want you to each take one. While both rooms have beds, don't assume that is where you'll be sleeping. However, I can assure you, you won't be sleeping in those beds together."

I knew they were in a relationship and had been living together prior to this, so I fully expected them to argue, to request to be in the same room, but neither did.

116

"Put your things up there for now, then come back down and join me."

Without waiting for them, I went to the kitchen and pulled out Tank's food bowl. While he had eaten earlier in the evening, I figured a late-night snack couldn't hurt, so I went to work preparing it. My dog was on a fresh food diet, no chemically processed kibble for him, so it took a few minutes to get it together. By the time I had it ready and sitting on the floor, Tank was back inside, his tail wagging enthusiastically because he considered this a treat.

My fuck toys—referring to them that way kept things less complicated for me—came down a few minutes later, looking exactly as they had when they went upstairs. There was still a gleam in the pretty boy's eyes, as though he hadn't quite come down from his high.

"It's late," I told them. "And I'm sure you're exhausted; however, I'm not sure when you last ate. Are you hungry?"

Both men looked at me and nodded. Now that I thought about it, until a few minutes ago, I wasn't sure either of them had said anything—except to answer my questions—since they emerged from the aftercare rooms.

"Good. So am I." I looked at the cowboy. "Since you're the chef, you have free rein of my kitchen."

His eyes widened as they should. My home had top-of-the-line everything, including a chef's kitchen. I wasn't the greatest cook in the world, but I could hold my own. Plus, my baby sister loved spending time in there, making a mess while she worked to concoct something amazing. I would admit, her cooking skills weren't any better than mine, but I generally suffered through simply because it put a smile on her face.

"The fridge is stocked, so make whatever sounds appealing. I prefer meat over vegetables and keep the carbs to a minimum. If there's anything you need for future meals, jot it down and I'll have it delivered."

"Yes, Zeke. Thank you," the cowboy said.

I stepped back out of the way, signaling for him to get started. While he took care of dinner, I had plans for the pretty boy. Plans that included him taking care of me.

"You. Back upstairs. I need to shower."

A smile formed on his lips as he said, "Yes, Zeke."

Case

(The pretty boy)

I WAS STILL TRYING TO wrap my head around the fact that Zeke Lautner lived in a fucking mansion. In fact, the long, winding road up to the place had me feeling as though I was about to greet royalty.

Okay, maybe it wasn't a traditional mansion but it was ridiculously nice. Honestly, I'd expected him to live in a loft warehouse of some sort. The type with concrete floors, exposed brick, and pipes running along the ceiling joists. This was ... not that.

In the living room, which appeared to be the focal point of the downstairs, there were two oversized black leather sofas with an iron coffee table between them. If I wasn't mistaken, that coffee table doubled as a cage. Whether it was for Tank (I somehow doubted that) or for his human fuck toys, I wasn't sure. The hardwood floors were sleek and dark, the walls gleamed white, and the fixtures appeared to be black iron. A couple of splatter-paint art pieces— black, white, and red—decorated the one wall that didn't contain floor-to-ceiling windows.

Based on what little I'd seen, I would venture a guess that it came in close to four thousand square feet with wide-open spaces and a monochromatic theme. I'd noticed two additional bedrooms upstairs when we headed down the hallway to the two guest bedrooms. One looked to be the master bedroom, the other very feminine, as though a woman lived there. However, there was no one else in the house. Not that I could tell, anyway.

I followed Zeke back up the stairs, admiring the impressive staircase as I went. The floating knotted-wood planks stained the same color of the hardwood and decorative wrought iron railing were unique by design. Very impressive.

I had a weird desire to snoop around, to see if I could find what made this guy tick. And maybe I would have, except once we reached the top landing, my body hardened at the thought of what was going to come next.

Honestly, I didn't care what he intended to do to me. After that scene at the club, I was ready and willing to bow at the man's feet. No one had ever made me feel what he'd made me feel. The pain, the pleasure. The intensity of it all still lingered even a couple of hours later.

Zeke stepped into the room I'd pegged as the master bedroom. The space was enormous, as was the furniture. Plush gray carpet covered the floor, a huge bed sat on one side of the room, several rectangular windows high up on the wall above it.

I noticed instantly that the bed was constructed of thick, black iron with posts that rose up from the corners and bars across the top. The headboard consisted of several rows of squares— capable of having chains hooked through them, which explained the huge cage beneath the bed, likely built to shelter one of his fuck toys, if I had to guess. It wasn't the sort of bed you found in a regular home, that was for damn sure.

On the opposite side was a full wall of windows with thick black curtains that were currently pulled back to reveal a sliding glass door. I couldn't tell what was outside, but I figured it had to be impressive for a room to be set up to overlook it.

There was a matching black dresser, two nightstands, a large armoire, and what appeared to be some sort of chest on the same wall as the dresser. Very modern, very open. *Very* unexpected.

I didn't know how I'd envisioned Zeke Lautner designing his personal space, but it wasn't like this.

"This way, pretty boy," he said, motioning toward the bathroom.

I turned and followed him through a set of double doors. On the other side of those doors was a huge open space. I was equally enthralled with the decor in here, noticing there were very few walls aside from the four that confined it. The double sinks were black—appeared to be quartz—sitting atop gleaming black cabinets. No hardware, just sleek lines. There was a Jacuzzi tub that looked like it would hold three people—or maybe just one Zeke—a single door that I suspected was the water closet, and a shower that took up almost half the space. No enclosure on it, simply gray, slate-tiled walls and floor.

"Undress," he said as he pulled his T-shirt off over his head before walking to the back of the room.

The way he moved captured my attention. All those hard muscles flexing even though he appeared relaxed. Zeke disappeared and I realized there was another door on the far end of the room, likely a closet.

Since he'd given me a command, I didn't hesitate, stripping off my T-shirt first, my shoes and socks next, then finally my jeans. The floors were warmer than I expected and I had to wonder whether he had radiant heat beneath the tile. I'd heard that was a thing in the northern states. Having grown up in Oklahoma and Texas, that was a luxury we hadn't needed.

When Zeke returned, the man was wearing only his jeans, his giant boots discarded in the room he'd emerged from. He moved with purpose, his long legs devouring the space on his way to the shower.

I waited, curious as to what he would do next.

The water came on and then he was stripping those jeans over his powerful legs. All corded muscle covered by smooth skin. His ass was a masterpiece, just like the rest of him.

"Over here." He pointed toward the shower floor. "Kneel by the wall. Facing me."

Swallowing hard, I did as he instructed, doing my best not to appear overeager. I was, but I damn sure didn't want Zeke to know that.

The wet slate floor dug into my knees, but I welcomed the pain. It blended with the delicious sensations still coursing through my body. While I had anticipated having open wounds on my back from our scene, I'd been surprised when Mistress D informed me there were only a few large welts that would likely disappear by morning. She had applied some soothing oil over my skin, outlining the huge dragon that covered my back.

Admittedly, I'd been a little disappointed when I learned the marks would go away so quickly. I had wanted to wear them for a little while longer. Perhaps fall asleep with them, feeling the sting as I settled into bed. It would've been a nice reminder of the scene from earlier.

While I kneeled obediently, Zeke stepped beneath the water, which was coming at him from multiple angles—a rain shower head above him and several others lining the wall at his back. I probably should've tilted my head down in submission, but I was entranced by the man's body. He was one of the biggest men I'd ever seen and I'd been around plenty, myself included. The gyms were full of powerful males and some females, all looking to enhance their physique to push their bodies to the limit.

There was no way Zeke didn't work out with a body as honed as his. That wasn't natural muscle tone, but it was admirable, regardless. His chest was broad and covered with various tattoos, but even from the front, you could see his lats. They flared out from his back, wider than his chest.

I tried to admire all the sleek lines and thick muscle, but my gaze inadvertently lowered, taking in his cock. He was hard as steel, the skin over the thick head glossy. I'd seen men with arms smaller than that man's cock. It wasn't just the length that was impressive, it was the girth. My ass clenched at the thought of him fucking me into oblivion. That damn plug he'd used today had absolutely nothing on him.

Soap suds began drifting down his body, gliding over his impressive dick before slipping farther until they washed down the drain. I had the strange urge to wash him, to let my hands roam over him, memorizing every inch to lock away for later.

"You didn't come tonight," he said, drawing my attention up his body.

His head was tilted back, his hands washing the soap from his bald head.

"No, Zeke."

Black eyes leveled on my face a second later. "Is that normal for you?"

"If I can reach subspace, I tend to hold off."

"That's your drug? Subspace?"

"Yes." I wasn't ashamed to admit it. "But it's rare that a Dom can get me there."

"Your pain threshold is high."

Although it wasn't a question, I answered anyway. "Yes. And it seems the more I play, the higher it gets."

"At what point did you realize you needed the pain?"

I hadn't expected the questions. "I was … a … uh … teenager." I didn't want to go into all the reasons with him. I didn't like talking about my childhood. While I wasn't abused or mistreated in any way by my parents, there were some things that had molded me into the man I was today.

"How long have you been in the scene?"

"A while. I went to my first club when I was twenty-two."

"And you're twenty-eight?"

He obviously remembered from the time he'd asked on the plane. "Yeah. I'll be twenty-nine in December."

The room was filling with steam from the heat of the water, holding back the chill from the air. But it wasn't the steam that had me warming. No, that was the way Zeke's hand drifted down to his cock, his big fist encompassing the thick shaft as he stroked slowly, leisurely. I was entranced by the damn thing, wondering briefly if he would split me open if he fucked my ass. While Brax's cock filled me completely, it wasn't as long or thick.

However, I got the feeling Zeke wasn't going to take my ass tonight. The way his eyes continued to linger on my face, I knew he was thinking about my mouth. I was almost disappointed when he didn't move toward me once he had rinsed off completely. Instead, he took a step back and sat on the wide tiled bench in the corner.

"Your turn." He motioned for me to get up.

My legs were trembling from anticipation, but I managed to remain steady as I got up and closed the distance between us. The water was hot but not scalding.

"Wash," he ordered.

I'd showered with plenty of men before—some intimately, some not—but never had I felt as exposed as I did when I stood before Zeke. His eyes were merciless, roaming over every inch of me, sometimes lingering for several seconds before moving on. I worked my soapy hands over my skin, trying to focus on breathing. My cock was so hard I hurt. My balls, still sensitive from the earlier torment, felt as though they were going to explode.

It wasn't until I was rinsed clean that Zeke spoke again.

"Over here, pretty boy. Kneel in front of me."

Again, there was that hint of condescension when he said pretty boy. As though he was making fun of me. The humiliation only added to my desire.

I eased down between his splayed thighs, not touching him as I did. I wanted to feel his skin, curious as to whether it was as tough as the rest of him, but I knew better than to touch without permission.

He stroked his cock several times before reaching out and cupping the back of my head, drawing me closer.

"Open your mouth, pretty boy. I want those lips on my dick."

He wasn't gentle as he guided me forward, but I hadn't expected him to be. I was still shocked that I was in Zeke's house, in his shower, about to devour his cock. My thoughts briefly drifted to Brax, who was downstairs cooking. I wondered whether he wished he'd come with us. If for no other reason than to watch.

When my lips were wrapped around the thick crest of Zeke's cock, he released my head and leaned back against the wall.

"Now suck me."

Hesitantly, I reached up to grip him with my hand. I half expected him to order me not to touch him but he didn't.

He growled low, an aggressive, albeit sexy sound that made my cock jerk and twitch. Forcing my jaw as wide as it would go, I worked his cock into my mouth, retreating slowly, then pushing forward again. His cock was velvet over steel, every vein and ridge slick beneath my tongue.

Zeke didn't move, but I could feel his eyes on me.

I briefly wondered if he ever lost control. Doubtful. Not based on the way he remained still as I worked him with my tongue and lips. I couldn't take all of him, but he didn't seem to want that, so I didn't gag myself. I lost myself in the smoothness of his flesh against my tongue, the way his cock flexed in my hand as I stroked in tandem with the bobbing of my head.

Seconds turned to minutes but Zeke didn't move. He seemed content to enjoy my mouth on him, but not once did I get the impression he was going to come. My jaw started to ache, but I embraced the pain, letting it fuel my desire to please this man in any way that I could. Giving back to him what he'd given me earlier tonight.

Time continued to crawl by as I sucked and licked, stroked and squeezed Zeke's enormous dick. I'd somehow gotten lost in the rhythmic movement, so when Zeke's hand curled around my head, it startled me.

"Wrap your lips around me and suck," he ordered. "Close your mouth."

I did and Zeke took over, holding my head as he forced his cock in deep.

"Relax your throat."

It was relaxed, but I couldn't tell him that.

"Take more of me, pretty boy." His tone was firm, lacking any emotion—aside from that patronizing superiority when he said pretty boy—whatsoever. "All the way in your throat."

Yeah. I wasn't sure that was even possible, but I couldn't argue with him filling my airway, the head of his dick brushing my tonsils. Every movement was controlled. Every thrust of his hips. Every pull of my head. He was using me. I was merely an orifice for his pleasure.

I fucking loved every second of it.

He became rougher as the minutes ticked by, but still controlled. He knew what he wanted and he was bound to take it from me. I was more than willing, eager. I wanted him to come down my throat, to taste him.

His cock pulsed a few times and I sensed he was close, but there was no sound coming from him. No grunts, no groans of pleasure. He used me roughly, fucking my mouth in earnest now, driving deep into my throat. I would gag and he would retreat but only slightly before pushing in deep again. My lips were burning from being stretched thin, but I had no way of asking him to stop.

"I'm gonna come," he warned. "And you're gonna drink it all down."

I moaned softly, encouraging him.

The force intensified and then he jerked my head all the way forward, my nose brushing his pubic hair, his cock brutalizing my throat. It was only when I thought I would pass out that I felt him shudder, his dick pulsing as hot cum splashed into my mouth. His cock head filled my throat and he groaned long and low.

He retreated shortly thereafter, releasing my head and staring down at me. My eyes watered from having my airway blocked.

"Now what do you say, fuck toy?"

I locked my gaze with his as I swallowed, my throat raw from his abuse. "Thank you, Zeke."

The approval I saw in his black eyes was all I needed. And I got the feeling it was all I would get.

ELEVEN

ZEKE

Saturday, October 13

I WOKE ON SATURDAY MORNING feeling as though I'd slept in a strange place. I figured it had to do with the fact there were people in my house. I was used to solitude. Just me and Tank. My subconscious seemed to know that the cowboy and the pretty boy were there, although I couldn't see them.

Having observed them at dinner, I opted out of having them sleep in the cage beneath my bed. I could tell they were exhausted, likely more so from their trip than the scene at the club. I wasn't one to be gentle on my toys, but I figured a full night's sleep would be good for them. It would prepare them for what I had in store.

The sound of metal clinking on metal mixed with the deep baritone of male voices rang up the stairs. Since I'd given the cowboy instructions to cook breakfast, I could only assume he was extremely obedient. I figured Tank was down there keeping him company because he was no longer sprawled out along the foot of the bed.

I glanced over at the clock on the nightstand.

"Fuck," I grumbled. It was already eleven o'clock. Granted, it had been a late night—I hadn't closed my eyes until right around three—but it wasn't like me to sleep late, regardless.

So, maybe the cowboy was making lunch, instead.

With the curtains pulled back, the sun shone in, the golden rays bouncing off the water of the lake a few yards below. I had bought the house for the view alone. It settled something inside me.

I spent plenty of time out on the deck or in the yard simply admiring the view.

My stomach growled, a direct response to the scent of bacon wafting up the stairs. Having enjoyed the cowboy's cooking last night, I was curious as to what he would come up with this morning. While beef stroganoff wouldn't have been my first choice, I certainly couldn't complain.

Swinging my legs over the bed, I stretched before heading into the bathroom to take a piss. My eyes fixed on the shower, the memory of the pretty boy on his knees. That fuck toy gave a phenomenal blow job, that was for damn sure. I'd fully intended to take my pleasure from both of them, but when I'd noticed the cowboy could hardly keep his eyes open during the meal, I'd decided to wait.

After all, I didn't want them to be bored today.

I finished up in the bathroom, pulled on a pair of jeans, then headed downstairs. My feet stopped on the bottom step when I noticed I had unexpected company.

"Morning, Zeke," Jamie said cheerfully, a wide smile on her face. "You sure slept late."

I glanced over at the cowboy, who was standing at the island cooktop, dutifully preparing what appeared to be breakfast. The pretty boy was setting the table. Everything appeared normal. Too normal. I wasn't used to having this many people in my house. I didn't bring fuck toys back here for a reason. I didn't care for them to interact with my sister, but those were things I'd considered before I propositioned these two.

Part of me was glad I hadn't ordered them to walk around naked. That had been my intention. I would have to figure out something if my baby sister planned on dropping in unannounced.

"What's up?" I asked her, accepting her hug when she danced over to me.

She took one step back, then reached out … and pinched my fucking nipple.

"Oww. What the hell was that for?"

Jamie's stern gaze met mine, the smile long gone.

Fuck.

"We have to talk," she demanded.

Great.

"Can we do it while we eat 'cause I'm starving?"

She pivoted toward the kitchen. "It looks like you've brought your toys home with you."

I glared at her. How the fuck would she know that? Had they said something? Did my kid sister know the details of my lifestyle? Or was she fishing? Hoping to get a rise out of me?

Deciding to ignore her, I put my hand on her back and steered her toward the breakfast nook. I didn't have a formal dining room because I'd had the space redesigned. There was one table where I consumed all my meals. No place for fancy get-togethers. I didn't need that shit. I was a simple man with simple tastes.

"Breakfast is ready," the cowboy announced.

"We really are gonna talk, big brother," Jamie hissed. "I'm mad at you."

"I figured that out already. Now sit."

"You want to do this in front of your guests?" she asked, her words lacking the usual chipper tone.

"Sure," I told her, motioning toward the table. "Why not?"

The cowboy's eyes swung over to me and I could see the concern there. God only knew how long Jamie had been here or how much she'd been pestering them this morning.

"Don't say I didn't warn you," she said as she spun around and headed in the direction she had come from. "Here, Brax. Let me help with that."

She was on a first-name basis with him? When did that happen?

The cowboy dished food on the plates, then Jamie delivered them to the table.

"Where's Tank?" My dog was nowhere in sight.

"In the yard," Jamie answered. "I fed him already. He's taking his afternoon stroll."

"It's not after noon," I argued.

"Same difference," she said, still glaring at me.

128

"Sit," I ordered the pretty boy when he shot those confused eyes my way. "Eat."

The four of us took our seats after the food, scrambled eggs, bacon, sausage, ham, and what appeared to be waffles, and drinks, orange juice, apple juice, and coffee, were set out. I watched the three of them carefully, wondering what the hell they'd spent the morning talking about.

Jamie was the one to speak first after downing half a glass of apple juice.

"So, imagine my surprise when I decided to go out to a club last night," she began. "Catrina and Elle got right in, no issues. But the moment I handed over my ID, I learned I'd been blacklisted."

I downed half my coffee, the heat scorching my throat. I ignored it.

"What did you do, Zeke?" she demanded, her hands fisting on the table.

"I..." Rather than answer, I shoveled eggs into my mouth and shrugged.

Jamie frowned. "You are such an asshole."

The pretty boy chuckled, his eyes remaining on his food. I contemplated punishment while I tried to come up with a response.

"Zeke, I'm serious," Jamie said, her tone changing from anger to disappointment.

"Fuck." I took another sip of coffee. "I changed my mind. I don't want to talk about it now."

"Too bad. I've spent some time with your new *toys* this morning. I think they can handle it."

Two sets of green eyes shot over to me. I imagined they were waiting for me to excuse them. While I wanted to, I figured it was probably best to have an audience. Less chance of my baby sister throwing knives at me.

Before I could answer, Jamie turned her attention to the boys.

"I'm not sure if he's told you, but yesterday, I asked my big brother if he'd let me go to Dichotomy."

The pretty boy damn near choked on his bacon, his eyes flying up to mine. I cocked an eyebrow. *Yeah. It's like that, pretty boy.*

"I took his rejection with grace," she said sweetly.

I snorted. "That's what you call your little tantrum?"

She ignored me. "Since Dichotomy's not the only kink club in town, I figured I had options. So, a couple of my friends decided we'd go check out one of the others." Her dark eyes shot my way. "I've been blacklisted, Zeke! From at least three clubs."

I narrowed my eyes. "I told you to stay away from the clubs, Jamie."

"Yeah. I heard you. Then I realized something."

I waited for her to continue, knowing I wasn't going to like it.

"I'm twenty-four years old. I live on my own. I'm actually an adult, adult-ing all day, every day. So, it's my right to do whatever I want to do."

"You have no idea what goes on in these clubs, Jamie."

"Actually…" Her gaze bounced from face to face before landing on me. "I kinda do. More so now that I've seen your new toys in action."

The cowboy dropped his fork and picked up his orange juice. I watched him closely.

"In action?" I asked, my gaze darting between the three of them.

"Let's just say, I don't think they were expecting company this morning," Jamie said with a grin. "They had to make a mad dash to get clothes when I walked in."

Oh, hell.

My stomach churned, my breakfast threatening to come back up. I reached for my coffee and downed it in one gulp, relishing the burn. When it was empty, I pushed to my feet and stomped into the kitchen.

"Case, how old were you when you went to your first kink club?" Jamie asked.

The pretty boy's eyes shot over to me and I frowned. I already knew the answer to that. As much as I wanted him to keep that to himself, I wasn't the sort who lied to my sister. Nor did I condone anyone else doing it. I offered a nod as I carried my mug back to the table.

"I was … uh … twenty-two."

Jamie's eyes flew back to me. "*Twenty-two*, Zeke. Did you hear that? He was twenty-two. That's—"

"Two years younger than you," I filled in. "Yeah. I get it, Jamie."

"If you don't mind me asking…" the cowboy interjected. He appeared to have composed himself. "What is it about a kink club that interests you?"

That was a damn good question.

All three of us turned our attention to my sister, eager to hear whatever nonsense would come out of her next.

Brax

(The cowboy)

JAMIE LAUTNER WAS ADORABLE.

Six feet of willowy brunette with a quick smile and a sassy side that had kept Case and me laughing for the past two hours since she'd arrived. Admittedly, I'd been shocked when she glided through the front door as though she owned the place.

Unfortunately, Case and I had been naked. Admittedly, it had been my idea. I figured it would be an interesting way to greet Zeke when he woke up.

Lesson learned.

The minute she appeared in the doorway, I had raced up the stairs with Case right on my heels. We quickly pulled on clothes while I tried to battle back the intense blush that had infused my entire fucking body. We returned a few minutes later to find she was still there, a brilliant smile on her face.

When she introduced herself as Zeke's sister, I had instantly noticed the resemblance. It was slight, but still there. Granted, there were some significant differences.

Such as Zeke was one hundred percent pure alpha male while Jamie had gotten all the softness in the Lautner line. And while Zeke wasn't big on chatting, Jamie did not have the same problem. She had pelted us with questions, curious as to how we knew Zeke and exactly why we were in his house—naked—gearing up to prepare him breakfast.

While I had wanted to wait until Zeke came down to share any details, Case had been far too willing to tell her why we were there, including the fact that Zeke referred to us as his toys. Thank God the guy had opted to leave out the term *fuck* from that description. I figured there was only so much a little sister needed to know.

Now, as the four of us sat at Zeke's kitchen table, I'd lost sight of the sassy girl I'd gotten to know this morning. In her place was a woman who had a beef with her brother about going to a kink club. I wasn't sure what prompted me to ask her such a personal question, but I was rather curious.

"I don't know," she admitted, her cheeks turning a rosy pink.

God had been good to the Lautner clan when it came to looks. More so when he had created Jamie, because aside from having the same smile and dark eyebrows, she didn't look anything like her giant brother. Sure, Zeke was appealing in his own right, but he wasn't exactly handsome. Jamie, on the other hand, would catch all sorts of attention when she walked down the street. And that sweet innocence she projected only enhanced her beauty.

"Something must've prompted your interest," Case implored. "Did you see something on TV? In the movies? You have friends who are in the scene?"

"I've been reading some books," she admitted, draining her apple juice. "And I'm curious."

"What sort of books?" Zeke asked, his full attention on his sister.

She offered a one-shoulder shrug. "You know. BDSM."

I grinned at Case and he smiled back. I was sure he was remembering the one girl we'd met at Dichotomy a while back. Sweet kid, very naive. Apparently, she'd started reading about BDSM and she'd decided to explore her kinkier side because it had captured her interest.

Zeke groaned as he leaned back in his chair. "Are you serious?"

"Well, yes," she practically shouted. "You're not the only one who's into this stuff, Zeke. I've always been … curious. And there are tons of books about it, so I read them."

"You know that shit's romanticized, right? It's not all about spanking some sweet little girl's ass while she giggles and laughs, then cuddling her close and telling her how wonderful she is."

Jamie glared at her brother again. She was the only person I'd ever seen look at him that way. And based on Zeke's reaction to her, they were close. It was interesting to see the dynamic between the two. I had a close relationship with my brothers and sisters, too. I could recall many times I'd been in the same room with them, engaging in conversations similar to this one. Well, not quite like this. My family wasn't aware of my kink side. However, we could give each other shit for days because we were close, always had been. Oh, sure, we'd had our falling-outs over the years. What siblings didn't?

"But it's not as scary as *you* make it out to be," she argued.

"Depends on who you ask," he countered.

"Okay, fine. We'll ask an impartial party." Jamie turned her attention to me and Case.

Shit.

My eyes remained fixed on her, but I didn't miss the warning look Zeke sent my way.

"I'm still curious as to what interests you about the clubs," I said, hoping to deflect. "I mean, are you interested in dominating someone? Submitting?"

"Submission," she said quickly. "And I don't know what the appeal is exactly, but when I read those books, I can relate in a lot of ways. Like I said, I'm curious."

Couldn't blame the girl for being curious. A lot of people were.

"Not just from a psychological perspective?" Case asked.

Good question.

"No, although I can't deny that's part of it." Her eyes shifted to me. "When did you start going to the clubs?"

"Not until I met Case," I admitted.

"But you knew on some level you were submissive?"

I shook my head. "No, actually. I didn't know anything about it before him."

"So, you didn't want to be roughed up by one of your sexual partners?"

Case choked on his juice and I sat stone-still, staring at the woman. How the hell was I supposed to answer that? Especially with Zeke glaring holes through me.

"I … uh…"

"Plead the Fifth, man. Plead. The. Fifth," Case mumbled loud enough for everyone to hear.

Surprisingly, Zeke chuckled.

"You stay out of this," Jamie bit out, pointing her fork at her brother. "But you went to a club anyway? And you liked it?"

Son of a bitch. She backed me in a corner there. I could feel the heat coming out of Zeke's ears.

"Yeah." I dropped my gaze to my plate.

Case, on the other hand, seemed to be quite content to watch the verbal volley. He hadn't said a word to help defuse this situation. I could understand Zeke's desire to keep his little sister out of the club. I wasn't sure what I'd think if one of my sisters wanted to venture into the world of BDSM.

"My brother's a hypocrite," Jamie said, her eyes swerving back to Zeke.

"No, your brother's protecting you," Zeke said roughly.

"From what? I didn't see anything wrong with Razor Wire," she said. "Unfortunately, I couldn't get inside."

Okay, so she'd evidently caught Case's attention with that one, because he put his forearms on the table and faced off with her. "Jamie, I'm not on anyone's side here, but I have to agree with Zeke on this one. You do not want to go to that club."

"Have you been?" she questioned.

"No. But I've talked to a couple of people who have. Submissives at Dichotomy. That place is bad news," he explained. "If you're interested in kink or whatever, I can assure you, that's not a place to learn about it."

She huffed and I suspected Zeke had already given her this spiel.

"Is that why you came over here?" Zeke asked. "To bitch at me for protecting you?"

Jamie sighed. "Yes. I did. And to tell you what an asshole I think you are. Why won't you just let me go to Dichotomy? That way you'll know where I am."

It was a good question. I could understand his reasons for wanting to keep her out, but if she was going to defy him anyway, letting her visit a place he was comfortable with seemed to be the only way to fix this.

Still leaning back in his chair, Zeke took another sip of his coffee. "I talked to a friend of mine last night," he began.

Hmm. Maybe he'd already considered it.

When Jamie's eyes widened and a smile pulled at the corners of her mouth, he held up a hand. "Now, don't get too excited. You're not joining a club."

"Whatever," she said, her smile not dimming in the least. "Who did you talk to?"

"Gregory Edge. He's agreed to give you an introduction to submission at Dichotomy."

"Seriously?" She was practically vibrating.

"Just you. Not your friends," he said firmly.

"When?"

Zeke shrugged. "I don't know. I told him I'd give you his number. He's the resident Dom at Dichotomy. He manages the place and he handles the submissive training classes."

"I know who Greg is," she said, her smile starting to dim slightly.

"Then I'm sure you know he's a busy man."

Jamie huffed. "So, you're telling me he's willing, but it might not be for a couple of years?"

Zeke laughed, a sexy rumbling sound that had the hair on the back of my neck standing on end. "I couldn't be so lucky. But I'll give you his number and you can contact him. You're only permitted to go on a night I'm not there. No way can I—" Zeke outwardly cringed.

He didn't have to finish that statement. I understood the big man's predicament. No way would he want to be at Dichotomy to watch his sister submitting to someone. Who knew what they'd be doing.

"What's his number?" she snapped. "I wanna call him right now."

Zeke shook his head. "You're far too impatient for your own good."

She was certainly that. Perhaps getting an introduction into submission wasn't a bad thing.

"Zeke," she said, dragging his name out into multiple syllables.

"Fine," he huffed. "It's under Gregory Edge in my phone."

Jamie jumped to her feet, but Zeke grabbed her arm before she could shoot by him.

"I want you to take this seriously, Jamie. I'm willing to let you see what Dichotomy's like, but you have to swear to me you won't go to one of those other clubs."

Her eyes softened. "I won't. I promise."

Seemingly pleased by her acquiescence, Zeke released her. I watched as she bounded up the stairs, her ponytail bobbing behind her.

"Oh, and Jamie?" Zeke called after her.

Jamie paused midway up the stairs. "Yeah?"

"The next time you come over, I suggest you knock. Otherwise, you'll get an eyeful of exactly what you got this morning. Only next time, I won't allow them to get dressed."

Her nose crinkled. "Eww." A quick smile followed and she darted the rest of the way up.

"Now finish eating," Zeke commanded, his voice low. "Because when she leaves, I've got plans for the two of you."

That now familiar sense of anticipation shot through me and I turned my attention back to my breakfast.

TWELVE

ZEKE

ALMOST THE MINUTE JAMIE GOT Greg's number, she came up with some excuse as to why she had to leave. Something about forgetting she was supposed to meet a friend at the library. I knew it was bullshit, but I didn't bother to stop her. I had other things on my mind and they involved two naked masochists.

"Once you've cleaned up," I told the pretty boy, "I want you to meet me in the basement." I turned to the cowboy. "And you go shower, then come down there."

While they took care of their assigned tasks, I headed down to the basement. Not only was it my home gym, it also held a few toys I'd acquired over the years. Granted, I had yet to use my personal stash of torture devices on anyone because I did not bring submissives to my house to play. Before the cowboy and the pretty boy, only one submissive had ever been in my personal space, but that was years ago. Before I'd decided to beef up my personal playroom.

I flipped on the music but kept it out of the ear-bleeding range while I got a few things set up for my new fuck toys.

Ever since my encounter with the pretty boy last night, I'd been eager to get my hands on the cowboy. I'd sent him to bed without touching him, despite the desperate urge I'd had. It was imperative that I show restraint when it came to them. Otherwise, they would get the wrong impression. And I was nothing if not controlled.

The pretty boy came down first, his eyes widening when he took in the space.

"This setup is impressive," he said, his gaze rolling over the racks of weights and the various machines I'd purchased. "Gym-quality machines?"

I nodded. I figured the pretty boy might approve considering his career choice. The man's entire life was built around helping people get into the best shape they could.

"You've got everything you need here," he said absently. "You don't go to a gym?"

"No. Not a fan of people wanting to sit around and chat." When I worked out, I worked out. I spent a few hours down here almost every day. Not only because I was intent to maintain my physique, but also because it allowed me to clear my head. Some people used alcohol, drugs, or some other vice to chase the demons away. I used weights.

"You've put a lot of thought into the setup," he said, his eyes still scanning the room.

"Glad you approve," I said blandly. "Now I want you naked."

He nodded. His gaze continued to bounce around the room as he removed his jeans, laying them over one of the nearby workout benches.

Good thing for him that wasn't the sort of bench I was interested in using today. Nope, we would be getting one hell of a workout, but it wouldn't be with weights.

I removed a cloth cover I kept over my most recent purchase—a steel spanking bench that I'd found online from a company that custom built BDSM equipment online. The A-frame legs were sturdy, designed to handle the abuse it would undoubtedly endure. It was magnificently designed, with roughly two dozen hooks that would allow me to restrain my toy any way that I saw fit.

The pretty boy's eyes shifted to the bench, but he didn't say a word.

"This isn't for you," I informed him, noticing his disappointment. "Don't worry. You'll enjoy what I've got in store."

After going into the closet and retrieving a set of iron cuffs, I motioned the pretty boy to follow me. I hooked the heavy iron manacles to a set of chains I had fixed to the concrete wall. I'd installed the hooks myself so I knew they would hold up to damn near anything.

"Put your back to the wall," I instructed.

The pretty boy got into position and I fixed the cuffs to his wrists, then pulled the chains until his arms were spread out to his sides, as taut as I could get them without pulling. I did the same with his ankles, forcing his legs wide. I wasn't using the cheesy padded leather restraints that would ensure his comfort for this scene. That wasn't my style. I had no intention of ensuring he was comfortable.

I stood tall and stepped up to him, gripping his jaw between my fingers, then held up a small round bell so he could see.

"As you probably remember, I'm not giving you a safe word. However, if something goes wrong, I do expect you to inform me. Since you won't be able to speak, this will be your only way of signaling if there's a problem."

His eyes shot to the bell. Once he got a good look at it, I tucked it into his right hand. It was small, but loud enough to be effective.

"Should you need to stop the scene, ring it. But it better be because you're bleeding or about to lose a limb." I shot him a malevolent grin. "If I hear that bell for any other reason, you will be punished. So I suggest you don't drop it."

His eyes were already glazing over, his desire evident. "Yes, Zeke."

I'd noticed the pretty boy had been quiet for most of the morning. While he *had* engaged with my sister, he hadn't spoken directly to me. I couldn't quite read his body language yet, but I didn't peg him for the strong silent type. Which meant he was likely adjusting to his new surroundings, attempting to figure out what I had in store for him.

I left him cuffed to the wall while I retrieved the other items I needed for him.

"Since the day I met you, I've thought about this," I told him as I held up the thick, stainless-steel ring. "Do you know what it is?"

"A cock ring," the pretty boy said, his breaths coming in a little faster.

"It's called a crown of thorns," I explained, holding it there so he could admire. "Each of these little screws has a point on it. Once it's in place, I'll show you what it feels like."

A minute later, I was working the steel ring over the head of his cock. It took a minute to get it in place because he was already semi-hard. This was a particularly fun toy to play with. The steel circle had six holes drilled through, where tiny, pointed screws were threaded, the sharp ends providing a similar sensation to the parachute harness I'd used last night. Only this was applied directly to his cock, just beneath the head. The pinpricks would stimulate the nerves in his dick, enhancing his torture.

"Relax," I instructed. "Think about algebra because I need you soft for a minute."

"Not sure I can do that, Zeke," he said through gritted teeth. "You're touching my dick and … well, that kinda does it for me."

I chuckled at his honesty. Even in a situation like this, the pretty boy kept his wits. He would be fun to play with.

Knowing I wouldn't have much time before he was rock hard, I worked the ring in place with lube, ensuring it was secure. The metal thorns were currently retracted, so he wouldn't feel them yet; however, the weight of the ring would be enough to keep his attention.

When I stood to my full height, I held up the small hex key that was used to tighten the screws. "Hold this for a minute." I placed it between his teeth. "Don't drop it."

I headed back into the closet to get the last item I would use to torture the pretty boy with. I was coming out when I heard footsteps on the stairs. The cowboy appeared, his hair still wet from his shower. His eyes went wide when he noticed the pretty boy already chained to the wall.

"Strip and then come here," I commanded as I made my way back to the pretty boy.

A minute later, the cowboy was by my side, both of us admiring my handiwork.

"He does make quite the art piece, huh?" I said casually.

"That he does," the cowboy confirmed.

Admittedly, the pretty boy was damn nice to look at. Thick and muscular, his body was meant to be on display. The way his biceps bunched as he shifted his arms, his thick thighs flexed when he attempted to shift his weight. I could probably stand there and look at him all damn day. From the alluring lines of his body to his sinfully beautiful cock.

"Tease his nipples until they're hard," I instructed the cowboy. "With your fingers, then your mouth."

"Yes, Zeke," the cowboy said obediently.

I stepped back and watched as the cowboy moved closer. Their eyes met and I could see the desire they ignited in one another. I was curious as to how two masochists had ended up together, but when I looked at them, it seemed rather obvious. They had a distinct physical attraction to one another, but there was something more. A connection.

The cowboy's fingers plucked the pretty boy's nipples as they stared back at one another. I found I liked that they had a connection. It meant scenes such as this one would have more of an impact on both of them. BDSM was as much mental as it was physical. Being that they cared about one another, they would likely have issues with the other being taken by a man like me. The concern for the other's well-being would be pivotal in the outcome.

The cowboy touched with the care of someone who knew what his partner enjoyed. He didn't hesitate to apply the necessary pain to get the pretty boy groaning in earnest. He wasn't rough, and he didn't tweak the pretty boy's nipples the way I would have, but he was getting the job done.

When he leaned forward and bit the pretty boy's nipple, my cock hardened. Strangely, I enjoyed watching one give the other pain. It was an aphrodisiac. Not quite as rewarding as doing it myself, but I could get used to this.

I gave them a minute before I stepped in.

With the precision of a man who was familiar with his own toys, I hooked the nipple clamps to the pretty boy, ensuring they were secured. These weren't the cheap little tweezer clamps that would fall off. These were stainless-steel nipple vises. Exactly what the pretty boy needed.

I watched his face as I checked the grips, his protruding nipple clamped securely between the small vise, paying close attention to his responses.

"Does it hurt?"

The pretty boy nodded, hissing when I squeezed the right clamp a little tighter.

I was after his pain, but it wasn't about injuring him. It took a couple of minutes, but I got the vises where they needed to be, compressing his nipples. Although the pretty boy made no sound, his teeth were clenched, a signal that he was feeling what I wanted him to feel. If he wasn't careful, he would bite that damn key in half.

After retrieving the last item and taking the cock ring key from between his teeth, I reached down and grabbed his dick, stroking firmly.

"Remember what I said about the bell, pretty boy. Don't let me hear it unless you mean it."

"Yes, Zeke."

"Anything I should know before I add this?" I asked, holding up the ball gag. "Any adjustments I need to make?"

"No, Zeke." His chest was expanding rapidly, his cock hard between my fist.

"Very good."

After pressing the ball into his mouth and connecting the strap behind his head, I used the key to screw the metal thorns through the cock ring, allowing him to feel the pressure of the spiked points. He hissed, his cock growing harder with every turn of the screw until he was moaning softly.

When I stood, I checked him one more time, observing his breaths, his eyes, the way his hands dangled from the manacles.

He appeared content, and that meant it was time to take care of the cowboy.

Case
(The pretty boy)

ZEKE LAUTNER WAS A VERY creative man, but I'd known that before he had invited me to his house to be his personal fuck toy and put a collar around my neck to prove ownership. I'd seen him in the club, attempted to get his attention a time or two, even.

However, I hadn't expected this.

When I agreed to what he wanted, signed a contract that offered myself up freely to this man, part of me figured we'd be spending quite a bit of time at Dichotomy. It seemed he was there often, so I figured that was where he chose to play.

I was wrong.

I wouldn't say I was disappointed, either. I liked the idea of playing at home, not saving that experience for an audience. It meant I would always be wondering what he had in store for us next.

The instant I stepped into his basement, I'd known he had something devious cooked up for me and Brax. Granted, I hadn't known what, and I hadn't considered being manacled to the wall with a torture device circling just below the head of my dick, vise clamps of hell on my nipples, or this fucking gag in my mouth.

It was heaven. Perhaps that made me sound warped and twisted, but that was exactly what I was.

If I were to get in a room with a therapist, I was sure she could pinpoint the exact reason I was the way I was. I couldn't deny one particular experience in my life had pushed me toward this path. I tried not to think about it because it was something that never should've happened. However, it had irrevocably changed me. I'd long ago stopped making excuses for who I was. I had no desire to change and that meant I had to embrace the man I'd become.

Zeke was going to be the one man who could possibly wipe everything away and give me something else to focus on. Unlike before, I was a willing participant. Eager and willing to see just how far he would push.

And he hadn't wasted any time either. In fact, I got the feeling he'd gone easy on us last night by allowing us to sleep in regular beds. The man who had restrained me to the wall had lost that subtle softness he'd allowed a glimpse of last night. In its place, the ruthless Sadist I'd been obsessing about lately.

Oddly enough, I had woken up with the feeling that I was out of my league. That probably had a lot to do with the rules and protocols Zeke had the two of us sign late last night—or rather, early this morning. Anyway. It was an amendment to the contract we'd signed at the club. Zeke had presented the rules to us after we ate one of Brax's phenomenal meals, laying it on the table with the instruction for us to read every word before signing. I had. It was more hard-core than I'd anticipated, cementing Zeke's promise that we would have no limits and no say. For lack of a better term, we were officially his slaves.

After I'd signed the form and handed it over to Zeke, he had insisted I go up to my new room and sleep. I'd spent the night in a strange bed, and for the first time in a very long time, Brax hadn't been beside me. I hadn't cared much for that part, but I understood it. Didn't mean I hadn't thought about sneaking into Brax's room and crawling into bed with him. I had refrained because before we went our separate ways last night, Brax had kissed me thoroughly and said he was looking forward to seeing this through, to enduring whatever Zeke had in store for us. No way could I deny the man I loved an experience like this.

But I was no martyr. We all knew I wasn't only doing this for Brax's benefit. After the scene at the club last night and the time I'd spent in Zeke's shower, I was looking forward to what he had in store for us. And based on this setup, Zeke had something wickedly kinky in mind. I got the feeling the restraints and various torture jewelry he'd applied to my body were nothing compared to the show he was about to put on.

145

"This, cowboy, is for you," Zeke said, patting the top of the vinyl-covered spanking bench.

I'd seen plenty of these in my day, having been strapped down to a number of them. This one, though, was top-of-the-line and appeared to be crafted for endurance. I'd even go so far as to say Zeke had this one built specifically with himself in mind. Based on the height, once Brax was in position, his ass would be at the perfect height for Zeke to fuck him if he so chose. I couldn't stop thinking about it, either. I'd watched Brax scene before, but I had never witnessed another man fucking him. The idea had both curiosity and concern warring inside me.

That was what was known as a mind fuck.

For me, of course. Not necessarily Brax. He would be at Zeke's mercy once he was strapped down, which would be a mind fuck of its own. I, however, would be forced to watch whatever it was Zeke decided to do to him.

With a swift go-ahead motion, Zeke urged Brax up onto the bench. He got into position on all fours, his chest lying flat on the vinyl-padded center, his hands and knees supported on padded bars that ran the length of it. The lower half of his body was at the end of the padded center, his cock hanging down, his ass tilted slightly upward.

"Get comfortable," Zeke said with a devious snarl. "You're gonna be here a while."

Brax shifted a couple of times, and the moment he stilled, Zeke went to work strapping him down. His wrists were cuffed so his hands wouldn't move, two straps were pulled over his back—one over his shoulder blades, the other right above his ass—and tightly secured so he couldn't lift up his chest. His calves were then banded to the bench beneath his knees and then his ankles, keeping his legs firmly in place. And finally, Zeke hooked something to Brax's collar, which kept him from moving his head to the side. He was forced to look forward, unable to see what Zeke would be doing to him.

From my position on the wall, I had a perfect view of Brax's ass, which was pointed upward as though in offering. I'd fucked that ass many, *many* times and I would never tire of seeing him in that position. His thick cock and heavy balls hung down, completely vulnerable to Zeke's devious intentions.

"I went easy on you at the club last night, cowboy," Zeke told him as he walked around, admiring his handiwork. "You're not gonna be so lucky this go-round."

I couldn't see Brax's face, but I could tell by the relaxed position of his body, he was okay with that.

Zeke disappeared into that closet once more, and when he returned, he was carrying a silicone paddle and a ball gag. He paused at the door, then reached over and turned up the music. It was loud, but not so loud we wouldn't hear Zeke talking.

He laid the paddle across Brax's back, then went to work fixing the gag into his mouth. It was a constant reminder of the gag I currently had stuffed in my mouth. I could moan and groan all I wanted, but it wouldn't make a damn bit of difference. Aside from that, I was pretty much limited to drooling, and the more I tried to say something, the more I would. Not a pretty sight.

I was effectively trussed up with no means of escape. And the thought alone made my dick hard. Something I was completely aware of since I could feel the pinprick of those steel screws poking into my dick. It wasn't unpleasant—yet—which, again, was a testament to how warped and twisted I was.

Zeke squatted in front of Brax and held up a bell similar to the one he had put in my hand. "There are no safe words. So unless you are bleeding or a bone is breaking, you better not use this." Zeke's smile was pure evil. "Considering your mouth is full, this is the only way I'll know."

After tucking the bell into Brax's hand, he stood and moved behind him. He took the silicone paddle and turned to face me. The man didn't say anything, but I could tell he wanted me to be fully aware of what he was about to do. He smirked, then turned his attention back to Brax.

I found myself holding my breath when Zeke set the paddle on the small of Brax's back before kneading his ass firmly. He pinched and grabbed his flesh, plumping it. The circulation would

147

be stimulated, which would make that damn paddle feel like the devil himself had taken to his ass.

Zeke picked up the paddle again and stepped to the side before rearing back and landing it firmly on Brax's ass. Brax cried out—the sound muffled by the gag—his body jerking. Zeke swatted him several more times. The music pulsing in the room added to the intensity. It wasn't loud, but it was effective. By no means did it block out the sound of that silicone slapping against Brax's firm ass.

After several swats, Zeke reached between Brax's legs and fisted his cock.

"I take it you enjoy having your ass beat," he said, pumping Brax's dick a few times before landing several more swats. He continued this for several minutes until Brax was effectively squirming, moaning unintelligible things through the gag in his mouth.

"I do like how red your ass gets, cowboy." Zeke slapped him again and again. He wasn't pulling any punches as he shifted and moved so not to focus on the same spot. By warning Brax that he wouldn't go easy, it was as though Zeke had all the permission he needed. Then again, he did because Brax and I had given it to him unconditionally.

After several minutes of turning his ass a bright shade of red, Zeke set the paddle down and retrieved a rubber glove. He pulled it onto his left hand, then resumed using the paddle again. A minute later, he paused once more, generously lubricating the fingers of his gloved hand.

"Let's see just how tight this asshole is," Zeke prompted before pushing one lubed finger into Brax's ass.

My cock jerked and swelled, drawing a ragged moan from me as the spikes pressed into the sensitive nerves under the head of my cock.

Zeke turned to look at me, another vicious smirk on his face. He shifted positions so I could see everything he was doing to Brax. The way he began fucking him with one finger, then two had Brax and me both groaning. It wasn't long before Zeke was scissoring his fingers, stretching Brax's asshole, and he wasn't gentle about it. He pounded his hand against Brax, thrusting those big digits in deep.

"It's not enough, is it?" Zeke asked, turning his attention to Brax.

Brax moaned something no one could understand, but I could hear the plea in his tone. He wanted more.

Hell, I wanted more.

"You like this, pretty boy?"

I cut my eyes over to Zeke.

"You like watching me fuck his ass with my fingers? You want to see my cock shoved in there? Giving him the sort of pleasure you'll never be capable of giving him?"

I shook my head although part of me did want to see it. The logical side of my brain said no because Brax belonged to me. He was mine in every way that mattered. The idea of Zeke claiming him had my insides coiling tighter.

"It's killing you, isn't it?" Zeke taunted. "The idea of me impaling his ass, shoving my dick so deep his thoughts of you are replaced with me. When he cries out in his mind, it's my name he screams. Not yours."

Oh, fuck. My cock jerked. The humiliation in those words ran deep, but they were effective.

"I'll take that as a yes."

Zeke shifted once more, his fingers still buried in Brax's ass. He moved so he could pick up the paddle. And while he thrust roughly into Brax's ass, he began paddling his flesh in earnest.

By the time Zeke yanked his fingers from Brax's asshole and stripped off the glove, I was sweating, my body rock hard.

Zeke produced a condom from his pocket, and a minute later, he had stripped his own jeans off, sheathed that enormous cock, and lubed himself up.

"Watch closely, pretty boy. Watch while I use him and abuse him. I guarantee, this'll be the best fucking he's ever had. The next time you fuck him, he's going to be screaming my name because I'll be etched in his memory forever."

Brax moaned when Zeke aligned the head of his cock with his ass. Without preamble, Zeke shoved in deep, stopping when he was lodged to the root. Brax's head moved back and forth the small amount he was allowed as he cried out. But not once did he use that bell. He was loving this as much as I was.

Fuck him. Pound his ass.

Those were the words screaming in my head as Zeke stood motionless, his hands kneading Brax's blistered ass as he spread his cheeks apart. He pulled out slowly, seemingly fixated on his glistening cock as it retreated, allowing those muscles to tighten before he pushed in again.

It was a damn good thing I was restrained. Otherwise, I would've been jacking my cock to the rhythm of Zeke's thrusts.

For a fraction of a second, I might've even been a tad jealous that it wasn't my ass Zeke was ramming his big dick into.

THIRTEEN

ZEKE

CHRIST ALMIGHTY!

The cowboy's asshole was strangling my dick and it felt so damn good. I'd known it would when I had fucked his ass with my fingers, burying them in deep while ensuring I massaged his prostate frequently. His muscles had locked tightly around my fingers as he tried desperately to buck against the restraints.

The cowboy was moaning loudly now, his words muffled by the gag. It was obvious he wanted more than I was giving him. Which was the exact reason I was taking my time. Well, that and I'd seen the look in the pretty boy's eyes when I'd started finger-fucking his lover's ass. He wasn't sure what to make of it, but it turned him on nonetheless.

I would give the cowboy everything I had, but not yet.

For now, I would simply enjoy myself. They would learn that I wasn't an expedient man. I didn't fuck simply to get off. I wanted that edge that came with a release. The buildup, the pure torture as my balls tightened and my muscles coiled.

Since the cowboy's ass was positioned at the perfect height for me to drive into him, I took the opportunity to pick up the paddle again. His ass was a deep cherry red already, but I wasn't sure he'd had his fill. I smacked him every so often as I plunged my hips forward, filling him completely.

I briefly considered removing the cowboy's gag so I could hear him beg and plead. Unfortunately, my dick wasn't willing to leave the tight, warm space it was currently tunneling into, so we would both have to deal.

"Your asshole's so fucking tight," I groaned as I slammed in again. "I thought for sure the pretty boy had stretched you by now." I cut my gaze over to the man shackled to the wall. "Doesn't look like you're giving this little boy what he needs." I smacked Brax's ass with the paddle. "You need a real man filling you. I can feel you trembling. You're so fucking hard, your cock ready to burst. But you won't. Not yet. Not until I fuck you the way you need me to."

The cowboy tried to move but I had him restrained with precision and care. The most he could do was flex his muscles while I used his ass for my own pleasure.

"You like watching me fuck him, don't you, pretty boy? Giving him everything you're not capable of giving?"

This was my tactic. Tormenting them both. I could see the humility on the pretty boy's face. He was wondering if he'd ever be able to give the cowboy exactly what he needed. Before me, I was sure they'd been satisfied with what the other brought to the table when it came to sex. Now that they were experiencing what I could offer, they would never be the same.

That was my end goal. By the time I discarded them, they would forever be impacted by me. Years from now, they would be dreaming about all the wicked things I'd done to them.

"You want me to go easy on you, cowboy?"

The cowboy jerked his head the few inches the restraints allowed, and I let out a satisfied chuckle. "Of course you don't. You need this ass fucked hard. You want to be impaled on me so that when you sit down later, you'll remember exactly who's dick was buried in your ass."

I dropped the paddle onto the cowboy's back one last time. I was done with that. It was time to take everything I wanted from this man. Gripping his hips, I began to fuck him harder, deeper, faster. I let their combined moans become the backdrop as I worked him over. It was highly satisfying to know the pretty boy was watching us, his cock so damn hard, brutally tortured by that crown of thorns.

It was a wonder the steel-framed spanking bench remained in place even as I pummeled the cowboy with my cock. A fine sheen of sweat coated my skin as the stirrings of my release ignited. I allowed the sensation to consume me, radiating through my entire being before I considered letting myself go.

"One of these days I'm gonna take your ass without a condom, cowboy. I'm gonna plow you bare so we can both feel the intensity of your tight ass squeezing the life out of me."

His muscles tightened as he groaned and I knew he was damn close to coming. I hadn't restricted him from coming, but I hadn't given permission, either. Since the rules and protocols he signed last night said he would ask permission, I could only hope he'd read the fine print. Otherwise, he would find out what punishment at my hands looked like. And despite the way I roughly used his body, he would think this was heaven compared to the hell I would put him through.

"Fuck," I growled, gripping his hips tighter. "I'm gonna come, cowboy. Then I'm gonna bend your boyfriend in half and take him the same way. Hard, rough. How does that make you feel? You wanna watch me fuck the pretty boy's ass?"

The cowboy nodded as best he could, his deep moans bellowing out of him. I plowed into him several more times before I stilled, draining my balls in the warm depths of his body. The condom was necessary, but a hindrance all the same.

After dislodging and disposing of the condom, I walked back over to the cowboy, shoving my hand between his legs and jerking his cock roughly. I worked him over well but stopped just short of his release.

Only then did I unhook the pretty boy from the wall and order him to move over in front of his boyfriend.

"Grab a mat and put it on the floor. Make sure the cowboy can see everything I'm gonna do to you."

The pretty boy did my bidding, grabbing one of the black vinyl mats and laying it on the floor. His chest was heaving, his muscles strained. He was close to losing it and I was eager to send him over the edge.

"On your back. Knees up by your chest."

The pretty boy was breathing hard, the steel ring squeezing his cock while the nipple clamps kept him on edge. He needed the pain, I could see it in his eyes. They practically glowed with that lascivious hunger building inside him.

Once he was in position, I sheathed my still-hard cock with another condom, lubed myself generously, then kneeled by his legs.

I leaned over him, smirking into his face. "I'm gonna remove the gag so you can hold on to the chain. Just remember, the more you move, the more those clamps'll pull your nipples." Having seen the pretty boy's pain tolerance firsthand, I figured that would be a bonus for him.

I didn't waste time. After removing the gag and placing the nipple clamp chain between his teeth, I gripped my dick and lined up with the pretty boy's ass.

"You ready for me, pretty boy? You ready to know what it feels like for me to fucking *own* you? Because that's what this is. I own you and your little boyfriend, too. I can fuck you whenever I feel like it and you'll take my dick and be thankful I've offered that much. Is that what you want? Me to fucking *own* you?"

His head jerked roughly in affirmation, a groan following as those clamps yanked his nipples, mercilessly pulling them away from his body.

I drove in deep, enjoying the way the heat consumed me. He was as tight as his lover, perhaps more so, but telling him that didn't suit my purpose, so I went with the opposite.

"Your asshole's loose," I lied. "Must mean the cowboy plows your ass frequently. You like when he fills you?"

He nodded again, unable to speak or risk that chain falling out of his mouth. He bared his teeth, showing how they were locked around the chain that connected his nipple clamps. Every shift of his head would cause those torture devices to tug on his sensitive nipples.

"But you like when I fill your ass more, don't you?"

He moaned, crying out, a torturous sound that pleased me more than anything. I slammed into him over and over.

"Answer me," I commanded. "My cock works you over better, doesn't it?"

He nodded, those clamps being pulled tightly.

"You want me to fuck you harder?"

He nodded again, his eyes glassy from the painful ecstasy that he craved.

Since I'd already come once, my dick wasn't quite as sensitive, which allowed me to fuck the pretty boy harder and deeper without the risk of coming too soon. I made sure to make eye contact with the cowboy, relishing the pain in his gaze as he watched his lover being fucked by another man. Although they were in this willingly and they knew what was in store for them, the heart wasn't always as eager as the body. He was tormented by the sight, even if he was enjoying the hell out of it.

"This time," I told them, "when I come, I expect both of you to come. If you don't, you will be punished."

This was a test for the cowboy since he had no way to stimulate his cock. The only thing that could send him over the edge would be watching the pretty boy shooting his load all over himself.

I let loose on the pretty boy then, not holding back. I had him practically folded in half, my full weight pinning him down as I slammed my hips forward, my cock tunneling into his ass over and over again. He was panting and moaning, begging without words for me to let him come. He knew better than to do so before I did.

I held out as long as I could, long minutes passing as the friction from his tight ass drove me closer and closer to the edge. When I finally roared my release without warning, I watched the pretty boy's cock. Without even touching himself, he came in a rush, cum splashing over his belly, his chest. A few seconds later, the cowboy groaned. I looked over in time to see his body jerking and twitching as he let himself go.

I was quite impressed with the scene. More so than I thought I would be. Perhaps a few more torture techniques were in store for them. I had noticed how they welcomed the humiliation. Perhaps I'd lay it on thicker next time.

I would have to come up with something even better, something to push their boundaries further. I was going to take advantage of having them around.

After all, that was why they were here.

My pleasure and my pleasure only.

Brax
(The cowboy)

Monday, October 15

BY THE TIME THE WORKWEEK started, I was feeling a little wrung out. Never since the day I learned the pleasure my dick could afford me had I ever thought the damn thing could possibly be the reason for my demise.

Yet I got the feeling Zeke Lautner was trying to prove that theory.

Not in a bad way, necessarily. But I did feel slightly worn. The one lesson Case and I had learned over the weekend was that Zeke was insatiable. He could fuck for hours and even then I wasn't sure the man's cock was ever fully satisfied.

After the scene on Saturday morning—likely the most intense thing I'd ever been involved in—he had found ways to keep us guessing throughout the weekend, taking his pleasure in whatever form he wanted. On Saturday night, when I was making dinner, Zeke had restrained Case to a kitchen chair, then pinned me to the kitchen cabinet and fucked me for all I was worth. On Sunday night, without warning, Zeke had strolled into the living room, insisted I drop my jeans and bend over. I had without argument, enjoying the hell out of the way he fucked me ruthlessly and without preamble.

Yesterday morning, Zeke had insisted I follow him outside when Case was playing ball with Tank. He had forced me to kneel beside him, then instructed my boyfriend to hug the wall of the house while he plowed Case from behind.

Last night, I had just settled into my bed alone—a place I had learned I would no longer be sleeping—when Zeke came in. The man proved his strength by flipping me onto my stomach before fucking me in earnest on the bed. For a brief moment, I had wondered if the frame was strong enough to hold us both. I was happy to say it had held.

I wasn't positive, but I thought Zeke had gone into Case's room shortly thereafter and done the same thing.

Needless to say, my body was on high alert, waiting for Zeke to make an appearance.

I had texted Trent last night to let him know that Case and I were currently staying with Zeke, but we were available for him should he need us. His response was simple: *I'm good for now. Enjoy yourself.*

I was certainly doing that. The suspense, though, was killing me. I had no idea what to expect. At any given moment, Zeke could walk into a room, command me to my knees so he could shove his dick down my throat or force me to bend over so he could pummel my ass with his giant cock. Oddly enough, I continued to hold out hope that he would, because I would take him any way I could get him.

On the other hand, I missed spending time with Case. Although we were in the same house, Zeke was keeping us apart for some reason. Not by ordering us to our rooms or anything, but he seemed to know whenever we were getting closer.

I wasn't sure if that was his plan. Perhaps he wanted each of us for himself. Or maybe he felt threatened by the fact we had a relationship.

Yeah, okay. So perhaps that was wishful thinking. I knew Zeke wasn't in this for a relationship. Despite the fact he was mindlessly fucking us both, it was always slightly impersonal. Not once had he used my name, referring to me only as cowboy or fuck toy. And he insisted I thank him for whatever he'd so kindly given me. Once I did, he walked away without a backward glance.

"How long until breakfast?" Zeke asked as he passed through the living room, which was separated from where I stood by the enormous granite-topped island.

He was sweaty from his workout, having spent the past two hours down in his basement with Case in tow.

"Half an hour," I informed him.

"I'm gonna shower. When I get back, I want you naked."

"Yes, Zeke."

Without pausing, the big man headed up the stairs to his bedroom.

Case appeared a minute later. He was wiping a towel over his face.

"Morning," he greeted. "Where's Zeke?"

I motioned toward the stairs with the knife I was wielding. "Shower."

Case made a beeline over to me. I paused, setting the knife on the counter when he pulled me into him, our lips pressing together. He was hot and sweaty but he was exactly what I needed right then.

"Mornin'," I said with a smile.

That was what I missed the most. Kissing. I had a thing for it and not once had Zeke kissed me. I was curious as to what it would feel like. It had me wondering whether or not Zeke had kissed Case. Not that I would ask. I was curious, but I didn't really want to know. How would I feel if I found out that Zeke had kissed Case and not me?

"I miss you," Case whispered as he kissed me harder. "I hate sleeping alone."

Gripping his hips, I pulled him into me, my heart swelling. "I miss you, too."

When he stepped back, his bright eyes scanned my face. "You still good with this?"

"Yeah." I hoped I didn't sound as giddy as I felt. I didn't want Case to think I was getting attached to Zeke. I wasn't. Well, I was and I wasn't. It was difficult not to develop some feelings for the big man. He might lack certain emotions, but he made up for it in the way he looked at me. I could tell he was thinking dirty things whenever his black gaze landed on me.

"You'll tell me if something changes?" Case asked, a hint of concern in his tone.

I frowned. "Of course. Why? Have you changed your mind?"

"Not at all." He smiled and my heart skipped a beat. "I'm supposed to set the table, then head up for a shower."

I nodded before turning back to the stove. Being mindful of Zeke's request to keep the carb count to a minimum, I was making egg white omelets this morning, stuffing them with red and green bell peppers and spicy sausage. Since I was merely using the ingredients Zeke had on hand, I could only assume he wouldn't be opposed to my choices. So far, he hadn't complained about the meals I had served.

Of course, that had my mind drifting to the restaurant. I'd started writing down some of my favorite recipes in an attempt to come up with a tentative menu. I was eager to get this endeavor underway even if I was enjoying the break from it all.

"Do you know what the plan is for today?" I asked when Case grabbed the silverware and headed to the small table in the breakfast nook.

"He hasn't told me."

Maybe that was a conversation we would have over breakfast.

"All right. I'll be back in a minute," Case declared before practically jogging out of the kitchen and over to the stairs.

I put the finishing touches on breakfast, hoping like hell Zeke would approve of my choice. Case wasn't a picky eater, and for the times he wanted something specific, he never hesitated to tell me. Being that he was a conscientious eater—paying close attention to balancing protein versus carbs and fat—I had learned to cook for him appropriately. Zeke was an entirely different beast. Aside from mentioning he didn't want carbs, he hadn't given me any clues as to what he preferred. And holy shit, between the two of them, they could put down some food.

I was just shucking my jeans off when the sound of footsteps coming down the stairs alerted me to Zeke's return. He walked into the kitchen looking like a shiny penny in his gray slacks and white button-down shirt, currently open at the neck. Since he'd spent the majority of the weekend wearing well-worn jeans and little else, it was a little shocking to see him so nicely put together.

The tats on his neck were still visible, but all the others were now covered up. Still, I had a hard time picturing him at his corporate gig, although I'd seen him there with my own two eyes.

Without a word, Zeke walked over to the refrigerator and pulled out several packages. I recognized them as Tank's food. I didn't offer to help because I had noticed Zeke enjoyed doing things for Tank. The man spent a ridiculous amount of time with the dog. They were outside for hours playing ball, sometimes going for a walk around the property. At night, when Zeke watched television, Tank curled up beside him on the couch, and when Zeke went to bed, Tank followed.

"Anything you need me to order?" Zeke asked, his deep voice startling me.

"Uh…" I glanced over at him, not sure what he was referring to.

"Food for the week," he said simply. "I'm sure you've run through most of what I had. Not used to feeding more than one."

A sheepish smile curved his mouth and I felt my insides tighten. I wasn't sure I'd seen Zeke smile at all. Ever.

"I made a list," I told him, keeping my tone firm. "I'm takin' into account your request for low carbs for the meals I've planned. If there's somethin' specific you'd like, I'll gladly amend my menu."

He stood tall. "No complaints. I'm actually impressed. You're a great cook."

I knew my eyes were wide, but I couldn't help it. That was the only compliment he'd given me, but considering this was my life, it meant everything to me.

"Thank you," I said, turning back to the pan before dishing out the last omelet. "Breakfast is ready."

"Great. I'm starving."

After setting Tank's food bowl on the floor, Zeke headed toward the table. He glanced around, obviously in search of something. A minute later, he returned with a carafe of orange juice and the stainless-steel coffeepot.

He waited to sit until Case was jogging down the stairs.

"Let's eat," Zeke stated. "Then we'll head to the office. Figured maybe you'd like to get out of the house for a bit."

My eyes darted to Case, curious as to whether he'd noticed the eerie change in Zeke. Gone was the stern, no-nonsense man and in his place...

I wasn't sure what this was.

FOURTEEN

ZEKE

"YOU LOOK DIFFERENT," LANDON STATED when he found me in the break room seeking my third cup of coffee of the morning.

"Got a haircut," I told him. Granted, my shiny bald head looked the same as it did every day.

"Not it."

"New tie," I said, keeping my attention on the cup as I poured.

"You're not wearin' a tie."

I smirked. "You're right. I'm not."

"So, that's not it, either," he said as he moved closer.

I glanced over to see Landon smirking at me. I knew what he was getting at and I wanted to tell him to go fuck himself, but I was in a damn good mood today. Perhaps I'd gotten plenty of sleep this weekend. Or maybe it was the food I'd been eating. Possibly the fact I'd had regular sex over the past two days. It could've been anything, but I wasn't willing to entertain the man. Even if he was technically my boss.

"How are the new toys doin'?" he asked, a teasing note in his voice.

I passed him the coffeepot. "Relatively well." I didn't have any complaints. Yet.

"I heard about the scene on Friday. Wish I'd been there to see it."

My cock twitched as I thought back to Friday night. That had been a damn good night. Saturday and Sunday had been rather pleasant, too.

"I'm sure there will be more," I told him, leaning against the counter as I sipped my coffee. "Plenty more."

"Luci's been beggin' to go back. I keep tellin' her she has to be good." He laughed. "She has a huge issue with that."

"Yeah, well. It doesn't seem to be causing too many problems." I grinned. I'd known Landon and Langston for years, and honestly, I'd never seen them as happy as they were with Luci. Whatever the three of them were doing, it worked well for them.

"What?" Landon asked. "No tips on how to keep her in line?"

"Not from me. It's about the submissive. Maybe she needs the discipline."

"And your toys? Have to discipline them yet?"

I thought back to the events of the weekend. Not once had either one of them done anything to earn punishment. That pleased me more than I thought it would. Not that I was fond of having to mete it out. The pets I played with knew that their reward was for doing as I wished, not going against my instructions.

"Not yet. I'm sure it's coming, though."

Landon sipped his coffee, his face losing the amusement. "I heard Case had a problem with the apartment."

I nodded.

"You know why?"

"He had an issue with the confined space," I told him. "More so the fact he couldn't get outside immediately."

"That the reason you decided to let them shack up with you?"

I knew Landon was trying to get a rise out of me. The Moore twins tended to do that. Every now and then I would give in, let them get the best of me. It was all in good fun.

"That and I like the idea of having a couple of fuck toys at my beck and call," I told him straight.

Landon laughed. "That, my friend, I believe."

"You should because it's true."

"They here today?"

"In my office," I told him.

"Are we gonna get a call from the boys across the way?" He motioned in the direction of the wall and I knew he was referring to the building across the street from ours. They had a perfect view of some of our offices.

"Probably." That was my goal anyway.

"Well," he said as he stood tall. "I look forward to that call. Just make sure the cops aren't sent our way."

"As long as they're not offended, shouldn't be an issue." Considering my fuck toys were currently blowing each other in the middle of my office floor, it was quite possible the uptight accountants were getting an eyeful.

After topping off my cup, I headed back down to my office. Tank was asleep on Addison's floor, his big head shifting when he heard footsteps. He didn't bother to get up as I passed.

"Traitor," I told him with a grin.

When I stepped into my office, I found the pretty boy and the cowboy exactly as I'd left them. They were sixty-nining one another with the pretty boy on his knees and the cowboy beneath him.

"Switch," I instructed as I headed over to my desk.

The cowboy rolled out of the way and the pretty boy lay down. A second later, they were back in position, filling each other's mouths with their cocks. It was a hell of a sight, I had to admit. They knew they weren't allowed to come, so neither of them was rushing.

I spent a few minutes working on a couple of emails I had to take care of. I had a call in fifteen minutes, so I wanted to get this out of the way before then.

Dividing my attention between watching the show and typing up information on governance, risk, cyber response, and defense wasn't as easy as some people might've thought. For whatever reason, I found my interest in the details of the email waning.

NICOLE EDWARDS

Finally, my computer chirped, alerting me of the appointment I had in five minutes.

"Cowboy, I want you over here," I said as I typed one last line in my final email and hit send. "It's my turn to enjoy that mouth." I glanced over to see them separating. "And pretty boy, I want you to stay just like that. Stroke your cock while I watch."

"Yes, Zeke," the pretty boy said.

I turned my chair to the side to allow the cowboy to kneel between my legs. As interesting as it would've been to shove his ass under the desk, he was too big to fit comfortably. Since I didn't want anything distracting him from sucking me, I figured this worked better.

"Free my cock," I instructed, leaning back in my chair.

The cowboy was up on his knees, his hands working my belt, then my slacks. When he had my cock in hand, I watched him.

"I've got a call to make, but I want your mouth on me at all times. Do not make a sound. If you do, you'll be punished. Understand?"

"Yes, Zeke." He peered up at me, his lips already swollen from having the pretty boy's dick between them.

I nodded for him to get started as I picked up the phone to make the call.

His hand was cool, his mouth warm. A definite distraction from the mundane task of rolling through my spiel on why it was important for a company to have the appropriate protocols in place when it came to data and what it was I expected from anyone who worked for me.

Yes, I had decided to pursue hiring a few employees. I'd already started feeling the strain on my time. Chatter PR Global was branching out and I suspected, if all went well, we would be branching cybersecurity into its own division, utilizing a name that better suited what we did. In order for that to happen, I needed to hire some people who were top in their field.

While the man on the other end of the line ran through all his qualifications, I kept my eyes on the pretty boy as he stroked his cock in front of me. Every now and then I would put my hand on the cowboy's head, urging him to continue. I liked the way his mouth worked me. It was different than the pretty boy's. Both of them were good at giving head, no doubt about that. But it was nice to have variety.

In fact, I found I liked having a choice between the two. They were similar in many ways, but still uniquely different. The pretty boy was all about pain while the cowboy didn't necessarily need it. He did succumb to humiliation in a way that fascinated me. Between the two of them, I hadn't gotten bored yet. That was a good sign considering my short attention span when it came to submissives.

"I'd like for you to come in for a personal interview," I said into the phone, "I'm setting them all up for Friday." I hit a button to pull up my calendar. "Right now, I've got times at ten thirty or two."

"I'll take ten thirty, sir."

"Perfect." I added the event to my calendar. "I look forward to chatting more."

"Thank you for your time, sir."

"Sure." With that, I hung up the phone and turned my full attention to my fuck toys.

"Pretty boy, I want you to come over here and lick his ass. Prepare him to take your cock." I rested my hand on the cowboy's head. "And you stay right where you are. I fully intend to fuck your throat in the very near future. I hope like hell you're ready."

Because I damn sure was.

Case
(The pretty boy)

WITHIN SECONDS, I WAS MOVING behind Brax, grabbing his ass as I leaned down to tongue his asshole. I knew how much he enjoyed being rimmed and I was ready to prep him for my dick.

Considering Zeke had kept us apart for the entire weekend, I was jonesing to get my hands on him, excited about the prospect of sinking my dick into his tight ass. Even the thought made my cock throb. It had been hell having his mouth on my dick and not being able to come. While I relentlessly teased Brax about how good my blow jobs were, he was the king of them. I wasn't sure what it was about him, but every damn thing his mouth did had my body coiling tightly.

"I do enjoy this mouth," Zeke stated.

Holding Brax's ass cheeks open, I buried my tongue in his ass, reaming him as best I could. Soft moans escaped him and I wondered if Zeke could feel the vibrations on his cock.

"That's good," Zeke said. "Keep it up, pretty boy. Fuck him with your tongue."

I worked Brax over roughly, giving him all that I had. I could feel the subtle way he pushed back against my mouth, trying to take more of my tongue.

"Oh, yeah. Keep doing that, cowboy. Right there."

This was the most Zeke had spoken during any of the encounters I'd been in aside from the way he'd taunted us on Saturday morning. I still remembered how it felt when he asked me if I was ready for him to own me seconds before he plowed my ass with his cock. I'd been as close to subspace as I'd ever been during sex. It had appealed to me on a carnal level.

Unless he was barking orders or humiliation, Zeke wasn't the sort to speak. Certainly not to lay praise for what we were doing to him. It was definitely interesting to see him in his everyday life. I'd been limited to seeing him in the club and he had a persona he upheld there. At home, he was more relaxed. The man wasn't one-dimensional like a lot of people believed.

"Take more of me, cowboy. See what it feels like for my dick to be in your throat. Because that's where I'll be in a minute."

Brax's moans intensified as I continued to lick his ass while he sucked Zeke's cock like a pro. I had no idea how much time passed, but I focused my attention on pleasing Brax, giving him what he needed.

"Pretty boy, take the condom and lube. Prepare his ass for your dick."

I lifted my head to see Zeke set the two items on the edge of his desk. Within seconds, I was sheathed and lubed, ready for Zeke's next command. I waited, knowing I had to have his permission before I fucked the man I loved. Some people would've thought that made me a pussy, but I preferred the instruction. I liked knowing that Zeke owned me and Brax.

I also liked knowing that someone was likely watching everything we were doing. Since there was a building directly across the way and no shades covering the windows in Zeke's office, anyone could have their own personal show if they chose. Maybe someone was taking a coffee break, watching as I prepared to fuck Brax.

"All right, pretty boy. Do your worst." Zeke's hand tightened in Brax's hair. "Don't you move, cowboy. And watch those damn teeth."

Brax moaned as though agreeing. I lined up my cock with his asshole before pushing in slowly, gently. His muscles tightened around me, squeezing hard enough to draw a ragged moan from me. It was fucking perfect.

"You like that, cowboy? You like when he treats you like you're made of glass? The way he inches his cock inside you as though you'll break?"

Brax moaned around Zeke's dick, but I had no idea what that meant.

"Fuck him," Zeke ordered, his black eyes pinned on me. "I know you've ached to get inside him since I purposely kept you apart. Show him how much you missed him."

Those words stirred something inside me. I gripped Brax's hips and slammed into him. He moaned again, pressing back when I thrust forward.

It felt fucking good to be inside Brax. Familiar. Like coming home. I had missed him this weekend although we'd been under the same roof. Having to keep my hands to myself was pure torture, another technique of Zeke's, I was sure. But this … being inside this man soothed something in my soul.

"That's better. Fuck him like the toy he is."

The hardwood had long ago bruised my knees, but I ignored the pain as I slammed into Brax, loving the way his asshole squeezed me. While I ruthlessly fucked him, Zeke lifted Brax's head by tangling his fist in his hair.

"You like that, cowboy?"

"Yes, Zeke." He grunted as I slammed into him. "I like it."

"Does he fuck you better than I do?"

"No, Zeke."

That had me slamming into Brax harder. I knew exactly what Zeke was doing and it worked the way he intended. The thought of not being able to satisfy Brax didn't sit well with me. And the logical side of my brain knew Brax didn't necessarily mean what he said, but that didn't stop me from fucking him harder, owning him.

"He doesn't need a sissy fucking him," Zeke growled. "He needs a man, pretty boy. Fucking own his ass."

Ah, Christ.

Zeke knew what he was doing to me.

"Fuck," I growled as I pummeled Brax's ass, slamming my hips forward, lodging my cock to the hilt before retreating. My fingertips buried in his flesh as I held him still. Over and over I fucked him as hard and as deep as I could. "Oh, God. Zeke." I groaned as my gaze shot up to Zeke's face. "May I have your permission to come?"

"No," he barked. "Not until the cowboy is satisfied."

Brax was moaning in earnest now, taking every punishing thrust.

"Do you want him to come, cowboy?"

"Yes!" Brax yelled as he jerked his mouth off the thick head of Zeke's cock.

"Tell him," Zeke ordered.

"Come in my ass, Case." He pushed back against me again. "Fucking come inside me."

I held Zeke's gaze, waiting for his permission.

"Come, pretty boy," he finally said, the rough edge in his voice the catalyst, triggering my orgasm. I groaned long and low as I held Brax's hips in my hands, my cock jerking endlessly inside him.

"Dispose of the condom, then I want you on your back, your head between the cowboy's legs. You're gonna suck him while I fuck his throat."

I quickly removed the rubber and tied it off before depositing it in the trash can. A minute later, I was on my back while Brax straddled my face. He buried his cock in my mouth, still kneeling before Zeke as the big man stood up.

From my vantage point on the floor, I could see Zeke's cock as it slid into Brax's mouth. The sight alone had me moaning.

"Now be a good fuck toy," Zeke told Brax. "You're gonna take all of me. The second I come, you have permission to do the same."

I worked Brax's cock while I watched Zeke face-fuck my boyfriend. He wasn't gentle, but Brax didn't seem to mind. He gagged a few times, but never did he try to get away as Zeke drove past his lips again and again.

"Oh, yeah. Swallow. Let me feel that throat work." Zeke grunted several times, clearly pleased by Brax.

Using my hand, I worked Brax's cock in tandem with my mouth. I could feel him pulsing. He was close. So close. I briefly wondered if he would come before Zeke, but he never did.

"Good boy," Zeke ground out, his hips driving forward. "Just. Like. That. Fuck yeah. I'm gonna come down your throat." A dull roar signaled Zeke's release, and a second later, Brax filled my mouth. I swallowed him down as I held on to his cock.

For whatever reason, I felt closer to Brax in that moment. Despite the fact I could've been anyone giving him a blow job, I got the feeling it had settled him, too, knowing that I was there. Or at least, I hoped that was the case.

"Now both of you go get cleaned up," Zeke said as he tucked his cock back into his pants. "After that, we'll grab a bite to eat."

"Thank you, Zeke, for allowing me to suck your cock," Brax said as he got to his feet.

Zeke's dark gaze slammed into Brax's face. It was evident he was surprised by the words. I hadn't expected them either and the submission I heard in them hit me in a way I didn't expect.

It had me wondering for the first time whether or not my boyfriend was developing feelings for Zeke.

Feelings I wasn't sure I could compete with.

FIFTEEN

ZEKE

AFTER SHARING A MEAL ON Monday night, I retreated to the living room to watch television. I had a thing for the legal dramas, although I wasn't sure why that was. Most of the time the characters irritated the shit out of me, but there was something about the legality of it all, the process and procedure perhaps, that kept me riveted to the screen. Sitting here, hanging out, mindlessly chilling, had become a thing for me and Tank. He would curl up beside me while I relaxed, unwinding from my day.

The pretty boy and the cowboy joined me, both sitting on the other sofa since Tank and I took up most of the space on this one. They sat together exactly as I'd expected them to. Their shoulders touched, and from time to time, they would absently touch the other when they spoke. Their affection for one another was palpable.

A couple of hours passed and I found it not nearly as irritating as I thought it would be to have them in the same room with me. In fact, I enjoyed their company even if they didn't speak except for to question something on the television. A couple of times I found myself having decent debates over why something happened. When it came to their point of view and reasoning, I found I didn't intimidate them. Their input was logical and they had no problem arguing their point. It was intriguing and I liked that.

By the time the cowboy had yawned twice, I knew it was time to head upstairs. Mornings always came far earlier than I wanted, and after a day like today, I was ready to hit the sack. Not to mention, tomorrow was going to test my patience, so every bit would help tonight.

Pushing to my feet, I stretched, then motioned for them to get up. "Come on. It's time for bed."

The pretty boy stood quickly, then helped the cowboy to his feet. I was taken by the way they interacted with one another. It was obvious they cared and that was endearing. Not that I wanted a relationship, but it was nice to see that it worked for some people. Even if, by engaging with me, they were doing something completely out of the norm for most people.

And I was about to introduce them to something else most people didn't do.

Before they could head to the stairs, I stopped them. "Tonight, and all nights going forward, you'll be sleeping in the cage beneath my bed."

For whatever reason, I fully expected an argument from at least one of them. Although I referred to them as fuck toys and I didn't think of them or speak to them by name, I was aware they weren't animals. Yet this was something I needed, something I craved. The question would be whether or not they could handle that.

Neither said a word, merely nodded as though my wish was their command. In a sense, it was. They didn't have a choice based on the agreements they'd signed and the understanding we'd come to.

Once we made it up to my room, I nodded toward the bathroom. "I want both of you to shower first. Together. One washes the other," I explained.

While I enjoyed watching legal dramas, I liked watching them touch each other more. It was an interesting twist to all of this. I'd never had two submissives at one time, so I was finding creative ways to entertain myself with them. Their connection to one another allowed me to push their boundaries and explore avenues I hadn't been privy to before.

After acknowledging me with a courteous, "Yes, Zeke," they went into the bathroom. I followed but I headed into the closet. The water turned on as I was stripping my clothes off. When I returned, they were standing beneath the water, their big, glistening bodies highlighted and shadowed by the many bulbs over the vanity.

There was a distinct difference in their sizes, but they weren't polar opposites as I'd initially thought. Both had green eyes and muscular bodies, although the pretty boy was bigger, his muscles more defined. The cowboy had dirty-blonde hair, the pretty boy short, dark hair. From a height perspective, they were equal, but when you looked at them, they were vastly different. The way they carried themselves for one. The cowboy walked with a slight swagger, the pretty boy more controlled. As for personalities, that was what truly set them apart. The cowboy was far more obedient. He was mindful of every move he made while the pretty boy seemed more laid-back, less stringent.

I took a position leaning my ass against the counter. I was as naked as they were, so there was no way to hide the desire they stirred in me. Not that I tried to, but aside from stroking myself leisurely—more to get their attention than anything—I ignored my dick all the same.

The cowboy washed the pretty boy first, starting with his hair, then running his soapy hands all over the pretty boy's muscular body, taking special care to soap the pretty boy's dick. He stroked him a couple of times but then moved on, dragging a low groan from the pretty boy. They alternated, then it was the pretty boy's turn to tease and torment the cowboy while efficiently getting him clean. Big hands ran over the cowboy's lean build, starting from his neck, down to his toes, then back again.

If they only knew what I had in store for them, perhaps they would've followed through with those hand jobs.

Once they were finished, both men rinsed off before shutting off the water. I motioned toward two towels sitting on the counter, then headed into my bedroom. I retrieved two sets of wrist and ankle cuffs from my nightstand drawer and the chains I needed to connect them to the bars on my bed. When the two naked fuck toys joined me in the bedroom, I grinned to myself.

"On the bed," I ordered.

Both men shot confusion-filled looks my way.

"No, you won't be sleeping there." I pointed toward the cage beneath the bed. "That's your new bedroom from now on. However, I do have something in mind for you first."

Apparently reassured by my explanation, they went to opposite sides of the bed and climbed up.

"On your backs. Hands above your heads."

Damn, but they looked good there. I could almost envision them sleeping on either side of me, within reach if I chose to torment one or both. I immediately shook off the thought. They would not be sleeping in my bed. That wasn't the reason I'd brought them here.

While I connected the chains to the metal frame, I admired them there in my huge bed. Other than me and Tank, no one else had ever slept in this particular bed. In fact, I had purchased it three years ago, wondering if I would ever get the opportunity to put it to good use. Never the one to hold out hope, I figured it would always be a reminder of the things I couldn't have but knew I wanted.

Not that I wanted these two fuck toys sleeping with me, but I did entertain the notion of using and abusing them in some form or fashion. I could envision the cowboy strapped to the mattress, facedown while I beat on him for a bit, then took his ass with the brutal force he would beg me to give him. I would have the pretty boy standing up, his arms shackled to the bars overhead while he was forced to watch me sodomize his boyfriend. My dick certainly liked the idea.

Once I had everything ready, I restrained their ankles and wrists in the cuffs, then retrieved the box I'd set on my dresser. When I returned, both men were watching me intently.

"Do you know what a chastity device is?" I asked, simply to get their minds working.

"A device to prevent masturbation," the pretty boy said.

"True. It prevents that. It also shows you who now owns your dick. It no longer belongs to you. It's mine to do with as I please." I selected two of the stainless-steel cock cages, which would cover their dicks completely. I then grabbed three rings—two medium, one large—just in case. I would have to determine which would fit each of my fuck toys.

"Going forward, you will sleep under my bed together. I don't give a shit if you spoon each other or not. However, these will be a reminder of who owns your cock. It's not there for your pleasure. It's there for mine." I looked up at the pretty boy. "Understand?"

"Yes, Zeke."

"Good. I'll fit you first. The harder you are, the worse it's gonna feel," I warned, ensuring he saw how much I would be pleased by the prospect of hurting him.

Since the pretty boy's cock was semi-hard already, it wasn't easy to fit the cage over him, but I managed. The large ring was easier because it was hinged, allowing me to open it so I could wrap it up under his balls and around his cock, effectively restraining them beneath the metal. The ends of the ring connected, then fit through a slot on the cage to hold it in place. I produced one of the stainless-steel padlocks and quickly snapped it shut. He would likely be running through some mundane shit in his head to fight the hard-on; otherwise, pain was going to become his friend.

"All done." I smiled, ensuring he saw the sadistic gleam. I got off on using them, controlling them. *Owning* them. It was a high unlike any other. "I have the key. It's your responsibility to pay attention. If you have any issues, I expect you to let me know immediately. You'll be wearing this to sleep in every night."

"Yes, Zeke," the pretty boy said as he relaxed on the pillow. If I had to guess, he was running through algebraic equations in an effort to keep himself under control.

"Now your turn, cowboy. You ever wear one of these before?"

"No, Zeke."

Ah. That pleased me.

I did enjoy being someone's first.

176

Brax

(The cowboy)

IF YOU'VE NEVER WORN A cage on your penis, I'd be the first to tell you, it's not fucking fun. Initially, the cold steel had been somewhat pleasant against my overheated skin. But it only went downhill from there. Between the all-encompassing metal contraption that constricted my dick and the ring that tightly cinched my balls, I could've gone my entire life without one and I would've died a happy man.

"Hmm," Zeke said with a smirk. "Looks like the cowboy needs a large ring like the pretty boy, after all."

I experienced a moment of relief while he switched the two out, but that didn't last long. Once again he was putting that vicious metal ring around my balls and my cock, effectively crushing them together. And, okay, fine. They weren't exactly crushed, but there was no way to ignore it, either.

Once that was finished and Zeke snapped the padlock on, he seemed rather pleased by the fact that he now held the keys to our ultimate happiness. Quite literally.

"Now under the bed," Zeke instructed once he'd taken his time admiring his handiwork before releasing the restraints on our ankles and wrists.

Another thing to note, moving with that torture device crimping your balls wasn't a walk in the park. I took several deep breaths as I inched off the bed and forced my legs to hold me up. Once I took a few steps, it wasn't horrible. I could get used to it if I had to. Hopefully, it wouldn't come to that.

Case didn't seem to have the same problems I was. That or he was entertaining himself by focusing on the cage now covering *my* dick, because his eyes seemed glued to the spot.

"Come on, ladies," Zeke taunted, motioning to the door leading to the dark space beneath his bed. "No time like the present."

I bent over and peered at the king-sized square of carpet where we would sleep.

I was a little concerned Case was going to have a panic attack once he found himself caged beneath Zeke's bed. While the bars were spaced apart and there was plenty of air circulating through the room, I wasn't sure he could withstand being locked inside. Not after what had happened at the apartment on Friday.

Case, on the other hand, did not appear at all fazed by the prospect of being treated like a dog. He quickly dropped to all fours and crawled through the cage door, then moved over to one side. Although there was roughly two and a half feet of space between the floor and the underside of the bed, there was no way for Case to sit up, so he leaned on his elbow. I followed, crawling like an animal into his kennel, not sure what else I could do. It wasn't like Zeke was giving us an option here.

I watched Zeke's legs retreat as he disappeared out of the bedroom. He returned a minute later, tossing two pillows and two large blankets onto the floor.

"Of course, I want you to be comfortable," he said with a sardonic laugh. "Come on, Tank. Time for bed."

Tank dutifully jumped up on the bed without giving us so much as a second glance. I wondered if the dog felt sorry for us. I'd never seen him caged before, but surely he'd experienced it a time or two.

Once Tank was out of view, Zeke's hand appeared on the cage door. It closed with a clang and then he snapped a padlock into place.

"Sleep tight," he said mockingly.

The bed groaned above us when Zeke crawled in while Case worked to spread one of the blankets out on the carpet. When he had it positioned to his liking, I peered over to check on him. Oddly enough, he was smiling.

"Why are you smiling?" I whispered.

He shook his head and then moved the pillows before reaching for me and pulling me down with him. In an instant he was spooning behind me and I let out a relieved sigh. He pulled the second blanket over us, then inched closer.

His mouth pressed to my ear. "I'll take sleepin' in a cage if it means I get to sleep with you."

The light suddenly clicked off, the room pitch-black in an instant. Case moved in closer, his arm going over me as he tucked me in close to his body. I tried to ignore the cage on my dick but it was damned uncomfortable. I figured that was part of it. I wasn't supposed to enjoy this.

"Good night, babe," Case whispered, his voice so low it was almost impossible to hear. "I love you."

"Quiet!" Zeke barked.

Rather than speak and risk angering Zeke further, I patted his arm and forced my eyes closed.

It didn't take long before I was drifting off, feeling oddly like an animal at the zoo while my boyfriend was practically wrapped around me.

I awoke to the repeated bleep of an alarm followed by a grunt. I slowly opened my eyes, taking stock of my surroundings. I was glad I didn't bolt upright or I would've probably knocked myself out. I was still imprisoned beneath Zeke's bed, Case's warm body pressing intimately behind me.

A few seconds after my eyes opened, discomfort registered in my nether region. It was then I remembered that damn chastity device. For those keeping track, morning wood did not do well with a chastity device.

Who the hell came up with that idea anyway?

Metal clanging on metal had me shifting to peer down at the bottom of the bed.

"Time to get up," Zeke called out before the door swung open and his footsteps retreated.

I nudged Case. He mumbled something back but didn't move.

"Get up," I told him. "Unless you want to endure his wrath."

"Hmm?" Case tried to move closer. The man wasn't a morning person.

"Up. Now," I told him before throwing the blanket off and crawling out from under the bed. I started to head for the bathroom but then paused. How the hell was I supposed to take a piss with this thing on my dick?

"Come here, cowboy." Zeke's deep voice sounded from somewhere behind me. I turned, searching the darkness for him. My eyes focused enough to see he was standing by the bathroom door.

A minute later, my dick was freed from its metal dungeon.

"Thank you, Zeke," I offered before rushing out of the room and into the bathroom down the hall.

After relieving myself, I washed my hands and my face and stared back at the guy in the mirror. He didn't look like a man who had spent the night sleeping on the floor beneath a monster's bed. A smile formed, but I wasn't sure why it was there.

I never expected I'd be the type to enjoy this sort of torture. I didn't think I would've fared well in an abduction scenario, but this was different. While Zeke had taken away my options, I knew I still had an out. Perhaps that was why I maintained my sanity, why I looked forward to whatever demented thing he had in store for me next.

I left the bathroom and headed to the guest room where I kept my things. I pulled on a pair of jeans and a T-shirt before padding on bare feet toward the hallway. I wanted to get started on breakfast. I knew it would be an hour before Zeke and Case came up from the gym, so I had some time. However, I wasn't the sort to rush things when I went to work.

As I reached the stairs I heard someone groan. I paused just outside Zeke's bedroom door.

"Who fucking owns you?" Zeke's deep voice bellowed.

"You, Zeke," Case cried out.

I took a step closer until I was in the doorway. Neither man saw me because they were facing away from the door. Zeke had Case bent over his bed, his cock shoved deep inside him.

"That's right. *I* own you. Your body belongs to me and only me."

Case grunted as Zeke fucked him roughly, slamming into him. It was hard to believe that we'd all been asleep not even ten minutes ago and now Zeke was brutally fucking Case as though he'd been storing up his energy for days.

"Who do you want plowing this ass, pretty boy?"

"You, Zeke. Only you."

My heart tightened at Case's words. They sounded desperate yet sincere. It caused a queasy feeling to ignite in my gut. Could that be true? Could Case be slipping out of my grasp already? We'd only been here a few days. Based on the way he'd curled up next to me, admitting he would sleep in a cage rather than a bed just so he could be near me, made me believe that wasn't true.

"I own you, pretty boy," Zeke growled.

The light spilling from the bathroom allowed me to make out both of them. Zeke's hands curled over Case's shoulders as he jerked him closer every time his hips thrust forward causing Case to grunt and moan. He did that with me, too. When I fucked Case, I could be as rough as I wanted and he was usually begging and pleading for me to come in his ass.

"You should be honored that I give you my cock, pretty boy. Grateful that I waste any of my time on you," Zeke continued.

"I am, Zeke. Fuck. I want you to own me. Every part of me."

That sickening feeling turned to dread as my heart lurched into my throat. It was one thing for Case to agree to those things when it was part of the game we were playing. Like the time in the basement. I had understood what Zeke was doing. The humiliation only made it hotter. But they didn't know I was here. Case didn't realize I was watching, listening. He was saying these things because he wanted to please Zeke. Not because humiliating me was going to get me off.

"By the time I'm done with you, I will own every part of you," Zeke declared as he reached around Case and jerked him upright, Case's back pressing up against Zeke's chest. The Sadist's hand wrapped around Case's throat as he continued to fuck him, his hips jerking forward while Case pressed against him.

"Every fucking part of you," Zeke reiterated. "You'll be begging me for scraps. I'll be the reason you wake up, the reason you breathe. I'll fill your every thought."

"Yes," Case groaned. "Fuck, yes."

"Tell me," Zeke insisted. "Tell me who you fucking belong to."

"You, Zeke. Only you."

For a second, I thought I would vomit, but I choked it down as I tore my gaze away. I forced my legs to move, rushing down the stairs. I stumbled through the living room and right to the kitchen. I needed water. Hell, I needed air.

When Tank stared up at me from his position by the back door, I took that as a sign. I hurried to let him out, then walked out onto the back deck. The sun was just coming up, the morning breeze cool, a new day starting.

Yet here I was, wondering if maybe we could go back to yesterday.

Better yet, last week.

SIXTEEN

ZEKE

Wednesday, October 17

AFTER BREAKFAST, I INFORMED MY fuck toys we would be going to Indiana for the day. The pretty boy seemed pleased by this information, the cowboy not so much. However, they both dressed when I instructed, then joined me in my truck.

I had asked that they dressed appropriately for a business setting and I was rather impressed. Both were wearing slacks and dress shirts, ironed and immaculate. I figured since they worked for Trent Ramsey, they were accustomed to dressing the part when necessary and I wasn't disappointed.

Because I was visiting a client, I had to leave Tank at home, but I spent a few minutes with him in the yard before I left.

The trip from Chicago to Valparaiso took just over an hour and we spent most of that time silent, aside from the radio. I noticed when the pretty boy tried to talk to the cowboy, he was met with resistance. I had no idea what that was about, but I made a mental note to deal with it tonight when we got home.

When we were five minutes out from our destination, I nodded toward the glove box. "Open that and get the two boxes out."

The pretty boy, who was riding shotgun, did as I requested. He pulled out the two boxes and stared at them with wide eyes.

"When we get to the building, I want you and the cowboy to go into a bathroom and insert those. Feel free to help the other out if necessary. There're a couple of small lube packets in the console.

You'll have five minutes. Should you take longer, you will be punished."

The pretty boy didn't say anything, but he did retrieve the lube when I moved my arm out of the way.

"Oh, while I'm thinking about it..." I passed the pretty boy my cell phone. "Once you've got them in, set up the app on my phone. Then test them to make sure they work."

"Yes, Zeke." He took my phone, then glanced down at the boxes. "Do I carry them in like this?"

"Up to you. You're more than welcome to take them out if that helps."

He tore into the boxes as I was pulling into the parking lot. I glanced in the rearview mirror, noticing the cowboy was staring out the window. He didn't seem at all curious about what I had planned.

I guess I would have to fix that.

Once inside, I signed in at the reception desk, then took a seat in the waiting area while my fuck toys disappeared into the bathroom down the hall. I was eager to see what they thought of those prostate massagers. More importantly, I wanted to see how well they could compose themselves while we were sitting in a room with other people.

Ten minutes later, the head of the IT department came out to greet me. He was an older man, probably in his early sixties, with a pair of wire-rimmed glasses and thinning white hair. He was kind, seemingly not at all intimidated by the three of us.

"I've secured a conference room," he informed me. "Are these your partners?"

I glanced over at my fuck toys. "They're just along for the ride."

The IT guy smiled. I'd already forgotten his name.

"Well, hopefully we won't bore them with the details."

184

I grinned. "I doubt they'll be bored at all."

Once we'd taken a seat in a small conference room, two other men joined us. The IT guy introduced them as his direct reports. They were going to walk me through the details of the security breach they'd experienced a month or so ago. He mentioned how his CEO had referred him to Ben, and I assured him I had the company's best interests in mind and would handle their issue with complete discretion and professionalism. I knew how to play the game even if I wished I had direct reports of my own who could handle this shit for me.

I took a seat on one side of the long, narrow table with each of my fuck toys on either side of me. I kept my phone on the table in plain view with the app that controlled those massagers open.

While the cowboy pretended not to give a shit that he had a toy shoved up his ass, I could tell he wasn't able to ignore it completely. I figured that would be doubly true when I turned it on.

Once the white-haired IT guy started in on his spiel, I turned my attention to the screen on the wall while they alternated speaking parts as they walked us through what had happened. I waited roughly one minute before I turned on the pretty boy's massager. Sure enough, it wasn't quiet as it rumbled inside his ass.

In fact, it was loud enough, the guy talking paused to look around. When his eyes met mine, I signaled for him to continue. He glanced at the pretty boy, obviously noticing where the sound was coming from before turning his attention back to the screen.

A minute later, I turned on the cowboy's.

Once more, the IT guy paused but not for as long as before. Now the sound was rather loud because it was coming from both sides of me. Personally, I didn't care if they knew exactly what I was doing. Granted, the pretty boy's ears were red, which meant he didn't feel the same. That or he was trying to fight the heat that was undoubtedly consuming him.

For a good thirty minutes, the IT guys walked me through their standard protocols and all the ways they'd come up with to combat the security breach. While they talked, I amped up the massagers a little at a time until there was no way for anyone to ignore it.

"Do you mind if I ask what that noise is?" the white-haired IT guy asked.

I grinned. "You really don't want to know."

He seemed oddly amused, then smiled. "All right. Now that we've told you everything, do you think you'll be able to assist?"

"Absolutely."

Before I launched into my business plan to help them along, I made sure to turn the massagers to the highest level.

I wanted to see the cowboy try to pout through that.

Case
(The pretty boy)

PROSTATE MASSAGERS WERE INVENTED BY the devil. Or an evil Dom. Either way. Sometimes I couldn't tell the difference.

That brutal device was shoved up my ass and causing all sorts of crazy tremors to race through me. It wasn't as comfortable as someone might believe and I damn sure couldn't ignore the fact that I had a silicone-covered massager inside my body. Not only was it loud enough the others in the room could hear, I had to maneuver my position because at certain angles, it was almost painful to sit on.

Not that Zeke seemed to care about my discomfort. He was clearly taking great pleasure in my torment. Throughout the meeting, he had glanced repeatedly over at me and at Brax. Every so often, he would tap the button to increase the speed. I had to focus on breathing and swallowed a handful of moans. There were certainly times when it came close to making me come.

While Zeke went through his spiel, talking about shit I had no idea about, I had tried to peek over at Brax. I'd noticed since yesterday that he was irritable, a condition he experienced from time to time. When I had tried to ask what was wrong, he shrugged me off.

Now, my boyfriend was certainly the moody type, so I always made a point to check in with him, see how he was doing, but I'd learned to leave him alone when he wanted to be left alone. Eventually he would share what was on his mind.

However, I got the sense Zeke wasn't all that happy about Brax's grumpy behavior. And thanks to one mood affecting the other, I was somehow caught in the crossfire.

"Well, thank you, gentlemen," Zeke said graciously as he got to his feet. "I firmly believe we'll be able to address the situation and ensure it does not happen again."

I had no idea what I was supposed to do, so I waited until Zeke motioned for us to join him.

"I'll be in contact as soon as I'm back in the office."

"We're looking forward to it, and thank you so much for your time."

The man who had introduced himself as Terry held out a hand and I reluctantly shook it, wondering if he could feel the vibrations that were still coursing through me.

A few minutes later, we were walking back to Zeke's truck and the massager in my ass had slowed significantly, although it was still on.

Because I had ridden shotgun on the drive here, I figured it was only fair to allow Brax the chance to sit up front. When he waved me off, I paused only for Zeke to insist that Brax ride shotgun. While the big man walked around to the driver's side, I tried to get Brax to talk to me, but he refused. Rather than push him, I got in the back seat and waited for them to join me.

By the time we were heading back to Chicago, the silence in the truck was deafening. Unlike the trip here, Zeke had even turned off the radio, making it doubly uncomfortable. There was no way to ignore the fact that Brax was in a pissy mood. While I was used to it,

I could tell Zeke wasn't. And the longer the silence ensued, the worse it was getting.

As he drove, Zeke picked up his phone and passed it back to me. "I want both massagers on high."

Great. Now I was in charge of my own torment. That was a first for me.

"Yes, Zeke."

He continued driving while I messed with the app, turning both massagers up as high as they would go. Other than a slight grunt, Brax showed no signs of acknowledgement.

"All right, cowboy. Two choices." Zeke glanced over at him. "You can either tell me what your problem is, or you can pull out your dick and stroke it until I tell you to stop."

Because I was sitting behind Brax, I couldn't see his face. I wished I'd opted to sit behind Zeke.

"Nothing to talk about," Brax grumbled and his lie was obvious.

"Lie to me one more time and your punishment will be severe."

Brax huffed.

"Pull out your dick," Zeke commanded, his tone rough.

I glanced out the window. Although we weren't on a deserted stretch of road, there weren't that many cars around and none that would've been able to see into the truck. At least not yet.

I could see Brax's arms moving and I heard the rough scratch of his zipper.

"Now stroke it. Slowly."

I had no idea how much time passed while that fucking massager drove me out of my mind, but it seemed like time stood still. I wished Zeke would let me stroke my dick. Maybe then I could've found some relief.

"Push your jeans down lower on your hips," Zeke instructed.

Brax shifted again, and I assumed he was shoving his jeans down. I kept my eyes on Zeke, watching the way his eyes darted over to Brax every so often.

A good half hour passed, possibly more, while the three of us sat silently, the road noise and the vibrations from the massagers the only sounds in the truck. Zeke could've turned on the radio to make it less tense, but he never did.

Not once did he instruct me to turn down the massager and I started to fear my prostate was going to be numb from this damn toy. Perhaps indefinitely. Which would likely ruin sex for the rest of my life.

Great.

And now I was thinking about it constantly.

It wasn't until we were on the backroads nearing Zeke's house that he finally spoke.

"Turn the toys off," he instructed. "Once we're in the house, I want you both to remove the massagers. Clean yourself up and join me downstairs. Cowboy, you can start dinner, and pretty boy, I want you naked and laid out on my coffee table. No questions. Understood?"

My dick throbbed, but I managed a firm, "Yes, Zeke."

Brax, on the other hand, merely grunted.

It was then I knew that whatever this was, whatever had put him in a bad mood, wasn't going to simply go away.

In fact, I got the feeling it was going to get worse before it got better.

SEVENTEEN

ZEKE

I DIDN'T LIKE THE COWBOY'S attitude one fucking bit. It pissed me off in a way that I didn't expect. For one, I shouldn't actually give a shit if he was mad. However, he made it damn near impossible to ignore.

Yeah, I probably should've left them at my house while I'd run to meet the client Ben had asked me to meet with. Unfortunately, I'd thought it would be good for them to get out of the house. It seemed to have backfired in my face. And now that we were back at my house, I was ready to dish out some severe punishment.

However, I decided against it.

In fact, I decided to give the cowboy the same treatment he was giving me. If he thought it was appropriate to ignore me and shrug off everything I said, I would show him exactly how it felt.

After I let Tank out into the yard to do his business, I headed upstairs to change out of my suit. Rather than jeans, I pulled on a pair of sweatpants after shucking my underwear. Clothing wouldn't be necessary for what I had in mind for the pretty boy.

As for the cowboy … well, I was going to let him watch. I damn sure wasn't going to reward him for his bad behavior. Which meant my only choice was to ignore him. While he worked in the kitchen to make us dinner, he would get a front row seat to me enjoying the hell out of his boyfriend.

I took my time changing. I even took a moment to check my email and to shoot Ben a note letting him know I had visited the client and I would be submitting my proposal for him to review.

That wasn't something he required from me; however, I was still new to the company, and while learning the ropes, I wanted to ensure I met or exceeded his expectations.

When I returned downstairs, the cowboy was in the kitchen, making more noise than usual. And the pretty boy was laid out naked on my coffee table.

"Mmm," I said when I approached. "Just how I want to see you." I glanced over at the cowboy. "When you get a chance, make sure you get Tank's dinner ready, too."

The cowboy nodded but didn't verbally respond.

I fought back the urge to confront him. I didn't approve of this childish behavior. But if I did say something, it would only provoke him. I expected him to talk to me when he had a problem, not bottle it up and pretend it didn't exist.

Not that I knew what his problem was. He'd been this way since I came down for breakfast yesterday morning. The more time that went by, the worse he got and I was starting to wonder if he even knew why he was pissed. At first he'd simply been quiet, somewhat melancholy. That had twisted and morphed into outright defiance today.

I grabbed the remote to the television and dropped down onto the sofa. Although I clicked it on, my gaze never strayed from the pretty boy. He was laid out perfectly, his cock hard and heavy against his stomach, his arms down at his sides, and his knees bent, feet on the floor. He looked comfortable. For now.

"Stroke yourself for me, pretty boy. I want to watch you touch yourself."

A shudder went through him as his hand moved to his cock. One big fist circled his dick, slowly working up, then down.

"Did you enjoy the prostate massager?" I asked, simply to make conversation so that the cowboy was curious.

"Yes, Zeke. Although, at one point, I feared my prostate would be numb indefinitely."

I chuckled. I hadn't thought of that, but the added mind fuck certainly didn't disappoint.

I made sure to keep an eye on the cowboy. He was working away, but he couldn't keep from glancing over to see what we were doing. I wanted him to watch, to see how I rewarded good behavior.

The pretty boy worked his dick for several minutes, not moving other than to fist his cock up and down. I couldn't resist the urge to lean closer, to admire what he was doing. My gaze darted between the cowboy in the kitchen and the pretty boy's hard cock. When I noticed the cowboy looking again, I leaned down and swiped my tongue over the head of the pretty boy's cock.

The pretty boy hissed, his hand stilling momentarily.

"I didn't tell you to stop," I said roughly.

He began working himself again and I used my tongue on the head of his cock, relishing the taste of him. While I tended to command my toys to suck me off, I happened to enjoy teasing with my mouth. I didn't indulge often because it gave the illusion that I cared more than I did. However, in this case, I was doing it to torment the cowboy.

"Hold your cock still," I ordered, ensuring my voice carried into the kitchen so the cowboy knew what I was doing.

The pretty boy's hand stilled and I leaned over and sucked the head of his dick between my lips. He groaned loudly and his cock pulsed against my tongue.

"You like my mouth on your dick, don't you, pretty boy?"

"Yes, Zeke," he replied breathlessly. "So fucking much."

I spent a few minutes torturing him with my lips and tongue. I never deep-throated him, didn't suck vigorously, merely teased. The longer I spent with my mouth on the pretty boy's dick, the louder the sounds in the kitchen became. Pots and pans clanging, silverware being dropped onto the counter. The cowboy didn't appreciate my tactics.

Which meant it was time to turn it up another notch.

Brax

(The cowboy)

I COULDN'T FUCKING BELIEVE THAT Zeke was sucking Case's dick right there in front of me.

He had teased me with that damn prostate massager all fucking day, made me stroke my dick during the ride home, then banished me to the kitchen so I could cook their fucking dinner.

I had half a mind to walk right out the front door and never look back.

And I would have if I didn't feel guilty about my stupid reactions to him. Ever since yesterday morning when I'd overheard Zeke and Case in Zeke's bedroom, I'd been in a state of chaos. My emotions were all over the map. I was hurt by the fact that Case admitted he wanted Zeke to own him. I was angry with Zeke because he hadn't confronted me that way, never gave me the chance to offer myself up like that.

It made no sense.

I'd known what this was when I agreed to it. Zeke didn't want strings, and I was supposed to respect that. I knew he was simply fucking with us. He didn't own us. Not for the long term anyway. Which meant I had overreacted to what I'd witnessed.

It would've been easy to simply lay it all out there for Zeke, to tell him how I felt. He could decide where to go from there. More than likely, he would make me feel like a jackass and then we could move on with our lives.

Except, I didn't want to risk Zeke throwing us out on our asses. Not because we didn't have somewhere to go. That could be easily rectified, even if it meant staying in a hotel in the interim. The truth was, I didn't want to leave. For me. For Case. For Zeke. I wanted to explore this. To have the experience if nothing else. We were just getting started and here I was about to ruin everything.

So, rather than talk, I had bottled it up. My anger would dissipate eventually. It always did.

Only now, watching Zeke suck Case's dick wasn't helping in the least. I wanted my dick to be in Zeke's mouth. I wanted him focused on me.

Did that make me selfish? Also-fucking-lutely.

Did I care? No.

Okay, yes.

I did care. I loved Case. And I knew he loved me. We had come into this agreeing to see it through. I had no right to be jealous, yet my stupid heart couldn't be swayed otherwise.

"Stand up, pretty boy," Zeke instructed.

My eyes shot up from the chicken Parmesan I was preparing. I watched as Case stood, his cock rock hard and bobbing proudly. Zeke stood, too, then shoved his sweatpants down his legs before he took a seat on the sofa once more.

"Come over here." Zeke patted the cushion beside him. "I want you on your knees, mouth on my dick."

I groaned, trying to be as quiet as possible. From the angle Zeke was in, I would be able to see Case's ass, not what his mouth was doing to Zeke.

"That's a good fuck toy," Zeke crooned, his hand sliding over the back of Case's head. "I want you to suck my dick until I tell you to stop."

I was well aware that Zeke knew I was watching them. Our eyes had met several times. I knew he was pushing me, rewarding Case while punishing me. I even understood why he was doing it.

Didn't mean I was happy.

Worse than that? My dick was hard. Watching Zeke and Case wasn't easy to do. It should've pissed me off, but it only turned me on. I was hard and horny and I knew there would be no outlet for me. Not tonight.

"Such a good fucking mouth," Zeke said. "Keep sucking me, pretty boy. Take my cock all the way in your throat. That's it. Just like that."

I tried to focus on the task at hand, but my gaze continued to bounce over to the sofa. I could see Case's balls and his asshole. He was spread out, as though in offering, but he wasn't mine to have.

I knew what was coming next. I knew Zeke had every intention of fucking Case. Probably right here in the kitchen, where I had no choice but to watch them, to hate myself for acting like a petulant child all damn day.

"Ah, fuck," Zeke groaned. "I need to feel that ass choking my dick, pretty boy. You want that? To feel me buried to the hilt inside you?"

Case groaned and my dick throbbed.

"Go grab some lube and a condom from my bedroom," Zeke told Case.

I focused my attention on finishing up while my mind wandered. I would simply excuse myself after dinner, go up to the bathroom, and jack off. Zeke wouldn't know and it would offer some much needed relief.

"Think I can't read your mind, cowboy?" Zeke asked.

My gaze shot over to him and I noticed he was walking toward me.

"I know what you're thinking," he continued, "but it won't happen. As soon as we're finished with dinner, I'm putting your cage on you. You won't get a chance to touch yourself. You will live with this discomfort for the rest of the night."

I groaned, not caring that he heard me.

"Come here, cowboy," Zeke insisted, his tone harder, more irritated than before. He motioned toward the kitchen table. "Pull out that chair and have a seat."

"I need to finish dinner," I retorted, my tone reflecting every ounce of my anger.

His eyes narrowed and I could tell I was pushing my luck.

"Sit. Down."

I had two choices. Sit down or piss him off royally. I had gotten away with more than I should have, so I knew Zeke was being lenient. However, the man was clearly getting close to his limit. If I pushed too hard, Case and I would be sleeping somewhere else tonight.

And honestly, that was the last thing I wanted.

So, I sat.

Case returned a minute later with lube and a condom.

"Bend over the table, pretty boy." Zeke quickly sheathed himself with the condom. "Give me your hand, cowboy."

I held up my hand and Zeke squirted lube into it.

"Grease me up so I can fuck the pretty boy's tight little ass while you watch."

Not having a choice, I did as he instructed. Once he was lubed, he pulled his cock from between my fingers, then walked over behind me. My chair shifted, moving closer to where Case was currently leaning over the table, his ass facing Zeke.

"You're gonna sit there and watch," Zeke growled, his voice low and deep. "Look away one fucking time and you can find another place to go tonight."

Case's head turned and I felt his eyes on me. I didn't look at him. I already hated myself for letting things get out of hand. It was all my fault, so I would take my punishment like a man.

I turned my attention to Case's ass, watching as Zeke lined up and slid inside him. My stomach twisted, churning as Case groaned and moaned.

Zeke took his time, fucking into Case slow and easy. He kept one hand on his cock, the other on Case's hip, ensuring I had a perfect view as he penetrated him.

"You like that, pretty boy? Feeling my dick deep inside you?"

"Yes, Zeke," Case confirmed.

Zeke's gaze shot to me, but I didn't look away. I wasn't going to risk his wrath. I'd already overstepped.

With my heart in my throat, I watched Zeke fuck Case. It started out slow, then became brutal. Zeke took his pleasure as easily as he gave it. They both grunted and groaned as Zeke pounded away at my boyfriend's ass. I had no choice but to endure.

Even as I wished like hell that was me bent over that table and Zeke was using me the way he was using Case.

I was so fucking jealous.

Jealous of Case.

Jealous of Zeke.

Just fucking jealous.

EIGHTEEN

ZEKE

Thursday, October 18

I SPENT THE ENTIRE NEXT morning trying to figure out what the fuck was wrong with the cowboy.

He'd had a bug up his ass ever since Tuesday morning when I ventured down for breakfast after my workout and shower. I wasn't sure what was bothering him, but he was standoffish, as though keeping me at arm's length. Then again, he seemed to be doing the same to his boyfriend. Last night, after I had fucked the pretty boy right in front of the cowboy, I half expected him to break. However, he hadn't.

So, I had followed him upstairs, allowed him to take a piss while I watched, then I put his cage on him and forced him to remain naked while we went back downstairs. We ate dinner and I had the cowboy clean up, although the pretty boy was usually the one to pitch in. He joined us in the living room when he was finished, and when we were watching television, the cowboy had put some space between himself and the pretty boy. That wasn't normal from what I'd seen.

Rather than go into the office this morning, I opted to work from home. Case mentioned he was scheduled to meet with Trent for one of his workout sessions, so I figured I could keep the cowboy company while he waited for their things to be delivered. Since they were currently residing with me, they had decided to put most of their belongings in storage. It made the most sense until they figured out where they would be living whenever this thing between us was finished.

I had briefly considered outlining a plan for them. Adding an end date so they had something to work toward. That thought was fleeting. I liked the idea of them not knowing. Wondering if perhaps today would be the day I would kick them out on their asses.

As with every sexual encounter I'd had with a submissive, I knew this would be ending. If the cowboy had his way, probably sooner rather than later. But I was expecting it, waiting for him to come to me and let me know he was giving back the collar because he was through. No matter how much I was enjoying having them here, I knew it was inevitable.

I was sitting at the kitchen table with my laptop when I heard footsteps behind me. A few seconds passed, but the cowboy kept his mouth shut. If he was waiting for me to greet him, he would be waiting a damn long time.

Finally, he cleared his throat and he began speaking to my back. "The movers said they'd meet me at the storage unit in an hour."

I pivoted in my chair to face him, curious as to what he wanted me to do with that information. When he wasn't forthcoming, I cocked an eyebrow and waited patiently.

His eyes went everywhere except mine when he finally spoke. "I just thought you wanted to know."

"I *do* want to know," I assured him, taking in his body language.

His arms were crossed over his chest, his hip slightly cocked as though what he was saying didn't mean a damn thing to him or me. His gaze darted my way briefly, but when he noticed me watching him, his eyes shifted again.

"Okay, then." He dropped his hands with a huff. "I guess I'll just go on up there and wait. Not sure when I'll be—"

"The pretty boy has your car," I told him unnecessarily.

"I know. I … I wanted to see if I could borrow your truck."

"No." I didn't see any reason for him to sit in my truck and wait for the damn movers. The place was five minutes from my house. It was obvious he was trying to get away from me and I wanted to know why.

His forehead creased and those emerald eyes finally settled firmly on my face, defiance glittering back at me. "No?"

"Did I stutter?"

"No. It's just … I was thinking … I figured I could…"

I pushed to my feet. "Don't think."

The cowboy's eyes followed my movement, his arms shifting in closer to his body. If he was trying to pretend not to be pissed off, he was doing a shitty job.

I nodded toward the basement stairs. "Follow me."

I was surprised he didn't ask me why. He wasn't nearly as obedient as he'd been a couple of days ago.

I marched down the stairs with him close at my heels.

"Strip and go stand by the wall."

"Uh … Zeke … I need to meet the movers."

Stopping in my tracks, I didn't turn to look at him. "Are you arguing with me, cowboy?"

"No, Zeke. It's just—"

I held up a hand to cut him off. When he stopped, I pointed to the wall. "Now."

It was time to address this situation. The man obviously had something on his mind, and if it meant torturing the information out of him, so be it. I certainly didn't mind. In fact, it was right up my alley.

I unlocked the closet so I could find one particular toy I'd been looking forward to trying out. It was rather brutal, but I figured the cowboy could handle it. Once I'd gathered all the parts, I carried the heavy items out to where the cowboy was currently waiting for me.

I set everything down on the vinyl-padded table in the corner, then began connecting the pieces until there was no mystery left regarding what it was for. Well, no mystery for me.

The contraption was rather large. Probably four feet in length, but sturdy on the six-foot table.

"Over here," I instructed the cowboy. "Do you know what this is?"

"No, Zeke. I haven't got a clue."

"It's a stockade." I motioned toward the front. "These two circles will restrain your wrists. This one your head." I patted the middle pad. "Your chest rests here since you'll be on your elbows and knees. Your ankles will be secured here and then this"—I pulled a thick black dildo out of the protective bag—"will attach to this part, converting it into a machine that's going to fuck your ass for as long as I want it to."

His eyes widened, but he didn't say anything. I knew what he was thinking. He was trying to determine if that dildo would actually fit in his ass. If my cock fit, this certainly would. But it wouldn't necessarily be comfortable.

"Get on up here."

The cowboy stepped closer and I gave him a hand when he crawled up on the table. It only took a couple of minutes to get him in position, then I went to work fixing everything around him so he was safely restrained.

"There's nowhere for you to go from this point," I told him once all the shackles were in place. "Which will help once this thing gets going."

I lubed the dildo and secured it on the rod, then lined it up with the cowboy's ass. He jerked when the cool gel lubed his asshole.

"Are you excited?" I asked, keeping my tone snide. "Because I am. I figure this'll do nicely as an attitude adjustment."

"Attitude adjustment?" he sounded skeptical.

"It appears we've got a problem," I told him. "You clearly have something on your mind. Since I don't tolerate bratty, sulking fuck toys, I'm gonna take care of that."

Once the dildo was where it was supposed to be, I grabbed the remote and hit the button. It was on its lowest setting, which was just enough to have the dildo inching forward ever so slowly, working its way into his ass.

The cowboy grunted as it breached the tight ring of muscles. Satisfied with the setup, I walked back around to stand in front of him. Since he was on the table, he was high enough to look me in the face without having to strain his neck too much.

"Now tell me, cowboy. What's the problem?"

He gritted his teeth as the toy fucked its way into him. "No problem, Zeke."

I stepped forward and grabbed his jaw, getting right up in his face. My patience was on the verge of snapping and his dishonesty had it hanging precariously in the balance.

I squeezed his jaw. "If you think this is punishment, you don't have a fucking clue who I am. Lie to me one more time and I swear to you I'll break you so fast you won't have a chance to think of a safe word, much less utter it. Understand?"

His eyes locked with mine, daggers shooting out of them. He was seething when he responded with, "Yes, Zeke."

Taking a deep breath, I released him and stepped back. The machine was doing its job, pulling out and pushing in. It was a steady rhythm that would have him wanting more but only I had the power to give that to him.

"You've been pouting for two days. What's the problem?"

His expression gave him away. He was pissed. Whatever had happened had angered him and he'd been walking around with it bottled up inside.

"I heard you and Case," he said, his words clipped as the dildo pushed into him.

"Heard us?"

"Yes. The other morning. In your bedroom. You were fucking him."

I'd fucked the pretty boy plenty of times, but only once in my bedroom. "And…?"

"You asked him who owned him. He said you did."

"And you have a problem with that because…?"

His lips formed a hard line but he didn't look away. "It bothered me that he said it."

"Feeling left out?" I taunted, smiling ferociously.

"Yes, Zeke." He grunted when the dildo penetrated him again.

202

I stepped closer, staring right into his eyes. "What is it you want from me, cowboy?"

"Everything, Zeke."

I wasn't sure I liked the sound of that.

"Everything?"

He tried to nod but the metal ring around his neck made it impossible. "Yes, Zeke."

"Define everything." This was what I needed to know.

While I had the pretty boy pegged, I hadn't quite figured out what fed the cowboy's true desires. He claimed to be a masochist, and in many ways, I saw the signs. He didn't mind having his ass spanked and the rough sex made his eyes glaze over. However, he wasn't into pain the way the pretty boy was. He took it when it was delivered, but the humiliation seemed to be what got him off. I wanted to hear him admit it.

"I get the feeling you don't have a clue what you need." I kept my tone cool, aloof.

"Not true." The dildo pushed in again and he breathed through it.

"Is your dick hard?"

"Yes, Zeke."

"Do you get off having a machine fucking your ass?"

"Yes, Zeke."

And there it was. The truth was in his eyes. He needed the humiliation.

I stepped in closer and curled my hand around his jaw. This time I didn't squeeze, merely kept his attention where it belonged. On me.

"That can be arranged. Would you like me to set this up so you can spend your evenings bent over with this toy drilling into your asshole? You can sit there and take it while I fuck your boyfriend. I can own him like the bitch he is, and you can take all the pleasure from a machine."

"No, Zeke."

"What? You're jealous that I'm fucking your boyfriend? Is that it? You don't like the idea that he gets off on it? Do you think I give him more attention than I give you?"

"Yes, Zeke."

I let that sink in. I considered all the times we'd played for the past few days. It was possible I'd given the pretty boy more attention. It certainly wasn't intentional, but part of me knew the pretty boy could handle anything I gave him. I had to rein myself in with the cowboy.

"He needs me," I told him. "He needs what only I can give him. That's why you're here, right? So I can give you both what you can't give each other?"

"Yes, Zeke."

"Do you think he wants me more than he wants you?"

"Yes, Zeke."

I took a small step back because the conviction in his tone caught me off guard. The cowboy was serious and *that* was the problem.

He honestly believed the pretty boy wanted me more than he wanted him.

Case
(The pretty boy)

AFTER SPENDING THE BETTER PART of the morning with Trent, I had finally finished up and hurried back to Zeke's so I could be with Brax when the movers arrived. He had mentioned wanting to get a few things—clothes, cologne, personal shit we'd packed rather than carried with us—before we locked it all up.

When I walked into the house, I noticed Tank on the sofa. He lifted his head enough to acknowledge me but he didn't move. Clearly I wasn't a threat.

There on the kitchen table was Zeke's laptop, but he was nowhere in sight. Since Zeke's truck was out front, I knew he was still here. And since I had taken Brax's car, he would've had no way to leave, so I assumed he was around, also.

"Where'd they go, boy?" I asked Tank, knowing he wouldn't respond.

I paused by the stairs to listen for noises coming from upstairs or down. I heard a muffled grunt, so I moved over to the basement stairs. When it sounded again, I knew I'd found them.

I started down the stairs and the sounds grew louder. Voices could be heard along with a strange whirring sound. I took one step at a time, moving slower, smiling at the idea of watching them scene together. I did enjoy watching Zeke torment him. Especially those times when he forced Brax to come on command.

Of course, last night had been weird. Like a battle of wits between Brax and Zeke, and I'd been caught in the middle. Not that I'd necessarily minded, but it had been rather awkward for Brax to be forced to watch Zeke fuck me.

I stopped on the stairs when Zeke's voice echoed from below.

"What? You're jealous that I'm fucking your boyfriend? Is that it? You don't like the idea that he gets off on it? Do you think I give him more attention than I give you?"

"Yes, Zeke," Brax replied.

"He needs me," Zeke stated. "He needs what only I can give him. That's why you're here, right? So I can give you both what you can't give each other?"

"Yes, Zeke."

"Do you think he wants me more than he wants you?"

"Yes, Zeke."

My legs turned rubbery beneath me when I heard the torment in Brax's voice. He was serious. Zeke might've been taunting him, but Brax was speaking the truth. He wasn't playing a role, he wasn't trying to push Zeke to give him what he needed. Brax honestly believed that I wanted Zeke more than him.

How could that be possible?

How could he doubt my love for him?

For the past three nights, I had curled up to sleep with Brax in my arms. I hadn't cared about the fucking torture device on my dick or the fact that we were being treated like animals, forced to sleep in a cage beneath Zeke's bed. I would take that any day over having to sleep separately from Brax.

And he thought I wanted Zeke more?

"What do you think he'd say right now if he came home to find you hooked up to that machine? That dildo penetrating your ass? Do you think he'd be jealous?"

"No, Zeke."

"Do you want him to be jealous, cowboy? Do you want the pretty boy to see you like this, to know you willingly crawled up on that table like a dog, let me strap you down so I could impale you with a fucking machine?"

"Yes, Zeke."

There was a long pause and I couldn't stay still any longer. I continued down the steps until I was in the basement with them. There was Brax, shackled to a table while a dildo hooked to a rod fucked into his ass. Zeke stood in front of him, far enough away that they could continue to make eye contact.

"What do you think would make him jealous, cowboy? What would make him hurt the way you're hurting?"

"I don't know, Zeke."

"Do you want him to hurt?"

"Yes. No!" Brax moaned. "No. I don't wanna hurt him."

"But you do. That's why you've been pouting. Because he's giving me what you want him to give you. Yet you're still here. Shackled in my basement while that machine drills your ass. Now tell me, what would make him hurt the way you're hurting?"

"I don't know!" Brax yelled.

"I do," I said, making my presence known.

To my shock, Zeke didn't move. He didn't look over at me.

I stepped closer until I could see Brax's face. His eyes shot to me and I could see everything he was thinking. Anger, confusion, doubt. It was all there. My heart slammed against my ribs.

"Tell me, cowboy. What will make him jealous?"

"I don't know. I honestly don't know."

"He said he knows," Zeke stated firmly. "Now I want to hear you say it."

"Nothing," Brax ground out. "Nothing will make him jealous. He needs us both equally."

"You think that's it?" Zeke taunted.

"Yes, Zeke."

"You think he needs me to hurt him as much as he needs the cuddling and kisses you shower him with?"

"Yes, Zeke."

Zeke's head turned and those black eyes pinned me in place. Something dark lurked there and I suddenly felt a chill in the air. I'd never seen him like that. I wasn't sure I wanted to see him like that again.

His attention shifted back to Brax and he stepped forward, closing the distance between them. When Zeke's lips brushed Brax's, I swallowed so hard I wondered if my heart had shot up into my mouth and then back down.

That ... *that* wasn't part of the deal, was it? Zeke hadn't kissed either one of us up to this point. I wasn't sure why I hadn't thought about that before.

Zeke's head tilted and he deepened the kiss. I could see the way their tongues slid together. It was erotic and dangerous for my sanity. My heart lurched, but I couldn't tear my eyes away. I was drawn to the way their mouths moved together in such an intimate way.

"I think that worked," Zeke said, drawing me out of my stupor. "Look at him, cowboy. He doesn't know what to think about that. He's the only one who's supposed to be kissing you. Not me. Not the big, bad wolf. I'm only allowed to use your body, to fuck your ass and your throat. To shove my dick inside you. Kissing's too intimate; it means more than anything else."

Zeke stood tall and stared into Brax's eyes. He was practically vibrating with barely restrained rage.

"And that's all bullshit, cowboy!" he snapped. "Kissing means nothing. It's merely fuel for the fire, but it does seem to get your boyfriend amped up. He doesn't like me kissing you. Now tell me, do you want that fake dick to move faster?"

"Yes, Zeke."

"Beg for it."

Brax's lips clamped shut and I held my breath, waiting.

"If you don't beg, I'll stop the machine while that toy's lodged in your ass. You want that? To be stuck there impaled on that fake dick?"

Again, Brax didn't respond, his eyes narrowed, his anger apparent.

"Beg me, fuck toy!" Zeke commanded, his voice deeper than before. "Fucking *beg*."

When the toy inched forward again, Brax moaned, the strain on his face lessening.

"Please," he groaned.

"Not enough, fuck toy. I said beg!"

"Shit!" Brax cried out, his body jerking within the restraints. "Please, Zeke. Fuck! I need more."

"Tell me," Zeke barked.

"Oh, fuck…" Brax moaned. "More. Please. More."

"You want that fake dick to drill you harder?'

"Yes. Please."

"Faster?" Zeke asked.

"Yes. Please, Zeke. Give me more."

Christ. Just hearing Brax's tortured pleas drove me damn near insane. Almost as much as watching Zeke kiss him, acting as though it didn't mean anything. It meant a hell of a lot more for me, that was for sure. I could get lost in Brax's kiss for hours. In fact, we'd done that before. Making out like teenagers on the couch on a lazy Sunday afternoon. Kissing, groping, fondling. I'd almost say I enjoyed those moments more than any other.

"Harder!" Brax cried out. "I need more."

Zeke moved around to the machine. He picked up the lube and squirted it on the toy, coating it liberally as it retreated from Brax's ass. When he stepped back, the machine sped up, pushing into Brax and retreating over and over. He was impaled on that damn thing, unable to move from the restraints. His hands were balled into fists, his teeth grinding together as he moaned and groaned, begging Zeke to give him more.

I watched in awe, loving the way Brax gave himself over to it, hating that I needed this.

Suddenly the machine slowed and Brax groaned.

"Tell me, cowboy. Tell me you won't let your petty jealousy fuck this up. Tell me you understand I'm not here as your lover or his. I'm using you both. Taking what I want when I want it. *How* I want it. It means nothing to me. When it's over, you and the pretty boy can go back to playing house all day long. I have no interest in that. Tell me you understand that."

"I understand, Zeke. I'm your fuck toy. That's all."

The machine picked up speed again, this time drilling into Brax again and again.

"May I come, Zeke?" He growled low in his throat. "Please let me come."

"Yes."

A few seconds later, a few more solid thrusts from that machine and Brax was crying out as his cock jerked. He came on a low growl, his eyes rolling back in his head.

I stood there motionless, my breaths coming in almost as rapidly as Brax's.

Zeke turned to face me, his eyes cold, his expression masked.

"He's your responsibility," he bit out before heading to the stairs. He tossed a key my way. "Get him off that thing and the two of you can go meet the movers."

He didn't wait for a response before he jogged up the stairs.

Out of sight, out of mind.

At least for him.

NINETEEN

ZEKE

Friday, October 19

"THIS IS A FIRST," JAMIE said when I walked into the diner that morning. She was already sitting at our favorite table, sipping apple juice. "I was surprised to get the text last night."

In an effort to avoid her feeling the stress that was a living, breathing thing inside my house, I had shot Jamie a text last night letting her know I had an early meeting and that I would meet her at the diner. While I could've forgone breakfast altogether, I hadn't wanted to miss the opportunity to spend time with her. There were too many excuses one could come up with not to spend time with those they loved. I wasn't about to make up one at this point.

"Sorry," I said as I took a seat across from her. "Busy at work. Got a day full of interviews."

Jamie stared back at me and it was obvious she didn't buy my bullshit.

"Or you didn't want me to have a chance to talk to your *toys*," she stated, her tone curious but not quite questioning.

I kept my expression masked. The last thing I wanted was for Jamie to worry about me. She might've been my kid sister, but I knew she worried about me as much as I worried about her. And after the debacle with my ex four years ago, she was always touchy when she thought I might be getting close to someone.

Not that I had. Not before the fuck toys and not now.

210

"So, how's school?" I asked after the waitress had delivered my coffee and confirmed my order.

"Good."

Of course it was.

"I have a question for you," she finally stated after a few minutes of strained silence.

"What's that?"

"Have you ever wondered why someone would need the pain you dish out?"

Okay. Wow. If she'd meant to shock me, she certainly achieved her goal. I frowned as I sipped my coffee. To be honest, I hadn't thought Jamie knew all that much about my ... kink. Sure, she knew I went to clubs, and she knew I was into BDSM, but I hadn't been aware that she knew of my desire to hurt people.

"And I'm not being judgmental, Zeke," she clarified. "I don't think there's anything wrong with your sadistic side."

"Is that the psychologist speaking? Or my sister?"

"Both," she said with a grin. "And yes, I've wondered what makes you tick. Why you get pleasure from ... doing what you do."

At least she was mindful of the others around us. Not everyone was okay with hearing that someone wanted to beat on someone else. I'd had people accuse me of being abusive but that wasn't the case. I didn't go around hitting people for the hell of it. And I never hit someone out of anger. Never.

"But I'm even more curious as to why someone would need it from you." There wasn't any accusation in her tone or her gaze. "Are people born that way? Or does their past mold them, make them desire it?"

I took another sip of my coffee. "Couldn't say. I don't have the desire to be hit."

"Nor do I," she said with a grin. "Although, I wouldn't mind being spanked."

"Okay." I set my coffee cup on the table. "That's TMI, my dear sister. Please don't sit here and tell me that shit."

Jamie laughed and I suspected she enjoyed getting a rise out of me. "Fine. I won't tell you. But have you ever wondered about the masochists you play with? What drives them? Why they need what they need?"

"No." And I wasn't about to start now.

"Liar." She giggled again and took a sip of her juice. "You might want everyone else to believe you're a hard-core badass, but I know you, Zeke. I know that you have a soft, mushy center."

I frowned. "Now you're just being a brat." It was time to change the subject. "Have you talked to Edge?"

Her face flushed. "Yes. I have."

"And...?"

"And what? If we're not going to talk about your kinks, we're certainly not gonna talk about mine."

I didn't want to believe my sister had kinks, but I didn't say as much. Thank God the waitress opted to bring our food because the mere thought of Jamie and Edge together ... yeah, I'd rather dig into my own psyche than think about that shit.

I got the feeling today wasn't going to be a good day.

"What do you think of the three we've talked to already?" I asked Ben as we sat at the conference room table after having spent an hour talking to one of the many interviewees scheduled for today.

"I don't think Mark's going to be what we're looking for," Ben explained. "As for the last two, I don't see any major issues. You?"

"Mark's out of contention," I replied as I set that resume aside before glancing over Lance Douglas's. "I'm worried Lance needs more handholding than I'm willing to give."

"Good point," Ben conceded. "I can see that." His eyes dropped to the copy of the kid's resume. "He's got quite the education, but not a lot of experience in the corporate world. Could require some molding to get where we need him to be."

This was the part I hated about hiring people. It wasn't necessarily the interviews, more so narrowing it down to who would be the right fit. You picked the wrong person and you were stuck with them, perhaps indefinitely. After all, you couldn't necessarily fire them for being a whiny asshole, especially if they were good at their job. I'd done my fair share of hiring over the years and it all boiled down to who was capable of excelling without needing someone there to walk them through every step. Training was one thing, being their mother was something else.

"Thoughts on Heather?" I prompted. "I think she's got what it takes."

"Agree. She lacks a lot of experience, but she's got quite the attention to detail."

The conference room door opened and Justin strolled in. "Any luck?"

"A couple of possibilities," I told him. "I'm willing to call Heather and offer her the job if you're both in agreement. Mark's off the list but I'll keep Lance in the running. This afternoon's applicants will be here shortly. We've got Chris Cavanaugh, the guy Edge referred, coming in at three."

Justin peered over at Ben, who nodded his agreement.

"Good," Justin stated. "Then I'm going to borrow my pup here for a little while."

I smirked. "I'll meet you back here in forty-five minutes?"

"I'll make sure he returns in one piece," Justin promised.

"As long as he can walk," I added with a chuckle.

Justin grinned from ear to ear. "Walk, yes. Sit down? Well, that's to be determined."

The two men left the conference room and I sat there staring at the resumes on the table although I wasn't really seeing them. My mind was on the two masochists who had successfully pissed me off to no end.

I'd made the cowboy and the pretty boy stay home today. In fact, I'd kept my distance from them since my scene with Brax and the fucking machine yesterday afternoon.

I still couldn't believe I'd kissed him. Not that I was opposed to kissing, but like aftercare, it gave a submissive the wrong impression. The worst part was I had enjoyed it immensely. It had been a damn long time since I'd slowed down enough to find that little bit of intimacy. Four years, to be exact. I hadn't kissed a man in four fucking years. And while I told him it meant nothing, I knew better. If it didn't mean anything, I wouldn't have thought about it endlessly since.

But I refused to give in to them. In fact, I was considering kicking them to the curb tonight when I got home. I didn't need this fucking hassle. I enjoyed what we had going on, but evidently, they were both seeing more than there was. Which surprised me considering the short time we'd been together.

The cowboy being jealous of the pretty boy spending time with me was a big red flag. I wasn't going to spend my time drawing up a timeline so that I fucked them equally. That wasn't how I operated. If they wanted that shit, they could find some baby Dom who wanted to smack them around a little and cuddle them after. They'd said they understood what this was, but I was beginning to doubt that.

"Zeke Lautner daydreamin'. Never thought I'd see the day."

I peered up at Langston as he stepped into the conference room. "Shouldn't you be working?"

"Takin' a break, actually. Landon's got Luci in his office. I was givin' them a little private time. All that yellin' was distractin' me, so I opted to come up here."

"Yelling? Landon or Luci?"

Langston chuckled. "This time it was Luci. From what I gather, the little brat put salt in Landon's coffee this mornin'."

"Ah. She's graduated to being a brat, eh?"

"Looks that way. We're gonna take her to the club tonight. String her up and show her the error of her ways."

"So, you reward her for her insubordination?"

"She's not like your boys," Langston said. "She doesn't particularly care for the pain."

"Fuck toys," I corrected.

Langston nodded slightly. "My apologies. Your fuck toys," he corrected. "How are they, anyway?"

I shrugged and stared out the window. "I'm thinking it's time to cut them loose."

"Yeah? They do somethin' wrong?"

"They're getting too attached."

"Translated to mean you're tired of them," Langston stated, his tone serious.

"No. Actually, that's not the case at all." Which surprised the hell out of me. I'd spent a solid week with them. I should've been ready to move on, but I found I wasn't. Even after the drama from yesterday, I didn't relish the idea of sending them on their way. I wanted to say that was due to the fact there were two of them. That broke up the monotony rather well. I had a million more scenes already planned out in my mind and I'd been looking forward to taking it one day at a time.

"You goin' to the club tonight?" Langston asked.

"Not sure yet."

"You talk to Greg lately?"

Langston's sudden topic change caught me by surprise. "No. Why?"

"Rumor has it he's bringin' a submissive to the club on a guest pass."

"When?"

"Tonight." Langston drummed his fingers on the table. "Found that interesting."

It was obvious Langston was fishing. I wasn't going to fall for the bait. "News to me."

Langston grinned. "Yeah? I talked to Ransom yesterday."

"Spit it out, Moore."

Langston appeared unfazed by my gruff command. "I'm pretty sure you and this submissive have a last name in common."

"Well, if that's the case, I guess you've got your answer as to whether or not I'll be at the club."

The man sobered somewhat. "She's in good hands, Lautner."

"I know. Hence the reason I asked him to show her around. Give her a taste."

"You don't think it'll stick, do ya? You're hopin' he'll scare her off?"

"I don't want Jamie going to one of those shit hole clubs. That's the only reason I asked him."

"Smart."

I wasn't sure about that. Allowing my baby sister into the club was a gamble. Perhaps she was more in tune with her desires than I wanted to believe. It was possible she was a true submissive. Which meant, once she got a taste of it, she might not be able to walk away. I could only hope Greg took care of her. Otherwise, the man would be walking with a limp.

A knock sounded on the door behind me. I spun my chair around as I called for the person to enter.

Dale appeared. "Mr. Lautner, your one o'clock is here."

I glanced at my watch. It was only twelve thirty. "They can wait. Once Ben comes back, you can send them in."

"Sure thing." He disappeared as fast as he had appeared.

"Any potential in the pool?" Langston asked when Dale closed the door.

"A little." I wasn't about to tell him I was having a hard time focusing on these damn interviews because my mind was back at my house with the fuck toys who had somehow changed the game on me.

Despite my better judgment, I couldn't help but wonder what it was they were doing.

And whether or not they were thinking of me while they did it.

Brax

(The cowboy)

"WE'RE GONNA HAVE TO TALK about this, Brax," Case said for the two-dozenth time.

Ever chopped vegetables? For me, this was therapeutic. Taking my time, focusing on the little things. That was how I grounded myself, remained in the here and now. Unless, of course, someone wanted to chat. At that point, focusing was nearly impossible.

"There's nothin' to talk about," I answered, exactly as I had every time he'd mentioned it since yesterday afternoon when he came home to find me strapped to a table with a machine gearing up to make me come.

Case sighed heavily and flopped onto the couch. I spared him a quick glance. He was swiping his phone repeatedly, as though scrolling through images. I had no idea what he was doing, but he'd been at it for a while.

"So, I've been lookin' for a place," Case prompted after a few minutes of blessed silence. "I think I might've narrowed it down to a few. Not easy when I don't know anything about the area, but I think we should go look at 'em today."

My gaze shot over the kitchen island to where Case was sprawled on the couch, one leg up, one leg down. He appeared casual, but I knew better. He was as stressed as I was. "What? We're not... No, Case."

I heard the rustle of the leather cushions as he got to his feet. "Look. I think Zeke's probably ready for us to go. So, while we're lookin' for a place, we should go back to the apartment for a while. Let's hire some people to move our things in and we can check out these places. If any of them strike our fancy, we can put in an offer. Be in our own house in a month and a half, tops."

I shook my head and turned my attention back to the meal I was prepping for tonight. "In case you forgot, you had a panic attack when we went into that apartment."

"I hear ya," Case replied. "But I'm all better now. I'm sure it was just an overreaction on my part."

Yeah, right. Case wasn't prone to overreacting. I stared at him as he neared. I was still curious as to what had prompted that panic attack. Something had triggered it, but I didn't know what. Never in all the time I'd known him had he had that sort of reaction to anything.

"We're not goin' back to the apartment," I stated firmly. "I say we stay put for now."

"What are you makin'?" he asked as he sidestepped the island, moving closer.

"Mustard-crusted boneless prime rib roast with cream sauce," I told him, although I knew he didn't want the specifics. The only thing he would've caught from that was prime rib.

Case's hand curled around my bicep and he tugged me around so I was forced to look at him. Placing the knife on the counter and picking up the hand towel, I gave him my full attention.

"What happened yesterday, Brax … in the basement… I heard what you told Zeke." He cupped my face and my chest constricted. "It's not true. I don't want Zeke more than you. I don't even want him *as much* as I want you."

My eyes focused on the center of his chest. I couldn't look him in the eye because I was embarrassed enough that I'd found myself in that position. Not that I had an issue with the scene. That damn fucking machine had done a number on me and not in a bad way. However, the fact that I'd broken down and admitted something so stupid still caused my cheeks to warm.

We'd officially been with Zeke for one week, and for some stupid reason, I was allowing things to move too quickly. What I said to Zeke was true, but I should've kept it to myself. I had no right to fuck this up for the three of us because of petty jealousy.

"Babe, I think it's time we did our own thing again," Case said. "This isn't working."

"But it is," I countered. "I know it is, Case. I see the way you look at Zeke, and I know what you need from him."

He frowned, his dark eyebrows shooting downward. "What do you mean, the way I look at him? I don't look at him any way. He's just a man who can… Regardless, that's not what I want from him."

I sighed, resting my ass against the countertop. "I get it, Case. I really do. Zeke's an enigma. He's the Prince of Darkness and he can give you things no one else can. You want to explore this with him, to see where it might lead."

Case jerked away from me and ran his hand over his short hair. "That's not true. I can get what I need from—"

"Anyone but me," I said, cutting off whatever lie he was going to tell me. I couldn't hide the sadness in my tone. "But I knew that going into it, Case. Zeke was right. It wasn't fair for me to get all butt-hurt over it. He's givin' us what we asked for. It isn't my place to ask for more, and I damn sure shouldn't be jealous."

Case turned back to look at me, something akin to grief written on his face. "This is what I didn't want to happen, Brax."

"I know. And that's on me." I motioned toward the food I was preparing. "Which is why I'll just focus on cooking for the two of you and … we'll figure it out from there. I just need to take a step back."

That much was true. I really did need to take a step back, to look at this objectively. Unfortunately, my emotions had always run hot. I was quick to get into relationships of any kind. Friends, lovers. I'd been accused of caring more than I should. And I couldn't deny that I did care about Zeke. Far more than he wanted me to.

"You wanna take a step back from me?" Case blurted, his eyes rounding as though horrified by my response.

"No." I stepped forward, needing to reassure him. "Not from you. From … the situation. I have to look at it objectively. Without emotion." I dropped my eyes to his chest. "But that's hard for me."

This time when Case cupped my face, I leaned into his hand. I needed his touch. It grounded me in ways I'd never experienced before him.

"I'm not good at this," I admitted. "I want to be, but I'm not."

Some people had the ability to shut off their emotions when it came to sex. I wasn't one of those people. While I tried to remain disconnected, to look at the situation with Zeke dispassionately, I found myself getting in deeper and deeper. When I looked at Zeke, I didn't just see the hardened Sadist. I saw the man, and beneath that rough, intimidating exterior, Zeke Lautner was still just a man.

I was drawn to him, curious about what made him tick. Did I want more time with him? Yes. Did I want him to spend less time focusing on Case? No. I just needed to learn how to deal with it.

"Neither am I," Case stated firmly. "Which is why I say we just go back to the apartment and forget all of it. We can even take a break from the club for a while."

I huffed a laugh, but the pain that consumed me wasn't funny in any way. "No, Case. That's not fair to you or me, and it's not fair … it's not fair to Zeke. We agreed to see this through the same way he did. I get that he's a badass and he acts like nothing matters to him, but I know better. He needs as much from us as we need from him."

And I was convinced of that. Otherwise, Zeke wouldn't have invited us into his home. He certainly wasn't the type of man who allowed people to see into his world. Not willingly.

Case didn't respond. His light green eyes never wavered from my face. I could see his concern, but I could also see the hope. He didn't want what he was offering. He didn't want to go back to that apartment or anywhere, for that matter. Case needed what Zeke was giving him. It settled that wild part of him. And I honestly believed that Zeke needed it, too. He could tell us all day long that he wasn't in it for friendship, but I didn't believe that. Perhaps he wasn't looking to fall in love, but at the very least, he needed us to see this through. Not to turn our backs on him.

"When he gets home tonight, I fully intend to apologize," I told Case. "I'm gonna own up to my mistake and ask for his forgiveness."

"You don't have to do that." Case's tone was threaded with pain. "I want you to be happy. That's all I've ever wanted."

"I know that." I pulled him into me. "And that's all I ever wanted for you, too."

I pressed my lips to his, sighing at the comfort I felt in his arms. This man made me feel things I'd never felt before. The same way Zeke made me feel things.

And yes, I was man enough to acknowledge that I was jealous of what I'd witnessed. But the more I thought about it, the more I realized I wasn't simply jealous of the way Case opened up to Zeke. I was also jealous of the attachment Zeke had seemed to form with him. I wanted that. For whatever reason, I wanted Zeke to want me the same way.

Perhaps it made me a glutton for punishment, or maybe it simply made me human. I didn't know. However, it was the truth.

And the only way for us to move forward was for me to own up to what I did. To admit it to Zeke and promise to remember our original agreement going forward.

Whatever we were doing here—the three of us—it wasn't time for it to end. I got the weird feeling there was a lot more in store for us. And I had to see it through.

Not just for Case and Zeke.

But also for myself.

TWENTY

ZEKE

I WASN'T ONE TO HANG around the office when I didn't have things to do; however, I found myself not wanting to go back to my house, not wanting to face the cowboy or the pretty boy.

For the better part of the afternoon, I'd given a lot of thought to how I needed to handle the situation with them. I figured it would be in their best interest if I cut them loose now. The selfish side of me wanted to lock them up and keep them for a while longer. To indulge in what they were offering for as long as possible.

Except, I wasn't a selfish man. I knew better than to encourage something that had no possibility of ending without a fallout. They were fun to play with, but like any toy, it was only a matter of time before I would discard them in lieu of something with more glitter and intrigue.

For the past four years, that was exactly what I'd done. I had indulged my desires. Sought the fuck toys who knew the score. I had kept my distance and it was working for me. Or it had been. Until them. For whatever reason, I was drawn to them.

And damn Trent Ramsey for sticking his nose where it didn't belong. He was the one who had set me on this path by putting the two of them in front of me. Before I'd found myself confronting them on Trent's private jet, I had managed to keep my distance. The couple of times I'd seen the pretty boy at the club, I had forced myself to limit my interactions with him. Even the cowboy. While I wanted to beat on the pretty boy because that was what he wanted, the cowboy triggered a different desire in me. I couldn't put my finger on it, but I couldn't deny that I wasn't ready for this to be over.

But, again, I wasn't a selfish man. I had no right to keep them when I knew in the end it would all work out the same. They would go their own way, and I would be back to being alone. Stuck in my own private hell of solitude and destruction.

On the drive back to my place, I considered calling Jamie, seeing if she wanted to come over for dinner. With her there, I could make a clean break with my fuck toys. Let the cowboy and the pretty boy know that I had too many balls in the air to continue this. They would understand because they had to. I wouldn't give them a choice.

Before I dialed my sister's number, I remembered Langston mentioning she was going to the club with Greg tonight. If I called her now, she would think I was trying to get in the middle of that. And while I had no desire for her to go to the club, I wasn't that much of an asshole. I'd set this thing in motion, the least I could do was see it through.

So, I kept my hands on the steering wheel and my eyes on the road. Tank sat in the back seat, sighing every so often. I wondered if he could sense my mood, the tension that had taken over my body. Maybe I could simply hide out in my gym for a while. I would tell the fuck toys they should pack up their things, and while they did that, I would work off some of this restless energy.

Of course, the mere thought of the basement had my warped and twisted brain coming up with other ideas. I could simply take the pretty boy and the cowboy down there and work out some of my frustrations on them. They would be willing because that was why they were there.

"This is bullshit," I grumbled as I pulled down the long, winding driveway that led up to my house. "This is the very reason I don't do this shit."

I hated where my head was at. Hated that the cowboy had put me in that predicament yesterday. Hated myself for falling for it. I had kissed him in an effort to taunt the pretty boy and it had backfired in my face. I found myself daydreaming about kissing him again. Tying him to my bed, letting loose on his body while I took my own pleasure. He would give himself freely because that was the agreement we'd made.

And all the while, he would be looking at me and wondering if I preferred the pretty boy.

Truth was, I didn't have a preference. I wasn't supposed to have a preference. I wanted them equally and for different reasons. The pretty boy struck my sadistic fancy. I wanted to explore his pain, to see how deep it ran. However, when it came to the cowboy, I didn't see his pain as the end goal. Sure, I'd spanked his ass and used various torture devices on him, but I could tell the hurt wasn't what got him off. He enjoyed the humiliation.

Perhaps that was the reason he'd set himself up for failure? Seeing something that wasn't there. Or was he a cuckold? Was he secretly enjoying the humiliation and degradation that came along with believing his boyfriend was being unfaithful?

When I pulled up to the house, I put the truck in park and stared out into the twilight. I let out a dull roar, angered by the situation. I needed to take back control. That was the only way I could operate effectively. If they thought for a second I might be caving, they would lose all respect for me.

After all, it had happened before.

With *him*. The last fuck toy I'd taken as my own. *He* was the reason I knew I would never fulfill anyone on a deeper level. I was as much a sex toy as the masochists were. He'd told me as much. I didn't have a heart, only a deep-seated need to inflict pain. I wasn't allowed to feel, to want more, to *need* more. If I ever stooped to that level, I was defying my role as the big, bad wolf, the evil lurking in the darkness, the alpha male, the primal seeking his prey, the man most men feared.

And that was what I was supposed to be.

According to *him*.

I wasn't a man who needed love, a man who wanted to wake up to someone else in my bed. I wasn't allowed to want those things because it negated my very purpose.

Over the years, my brain had worked diligently to blank out his face until he was merely a body I'd used for eighteen months. It had worked for him and for me.

Right up until I realized I'd fallen for him.

I'd given him more of myself than he'd ever wanted. When I called him my fuck toy, his eyes lit up with excitement. And when I called him by name, he shut down and sulked. He didn't want to be mine in every sense of the word. He merely wanted me to use and abuse him. I wasn't allowed to take more than I'd initially agreed to. And the day I told him I loved him, that I wanted every piece of him in return, he had sneered back at me, telling me I was weak and pathetic, just not in so many words. I wasn't allowed to love because I was a monster. That hadn't been the deal.

For a year and a half, I'd thought I was building something real, something lasting. I gave him what he needed and in return he gave me … nothing.

And that was the reason I couldn't allow this to go any further. The cowboy was already seeking more, looking deeper than the surface. Jealousy was an emotion I couldn't allow. It provoked feelings, desires that went deeper than pain. I had to end this before it went too far. I could never be what either of them needed.

They wanted the Sadist, not the man beneath. They were content with each other and I had to respect that, not come between them. If I ever made the mistake of wanting more again, I would quickly learn my place.

Once had been enough for me.

It was time to move on. Back to the lackluster scenes, the submissives who didn't want anything other than the pain I was capable of inflicting. That was my worth, the value they'd put on my head.

No one would ever love me, because if they did and I loved them back, I would no longer be the nightmare they dreamed about.

At that point, I was merely human.

The Sadist completed them.

The human was a failure.

Case

(The pretty boy)

"ZEKE'S HOME," I TOLD BRAX when I heard the man's truck pull into the driveway.

I strolled over to the window, watching as Zeke sat in his truck, his eyes forward, his hands gripping the wheel.

"Something's wrong, Brax," I muttered, unable to look away from the sight.

"What do you mean?" He stepped up beside me.

"He looks … upset."

Brax took a deep breath. "He's upset at me," he said, as though that was the only logical explanation. "It's time I fix this."

I turned to the man I loved, watching his face, trying to read his mind. He'd been melancholy all day, sulking in a way I wasn't familiar with. Whatever his reasons for provoking Zeke yesterday afternoon, he was regretting that he had.

"What are you gonna do?"

"Apologize." He peered over at me. "Like I said, I owe it to him."

My attention returned to the window when Brax started undressing right there in the living room. I watched Zeke, wondering what he was thinking about. He'd been pissed yesterday, storming out after his scene with Brax. He'd been prickly for the rest of the day, too. He'd sent Brax and me to bed early, instructing us to put on the chastity devices and sleep in the cage, but he didn't join us.

At some point during the night, he must've come up, but I didn't know when. This morning, when I woke, the door to the cage was still open. Zeke hadn't locked it the way he normally did. When I finally shook off the desire to curl back up with Brax and sleep for a few more hours, I'd crawled out from under the bed to find Zeke gone. The sheets were in disarray, as though he'd slept there, but he wasn't.

I found him in the gym a little while later, finishing up his workout. We'd been spending that first hour of the morning together in complete silence except for the few times I gave him tips for additional exercises that might interest him. He'd taken my suggestions with grace, smiling and thanking me after he worked to get the form down. We had found a way to coexist in peace during those times. I wasn't the masochist and he wasn't the Sadist. We were men who enjoyed one another's company.

He had seemed almost human to me, a man beneath the monster.

Honestly, I'd enjoyed those moments as much as all the others. I liked seeing that side of Zeke. While I got off on his torture techniques and I actually enjoyed the fact that he wanted to keep us caged like animals from time to time, I did like seeing what was hidden beneath that hard outer layer. In fact, I had been looking forward to getting to know him better. Most people would see the sex and the scenes as a perversion, but for us, it was a way of life. We opened up during those moments. No shields, no barriers. And it was bringing us closer together.

Or so I'd thought.

Zeke suddenly opened his truck door and stepped out. He looked a little forlorn, as though he'd had a shit day. I glanced over to see Brax was already in position, naked and kneeling by the door, his head down.

I had no idea what to do. Was I supposed to give them a moment? Should I go upstairs? Downstairs? Sit on the couch? I had no idea what Brax needed from me right now, so I stood there like a dumb ass, unable to move, oddly fascinated to see how this would play out.

One more look out the window and I noticed Zeke waiting for Tank to do his business. When that was out of the way, they both headed for the house and I pivoted back to Brax.

The knob turned, the door opened. Tank trotted in, giving Brax a quick sniff before making a beeline for me. I squatted down to pet him as Zeke stepped into the house.

"What the fuck?" Zeke grumbled.

His words were clipped, an edge of anger I wasn't familiar with. The Sadist was generally good-natured, which I figured was an oxymoron. He could dole out pain in a way that scared the shit out of me, but I sensed there was no anger fueling him. I'd been with a few Doms who had used that anger to drive their need to punish. But it was different with Zeke. He was creative with his scenes. He wasn't simply beating on us because he could. He got off on it, and he enjoyed it as much as we did. The man didn't hurt us because he was battling some internal rage.

I figured that was what made him the best of the best. You could trust Zeke with your safety. Give yourself over to him without worrying about the consequences. He took special care to heighten the senses, ratcheting up the fear and the need. Yet I never felt as though he would go too far. Believe it or not, that was a skill some Doms didn't acquire. To be a Sadist, they had to be in the right headspace because it wasn't about abuse. It was about the power exchange, the give and take from a Sadist to a masochist.

"Why're you kneeling?" Zeke questioned as the front door closed behind him.

Those black eyes shot over to me, but I shrugged and looked away. This was between Brax and Zeke. While the three of us were involved, I knew Brax was taking responsibility for his actions yesterday. Whatever Zeke opted to do was up to him. I couldn't be part of it, even if I wanted to.

"I owe you an apology, Zeke."

I watched in awe, my stomach churning with fear. Fear for Brax. Fear for Zeke. I wasn't sure either one of them knew what they were doing. I sensed Zeke was battling something internally while it was obvious Brax wanted a do-over. The question was, could we? Could we start over with Zeke? He already knew Brax wanted something he had never agreed to offer.

Not that I knew what that was. For the first time in the two years Brax and I had been together, I couldn't read him. I wasn't sure what his angle was. Did he simply want to submit to Zeke? Was he doing this for himself? Or was he being a martyr here? Giving Zeke and me what we needed? I wouldn't put it past him. Brax was one of the most selfless men I'd ever met. He was so fucking good to me, sometimes I wondered how I'd gotten so lucky.

"What're you apologizing for?" Zeke asked, his tone neutral.

"For my actions these past few days, Zeke. You deserve more from me."

Zeke seemed to wave him off, as though what he was offering didn't matter.

"It's done and over, cowboy. I don't care anymore."

That had my back straightening. How could he be so aloof? Was I right? Was Zeke writing us off already?

"But *I* care," Brax said, his head still down.

"And that's the problem," Zeke snapped, his eyes blazing with restrained fury. "You're not supposed to fucking care. This isn't about feelings, fuck toy."

While his words said otherwise, I got the sneaking suspicion that Brax wasn't the only one concerned about the direction this was headed. Try as we might, no one could predict how this would turn out. Sure, the three of us had walked into this with our eyes wide open.

So why did it feel as though everything was changing?

TWENTY-ONE

ZEKE

THE LAST THING I EXPECTED to find when I came home was a naked masochist kneeling in my entryway. I wanted to be angry at him for fucking this all up, but I had to respect his ability to own up to it. I hadn't gone easy on him yesterday, even less last night when I dismissed them both.

In my defense, I had needed time to stew in my own frustration. I had gotten nothing out of that scene. It was one of the rare times I'd been intent on punishing. That wasn't the man I was. I didn't do things because I was pissed. Those who said I did were ignorant. They knew nothing about me. And I liked it that way. It allowed me to keep my distance. That way I could pick and choose who I wanted to play with, and when they always expected the worst, they would never be disappointed.

However, I had no idea what the cowboy expected from me. Did he think I gave a shit that he'd pouted and sulked, jealous of something that wasn't even there? Because I didn't. He already had a relationship with the pretty boy. He didn't need that from me. I was the instrument they were using to live out the fantasy. In the grand scheme of things, I was nothing. More importantly, I was temporary.

"Get up, fuck toy," I demanded.

Brax slowly got to his feet, but he didn't lift his head.

"What do you want from me?" I asked, glowering at him, my anger morphing into something potent.

"I deserve your punishment, Zeke," he said softly.

230

"Punishment?" I barked a laugh. The cowboy was off his meds. No one in their right mind would ask me for punishment. The pain was for fun. It fueled the flames that lived within us all. Punishment at my hand was a world unlike anything they'd ever experienced before.

"Yes, Zeke," he confirmed.

"Do you even know what you're asking for?"

The cowboy's eyes lifted to mine for the first time since I walked in the door.

"No, Zeke. But I still deserve it."

I hated that I saw the truth in his eyes. The emerald depths glittered with honesty. He truly believed he wanted my punishment and it struck a chord deep down. I fought it back, refusing to give in to that niggling feeling. The one that had me wanting more, wanting to explore this to see if it could possibly be real. I knew better. It wasn't real. And I wasn't stupid.

"You understand my punishment is its own brand of hell? I'm not gonna play with your little dick or beat on you until you come. That's not how it works. I reward good behavior. That's the only time I'll touch you."

"I understand, Zeke."

Although *I* didn't understand it, the cowboy seemed sincere. He was willing to take my punishment in an effort to make amends for his stupidity.

Tucking my finger beneath his chin, I forced his eyes to remain on me. "Do you understand I will not go easy on you?"

"Yes, Zeke."

"You will likely hate me when this is over," I informed him.

"I won't hate you, Zeke."

Oh, he would. He would wish he'd never laid eyes on me.

"Is dinner ready?" I asked because the delicious aroma filling the house was making my stomach rumble.

"Yes, Zeke. It's warming in the oven."

I turned my gaze to the pretty boy. "Set the table. For two."

The pretty boy shot a confused look my way but he quickly nodded. "Yes, Zeke."

"You, cowboy, I want you to kneel by the sofa. Do not move until I return."

"Yes, Zeke."

While the cowboy traipsed over to his new spot, I headed up the stairs to change clothes. Gone was the starchy shirt and slacks. In their place, a pair of comfortable jeans. No shirt was necessary. As it was, I would be naked later, too.

I was now fueled by something else. Desire and lust had stopped flowing in my blood. In their place, a menacing cold, a darkness that was as foreign to me as having two masochists living in my house. I embraced it, allowing it to consume me. If the cowboy wanted punishment, I would give it to him.

Before heading back downstairs, I went into the hall closet and retrieved one of the rubber-backed blankets I used for those times when things would get messy. I returned to find the cowboy still kneeling by the sofa and the pretty boy was standing near the table, clearly waiting to sit down until I joined him.

"I need you over here, pretty boy."

He walked over and I handed him the blanket. "Put this over the sofa. Ensure it covers as much space as possible."

While he did that, I headed down to the basement. To pull this off, I needed a few things from my stash. I gathered the spreader bar, a ball gag/blindfold harness, a feather tickler, a single vampire glove, a bottle of toy cleaner, and the ever-desirable prostate massager. Oh, and lube. I would definitely need that.

When I returned to the living room carrying my loot, I saw the cowboy still kneeling exactly as he was supposed to.

I motioned the pretty boy back over with the crook of a finger. I passed off the prostate massager, the one the cowboy had used previously, along with the bottle of lubricant and spray cleaner.

"It's been cleaned, but use this to clean it again, then lube it up and put it in his ass," I instructed.

"Yes, Zeke." He turned to the cowboy. "You'll need to lean over, put your ass in the air."

The cowboy followed instruction, putting his head and chest down on the floor, his ass open and eager for what was coming next.

Yeah, my dick stirred. So what? I found it hot that the cowboy was so willing, even if he had no fucking clue what he was in for. Didn't mean I was going to do anything about it.

The pretty boy went to work opening the toy and prepping it for the cowboy's rectum while I set everything else on the table.

It took roughly ten minutes to get everything ready. The cowboy had the prostate massager in his ass while he sat on the sofa. The spreader bar kept his legs open. The vampire glove was covering his right hand—his dominant hand. I held the blindfold that would cover his eyes, which was connected to the ball gag that would rest between his lips. While he wouldn't be able to see or speak once we got started, he would be able to hear, which was all I needed.

"In about five minutes, you're going to hear a chime," I explained to the cowboy, ensuring he was paying close attention. "When it sounds, you have one minute to come. Which means you'll be jacking yourself off. From that point, the chime will sound every fifteen minutes. Again, when you hear it, you have one minute to come.

"You are not permitted to come before the chime. Your punishment begins after you come the first time and will continue for two hours, which means you'll come a total of nine times. Should you come before you're allowed, or should you *not* come within the allotted minute, you will spend the entire weekend as a dog. That means you'll be wearing a mask, paws, a tail, a leash, and you'll be on all fours just like a dog. Other than those items, you will be naked.

"And this goes for wherever we are, and I assure you, I will take you out in public. Like Tank, you'll piss and shit outside and you will not bathe. You'll sleep in a kennel by yourself and your food and water will be given to you in a bowl on the floor. And you won't be able to speak a single word. Dogs don't talk."

The cowboy's dark green eyes were wide with genuine fear. He knew I was serious.

And I suspected he also knew that coming four times an hour wasn't going to be nearly as easy as one would think.

Brax
(The cowboy)

FUCK.

When I decided to request Zeke's punishment, I obviously hadn't considered how sadistic the man truly was. While my brain and my body were willing, I knew it was going to become difficult the more time that passed.

"Do you understand?" Zeke asked.

"Yes, Zeke."

"Explain it back to me."

"When the chime sounds, I have one minute to come. This will last for two hours after the first time I come. If I do not meet the requirements, I will spend the entire weekend as a dog."

That was the part that scared me the most. Having to crawl around on all fours was one thing, but having to piss and shit outside and to eat from a bowl on the floor, not being allowed to bathe… That was a horrifying notion.

Part of me wished I'd listened to Case and headed back to the apartment, leaving Zeke in the past. However, I knew I couldn't do that. I had to see this through, and quite frankly, this punishment would be a good incentive to not fail him again. That didn't mean I wouldn't do everything in my power to avoid it. I had one chance, and I couldn't blow it.

Zeke skirted the coffee table then leaned over and placed the harness over my face. The blindfold covered my eyes, blocking out all the light. The ball gag filled my mouth, making it impossible to speak.

"At no time will you be left alone," Zeke said as he connected the buckle at the back of my head. "Your only responsibility is to do as you've been instructed."

I mumbled my affirmation around the gag.

"I suggest you start stroking, cowboy. You've got less than a minute before that chime goes off."

Fuck.

I gripped my dick with my left hand, stroking firmly. I was already hard, so it wouldn't take much to get me off the first time. Simply being in the same room with Case and Zeke did it for me. Not to mention, I'd been so worked up from Zeke fucking Case on the kitchen table last night. I probably could've relieved my tension today, but I hadn't.

So, here I was, sitting on the sofa, naked while they were both dressed, blindfolded while they watched, and gagged while they could speak freely. It left me with a heightened sense of vulnerability. Oddly enough, I liked it.

I was getting used to the sensation of my hand when I felt something cold land on my dick. I hissed when the lube coated my skin. At least he'd given me that. I figured after two hours of stroking myself, I would have friction burn at the very least.

I had no choice but to block out everything since I couldn't see. I allowed my mind to drift, pretending my hand was Case's. He was stroking me roughly, just the way I liked it. My breaths increased, pure bliss coiling inside me. I would be ready when—

The chime sounded and I felt a sudden sense of panic. Seconds felt like hours and the familiar jerk of my hand became foreign, as though I hadn't spent a large portion of my life getting myself off. I tried to block out my thoughts, working myself into a frenzy. I thought about Zeke and Case, the way they looked when Zeke was fucking him. How their giant bodies came together, Zeke's dick inching deep inside Case's ass.

I came in a rush, my lungs expanding and contracting, matching the rapid pace of my heart.

"Very good, cowboy," Zeke said, his tone full of approval. "Your two hours starts now. Remember, you'll have fifteen minutes. You are not allowed to come until you hear the chime."

I nodded, although I wasn't sure whether he was looking at me or not.

"Come on, pretty boy. Let's eat. Oh, one more thing."

I heard footsteps, but I wasn't sure who it was or where they were going. A second later, the television came on. It sounded like the nightly news, but that stopped a moment later. The next thing I heard was moaning and groaning. I smiled to myself. He'd turned on porn. A man's voice sounded. He was giving instructions. His tone was rough, angry almost. He was ordering his charge to open wider, to take his cock.

I hadn't anticipated this. The sounds alone were making my dick hard once more. I was hoping to take advantage of some of the downtime. Fifteen minutes would be plenty of time to recover. Except now I had the insane urge to stroke my dick.

The clink of silverware on glass sounded from across the room and the glorious aroma of prime rib wafted through the air. I took that to mean Zeke and Case were eating. I heard the soft rumble of voices, but I couldn't make out what they were saying because the television was turned up loud.

I allowed my attention to stray back to the television. At least that would keep my libido from drying up right away.

I worked myself slowly with my left hand. I couldn't use my right because of the vampire glove that covered it. I tested out the feel on my thigh. All those little tacks that poked out along the fingers and thumb definitely turned me off the idea of trying. Obviously, Zeke's intention. When it came to jacking off, I was ambidextrous. Neither hand saw more action than the other. However, I did usually alternate. Since that wasn't an option, I could only hope my arm wouldn't tire before this was all over.

More moaning came from the television. A few rough commands, the man speaking about eating his partner's ass. My insides started to coil tightly and I fought it. I couldn't come until the chime sounded, and at this point, I had no idea when that would be. I probably should've started counting down so I could predict it. Unfortunately, there were too many distractions.

Taking deep, cleansing breaths, I relaxed against the cushions, the rubber-backed blanket squeaking against the leather when I shifted. I stroked myself leisurely, imagining I was sitting here watching Zeke and Case share a meal. The sounds from the television intensified. Grunts and groans, pleasure being sought.

The next thing I knew, the chime sounded and I raced against time to get myself off. Once again, I thought about Zeke and Case, imaging Case on his knees taking Zeke's big dick in his mouth. The way the two of them looked, all those tattoos on their sweat-drenched skin. The intensity in Zeke's black gaze as he stared at Case, willing him to get him off. Several more strokes and I came, warmth splattering on my stomach.

This time, no one said anything. I started to wonder if I hadn't come in time. Was that more than a minute? Was I already doomed? Was Zeke prepping my dog costume while I sat here and caught my breath?

I couldn't ask because of the gag, so I had to assume I was safe. That was the only way I would be able to continue.

Admittedly, this was a mind fuck like no other. I'd mistakenly thought this would be a simple task. I could come without even touching my dick, so using my hand was easy, right? It was as normal to me as breathing, something I'd been doing since I was a lusty teenager who didn't understand his own body.

I teased myself from time to time, cupping my balls, then swiping over the sensitive head of my dick, once again wondering why I hadn't started counting when I was finished. Had it been two minutes? Ten? Would that damn chime sound any second now? Could I come again if it did?

The sounds from the television were still assaulting me. Only now the man was verbally humiliating his partner. It was evident they were fucking at this point, and it sounded brutal. That helped to amp me up.

But should I be ready to shoot again? Or did I still have time? I didn't want to get too close before it was allowed.

As I was thinking, a sensation erupted in my ass. I'd almost forgotten about that damn prostate massager. Right up until it began vibrating against that sensitive spot inside me that had my spine tingling, a glorious electric sensation causing the hair on my arms to stand on end. It was pleasure and pain morphing into bliss.

I moaned, caught completely off guard by the pure pleasure it ignited. I gripped my dick, squeezing firmly. I couldn't come until the chime sounded. I figured that wasn't going to happen because this would be just another way for Zeke to torture me. To send me closer to the edge when it wasn't allowed.

Oh, fuck.

Oh, fuck.

Oh, fuck!

TWENTY-TWO

ZEKE

I WAS IMPRESSED.

The cowboy was halfway through his punishment, and all five times, he'd come on command like a good little fuck toy.

However, it was obvious he was tiring. He could only use one hand thanks to the vampire glove, and I was sure the muscles in his forearm and wrist were growing weaker. Not to mention, the overstimulation he was receiving from the television and the prostate massager.

But there was still time. I had no doubt he would fail. After all, I hadn't set this up for him to succeed. That was part of the punishment. He would spend the entire weekend crawling around on hands and knees like a dog. *That* was the sort of punishment he could expect from me. *This* was simply the mind fuck that would allow us to get there.

"You clean up," I ordered the pretty boy. "Then join me in the living room." I smiled over at him. "But first I want you to strip."

"Yes, Zeke."

During dinner, I had ensured the pretty boy and I could both watch the show. For one, I was not about to take my eyes off the cowboy. Although there was nothing that put him at risk, his safety was paramount. And while I doubted he could hurt himself doing what he was doing, I still insisted on keeping an eye on him. And two, it was enjoyable. The way his hand moved over his dick when the chime sounded, the way he seemed to panic, knowing time would run out. And the fact I wasn't telling him whether or not he had succeeded. Those things were coalescing into fear, causing the cowboy to overthink things, which would be ultimately what tripped him up.

The pretty boy started rinsing the dishes and loading them into the dishwasher while I took my water glass and joined the cowboy. I glanced down at the timer. He still had eight minutes before he was allowed to come again.

I punched the button on my phone app to kick the prostate massager into high gear. A startled groan sounded from the cowboy, his hand squeezing his cock. He wasn't hard, but that was expected. It was inevitable that he would soften despite the erotic noises sounding from the television. A man could only come so many times. Quite frankly, I was impressed by the cowboy's stamina. Then again, he was still young.

I grabbed the feather tickler and perched my ass on the coffee table in front of the cowboy. I brushed it along his thighs, earning a soft hiss. I worked it over his chest, brushing his nipples before pressing it between his legs and tickling his balls. He groaned around the ball gag.

Turning off the app and removing the feather, I left him to hang precariously in the balance. His hand was stroking firmly although he still had ... four minutes left.

Yep. This was rather enjoyable.

I took a seat on the opposite sofa and alternated between watching him and the television. The chime sounded once more and the cowboy began pumping his dick in earnest. I watched the seconds tick on my watch. They inched closer and closer to his time limit. He began furiously pumping, but he was still going when the second hand passed the one-minute mark.

Triumph erupted inside me, but I kept my thoughts to myself. He had failed. His time was up.

I continued to watch, smiling to myself as he finally pushed himself over the edge, his cock jerking and twitching, but nothing shot out of his dick. He was dry at this point and he still had three more times to go.

The pretty boy appeared and I motioned for him to sit beside me.

"Spread your legs, pretty boy," I instructed, ensuring my voice was loud enough for the cowboy to hear. I wanted him to be aware we were there, that we were watching.

I put my hand on the pretty boy's dick and started stroking firmly.

"I expect to hear you, pretty boy. Make sure your boyfriend knows how much you enjoy my hand on your cock."

The pretty boy groaned loudly, his hips jerking as I worked him easily. I wasn't about to make him come. That would take place while he was bouncing up and down on my dick.

Minutes passed as the three of us sat there, the television providing an erotic backdrop. That, combined with the sensual moans from the pretty boy, was enough to have the cowboy's cock firming up nicely. I flipped on the prostate massager again, smirking when he began moaning, his ass shifting around on the blanket.

He was covered in his own dried jizz, and at this point, he had nothing to lube his cock as he stroked. His arm remained limp at his side, but his head was cocked in our direction, as though whatever it was we were doing was going to assist him in accomplishing his task.

"Get on your knees, pretty boy. I want your mouth on my cock."

When he stood, I quickly shed my jeans, tossing them onto the floor by the cowboy's feet so he could feel the denim touching him. He would know I was naked, would likely wonder what I was doing to his loving boyfriend.

"Ahh, that's it," I urged, palming the pretty boy's head when his lips wrapped firmly around my cock. "Suck me like a good little fuck toy. Then you can lube me up so you can ride my dick."

The pretty boy moaned.

"You like the idea? Bouncing up and down on my cock while you watch the cowboy jack off?"

The pretty boy groaned, but he didn't release me. I patted his head, showing my approval.

I relaxed into the cushion, allowing the minutes to tick by as we all waited for the chime that would signal the cowboy's next release. He was almost finished.

The pretty boy was slurping all over my dick when the chime sounded. I kept my hand firmly on his head as I watched the cowboy work to make his deadline. He was panting and groaning, but it was no longer fueled by pleasure. I had warned him. He didn't want to ask for my punishment. He would hate me by the time this weekend was over. But it would be worth every humiliating second.

"Keep sucking," I urged the pretty boy, figuring I could help the cowboy along a little. "I fucking love the way your mouth feels on my cock. That strong throat taking every inch. Your boyfriend's trying to come. He's working so hard, probably picturing you in his mind. Your mouth stretched wide around my cock. It's not working, is it, cowboy? You can't come anymore because it hurts."

The cowboy groaned, his cock jerking as his head fell back. He came once more, but there was only a small drop of cum, not even enough to lube his dick for the next round.

"Get the lube, pretty boy. I want you to coat my dick. No condom this time. You're gonna ride my cock bare while your boyfriend plays with his own dick."

My rock-hard cock fell from the pretty boy's mouth as he turned to grab the lube from the coffee table. I watched him as he slicked me up. His eyes were hot. I had yet to take either of them without a condom despite the fact the three of us had shared our most recent test results. No one was at risk here.

"You know what?" I mused. "I want you to get up on the coffee table first. On your knees, chest down. I'm going to eat your ass, to work you open so you're ready for my cock. Would you like that, pretty boy?"

"Fuck yes, Zeke," he hissed, my words clearly taking him by surprise.

"Good." I patted the table and he quickly got into position, his ass pointed toward me.

"You wish you could see this, don't you, cowboy? Me tongue-fucking your boyfriend? Do you do that for him? Do you rim his asshole?"

The cowboy groaned, but I had no idea what he was saying. Nor did I care.

I dropped to my knees behind the pretty boy and gripped his hips firmly in my hands before burying my face in his ass. I worked him roughly with my tongue, ensuring my beard abraded his sensitive skin.

"Make sure he hears you, pretty boy," I commanded.

The pretty boy began rambling. Begging and pleading for more, telling me how much he loved that I tongued his asshole, getting him ready for my dick. I gave him my full attention as the minutes continued to count down. We were closing in on the next chime and I pushed it close before I perched my ass on the couch and pulled the pretty boy into my lap.

"Sit on my dick," I growled, my tone reflecting the driving need in my balls.

The pretty boy was facing away from me as he inched down onto my cock. He groaned loudly, as did I. Taking him bare was incredible, feeling the tight heat as he sheathed my cock.

"Oh, fuck, Zeke," the pretty boy moaned. "It feels so good."

"Come on, pretty boy. Take all of me."

The chime sounded and the cowboy moaned around the gag. I watched him as undiluted pleasure assaulted me when the pretty boy took me all the way to the hilt.

"Stay right there," I ordered. "Watch your boyfriend as he tries to come again. He wishes he was sitting on my cock. He wishes I was fucking him. He needs it more than anything, but the only thing he's got is his hand. And it's failing him now."

The cowboy didn't stop groaning but he tried extremely hard to make himself come. It wasn't working and he knew it.

"Lift up and drop down on me," I instructed the pretty boy. "Fill your ass with my dick. Take your own pleasure from me."

He did. Slow and steady, the pretty boy began fucking me, taking my dick to the root before lifting up, then dropping down again.

The cowboy yelled, his disappointment obvious. He couldn't come no matter how hard he wanted to. I didn't bother to tell him his minute was up. He would figure that out eventually.

I kept a firm hand on the pretty boy's hips guiding him up and down, not wanting him to hurry. I didn't intend to come yet. The timer was counting down again, ticking closer and closer to the last time the cowboy would be forced to jack off. He was breathing heavily and I sensed his disappointment. He knew he had failed. There was no way to deny it.

I purposely kept the pretty boy working himself on me until there were only two minutes left. At that point, I flipped on the app, turned it to high so the massager was vibrating against that sensitive spot inside the cowboy.

"Keep going, pretty boy. Pretend I'm your boyfriend. Talk the way you would talk to him when he's fucking you."

"Oh, God, Brax," he growled. "It feels so fucking good."

Those words drew a long, desperate groan from the cowboy.

I smacked his ass hard. "Fuck me," I demanded. "Make me come in your ass."

Leaning into the sofa cushion, I watched the cowboy as I allowed the pleasure to build inside me. The pretty boy did all the work. His finesse disappeared as he fought to get us both to the breaking point.

"Talk to him," I insisted.

"Fuck, Brax. It feels so good. I can't get enough. I need more …" He moaned long and low. "Brax. Baby. Fuck. I … need you to make me come. I need…"

The chime sounded and this time the cowboy growled when he fisted himself.

"Harder, Brax," the pretty boy urged. "Harder, baby. I need you to come inside me. Fill my ass, Brax."

The cowboy's triumphant shout signaled his release and it was enough to send me cascading over the edge. I gripped the pretty boy's hips, jerking him down on me as I slammed upward until he was screaming his boyfriend's name over and over again. I came hard and fast, my orgasm nearly leveling me.

When I was spent, I wrapped my arm around the pretty boy and jerked him back against me, his back to my chest. I reached for his cock, jerking roughly until he was moaning.

I nipped his ear with my teeth. "Come for me, pretty boy. Right fucking now."

The pretty boy growled as his cock jerked in my hand, cum splashing onto his chest as he heaved in deep, labored breaths. When he stopped spurting, I dropped my hand and held him there.

As I fought to catch my breath, I looked over at the cowboy wondering if he was ready to bolt. I wouldn't put it past him. He'd thought he would succeed, but I never meant for that to happen.

After all, when it came to punishment, my Sadistic side had no bounds.

Case
(The pretty boy)

AFTER EXCUSING MYSELF AND HEADING to the main-floor bathroom to clean up, I returned to find Brax still sitting on the couch. He looked completely wrung out, his arms hanging loosely at his sides, his head back on the cushion. The blindfold and gag had been removed, and Zeke was working the vampire glove off his hand.

I knew what was coming next. Brax had failed to do as he was instructed, which meant he would spend the next two days crawling around like a dog. I couldn't help but feel sorry for him. Humiliation to a degree was erotic, but there was a limit, I knew. This would push Brax's boundaries and the only thing I could do was sit back and watch it happen because the man I loved had asked for this.

Not that Brax could've possibly known the extent of Zeke's Sadistic desires. If he had, perhaps we would be on our way to the apartment while I did my best to prep myself for the inevitable panic attack that would follow.

I had been sincere when I made the offer to Brax. I'd been willing to suffer so we could figure this thing out. No matter what I told myself, I was getting in deeper where Zeke was concerned. I wanted more from him. Hell, I wanted everything. During those moments when he fucked me, I could imagine spending the rest of my life with Brax and Zeke, having everything I'd ever wanted and all I'd ever needed. It was a selfish train of thought, no doubt. I wasn't sure I deserved both. That didn't mean I didn't want it.

Once Zeke removed the spreader bar from Brax's ankles, he motioned toward the stairs.

"Pretty boy, take him upstairs and shower with him. Remove the massager and get him cleaned up." Zeke's attention remained on Brax. "This is the last shower you'll get until Monday morning. Your punishment starts when you're finished."

"Yes, Zeke," Brax whispered, his eyes hooded.

He had to be exhausted after that. Hell, I was just from watching him.

When Brax stood, Zeke did, too. They were still facing each other when Zeke gripped Brax's cheeks and forced him to meet his gaze.

"Remember, cowboy. You asked for this. You wanted my punishment. Should you change your mind before Monday morning, you and the pretty boy can leave. You can go back to your sweet little life where the big, mean Sadist doesn't exist. Understand?"

"Yes, Zeke," Brax whispered, his eyes wide, his cheeks flushed.

"Take him," Zeke ordered. "Get him washed up and then the two of you can meet me in the basement."

I agreed, then took Brax's hand and led him up the stairs and into Zeke's massive bathroom. I turned on the water while Brax used the restroom. When he returned, he looked a little better. More in control but still beaten down.

"We don't have to do this, you know," I told him when I pulled him beneath the shower spray with me. "We can do what I said. Go back to the apartment, take a break from the club, and get our shit in order."

"No," Brax said, his tone firm. "That's not why I did this, Case." His eyes were focused on my face. "I knew jacking off for two hours wasn't my punishment. Zeke set it up that way. I wasn't supposed to succeed."

"But you tried," I said as I began running my soapy hands over him.

"You're damn right I did."

"What was it like?" I asked, curious.

"Hell." His smile said he had at least enjoyed it. "I never knew whether or not I came within that minute. And the more time that went by, the harder it got."

"From what I tracked, you only missed the mark twice. You made it through the first hour."

Brax grinned. "Figures."

"Was it painful?"

"Yeah. My dick's gonna be sore for a while." He chuckled.

I reached for his cock to wash it and he hissed.

"Seriously, Case. It's extremely sensitive."

I leaned over and kissed him, enjoying the feel of his mouth on mine. I wouldn't get the chance to kiss him again for two days and that bothered me. I knew how much Brax enjoyed those little intimacies. Until him, kissing hadn't been a big deal for me. Since him, I'd learned to crave it as much as he did.

Curling my hand behind his head, I pulled Brax closer, letting my tongue slide against his. We stood there for several minutes, lip-locked while I tried to get my fill.

Brax was the first to pull back and he was smiling when he did. "What was it like?"

"What?"

"Fucking Zeke while I was blindfolded and gagged right beside you?"

I let my eyes roam over his face, trying to determine if he really wanted to hear the truth.

"Tell me, Case. I want to know."

"Amazing," I admitted. "Feeling him inside me ... bare." My stomach muscles clenched, the sensation still ghosting through me. "And having you there ... when Zeke forced me to talk to you... Damn."

I had never felt anything like it before. I had even mentally traded places with Brax. The thought of hearing Brax fuck Zeke while I couldn't see them made my dick twitch.

I pulled him closer.

"No matter what, Case, I'm gonna see this through. Zeke's right. I asked for the punishment. It's only fair."

"If you need to use your safe—"

Brax's hand covered my mouth, effectively shutting me up.

"We don't have safe words, Case. We agreed to this, remember? No safe words. No limits. That's what I want." Brax's hand fell from my mouth. "He expects that," Brax whispered. "Zeke's tryin' to push us away. I'm not gonna let that happen." His eyes dropped. "I want him too much."

"Him?" I asked, taking a step back and staring while my jaw felt as though it would unhinge. I willed Brax to look up at me. "What does that mean?"

"I don't know exactly. The more I thought about it, the more I realized I was jealous of both of you. Not just of you being with him. I want more of what he has to offer."

That sounded like a confession. As though Brax had feelings for Zeke. Or he was starting to have them. Either way, I wasn't sure what to do with that information. Part of me was happy because this was what I wanted. I needed more time with Zeke. I needed to explore his sadistic side in depth, to get him to give me the pain I sought. The humiliation was all part of the game, but Zeke had yet to push me to my limits.

248

"Now kiss me one more time," Brax insisted with a smirk. "You won't be able to once we go downstairs."

I jerked him to me and did as he requested. When we pulled back for air, I smiled at him.

"I love you, Case," he said softly. "I won't be able to say that for two days, but know that I do. I'm gonna see this through and so are you. No matter what he does or what he says, we're in this together."

"Understood." I kissed him one more time, letting the water rinse us before turning it off.

Once we were dried off, I followed Brax—both of us still naked—down to the basement. Zeke had the music playing as he stood by the padded table, where he had accumulated a vast number of items. He had pulled on his jeans, so he was the only one of us who was clothed.

He turned, obviously hearing us approach. His attention shifted to Brax first and he smiled. It was an evil grin that had my insides twisting. He was going to enjoy this far too much.

I glanced over at Brax and wondered if he would, too. Humiliation was a huge thing for Brax. He enjoyed it in ways I didn't understand, so maybe this wasn't as bad for him as I was thinking it would be. Personally, I couldn't do it. Wearing a dog mask would be a limit I would have to think long and hard on.

Zeke motioned for Brax to join him. Not knowing what he needed me for, I remained where I was.

"Are you ready for this, cowboy?"

"Yes, Zeke." His back was straight, chin slightly tilted. He looked better than he had when we'd gone up for the shower.

"From the moment your knees touch the floor until Monday morning when I remove the items from you, you will not be allowed to speak unless it's because you are in pain. This is meant to be humiliating. If at any time something doesn't feel right, I expect you to tell me."

"I will."

"Come here, pretty boy. I want you to put the knee pads on him."

Crossing the space slowly, I took the knee pads Zeke held out. I dropped to my knees before Brax and began fastening them in place.

"You will be naked the entire time. You will wear the plug for two hours at a time during the day with an hour off. You will not sleep with it in. The mask will remain on at all times, but the muzzle will be removed so you can eat."

Wow. The man had seriously thought this through.

I knew that puppy and pony play were big things for some although I didn't quite understand the fascination with it. It wasn't uncommon to see at the clubs, either.

"And I've decided you will not sleep in a kennel. While that would be ideal, your height makes it almost impossible," Zeke told him.

"Where will I sleep?"

"In my bed. After all, that's where Tank sleeps."

I wasn't sure whose inhale was louder, mine or Brax's. That was an interesting twist. I had to assume I would continue to sleep under the bed in the cage. I wasn't opposed to it and found it didn't freak me out the way the apartment had. Then again, I'd given a lot of thought to what had caused me to panic at the apartment. It had taken some time but I finally realized why. Granted, it wasn't something I wanted to dwell on, so I kept it to myself. Sleeping in the same room with Brax and Zeke, even caged by myself, was doable. However, I would definitely miss having Brax's body against mine.

"Not only will you not speak, but you will not touch yourself in any way. You will not be asked for any sexual favors for the next two days. You will be a dog, and quite frankly, that's not appealing to me in any way, shape, or form."

Well, that was interesting.

"It'll give my dick time to heal," Brax said with a soft chuckle.

I was surprised that Zeke laughed, too. "True. Remember what I said. The goal isn't to have you in unnecessary pain, so if at any time you have a problem, I want to know."

"Yes, Zeke."

"Give me your hands."

Brax held up his hands and my eyes widened when I noticed the leather "paws" that Zeke was holding.

Holy shit.

This was about to get really … weird.

EDGE

IF SOMEONE WOULD'VE TOLD ME I would one day be willingly waiting for Zeke Lautner's sister to meet me at a kink club, I would've told them to lay off the sauce.

Seriously.

No one in their right mind would entertain the thought of engaging Jamie Lautner in any sort of kinky activity. Not if they wanted to live, anyway.

Except, that was exactly what I was doing.

Didn't matter that I had an entire club to manage. I had somehow been roped into meeting sweet little Jamie so I could show her the ropes at Dichotomy. Not literally, of course. No way was I going to tie that girl up. I valued my balls far too much to allow that to happen. Zeke would castrate me in a New York minute if he found out.

Yet I couldn't deny some sense of anticipation. I had known Zeke for some time, and I'd had the privilege of meeting Jamie a time or two. More so in recent years when it seemed Zeke used her as his plus one whenever there was a function that wasn't club related.

I tried to picture her as my little sister, but I had a hard time. It would've made tonight a hell of a lot easier if I could. Only then it would be weird because I couldn't fathom introducing my sister into this world. In fact, that would be rather creepy.

Not helping, Edge.

Yeah, yeah, yeah. That inner voice was being a pain in the ass. Had been ever since Ransom Bishop had come up with this absurd idea and Zeke had gone along with it. I had to believe Zeke was suffering some sort of mental breakdown. The man was so protective of his sister, I wouldn't be surprised if there were a long list of injuries sustained at that man's hands. Any man who wanted to so much as take the girl for coffee probably had endured a broken finger or two.

I shook out my hand. Like my balls, I'd grown quite attached to my fingers.

For fuck's sake, Edge. Grow a pair, would ya?

"Master Edge?"

I turned to see Angela Evans strolling my way. She was one of the submissives on duty here at Dichotomy, the red studded collar around her neck a sign that she was here in an official capacity.

"Yes, Angela?"

"There's a guest waiting for you at the check-in point."

Fucking lovely.

Part of me had been hoping Jamie would freak out at the last second and be a no-show. I couldn't get that lucky.

"Thanks," I told Angela as I took a deep breath and tried to calm myself. No way could I give Jamie the proper introduction if I was a freaked-out mess.

You're a Dom, for fuck's sake. Act like one.

I hated that damn voice, but it seemed to be there more and more these days. I wasn't sure why it thought I needed a mental push, but there it was, always shoving me forward. It was almost as though I was stuck in a rut, and without it, I would likely find myself sitting at home, my hand down my pants as I ate pizza in front of the television.

And what? Have a beer or two? Get fat and lazy? Come up with an excuse to be alone?

As I was making my way to the front entrance, I passed Ransom and I couldn't miss that wicked grin on his face.

Yeah, buddy. We're doing the death march. Are you happy?

Ransom Bishop was an instigator. He enjoyed the hell out of setting things in motion. He was always inserting himself in various situations, motivating people to do things they likely wouldn't do otherwise. All so he could sit back and laugh.

Somehow, I'd fallen into his trap and I hoped for his sake I walked out the other side in one piece. Otherwise, I was going to beat him within an inch of his life.

I approached the front entrance, fully expecting to see Jamie standing there. Probably decked out in jeans and a T-shirt, not understanding what fetish wear was or why it was standard protocol in a club of this nature. However, I didn't see anyone out of place as I scanned the area.

My eyes shifted to the bar. Two Doms were standing there chatting. No submissives. I peered into the Dom lounge but I only noticed Mistress Jane speaking to Mistress D while four male submissives knelt on the floor at their feet.

Maybe she bolted before you could get here.

I turned, ready to head up to the front desk to see if she'd done exactly that when my gaze landed on a young woman standing to the left of the scanning room where everyone was patted down to ensure they didn't have weapons or video equipment.

Holy mother of God.

Yeah. I really needed that voice to shut the hell up. It was hard enough to breathe without his interference because … holy mother of God.

There was six feet of lithe brunette watching me, her long limbs drawing my attention as I took her in from head to toe. Not an inch of denim was covering her. Then again, the brown and gold corset she wore didn't cover much of her, either. It cinched in her trim waist and highlighted her breasts, cleavage cascading deliciously over the top edge, which hugged her breasts lovingly. The brown spandex boy shorts covered her private parts but did nothing to hide those long, long legs.

For fuck's sake. Say something, dumb ass.

"Master Edge?"

253

I forced a smile as I composed myself, allowing my Dom face to fall into place. Ogling this woman wasn't an option and I needed to remember that.

"Jamie, you look ... lovely."

She smiled and her face was so radiant it damn near blinded me. On a normal day, I wasn't one to wax poetic about a woman's smile, but I couldn't help it.

"Thank you." Her chest bloomed with color and the sweet rosy red inched upward until it highlighted her cheeks. It was in that moment that I noticed how fucking young she was. She was ten years younger than Zeke, which made her twenty-three or twenty-four.

Twenty-fucking-anything was insane for me to consider. I was thirty-six, which made this girl twelve years younger than me at the very least.

It's not like you're old enough to be her father.

Well, technically, I probably was. Not that I'd been having sex at the age of thirteen, but it would've been shortly thereafter.

"Thank you so much for allowing me to come here tonight," she said sweetly.

"It's my pleasure to have you as my guest."

Her brown eyes darted around and the curiosity I saw there made my dick stir with anticipation. I fought it back, reminding myself she wasn't just any submissive who was looking to explore this world for the first time.

She was Zeke Lautner's sister.

She was an innocent.

She was off-limits.

How the hell had I allowed Zeke to talk me into this?

TWENTY-THREE

ZEKE

BY THE TIME I HAD the cowboy decked out as a dog, I was glad I'd had the forethought to prepare for all sorts of scenarios.

I'd never had the desire to dress a submissive up like a pet, but there was something about the cowboy that told me he was the perfect submissive for it. And I enjoyed the hell out of it. Especially seeing him like this. Not in a sexual way, mind you. I had some serious kinks, but that didn't work for me, for whatever reason.

However, everyone knew I loved Tank like my very own child. I could see taking care of the cowboy the same way. Ensuring he was protected and cherished. Giving him the full experience of being my pet.

"All right, time for bed."

I resisted putting the cowboy's leash on him. There was no point since we were inside. However, tomorrow night at the club I would find great pleasure in leading him around while he crawled on all fours.

The cowboy was completely naked, which was necessary to ensure he felt vulnerable. The mask he wore covered his entire head, only his eyes visible. The ears were a nice touch, too. I would take the muzzle off the mask so he could sleep. Otherwise, I would be concerned he couldn't breathe. Like I'd told him, pain wasn't the end goal here. He should be mentally challenged, not physically uncomfortable.

Rather than wait for the cowboy to crawl his way up the stairs, I went ahead of them. While they took their time navigating the hard wooden planks, I let Tank out into the yard to take care of business. He hurried and returned in time for us to see the cowboy making his way up the second flight of stairs to the bedroom.

Was he already regretting his request for punishment? Would I wake up to find them both gone in the morning? Would they slip out in the middle of the night in order to avoid having to endure my wrath? It wouldn't surprise me in the least if they did.

The crawling on all fours—even with the pads on his knees and hands—certainly didn't look comfortable. But I wasn't worried. After all, I was allowing him to sleep in my bed. Like I'd told him, the cage would've been ideal, but with his six-foot-three-inch frame, it would've been impossible for him to shift. I wasn't worried about his comfort, but I didn't want to put unnecessary strain on his body. Crawling and kneeling at all times was going to be hard enough.

Perhaps I was soft in that regard.

Then again, I had a human crawling on all fours like a dog. And in a few hours, I suspected I'd be letting him out to do his business in the yard. That was going to be an interesting feat.

The thought made me smile.

Saturday, October 20

"Holy fuck, man. That is some hard-core shit," the baby Dom said when he approached me in the main-floor Doms' lounge.

I didn't know this one's name, but that wasn't unusual. I wasn't the sort to befriend a lot of people at the club. While I cherished those I had become close with, I didn't make a point to make more friends, because that wasn't why I was here. Not the biggest reason, anyway.

I tried to ignore the baby Dom as he stepped closer to the cowboy, who was kneeling at my feet, his mask covering his entire face, his eyes the only thing visible. With him and the pretty boy so close, any Dom would know they belonged to me. However, if that wasn't enough, the fact they were collared and I was holding the cowboy's leash should've been a telltale sign, which meant they were off-limits.

The baby Dom was pushing his limits.

Plus, I was in the middle of a conversation with someone, so the interruption was rude.

"Does he bite?" the baby Dom laughed, and I shot him a glare.

When he reached to touch the cowboy, I shot to my feet and stared him down. "I don't recall giving you permission to touch my submissive. If you want to keep the hand, you'll keep it to yourself."

Wary eyes shot to my face, but the smirk said he thought I was kidding.

"Whatever, man. You're too uptight. I was just admiring your work. If you didn't want anyone to pet him, you should've left him caged at home."

I took another step closer, but before I could get there, Trent inched between me and the guy who was about to have his face rearranged.

The baby Dom's face lit up. "Hey, Trent. How's it going? Haven't seen you in a while."

I growled from behind Trent.

"It's going well." Trent motioned for the baby Dom to head out of the lounge. "Come on, let's go chat at the bar."

The baby Dom was smart enough to keep his eye on me as he headed out. I snarled, a silent warning that my submissive pet wasn't the animal he should fear most.

"Who the fuck do these newbies think they are? And who teaches them it's okay to touch another Dom's submissive?" Ransom grumbled from his spot across from me.

I took my seat once more and placed my hand on the cowboy's head. I had to admit, he had done far better than I thought he would. Not once today had he done anything he shouldn't have. I knew it had to be difficult to move around on all fours. But that was likely the easy part. The fact I had a plug in his ass and he was forced to eat and drink from bowls on the floor was likely driving him insane. But honestly, I figured the no speaking part was the hardest. Not once had he so much as uttered a word.

He was taking his punishment like a champ.

"It's disgusting," Mistress Jane said, crossing one shapely leg over the other. "I'm not sure how they get into this place, either."

That comment had me looking around, because I knew exactly who was responsible for allowing the baby Doms in. "Where's Edge at, anyway?"

Ransom's eyes shot from my face to the far wall. He was hiding something. Something big, but I didn't know what it was.

I inhaled sharply when I remembered my sister had been here last night.

"What aren't you telling me?" I growled, leaning forward as I pinned him in place with a stare. "Where the fuck is Edge? If you tell me he's with my sister, I'm gonna castrate him. His last meal will be his own balls."

Mistress Jane laughed. "It's fine, Zeke. Your sister was in good hands last night. I'll spare you the details, but I was here the entire night, and I assure you, you would've approved."

I seriously doubted that.

I leaned back and took a deep breath. I promised myself I wouldn't get involved with Jamie and her interaction at the club. I didn't want to know the details of what transpired. That was why I had stayed away.

"Master Zeke?" one of the submissives on duty said when she came to stand in front of me. "Your scene is set up and ready for you."

I nodded my head in acknowledgment, then glanced down at my fuck toys. The cowboy was kneeling on my left and the pretty boy sitting on my right. I didn't usually permit submissives to accompany me into the Doms' lounge, but tonight I made an exception. I figured they deserved it after last night.

"I'm betting this is gonna be good," Mistress Jane said, sliding her hands together. "I'm looking forward to this one."

"Everyone enjoys a good caning," Ransom noted as he pushed to his feet.

I felt the pretty boy stiffen near my leg. I had yet to fill him in on the details, but it appeared the cat was now out of the bag. Leave it to Ransom, the instigating fucker.

"Oh, sorry." His smile was wicked and held absolutely no apology. "Did he not know?"

I flipped him off, then pushed to my feet.

"Just for that, I'm gonna leave you in charge of my pet," I told him as I passed over the cowboy's leash. "Do not let him out of your sight and do not let anyone touch him."

"It'll be my pleasure to look after him." He took the leash and tugged. "Come on, Rover. Let's head that way. We may need a few extra minutes."

I turned to Jane. "Would you mind handling aftercare?"

"Not at all," she said sweetly, but there was a look in her eyes, something I'd never seen before. As though she was expecting me to be different.

In fact, I'd noticed several of my good friends watching me closely tonight and I wasn't sure why. Nor did I care for them to enlighten me.

"Come on, pretty boy. Let's get you taken care of."

Brax
(The cowboy)

WHEN I DIE, I HOPE like hell I don't come back as a dog.

That thought continued to run through my head because this shit was not for the faint of heart.

And it wasn't necessarily being naked or sporting leather paws or even the uncomfortable plug in my ass. I'd gotten used to those relatively quickly. Granted, the fact that Zeke insisted on removing the plug and reinserting it later wasn't my favorite thing in the world, but I understood his reasoning.

Of course, taking a shit outside … yeah, that was a memory I hoped to banish from my mind right quick.

Honestly, the most difficult part was having to eat from a bowl. Drinking water had proven to be damn near impossible because I was expected to lap it up, which meant by the end of the weekend I would definitely be dehydrated. However, it wasn't necessarily *how* I was being forced to eat but *what* I was being forced to eat.

No, Zeke wasn't insisting that I eat Tank's food, although it might have been better than Case's cooking. The man was not meant to be in the kitchen. Of course, since I couldn't speak, I couldn't complain, nor could I tell him how to do it right. I figured that was just another way for Zeke to punish me.

I couldn't wait for Monday morning to get here. I was ready to stand up again. If Zeke allowed, I would spend the entire day in the kitchen, working on a masterpiece that would ensure Case would never be allowed the opportunity to wield a spatula ever again.

"Your master wants to ensure you have a front row seat," Master Bishop informed me when we finally made it down to the dungeon.

My knees, although protected by the pads, still ached. Every move was a painful reminder that I had learned to walk for a reason. Not only did crawling wear on the bones, it required a ridiculous amount of time to get from one place to another. The sidewalk had been especially brutal. And yes, Zeke had required me to crawl in from the truck on my hands and knees. Thankfully, he'd at least draped me with a blanket. Otherwise, I would likely be in jail for public indecency.

I noticed people were getting out of my way quickly, their gazes slowly inching over me as I passed. I'd garnered a lot of attention since we walked into the club. Thankfully, the dog mask covered most of my face, which helped because I was sure I was red as a beet. This wasn't my finest moment. When I had requested punishment, not once had this scenario crossed my mind. Then again, I'd learned not to attempt to figure Zeke out. His mind was its own brand of warped and twisted, so it didn't necessarily surprise me, either.

On the plus side, I was getting to sleep in a bed. The negative to that was that Case was still sleeping under the bed by himself.

The one thing I'd learned in all of this was to never, ever, *ever* ask Zeke Lautner for punishment and do everything in my power not to earn it in the future.

Truth was, I didn't mind being forced to crawl around like a dog or to be treated like one for that matter. The humiliation was its own perverse brand of eroticism. I couldn't explain it if someone forced me to, but I had long ago stopped making excuses for my desires. I figured we were all programmed the way we were for a reason. I was a much happier man having accepted that. And I had Case to thank because he had opened my eyes to a whole new world.

Speaking of Case...

Zeke appeared in front of me, Case following close behind him. My peripheral vision was blocked by the mask, but I could sense there were people gathering around us. As long as no one stepped in front of me, I would have a front row seat for Zeke's special blend of torture. I had never been caned before, and honestly, if I had a hard limit, that would be it. From what I'd heard, it wasn't all that fun. Then again, neither was being a dog.

"Have you ever been caned before, pretty boy?" Zeke asked, his voice low and menacing but loud enough everyone around me stopped talking.

"Yes, Zeke," he answered easily.

From what I could tell, Case was relaxed, perhaps even eager. Knowing him, he was already floating on a cloud.

"Then you know how this will work," Zeke said. "Which position do you prefer? Lying flat, bending over, or standing?"

"Bending over, Zeke."

"Very nice." He motioned toward the spanking bench, which, oddly enough, seemed to be the piece Zeke had selected already.

Had he somehow known that would be Case's preference?

"Strip," Zeke commanded.

I admired Case's physique as he stripped off the jeans he was wearing before walking closer to the spanking bench. The dragon on his back seemed to come to life when he moved, arching and shifting. It was a masterpiece, really, something I had admired since the first time I saw it.

My focus moved to the spanking bench. It wasn't quite as intricate as the one Zeke had in his basement, but it was sturdy enough to hold Case's large body. He stood there, still as a statue while he waited for Zeke to instruct him what to do next.

Zeke joined him, then motioned him into position, assisting as needed. Rather than have him kneel on the padded leather bars, Zeke had it turned the opposite direction, allowing Case to drape himself over the bench while his feet remained on the floor. His head was angled downward, but only slightly. Enough to ensure his ass was in the air.

"Do you prefer to be restrained?" Zeke questioned.

"Yes, Zeke."

I noticed Zeke was taking this very seriously. He wasn't smiling or laughing and he wasn't taunting Case the way he normally did. I found that interesting.

He moved around Case as he secured his wrists and ankles to the metal frame. Zeke checked the restraints a couple of times before he went over to the table, where his toy bag was sitting.

When he picked up the long, thin cane, my breath halted in my lungs. I'd heard that thing left bruises when done correctly. I had yet to get to that frame of mind when I wanted to wear the stripes of my master. I enjoyed some pain, but I couldn't handle even remotely close to what Case craved.

And now, I was forced to kneel here on the floor and watch as the man I desired beat on the man I loved.

TWENTY-FOUR

ZEKE

THERE WAS A TECHNIQUE TO caning. While most submissives, even masochists, would enjoy the thud of the rattan cane against their backside, it was one of the more impactful tools. It would leave bruises under the skin and welts on the top provided it was used correctly. But it wasn't about the visible marks it would leave as much as it was the pain it would cause. A Dom had to be mindful of how hard and how often they were striking the submissive in order to have the desired effect.

When it came to caning, it wasn't about constant hitting. If struck too quickly, the submissive wouldn't experience the full impact. The point was to allow the submissive to feel the thud of the cane and the reverberation that came from it. Striking too quickly defeated the purpose. The same went for how the cane landed and where.

I'd done numerous canings in my BDSM lifetime. I'd even been caned myself more than once. I found it important to understand how the tools felt in order to deliver what was needed for a particular submissive. Hence the reason I'd endured having every tool in my arsenal used on me and by more than one Dom. It was about understanding the various techniques and the outcome.

I took my cane—I preferred a three-eighths-inch rattan cane—and held it firmly in my hand as I walked around the pretty boy. I admired the lines of his body, the way he looked restrained to the bench. His ass and the backs of his thighs were on display and very soon everyone standing near would be able to see the wicked stripes delivered by my hand.

Due to the height of the bench, the pretty boy was exactly where he needed to be for my swing to land perfectly on the fleshy part of his body. It would allow me to hit him accurately and as easy or hard as I chose.

I wouldn't be going easy on him.

Because I knew my submissive well, I didn't feel the need to confirm his safe word for club protocol. Although he technically didn't have one, he would know I would heed it should he need to use it, so I trusted him to do so. My only objective was sending him into subspace.

It was easy to block out everyone and everything around us. Out of respect for me, no one was speaking. The only sounds were the music pulsing through the speakers and the noises from the other scenes taking place a short distance away.

After one more pass around the bench, I placed my hand firmly on the pretty boy's back, silently signaling I was ready to start. After a light squeeze of my fingers, I removed my hand and placed the cane against his ass, exactly where I intended to land the first blow.

I pulled back and delivered perfectly, allowing the cane to bounce lightly and remain on the mark I'd made. As for whether the pretty boy experienced the white-hot heat that bloomed on the line I'd made or if he'd focused on the searing sensation or the vibration through his body, I didn't know. I turned and landed another blow on the opposite side in the same place. After allowing it to sink in for a moment, giving the pretty boy an idea of what he could expect from me, I decided it was time to proceed.

I focused on pacing and rhythm, delivering each blow in a different spot along his ass and the backs of his legs. The marks were appearing beautifully, red welts marring his skin. Every so often, the pretty boy would grunt or groan, a definite sign he was enjoying himself.

I allowed myself to drift into that mindset some called Domspace. It was a high unlike any other, the ability to deliver pain to someone who craved it. These were the moments I looked forward to. The way I felt, the invincible feeling. My cock swelled behind the zipper of my jeans, pure pleasure pulsing through my veins. Like the pretty boy, I, too, craved the endorphin high more so than the release.

As I moved along, I began dragging the cane over the mark I'd just made, drawing an agonizing groan from the pretty boy. My eyes never strayed from what I was doing, paying attention to the marks, ensuring I hadn't split the skin. My cock twitched and jerked with every mark that appeared, proof that I was taking my pleasure from his pain. I'd been taking my time, purposely keeping him from soaring too high, but I knew he was ready for the encore.

Pure, raw satisfaction radiated from my insides as I released the last of the vicious blows that would send him into subspace, his mind detaching from his body as endorphins flooded his system, that natural high he worked so hard to receive taking over.

When I was finished, I set the cane down and returned to the pretty boy. I ran my hand over the marks, admiring my work, enjoying the way he hissed and flinched. I couldn't wait to see the bruises that would appear later on.

I caught Mistress Jane's attention and motioned her over. She brought along two male submissives who went to work unhooking the belts holding the pretty boy down. When they got him upright, I looked into his eyes. They glittered with heat, his cock rock hard from the experience. For the first time, I was tempted to lead him into an aftercare room and finish what we started. I could take care of him while he took care of me.

My gaze strayed to the cowboy, still kneeling at Ransom's feet, and I decided against it. Aftercare was for someone else to handle. Once he was feeling more like himself, I would take them home and lose myself in the pretty boy for a little while.

Mistress Jane nodded toward me, her signal that she was taking my charge into her care. I didn't nod back, choosing to go back to my toy bag and load up my gear, forcing my mind to detach from the scene.

The pretty boy was in good hands. I had to dispel the absurd discomfort I suddenly felt knowing someone else would be touching what belonged to me, caring for him. There was a reason I'd selected a Domme. My fuck toy would find her care clinical at best, nothing arousing.

For some reason, although I knew that deep down, it did little to assuage that strange possessiveness that erupted in my gut.

"Master Zeke? May I clean up for you now?"

Without looking at the submissive, I growled a confirmation, my eyes remaining on my bag. I inhaled deeply, let it out slowly. This wasn't the time or place for me to get caught up in some misplaced feelings. In fact, as far as I was concerned, there was never going to be a time or place.

I simply had to figure out how to remind myself before I went and did something stupid.

Case
(The pretty boy)

MY ASS WAS ON FIRE. Even three hours later when we were back at Zeke's, I could still feel the singe as that cane struck my ass. My jeans were causing friction, which made me grit my teeth. And yet my insides were glowing like hot coals. I wasn't sure the last time I'd felt this damn good.

Zeke had been silent ever since he'd come to get me from the aftercare room, his body present but his mind somewhere off in the distance. Once I had floated back to earth and Mistress Jane had coated my welts in some ointment, we had returned to the Doms' lounge, listening as everyone wanted to discuss the scene. I had kept my mouth shut while my ass blazed from the pain that lingered. The marks were there, the bruises already appearing, and I felt an odd sense of attachment to Zeke because he'd given them to me. Yet I had noticed he hadn't acknowledged me since we left the club.

It was evident he wasn't angry but he was rather morose, despondent. Brooding, maybe. Or perhaps he was simply reflecting back on the scene and this was how he did it. I wasn't sure what it felt like for him to go through something like that because I'd never been in his shoes. I only knew how fucking incredible it was for me. And that had been, by far, the best caning I'd ever received. Zeke was a master when it came to delivering the painful blows. He hadn't rushed, allowing the cane to sit on my skin, the delicious sensations coursing through me, vibrating in my balls, then working their way over my entire body. Every hit had been exquisite torture and I'd wanted it to go on forever.

Granted, I had seen my ass and my legs. I knew the damage that had been done. I knew Zeke had stopped because any more would've risked breaking the skin.

"Let's shower," Zeke said to me as we were heading up the stairs. "Cowboy, you can come upstairs and watch."

Sweat prickled my skin at the thought of warm water on my hypersensitive ass, but I wasn't about to deny him whatever he needed.

I thought for sure he would send me to bed despite the fact my dick was still rock hard from that scene. Zeke knew I preferred subspace to an orgasm, so he hadn't demanded I come and he hadn't yet taken his pleasure from me, either. The thought of wearing that chastity device to sleep in while my dick was so fucking hard it hurt made my head swim.

Without waiting for Brax to crawl up the stairs, I went into the bathroom and started the shower while Zeke disappeared into his closet. I stripped off my clothes, the denim scraping over the tortured nerve endings causing the marks to burn hotter than before.

When Zeke returned, he motioned for me to get in the shower as he followed.

I did like this bathroom. It was designed with a man his size in mind. The lack of walls left the space open. The numerous shower heads allowed him to move about freely while getting clean.

"Put your hands on the tile. Ass facing me," he stated roughly. "I want to admire my work."

Without hesitation, I did as instructed, bending at the waist and putting my palms flat on the tile. My cock thickened as I put myself on display for this man. I wanted him to move up behind me, to take me in that wild way that kept me hanging precariously close to an orgasm strong enough to blow my head off my shoulders. Knowing Brax was there, watching, only made it hotter. If Zeke wasn't prepared to fuck me, I hoped he would touch me, run his hands over my skin. It would intensify the fire in my skin, but I didn't care.

I could hear the water being displaced as Zeke showered. I didn't move, my knees locked, my back straight. I was rewarded a short time later when Zeke's soapy hands stroked over my back.

"You did good tonight, pretty boy." His tone was soft, his words laced with what sounded like wonder.

"Thank you, Zeke."

He washed me slowly, as though he had all the time in the world. My shoulders, my neck, my back. He disappeared only to return with more soap.

My breathing increased as I silently urged him to go lower, to run those callused palms over my abraded skin. The friction alone would make me see stars, but I needed that. In that moment, I needed *him*. Something to solidify the experience, to increase the connection I felt to him.

When his palms finally inched lower, down my spine, I held my breath. He paused momentarily at the lowest part of my back and I squeezed my eyes closed. Hoping for more while preparing myself for the blistering heat to bloom on my skin.

"Oh, fuck," I cried out through clenched teeth when his hands finally shifted. "Holy shit."

"It hurts." It wasn't a question.

"So fucking good," I admitted.

His soapy hands wandered over my ass, down the backs of my legs. I groaned and hissed, letting the blessed warmth radiate throughout me. It was enough to make me light-headed, but I welcomed the sensation, relishing the fire blazing along my nerve endings.

I wanted him to fuck me, to fill my ass, to use me in the way only he could. I needed his brutal touch, the overwhelming way he controlled both my pleasure and his. He was driving me insane.

But Zeke didn't fuck me. His hands continued to wander. Down my legs, my ankles, around to my calves. He washed me thoroughly, working his way back up, fisting my cock a few times but not offering relief.

"Stand up."

When I did, his chest pressed against my back, his thighs brushing mine, his groin smashed against my ass. He kept me steady on my feet with his strength and security. I hissed again as the hair on his legs had fire licking every nerve ending. Big arms wrapped around me as he washed my chest and my stomach. His hips rocked against me, his cock trapped between our bodies.

"Zeke ... oh, fuck ... I need more."

"I know you do," he growled, his mouth close to my ear. "You need to feel my cock filling you."

"Yes." So fucking badly.

His big hand curled around my throat as he held me against him. He wasn't cutting off my air, but there was no denying who was in charge here.

Zeke walked us backward until we were both under the spray, water cascading over me, rinsing the soap from my body. His mouth moved to my shoulder and I hissed when he nipped me with his teeth. He didn't stop, those stinging bites making my dick throb as he worked his way up my neck.

This man made me feel things I'd never felt before. Maybe not the sweet intensity I felt with Brax, but there was something about our connection. It was palpable, a living, breathing thing that had me hoping for more, wanting him to embrace whatever this was building between us.

Zeke held me tighter, his teeth nipping my skin, his breath warm against my shoulder. I could feel a soft rumble in his chest. He was as worked up as I was, but he was still holding back.

Ah, fuck. This was not what I expected. The pleasure coiled hot and fierce inside me. This man had never touched me like this. He was always so impersonal. This felt like more.

Once the soap was gone from my skin, Zeke spun me around and backed me up against the tile. I cried out as the rough pieces scraped against my ass. The pain ignited sparks in my eyes, small white flashes dancing there.

Zeke's hand remained on my throat as he pinned me against the wall, his eyes fierce as he stared back at me. I couldn't look away even as the pain morphed into something more intense.

When he leaned forward and crushed his mouth to mine, all thought fled. The only things I was aware of were his lips, the brutal way he thrust his tongue into my mouth, his hand tightening, air becoming scarce. Still, I kissed him, desperate and eager for *this* man. I got the feeling I wasn't kissing the Sadist. This was the man beneath it all. While he was still in charge, still dominant in every right, he was seeking something from me. Acceptance? Desire?

I wanted to give it to him. Whatever he needed.

But I didn't touch him, fearful he would stop touching me if I did. I settled for having his lips brutally crushing mine as he owned the kiss.

When he finally pulled away, oxygen seeped back into my lungs as I stared into those glittering black eyes. I thought he would be angry, the way he'd been after he kissed Brax.

Anger wasn't staring back at me.

No. Something else. Something potent.

Something that I feared was going to bring me to my knees.

.

TWENTY-FIVE

ZEKE

I COULDN'T EXPLAIN WHAT WAS going through my head as I kissed the pretty boy. I wanted him with a ferocity I hadn't experienced in a damn long time. I thought back to the scene at the club, my mind automatically drawing on the memory of Jane walking the pretty boy away to an aftercare room. For the first time, I had felt as though I should've been the one caring for him.

And now, as I feasted on his mouth, the warmth of his body lured me closer. I couldn't stop myself. Even knowing the cowboy was kneeling feet away, I didn't want to stop. It was insanity in its purest form.

But I did have to stop myself. I couldn't allow this to go too far.

Pulling back, I took a deep breath, then shut off the water. I grabbed a towel, pretending the pretty boy wasn't standing there staring at me with wild eyes and swollen lips. My cock was so damn hard, yet for some reason, I wanted more than a quick fuck.

After drying off, I wrapped the towel around my waist and went to the mirror over the sink.

"Both of you can go to the bedroom," I said absently, refusing to make eye contact with either one of them.

When they left me in peace, I grabbed my toothbrush and went through the motions. I stared at myself, trying to figure out what was different. The past week had been phenomenal. Aside from the minor setback with the cowboy, I'd thoroughly enjoyed myself. And even that ... the way the cowboy had admitted he was jealous... That hadn't been so bad. It was my reaction to the situation that threw me. I didn't want to get close to them, because once I did, once I made the mistake of wanting more, they would be gone.

After rinsing my mouth, I shook my head and glared at the man staring back at me. I wouldn't want more. That was all there was to it. I had to move forward the way we had been. I didn't necessarily have to toss them to the curb to maintain my control, either. We could simply enjoy this for as long as it lasted.

I glanced down to see my cock was tenting the towel. It needed some attention and it was no longer waiting. I freed my cock from its cotton cavern, tossing the towel over the rack before I headed toward the bedroom.

The cowboy was still kneeling on the floor, his eyes following me as I walked. He had yet to say a word, and I had to admit, I was rather impressed with how he was handling this. Only one more day to go before he could get back to his normal life. Admittedly, I couldn't wait for that to happen because I had a few things in mind for him. Things that wouldn't require him to play dress-up or eat out of a bowl on the floor.

"Come here, pretty boy," I commanded, ensuring the edge in my voice was pure steel. "Get on the bed. Facedown." I stood beside the bed and motioned toward my cock. "Head over here."

The pretty boy did as instructed, moving into place until his head hung over the edge of the bed, his big body sprawled across the mattress.

"Put your mouth on my dick." I glanced at the cowboy. "You're welcome to move over to this side of the room if you'd like a better view."

Without a word, the cowboy crawled over near us, kneeling so that he could watch his boyfriend deep-throat my dick.

Damn, but the man was good at that. His lips circled the head, his tongue stroking leisurely at first. When I placed my hands over his head and pulled him down while thrusting my hips upward, he groaned, the vibrations going straight to my balls.

I did enjoy using his mouth. I would have to take advantage of the cowboy the same way once he was finished with his punishment. I'd been thinking about all the things I intended to do to him when he wasn't wearing that fucking costume. Needless to say, the cowboy was in for a treat. I respected his courage and I intended to reward him for it.

Eventually.

My eyes darted down the pretty boy's long body, coming to rest on his ass. The marks were still there, bruises now appearing where the cane had brutally smacked him. I'd been surprised in the shower when he had wanted me to hurt him more. It wasn't the usual response. Not that I'd seen anyway. However, the pretty boy wasn't a usual man. He sought pain for whatever reason. I hadn't figured out whether it was a coping mechanism or merely some deep-seated perversion. I found myself oddly curious as to how it came about, but it was a question I knew I couldn't ask.

I pulled my cock from between the pretty boy's lips and took one step back.

"Turn over."

His eyes lifted to mine, but he did as I asked, flipping onto his back. He hissed when his ass came in contact with the blanket. I placed my hands on his chin and tilted his head all the way back until it was hanging over the edge. Without preamble, I shoved my cock in his mouth. This allowed me a little more leverage while he could do nothing more than open wide.

"Suck me," I growled as I held his head still by cradling his face. "Let me feel that throat work the head of my cock."

I tugged on his neck, forcing him to lean over the side so I had a better angle. I pushed in as far as I could, held myself there until the pretty boy's throat began working hard. He gagged and I retreated, but I didn't wait long before shoving in deep again. I growled low in my throat when my cock pushed in deep.

Fuck, Case. It feels so good.

I shook off the thought. I couldn't think about him by name. It wouldn't suit my purpose.

The pretty boy held still, allowing me to use his mouth for my pleasure. I couldn't help myself, fucking him firmly as the suction of his lips worked me over good. I allowed several minutes to pass as I kept him immobile with only my hands on his neck. When that telltale tingle started in my spine, I pulled back.

"Move up on the pillows," I instructed. "And stay on your back."

While this wasn't my first choice in position, I wanted to ensure he felt the sting for as long as possible. His ass would rub against the blankets, which, in turn, would heighten the sensation for him.

After retrieving the lube from the nightstand, I joined him on the bed. I easily shifted between his legs, positioning him exactly as I wanted. I wasn't gentle, but I doubted he expected me to be.

I watched his face while his gaze was trapped on my hands stroking my cock, lubing myself up. He never looked away and my attention trailed down between his legs as I guided my cock to his asshole.

"Pull your knees up to your chest."

The pretty boy moaned softly when I inched closer, my thighs brushing the abused, reddened skin on his backside. I should've taken pictures, something to look back on in the future, because damn, it was a nice sight.

"Look at me, pretty boy."

His eyes flew up to my face, the light green irises glittering with heat.

"You like when I fuck you." It wasn't a question. I didn't have to ask, I already knew.

"Yes, Zeke." The pretty boy grunted when I pushed my cock in deep. His ass was tight, gripping me firmly, dragging out a long exhale as the heat consumed me.

"I like fucking you, too," I admitted as I leaned over him, placing my hands on both sides of his head. "The way your ass strangles my cock, trying to take more of me. And that's exactly what I'm gonna do." I held his stare for a moment. "I'm gonna give you all of me. And when I come, you have permission to come. But not until then."

"Yes, Zeke." His eyes softened, and for a brief moment, I swore I saw more than lust looking back at me.

I tried to shake it off, but I was trapped in his gaze. I thrust my hips forward, then retreated slowly, allowing my cock to drag along all those sensitive nerve endings. When only the head remained lodged inside him, I slammed forward again. I repeated the slow drag once more. I fucked him just like that, maintaining a steady rhythm as the scalding heat consumed me.

The pretty boy's jaw clenched, the muscle flexing as he held back while I impaled him again and again. I allowed the pace to quicken, the thrusts to become more forceful until I couldn't restrain myself any longer. I fucked him hard, driving him into the mattress as I angled my hips for the best penetration. Sweat coated my skin as my orgasm neared, but I still held out. It wasn't until I curled my arms behind his knees and held him firmly beneath me that I let loose. He took every punishing thrust, grunting, groaning, his eyes pleading for me to send him over the edge.

"I'm gonna come in your ass, pretty boy," I growled, my mouth close to his. "And when I do, you're gonna thank me for it."

"Yes ... Zeke." His breaths sawed in and out of his lungs, our hearts pounding in time with the driving force of my hips.

When my release barreled down on me, I impaled him one last time, keeping my eyes locked with his as my cock pulsed deep inside him. A dull roar escaped me, but he took every drop before he fisted his cock and came all over his chest. I watched, mesmerized by the sight.

I wasn't sure what made me do it, but I released his legs, then leaned down and licked the cum from his chest. The pretty boy inhaled sharply, his hands suddenly on my shoulders. He wasn't pushing me away and it sent a chill down my spine.

"Thank you, Zeke," he whispered hoarsely.

I lifted my head one last time, wondering what the hell was coming over me. Although I knew I was moving in a very dangerous direction with these two, I couldn't seem to help myself.

Weak, unsteady legs carried me off the bed and into the bathroom. I cleaned myself up, refusing to look at the man in the mirror. I didn't want to see what was in his eyes. The pep talk from earlier had done absolutely no good, and quite frankly, I wasn't sure what the hell I was supposed to do about it now.

Man up, an inner voice said.

Good advice. Except that could be taken in more than one way.

The question I had was which direction did I go? And how long before I fucked it all up?

Because that, I knew, was inevitable.

Brax
(The cowboy)

Monday, October 22

MY EYES FLEW OPEN ON Monday morning. The room was dark. The whisper of deep breathing sounded all around me. Tank was curled up beside me, his doggy snores soft and even.

I was lying in Zeke's bed, where I had slept since I had donned the dog paraphernalia on Friday night. My brain obviously registered my punishment was over, which explained why I had jarred myself awake so quickly. I was so done with this mask and these paws. Of course, my punishment wasn't over until Zeke removed these things from my body, and I would've been lying if I said I wasn't eager for that to happen. The damn leather head mask caused me to sweat profusely and I desperately wanted a shower.

I cut my gaze across the semi-dark room and found the big man asleep on his back. That was his normal position. Flat on his back, hands at his sides. Mostly. Once or twice, Zeke's hand had ended up on my arm or my chest when he slept. I'd woken the first time, surprised by his touch. I hadn't been sure he'd meant to do it, but it was oddly settling to have him casually touching me.

Right now, though, he wasn't touching me and I wished that he was. It was odd to see him so peaceful, but I'd actually admired him yesterday morning for a bit before he opened his eyes and caught me looking.

Since he wasn't moving and he wasn't talking, I assumed he was still out, so I allowed my gaze to rake over him. The tattoos that covered his neck, chest, and arms captivated me as they always did. I could spend hours looking at them. While Case only had the one dragon tattoo covering his back and curling over his shoulder and onto his chest, Zeke had many. Various things: a skull, a whip, an eight-ball, a hammer, a flower, just to name a few. They were random yet somehow made me believe I was getting a glimpse at more of the man. The overall design was unique. Like him.

"You're staring at me," his deep voice rumbled from beside me.

His eyes were still closed, so I smiled to myself. I had hated every second of being his pet, but now that it was over, I couldn't find it in me to hold it against him. I only hoped we would be taking a step forward and not back. I had taken my punishment like a man, following every order and not trying to get away with anything. I figured that was the only way to please him, so I had obeyed.

Zeke yawned, then stretched before his eyes opened and he turned his head toward me. "Time for a shower, cowboy. You, me, and the pretty boy."

My heart hammered in my chest. Having watched the two of them in the shower last night, I had dreamed about being part of it. Zeke inviting me to join them, his hands, his mouth, all doing wicked things to me while we cleaned up.

"Yes, Zeke," I said, my voice rough from disuse. "I'll turn the water on."

He nodded before sitting up and swinging his legs over the edge of the bed.

Wanting to be there before him, I scrambled off the bed. My knees ached from having spent two days on them, but I ignored the pain. I was upright now and that was all that mattered.

Zeke joined me a minute later, finally removing the various pieces of the costume from my body. The relief was instant, not having the leather mask over my head or the gloves on my hands. The only thing that remained was my collar, which oddly enough wasn't part of the costume.

"Brush your teeth," Zeke instructed before he carried the stuff out of the bathroom.

I hurried to the second sink, which Case and I had been using when Zeke allowed us in this bathroom. I quickly went to work, the minty toothpaste like ambrosia. Not only had I not been allowed to shower, I hadn't been allowed to brush my teeth, either. I remembered those weekends when I was a kid. Attempting to get away with not bathing or brushing my teeth because it was a pain the ass and the only thing I'd wanted to do was play.

I was no longer that kid. Hygiene was important and I was salivating at the thought of a shower.

Once my teeth were shiny and clean, I made a beeline for the toilet and took a piss. I sighed in relief. Peeing outside might've been an interesting thing to do when I was a kid, but it damn sure wasn't something I enjoyed now.

When I came out of the toilet room, I found Case and Zeke already in the shower. Zeke was washing up while Case stood there. I could tell he was still half-asleep, probably wishing like hell he could curl up for a little while longer. My man certainly wasn't a morning person.

Both sets of eyes shifted to me and a strange sense of anticipation filled me.

Without hesitation, I joined them, my skin warming as the water from the various jets hit different parts of my body. I moaned in response. I wasn't sure a shower had ever felt this good before.

"Over here, cowboy." Zeke crooked a finger, motioning me toward him.

I padded over, feeling every inch of the difference in our sizes. He was a big man. Huge. Although I wasn't small, compared to these two, I was. Oddly enough, I liked that about them. They made me feel protected in a way I didn't expect.

Zeke used a spinning motion with his hand to tell me to turn around, so I did. Once my back was to him, Zeke pulled me in close until his chest was against my spine, his big arms wrapping around me, holding me against him.

"Clean the cowboy," he instructed Case.

The smile that curled Case's lip was wicked and mischievous. The way he moved toward me was pure sex. He poured soap into his hands, then proceeded to wash me from neck to toe, rough hands scraping over every inch. His movements were as sensual as the gleam in his eyes. I found myself leaning into Zeke, enjoying the warmth of them, the way they were giving me every ounce of their attention.

The soap was rinsed away as soon as Case rubbed it over me, causing him to do it again and again. He was working me up, making me hyperaware of how close they both were.

Big hands fisted my cock and I looked down to see Zeke was the one jerking me off. Slow, steady. I watched his hand as it stroked the length of me, soft grunts sounding in my chest. I prayed I wasn't still dreaming.

"Feed him your cock, cowboy," Zeke mumbled in my ear, his breath warm, his words raspy.

Case dropped to his knees instantly, his bright eyes locked on my face as I guided my cock toward his mouth. I hissed in a breath when he wrapped those succulent lips around the swollen head. I felt as though it had been a lifetime since anyone had touched me. Every movement had my skin sparking.

Zeke began nipping my neck while Case swallowed my dick. They were overwhelming me with sensation and I never wanted it to end. I needed this. Needed both of them focusing only on me. My balls were heavy, my cock hypersensitive.

"Do you want to come in his ass or his mouth?" Zeke whispered, his hand winding around my neck, holding my head back as he nipped my earlobe.

"His mouth," I said on a rush of air. I was dizzy with lust, my entire body succumbing to the brutal pleasure. "I wanna come down his throat."

Zeke's lips disappeared from my skin, but only for a brief moment as he instructed Case to make me come. Once his words were out, Zeke turned my head as he leaned around and pressed his mouth to mine. I shifted slightly to allow him a better angle as he thrust his tongue inside.

A deep, ragged moan escaped me as Case devoured my cock and Zeke tongue-fucked my mouth in the sweetest, most devastating way. Without thinking, I wrapped one arm behind Zeke's head, holding him to me. He stiffened momentarily but then unleashed on me. The kiss went nuclear, my body trembling as my orgasm neared. Case wasn't gentle. He sucked me hard, his hand roughly kneading my balls until the pleasure was too much.

I cried out as my cock jerked in Case's mouth. Zeke's lips released mine, but he didn't turn away. Our eyes met and I saw a hunger there. Something dark and promising. I wasn't sure what had spurred this, but I didn't want to question it. It wasn't much different than what I'd witnessed last night between Zeke and Case. And now they were including me.

They brought me down gently, allowing me to regain my senses as I stood beneath the hot water. Case was back on his feet, his mouth melding with mine. I could still hear Zeke breathing against my ear and a tremor raced through me. I'd never experienced anything like this in my life.

And I prayed like hell I got the chance to experience it again. Soon.

TWENTY-SIX

ZEKE

WHILE I HAD FULLY INTENDED to walk out of that bathroom and not seek anything from the cowboy, giving him time to recover from his traumatic weekend, I couldn't bring myself to do it.

After he blew his load in the pretty boy's mouth, my desire had escalated tenfold. The kiss we'd shared had only ignited something hotter, brighter, far more intense than I'd expected.

"On my bed, cowboy," I commanded when his legs were steady beneath him. "Right now."

Emerald-green eyes locked on my face and I could see the same desire staring back at me. He wanted everything I had to offer, and for the first fucking time since I'd met him, I wasn't worried I would hurt him more than he wanted.

"Yes, Zeke," he said, an urgency in his tone that I related to.

When he stepped out of the shower, I glanced at the pretty boy. "It's your turn to watch."

He smiled, seemingly pleased with this command.

I didn't wait for the pretty boy. I simply walked out of the shower. I didn't bother with a towel, either. I followed the cowboy into my bedroom, catching up to him before he reached the bed. With one hand on his shoulder, I spun him around to face me, then slammed my mouth down on his.

The cowboy's arms flew around my neck as I crushed him to me, assaulting his mouth with brutal intent.

"Fist my cock," I commanded between kisses. "Rub it against yours."

He whimpered but did as I said. Both arms released me and he grabbed my cock, sliding it against his as I pumped my hips to increase the friction. I wasn't sure what had gotten into me, but I couldn't bring myself to stop. I wanted him. Hell, I'd go so far as to say I fucking needed him.

If I didn't know better, I would say that these two broke me. All my good intentions of dominating them, hurting them, abusing them… They had gone out the window. At least in that moment.

"On the bed," I muttered, gripping his hips and pushing him up onto the mattress.

I had enough sense to grab the lube as I crawled onto the bed with him. Seconds later, my cock was slick as I aligned with his body, eager to thrust inside.

"Hold on, cowboy," I growled. "Fucking hold on."

Without waiting a second longer, I impaled him on my cock. His knees shifted back as I pressed him into the mattress with my weight. I fused our lips together as I began pumping my hips, fucking him as though my life depended on it.

The cowboy whimpered and moaned, his arms tightly twined around my neck as he held on to me. I kept at it, fucking him roughly, not caring about anyone or anything except for his pliant body beneath me and his tongue warring with mine.

Unchecked groans escaped me as I fought the overwhelming urge to come hard and fast. I wanted to enjoy this, to ride it out for as long as I could.

Finally, I managed to break the kiss and pushed up onto my knees. I gripped the cowboy's hips and jerked him toward me as I thrust forward, driving my cock deep into his ass. I was possessed and I didn't give a shit. His body clamped onto my cock, hot and so fucking welcoming. It was driving me out of my mind.

Our eyes locked and I held his stare as I continued to fuck him.

Goddamn it, Brax. What the fuck are you doing to me?

As soon as his name registered in my mind, I threw myself forward again, bending him in half as I held myself over him and slammed my hips downward, driving as far as I could inside him before retreating. I pummeled him over and over, relishing the sharp gasps and desperate groans my thrusts earned me.

The sudden urge to have him riding me had me wrapping one arm beneath his back.

"Hold on," I commanded again as I rolled onto my back.

Without dislodging my cock from his ass, the cowboy repositioned so that he could fuck me, lifting and lowering on my cock. I reached for his dick and stroked him roughly, our eyes once again fixed together.

"Fuck me," I ordered. "Make me come, damn you."

The cowboy rode me like a fucking bull, driving me closer and closer to release until I couldn't hold back a second longer.

Without warning, I roared my release, slamming my hips up into him. He cried out as his cock jerked in my hand, cum splashing over my belly and my chest.

When I could take a breath without fearing I would pass out, I smiled up at him.

"Clean me, cowboy."

He smiled in return. "Gladly, Zeke."

And he did.

Friday, October 26

Jamie surprised me on Friday morning when she showed up just after six in the morning. Like usual, she caught me during my workout. Thankfully, I'd been mindful of the day, figuring she would show up since I had purposely kept her away from the house last Friday. I had made sure both the cowboy and the pretty boy were dressed just in case.

283

"So, what's for breakfast?" she teased when I finished the last of my set.

"Your choice. I just need to shower."

Jamie stared back at me, her head tilting to one side, then the other.

I frowned. "What?"

She shrugged. "I'm not sure but I think something's different."

I waved her off. "Don't be ridiculous. Nothing's different."

"You're smiling more," she teased.

"I'm always smiling."

"If you say so."

Not wanting her to throw out some of that psychobabble she was fond of, I motioned toward the stairs. "After you."

With a grin, she jogged up the stairs and I followed close behind.

"My brother's treating the three of us to breakfast," Jamie announced when we were on the main floor.

The cowboy grinned from his spot in the kitchen. This week, he'd taken to cooking Tank's food, coming up with dog-friendly meals that had shocked the shit out of me. Tank certainly didn't object to the new dishes he'd been given. While the cowboy would deliver Tank's breakfast to him, I handled his dinner. The pretty boy had contributed by spending an hour outside in the evenings, throwing the ball until Tank could hardly walk from exhaustion.

I'd gone to the office with Tank every day this week while they were getting back into a regular routine with Trent. Although I wanted to take them to the office simply because I could play with them all damn day, I'd taken a step back and allowed them to get back on some sort of schedule. Oddly enough, it was working for us.

From what I'd gathered from Justin and Ben, the restaurant was underway, the interior demolition already complete. As for the gym, the last of the tenants who had previously occupied those two floors would be moving out at the end of the month. Once that took place, they would be full steam ahead on it, too.

"Where're we going?" the pretty boy asked when he came down from taking his shower. His smile was bright when it landed on Jamie.

"There's this diner," Jamie began telling them. "The waitress flirts with Zeke. It's kinda cute."

I rolled my eyes. "I'm gonna shower. Be back in a minute."

While she started rambling about pancakes and shit, I went upstairs to take care of my morning business. Twenty minutes later, I returned to find the three of them sitting at the kitchen table sharing coffee.

Jamie spun around to look at me. "You ready?"

"Yeah."

"Great. I'm driving!"

"The hell you are," I grumbled. I'd seen my sister drive. No way was I getting in a car with her.

"Can't blame a girl for trying," she said with a giggle.

She seemed in an even better mood than usual and I couldn't help but wonder what had her so chipper. Jamie always had a quick smile, but this was different. *She* was different.

"How many brothers and sisters did you say you had?" Jamie prompted the cowboy when we were all piled in my truck.

"Four brothers, three sisters."

"And what do your sisters do?"

"Two are in the military, one owns a bakery."

"Ah, so she got the cooking gene, too?"

I peered in the rearview mirror to see her wide smile as she stared over at the cowboy.

"She did."

"And what do your brothers do?"

"The oldest is a divorce lawyer, the next two own a landscaping business, and my younger brother's ... well, he's not doin' much of anything these days."

I noticed the way the pretty boy grinned when he listened to the cowboy speak. I found myself doing the same. This was one of those rare chances for me to learn something about them without meddling. My sister would do that for me so I could sit back and pretend not to care.

Oddly enough, I was starting to care. More than I should. Not that I was going to let them in on that little secret. Throughout the week, I'd continued to play with them. Sometimes in the basement, sometimes in the living room while we watched television. One time, I'd had the pretty boy sit under the kitchen table and blow me while the cowboy and I ate dinner.

I had to continuously remind myself that they were my fuck toys and I had to take advantage while I could. At some point, they would be ready to leave, to find a place here in Chicago, where they would be working full-time in the future. I tried not to think about that end date, but I knew it was lurking.

They needed what I could offer them and I wasn't willing to give them more than that. While I found myself fascinated more and more, I knew my place. I was the alpha in this thing and they already had a relationship. Since the cowboy's punishment was over, they'd gone back to sleeping beneath my bed. Once or twice I had considered having them join me. Fortunately, I'd shaken off the ridiculous idea before I opened my fucking mouth and said something stupid.

"Are they here in Chicago?"

The cowboy chuckled. "Oh, no. They wouldn't last a minute in the city. We grew up in North Carolina, but we moved to Texas when I was twelve. My parents have a small farm, a couple of horses, some goats and pigs. The two sisters in the military are both deployed—one army, the other navy. The bakery owner lives in the suburbs of Dallas. My parents are a little farther north. My landscaping brothers moved to Arkansas about eight years ago. And the divorce lawyer lives in California."

"That's a big family. Was it hard growing up with that many people in the same house?"

"Even when we had two bathrooms, it wasn't easy."

Jamie huffed a laugh. "Only two bathrooms? For ten people? That would've been miserable. What about you, Case?"

He turned his head to speak to her. "No siblings. I was more than enough for my parents."

I glanced his way, silently wishing he would elaborate. Perhaps he could delve into the reasons he needed pain.

"So, you grew up alone?" Jamie asked.

"Not really, no." The pretty boy turned to face the front, his gaze straying out the side window. "After we moved to Texas, I met John. He and I were inseparable for years. He died of leukemia when he was seventeen."

The way he spoke said that was a time in his life that wasn't easy to remember.

"I'm so sorry," Jamie said kindly. "Were you close to his parents?"

I glanced in the rearview mirror to look at my sister. That seemed an odd question to ask.

"I was. After John died, they moved to the city. Got an apartment. They wanted a change of scenery. Not long after, they split up. I visited them from time to time."

An apartment? In the city? Perhaps that was the reason he'd had a strange reaction to the apartment here. Had something happened there?

Shit.

That was a question I didn't need an answer to. It wasn't my business.

"Well, I had Zeke," Jamie noted. "Our parents died when I was six, so he took care of me mostly. Him and Opa. We went to live with my grandfather after they died. But it was Zeke who took care of me most of the time."

"Is that right?" the cowboy questioned, sounding strangely fascinated.

"Yep, without him, I don't know where I'd be."

When I heard the sadness in her tone, I turned my attention to the road.

I felt their eyes on me, knew the pretty boy and the cowboy were attempting to humanize me in some form. I doubted they'd done so before now. Part of me wished they wouldn't. They could continue to see me as the monster everyone believed me to be.

Thankfully, I pulled up to the diner in time to put an end to that conversation. Without a word, I threw the truck in park and hopped out.

My overly cheerful sister was at my side a moment later, hooking her arm into mine and leading the way into the restaurant. While everyone seemed distracted by her giddiness, I did my best to allow the mask to fall back in place.

I hoped like hell the cowboy and the pretty boy didn't start looking at me differently. If they did ... well, if they did, then perhaps it was time for us to move this to the end phase. Maybe that was what was best for everyone.

Especially me.

Case
(The pretty boy)

JAMIE LAUTNER WAS CUTE AS could be. The way she mooned over her brother, as though he was the greatest man she'd ever known... It gave me tremendous insight into Zeke. A glimpse I honestly never thought I would have the opportunity to see. There was a hell of a lot more to him than most people realized. Sure, he was a sadistic man, but there were so many other qualities about him that intrigued me.

The way he carried on a conversation with Jamie made it obvious he was highly intelligent. Of course, I'd gathered that merely from his position at Chatter PR Global. I'd heard him talk to clients, knew he was well-versed in what he did. But it was more than that. He had something to say on nearly every subject she brought up. Unless it pertained to something personal. Especially regarding Brax or me. He did not seem pleased by Jamie's inquisitive nature when it came to our history.

Yet he listened without interruption as Jamie asked about what we did for a living, how we'd come to be in the industries we were in. How we'd met Trent Ramsey, what was it like working for him. And so on and so forth.

When she finally fell silent for a moment, I decided to get in a question of my own.

"So, were you able to make it to Dichotomy?"

A deep growl sounded from Zeke and I looked over to see him glaring back at me. I smiled because why not. I knew this wasn't a subject he was fond of, but I wanted to know how it had turned out.

"I was," she said hesitantly, her eyes darting over to Zeke, who was sitting beside her in the booth.

"And…?" I prompted.

"It was…" She took a deep breath and then a brilliant smile transformed her face. "It was amazing, Case. Truly amazing. I've never experienced anything like it. I couldn't believe half of what I saw. It was far more intense than any book I'd read."

I watched Zeke as she spoke, noticed the way his hand tightened around the handle of his coffee mug. If he wasn't careful, he would break the damn thing.

"So you spent time with Master Edge?" Brax asked.

There was a dreamy look in her eyes and I was suddenly grateful Zeke was sitting beside her. Otherwise, he would've seen that look and poor Master Edge would probably be missing a few fingernails at the very least. I imagined Zeke torturing the man, tying him to a chair, demanding answers before plucking out his fingernails one by one when he didn't say what the Sadist wanted to hear.

"I did," she said, her tone steadier than her gaze. "He showed me around, let me watch some scenes. We talked for what felt like hours. I had a fantastic time."

"So I take it you related to the submissives?"

"Yes. Very much so. In fact, I'm going to go back."

Zeke grimaced, but he didn't look at his sister. I could see the strain on his face. He was holding back whatever he wanted to say. I had to admit, I was proud of him. I could tell this wasn't easy, but he was giving his sister the chance she had asked for.

"Do you know when?" Brax asked.

"No." She smiled, but it appeared sad. "I was hoping Master Edge would call me, but he hasn't."

Zeke's eyes cut to his sister, but he didn't turn his head. I couldn't tell what he was thinking. Was he happy Master Edge was blowing her off? Or was he planning to beat the man to a pulp for it?

There was no telling with Zeke.

"So, tell me what it is you're studying," I prompted, hoping by changing the subject the big man would get in a better mood.

That or he wouldn't decide to take his frustrations out on us for bringing it up in the first place.

"Hmmm. Where should I start?" There was a mischievous gleam in Jamie's eyes when she spoke.

I was almost positive I'd seen that same gleam in Zeke's a time or two.

"What's your plan for the day?" Zeke asked Jamie when we were heading back to his house an hour later.

"I've got class this afternoon," she told him. "What's your plan?"

"Work."

Since Jamie was riding shotgun, she turned her head to look back at me and Brax.

"And you two?"

"They're going to the office with me," Zeke stated before either of us could respond.

This was the first I was hearing of the day's plan, but I wasn't bothered by it in the least. I was hoping to spend more time with Zeke, not less.

"Yeah? That sounds fun."

Oh, I got the feeling it would be anything but fun. However, I certainly didn't mind the idea. I'd spent the better part of the week with Brax. During those times I wasn't with Trent, anyway. Not that there had been a lot going on, but it was nice to settle back into work.

Still, I couldn't deny that I welcomed the chance to spend some time with Zeke. I didn't even care what he had in store for us. Based on his solitude this morning, I got the feeling he was cooking up something interesting.

When we pulled into the driveway, Jamie smiled back at us. "Thank you both for having breakfast with me. I had a great time."

"Likewise," Brax told her.

"Same here," I said. "And good luck with Master Edge."

Zeke's gaze shot up to the rearview mirror and I knew he was looking back at me.

Jamie unbuckled her seat belt, then leaned over and kissed Zeke on the cheek. "I'll talk to you later. Be good."

He chuckled, a rough sound that had my balls trembling.

"I'm always good."

"Right." With that, Jamie hopped out of the truck and headed over to her car.

"Cowboy. Go on in and get Tank."

Oh, shit.

"Yes, Zeke." Brax shot me a concerned look before he got out of the truck.

When the two of us were alone, Zeke glanced back over his shoulder. The smile he shot my way spoke of dark promises.

"I've got something in store for you once we get to the office."

I couldn't look away from him. "Whatever pleases you, Zeke."

I knew it sounded like I was taunting him and maybe I was. Just a little. The truth was, I felt more comfortable with Zeke. Although he wasn't sharing anything about himself in words, he was opening up in other ways. I found him to be a fascinating man and I didn't care how he interacted with us, just as long as he did.

And I suspected whatever he was cooking up was going to have me wishing I'd kept my mouth shut that morning.

Still, I was looking forward to it all the same.

TWENTY-SEVEN

ZEKE

DESPITE HIS CHOICE OF TOPICS of conversation, the pretty boy amused me. Although irritated that I had to listen to my sister discuss her visit to Dichotomy, I had to admire the way the pretty boy launched right into it while I was sitting directly across from him.

And with a smirk on his face, to boot.

The pretty boy was going to pay for that later and I was going to enjoy the hell out of it.

But right now, I was allowing the pretty boy and the cowboy to chat it up with Luci, Addison, and Dale up in the break room. I figured I'd give them some time. Allow them to relax before I sought them out and made them beg.

A knock sounded on my office door and I peered up to see Ben standing there. He was holding a mug of coffee and leaning against the doorjamb.

"Morning," he greeted.

I leaned back in my chair and smiled. "Morning."

For a brief moment, his eyes roamed over my face and I wondered if he was going to launch into something about how I looked different. My sister had already called it out this morning, and since I was known to give everyone shit, I figured Ben was gearing up to launch into the same thing.

He didn't. He simply smiled, white teeth flashing in his dark face. "I thought I'd check in, see what you decided on the hiring front."

I sighed heavily. "Heather accepted the offer and I'm still on the fence about Lance. Because I wasn't thrilled with the other interviews, I've got a couple more coming in this afternoon."

"Want my help talking to them?"

"If you've got time, sure."

"Always have time for you." He stood tall. "Send me the calendar invites and I'll block out my afternoon."

"Will do." I fully expected him to say something more, but Ben simply turned and disappeared.

I stared at the empty space, which was the only reason I caught Greg trying to slip by unnoticed.

"Edge!"

He grumbled something but then appeared in my doorway.

"Come in," I urged. "Let's chat."

Electric-blue eyes shot to my face momentarily, then darted down the hall. I expected him to come up with an excuse. I couldn't blame him. I would run from me, too.

When Edge peered back over, he looked... I'd go so far as to say the man looked scared. Which could only mean something had happened with my sister.

"Sit," I commanded.

A smile pulled at his mouth but he did join me. "I'm not one of your submissives, Zeke."

"Nope. You're not. However, you are the Dom who introduced my sister to kink."

He practically fell into the chair across from me. "Is this where you give me shit about it? Keep in mind, that was your idea."

"Technically, it was Ransom's."

"But you went along with it."

True. I did.

I stared at him for a moment, hoping the silence would intimidate him. I should've known better. Edge wasn't intimidated easily. He had a backbone of steel, which I actually admired.

"So, how'd it go?" I held up my hand quickly. "But spare me the details. I mean overall."

He seemed to consider his words carefully. "It ..." Edge thrust a hand through his thick, black hair. "Fuck, Zeke. Why'd you have to go and do this?"

I sat up straight when I heard the torment in his voice. "What happened, Edge?"

He dropped his head in his hands and I instantly came up with worst-case scenarios, hating myself for doubting my friend. He was right. This had been my idea. I thought back on Jamie's responses at breakfast. She had seemed so happy. Well, except for the fact that she'd obviously been waiting for Edge to call her and he hadn't.

Leaning back in my chair, I forced myself to relax, to take deep, even breaths. "Talk to me, Edge."

"What do you want me to say?" he snapped, his eyes lifting. I shrugged. "I don't know. Tell me how it went."

"I assume you've already talked to Jamie?"

"Not in depth, no." That much was true. I'd only heard what I had to hear and even then I had tried to block it out.

He huffed out a breath. "Fine. You want to know?"

I tilted my chin as a confirmation.

"It was great. Your sister's a beautiful submissive and I enjoyed her company far more than I thought I would. She was eager, attentive." He raised his hand quickly. "And no, there was nothing sexual about the encounter. I answered her questions, listened when she wanted to talk and..."

And holy fuck, Edge had a thing for my sister. It was so fucking evident I could hardly breathe.

"You know how old she is, right?" I asked, my tone curt.

"I do," he quipped. "She's thirteen years younger than me. Yeah. I get it. I'm too old for her."

"Twelve," I corrected, not that it mattered. "She's twenty-four."

"Fine. She's twelve years younger than me."

It was obvious he hated that fact.

"She mentioned she's going back?"

Wary blue eyes locked on my face. "She asked. I told her I'd call her."

"And you haven't called."

"Fuck," he growled before launching to his feet. "What the fuck do you want me to do Zeke?"

"What do you want to do?" I was surprised by how calm my voice was.

His head snapped around to me. "I want to call her. I want to invite her back to the club or out to dinner. Fuck. It's all I can think about, and I know you want to punch me right now. Sadly, I can't blame you. I want to punch me, too. But don't worry. I know what you wanted from me and I did it. My obligation's over."

"Call her." I shook my head quickly. "Wait. No. I didn't just say that."

Edge was staring at me, his eyes wider than I'd ever seen them. There was a glint of hope there.

"Zeke."

"No, I know." I sat up and stared at the hard surface of my desk before taking a deep breath and looking up at him. "It's not my place. Jamie's told me that a million times. And she's right. She's an adult. She can make her own decisions."

Edge was still staring, but now his mouth was hanging open.

I laughed because *fuck me running*. I couldn't believe what I was saying. I was giving this man permission to... Hell, I wasn't even sure what I was giving him permission for. To talk to my sister? Have dinner with her? Chain her up and— Nope, not going there.

"Zeke? I need you to open your mouth and tell me what's on your mind," Edge said, his tone pleading.

Swallowing hard, I forced myself to maintain eye contact. "You like her?"

"More than I should," he admitted and I had to admire the man. He had balls of steel. No one had ever admitted as much to me. "And not in a one-night kink club encounter sort of way, either."

Son of a bitch.

I pushed to my feet and stepped around my desk. "Fine. Call her. Take her out. Wine her, dine her. Do whatever the fuck you feel you need to do." I stopped when I was right up in his face. He was only a few inches shorter than me, so we were nearly eye to eye. "But you hurt her, Edge, and I will break every fucking bone in your body. Then, I'll wait for you to get out of traction and I'll do it again."

His eyes were stone-cold serious when he said, "The last thing I want is to hurt her, Zeke. I swear to you. That's the last thing I want."

I could hear the sincerity in his words but I couldn't speak. I had just given this man—one of my best friends—permission to date my sister. And I knew deep down that he wasn't some blowhard college kid who wanted to take her for coffee and stare deep into her eyes while they chatted about mundane bullshit. This man was into kink, which meant he would likely—

Nope. Not going to think about it.

"Just promise me one thing," I said on a sigh.

He looked skeptical. "What's that?"

"That'll you'll warn me when she's coming to the club. Because … no. If you forget, and I show up to find my sister… I mean it. If I walk into Dichotomy and see her, I swear to God, I will kill you, then resuscitate you and do it again and again."

A small smile pulled at Edge's mouth. "You've got my word."

There was gratitude in his eyes and I found myself oddly relieved. My sister could do far worse than Gregory Edge. I just had to remember that this was my idea when things went south between them. And when that happened, I was going to lose one of the closest friends I had, because no matter what, I would never turn my back on my sister. Not for anyone.

Edge nodded, then turned to go. He cast a quick look over his shoulder as though expecting me to launch myself at him and beat him to a pulp. It was surprising that I didn't want to. I'd never felt as though anyone was good enough for my sister. However, Gregory Edge was one of the finest men I knew.

When he walked out, I stared after him.

It was time I found my fuck toys.

Brax
(The cowboy)

"I HATE TO INTERRUPT THE party," Dale said when he popped his head into the break room, "but you two are being summoned."

He was looking directly at me, so I assumed he was referring to me and Case.

"Well, ladies," Case said with a smirk. "That's our cue. It seems our Sadist is ready to inflict some pain."

He didn't appear at all bothered by the notion.

"Good luck," Addison teased. "I think I'll go back down to my office, too. Maybe I'll get to hear some moans and groans coming from that direction."

"Not if he gags them," Luci noted. "Does he enjoy that? Gagging you?"

Case waved her off. "A masochist never tells."

I was the first to get to my feet, but Case was right behind me.

"Maybe we can grab lunch later. You know, if we can walk," I told them with a smile.

"I'm down." Addison smirked. "Even if you can't walk. That way I can make fun of you."

I couldn't help but like Addison. She'd come out of her shell ever since she hooked up with her two Doms, her rebellious streak shining brightly.

"Come on," I urged Case. The last thing I wanted was to keep Zeke waiting.

I practically had to run to keep up as Case darted for the stairs. We arrived at Zeke's office to find him sitting in his chair, staring out the window.

He must've heard us because his attention redirected our way when we stepped into the room.

"Close the door," he instructed.

Since I was the last to enter, I closed the door behind me, then turned and gave Zeke my full attention.

"Do you know what a humbler is?"

I frowned but not because I was confused. I knew exactly what a humbler was, and while I'd never used one, I knew from research that the damn thing was brutal.

"Yes, Zeke," Case replied, an edge of excitement in his voice.

Zeke's grin was ferocious. "Have you worn one?"

"No, Zeke," we both said in unison.

"That's about to change. Now strip."

Instinctively, I glanced out the window, noticing all the windows across the way. Thanks to a thunderstorm brewing, it was darker outside than it was inside, which meant everyone within range would have a perfect view of what was about to happen. Oddly, this excited me. More so than that damn humbler.

Case and I made quick work of removing our clothes. By the time we were finished, Zeke was on his feet.

"I want both of you on your knees." He motioned toward the opposite side of the room. "Over here. Asses toward me."

At least the people across the way wouldn't have a front row view of my asshole.

I dropped to my hands and knees, my breaths already becoming more labored. I wasn't sure if it was excitement or fear that had me breathing roughly. Maybe a little of both.

"The intention is to keep you on your knees. Once your balls are secured between the two wooden slats, you are not going to want to get up. If you do, you could cause serious damage. Understand?"

"Yes, Zeke," I said on a harsh exhale.

Why he opted to hook me up first, I wasn't sure. My breath lodged in my throat when I felt the cold wood as he shifted one side in place. A humbler was a handmade torture device that secured a man's ball sac between two pieces of wood that were locked together. It was only the length of both of my thighs, curved so that it fit against the backs of my legs, which kept it in place.

Zeke's warm hands curled around my balls, pulling them away from my body. I could feel the press of the wood against my thighs, where it horizontally curved across the tops of my legs, right beneath my ass cheeks. When my balls pressed against the wood, I sighed, but that quickly transformed into pain as they were compressed by the two pieces of wood. Not crushed completely, but there wasn't much room, that was for damn sure.

I groaned softly, inching my knees closer to my chest to keep the damn thing from pulling too hard. I gave up trying to hold myself up with my arms, choosing to rest my chest on the floor. The smaller I made myself, the less painful it was.

However, it also meant my ass was completely vulnerable to whatever Zeke had in mind.

"Your turn, pretty boy."

Case didn't make a sound as Zeke got the device set up. Before he was done, Case had taken up the same position as me. I was looking at him and he was looking at me. That was a nice twist. At least I would be able to watch his expressions.

"Very nice," Zeke said, his tone full of approval. "I definitely like this."

His footsteps sounded on the hardwood but I couldn't turn to see where he went. The sound of him rummaging through a drawer had anticipation curling inside me.

"Today you're gonna experience my crop," Zeke said, his voice deep, his words unhurried. "This particular one is my favorite. Split leather end, which adds a bite."

Ah, damn.

"Just remember, if you move, that humbler's gonna pull your balls."

Yeah. That was a reminder I didn't need. Unfortunately, it was likely inevitable since that crop was going to be vicious. I could already imagine myself jerking forward, attempting to get away from the sting. It would've been easier if Zeke had restrained me. Of course, that defeated the purpose of the humbler.

Damn it.

"Hmm. Who should go first?" he mused, his footsteps sounding behind me.

I felt the leather stroke across my ass as he passed. I held my breath, anticipating the first slap. It didn't come and my nerves ratcheted up, dread warring with anticipation.

Suddenly, a loud smack had me flinching. I inhaled, but the sting never came. Beside me, Case closed his eyes and moaned, a smile tugging on his lips.

Again, I waited, expecting to be hit next, but still it didn't come. Then a loud smack and Case moaned again. I was driving myself insane waiting for impact. Zeke obviously knew what he was doing, because when that crop hit Case, I couldn't keep myself from flinching, the humbler tugging on my ball sac. It wasn't painful but it could be if I moved too much.

Before I could inhale, a slap sounded and this time the pain rained down on my ass. I moaned softly, surprised by how much I enjoyed it. Case's eyes were open, focused on me. I felt a strange connection with him right then. He was my anchor in the sea of chaos.

While the pain sank in, I breathed in and out, letting it consume me. I was just getting used to it when another slap sounded, but it wasn't on me this time.

The anticipation was the hardest part. I had no idea what Zeke would do or when. The next few minutes ticked by painfully slowly. Zeke hit me several times, but not nearly as much as Case. I could see the euphoria on my boyfriend's face. He was enjoying this immensely.

Suddenly, the crop bit into my ass again and again, over and over as Zeke hit me numerous times. The pain was intense, all-encompassing. I hissed and groaned, forcing my body to remain as still as possible. The pleasure radiated through me, again surprising me with its intensity.

Zeke landed the same blows on Case in rapid succession until he was gritting his teeth, his eyes closed. Still, he looked peaceful, as though this was exactly what he needed.

There was something eerily calming about this moment, bent over and held captive by that torture device while Zeke landed swat after swat on each of us. Part of me wondered if maybe there *wasn't* a reason for Case's need for pain. That he hadn't experienced

something at some point in his life that drove him this direction.
Maybe he simply enjoyed how it felt.
Because oddly enough, I was enjoying it.
Right up until Zeke smacked my balls.

TWENTY-EIGHT

ZEKE

Tuesday, October 30

"WHEN YOU'RE FINISHED CLEANING UP, join me in the living room," I instructed my fuck toys after we'd consumed one of the best meals the cowboy had cooked thus far.

He seemed to be working hard to ensure he pleased me, and I couldn't deny he was doing a good job. It didn't go unnoticed, either. Hence the reason I had something rather pleasant in store for them this evening. Something that would allow me to sit back and relax. I was going to take advantage of watching them torment one another.

I flopped onto the sofa and flipped on the television. Rather than finding one of the legal dramas I enjoyed, I flipped it to porn. I mean, why not? It was meaningless, and since it would merely be a backdrop to my plan, I figured what the hell.

I could admit, I was loosening up a bit around them. My guard wasn't as firmly in place as it had been before. I still refused to think of them by name, but that wasn't uncommon. I'd known the damn waitress at the diner for roughly three years and I still thought of her as the waitress.

However, I didn't find myself thinking about her the way I was constantly thinking about my fuck toys. Day, night. At home, at work. It didn't matter. They were always on my mind. We'd settled into a routine and I'd come to trust them enough that I allowed Tank to stay home with them when they weren't going to be coming and going all day. It was working for us for whatever reason.

The cowboy appeared before the pretty boy. When he went to sit down on the sofa, I stopped him with a hand.

"Don't sit. I've got something for you."

His eyes wandered around me as though he expected me to have his surprise behind my back.

"Lift up the towel," I said, motioning toward the hand towel I had laid on the coffee table.

The cowboy raised it and revealed my most recent purchases. There on the table were two ball stretchers and a handful of small circular weights that would be added for maximum discomfort.

Emerald eyes took it all in before looking up at me.

"What's goin' on?" the pretty boy asked when he joined us a few seconds later.

His gaze fell to the table and a smile pulled at his lips.

"This looks like fun," he said with a chuckle.

"It will be," I confirmed. "For me. Now strip each other. And do it slowly. This show is all for me, and I expect you to keep that in mind from this point forward."

"Yes, Zeke," the pretty boy said with a certain level of enthusiasm.

He turned to the cowboy and stepped closer, his hands rising so he could slide beneath his T-shirt. He didn't rush, simply pulled the cowboy to him before kissing him gently.

"It's been a while since I've had the pleasure of undressing you," the pretty boy said.

I liked that he could pretend I wasn't there. It heightened the voyeurism aspect for me.

The cowboy clearly wasn't finished kissing, because he pulled the pretty boy into him and crushed their mouths together. They were a fumble of hands and lips for a minute or two, working their shirts up higher on their chests until they had to break apart to remove them.

There was something fascinating about the two of them together. They seemed to fit well, as though they were two puzzle pieces that had been designed to go together. The way they touched, moved, kissed. It wasn't choreographed, but it didn't have to be. It worked for them and I liked that I had the opportunity to watch.

Once their shirts were removed, they were kissing again, hands fumbling as their body temperatures heated from the steady groping. Another few minutes passed before they managed to relieve each other of their jeans, both men breathing roughly.

"Now, I want you each to put the ball stretcher on the other. This one's relatively easy. It's in an upside-down U-shape, which will allow it to hook around the top of the scrotum."

Neither man said anything as they each took one of the ball stretchers. These were stainless steel rods that had been formed into a unique design. They resembled a very skinny inverted U. The top was curved forward so that it would hook over the ball sac and remain in place while the long rods hung behind their balls and down about five inches or so between their legs. There was a chain that dangled from each rod, which would allow weights to be added.

"When you're putting it on him, I want you on your knees," I instructed.

The pretty boy dropped to the floor, his eyes wide with amusement.

"Be sure to make it pleasurable," I told him. No reason they couldn't enjoy the moment before the torture began.

While he hooked the ball stretcher in place, the pretty boy licked and sucked the cowboy's cock. He was firming up quickly, growing harder from the pretty boy's ministrations. It didn't take long before the ball stretcher was hooked around his scrotum and they traded places.

I reclined, enjoying the show while the cowboy returned the favor, getting the pretty boy worked up with his mouth while he hooked the rod around his balls.

"Now for the fun part." I nodded my head toward the table. "See those weights? Each one is eight ounces. Might not seem like a lot until you have them dragging your balls to the floor." I grinned for effect. "Each of you will suck the other one, and for every minute you don't make the other one come, I will be adding another weight. So, the objective is to make him come as fast as possible to keep from having more added."

I sat up and pulled out what I'd hidden beneath the cushion.

"However, to make it fair, you'll both be handcuffed because your hands are not allowed."

After pushing to my feet, I moved around the coffee table to where they were standing.

"Who wants to suck first? Keep in mind, that person will wear the weights the entire time, even when it's his turn for the blow job."

They looked at each other and the pretty boy smirked. "I'll go first."

I had figured he would say that. A masochist through and through.

I hooked the leather cuffs to the cowboy's wrists and connected them behind his back, then gripped his bicep firmly. "Up on the table."

Good thing my furniture was top-of-the-line.

The cowboy stepped up onto the coffee table. I released him so I could restrain the pretty boy.

The table height was enough that the pretty boy wouldn't have to lean over too far to get the job done. However, it would require me to hold on to the cowboy to keep him from toppling over since his balance would be off from having his hands behind his back.

I pulled my phone from my pocket and opened the stopwatch app. It would allow me to watch the time easily. I set it on the table beside the cowboy's feet.

I turned to the pretty boy. "For every minute you don't get him off, I'll add another weight to the chains. You will maintain that weight even when the cowboy sucks your dick."

Both men were rock hard as they stared at one another. I figured they enjoyed the challenge. I know I certainly did.

Case
(The pretty boy)

I HAD TO ADMIT, THIS was a rather creative scenario. Wearing the ball stretcher while sucking Brax's dick in an effort to make him come was intriguing. I was curious to see how long Brax could hold out. I could take my time in order to have more weight added, or I could try and push him to the finish line early. Either way, it seemed like a win-win situation.

I briefly glanced down at the weights. There were a couple dozen. More than enough to torment us both should the other manage to hold out.

"Timer starts ... now."

Zeke hit the button on his phone, then moved to stand behind Brax while I leaned forward and slowly wrapped my lips around Brax's cock. I didn't rush, wanting to tease him. I knew exactly what he liked. How to draw out his pleasure or to push him over the edge. We'd been together for just over two years, and during that time, I'd learned so many things about him. All of which made me love him more with every passing second.

Brax moaned when I teased the slit with my tongue, working the sensitive head first. Without the use of my hands, I had to move quite a bit to maintain my momentum, which caused the chains on the ball stretcher to sway. It wasn't an unpleasant feeling. Not by a long shot.

"One minute passed," Zeke stated as he moved around behind me.

A second later, I felt the weight pulling the chains down. It wasn't nearly enough, but it would have to do for another minute.

I continued tormenting Brax, sucking and licking while he moaned softly above me. He was enjoying this as much as I was.

Truth be told, this was one of my favorite things. I could suck Brax's dick for hours because of those soft grunts he emitted. I loved hearing what I did to him. It spurred me on.

Several minutes passed and several more weights were added until I could no longer ignore the strain on my ball sac. The pain was pure bliss, firing in my bloodstream, spiking my lust. While I wanted to hold back to see how much I could take, I found my pace had increased. I was sucking furiously. Zeke stood behind Brax, holding him firmly while his big hands ran over his hips. I was sure that was driving Brax insane. I knew what Zeke's touch was like. Gentle or rough, I always wanted more.

What it was about the man, I wasn't sure, but I found myself falling for him. Not merely the Sadist either. I saw the other parts, too, and they drew me in, made me want more. I hated to think about the day this all might end. I'd come to rely on the safety and security I felt with the two of them.

"Oh, fuck," Brax growled. "That feels so damn good."

Inspired by his words, I sucked harder, bobbing my head faster as I took him to the back of my throat. I gagged and retreated. Over and over I worked him furiously, no longer worried about the fact my balls were damn near tearing from my body.

Zeke added another weight and it seemed evenly distributed at this point, but I focused solely on driving Brax over the edge just because I wanted to hear him when he came.

"Shit ... Case ... that feels too good. You're gonna make me come."

"Come down his throat, cowboy," Zeke urged. "Give him what he's seeking."

"Swallow my dick, Case. Give me more," Brax pleaded.

I took him to the back of my throat and remained there, swallowing around the intrusion. I could feel him pulsing in my mouth, knew he was close.

A second later, Brax roared, hot cum spraying down my throat. I pulled back enough to drink him down before licking him clean. When I released him from my mouth and looked up into his

308

eyes, I saw the love I'd come to expect. Despite the raunchy scene, it was still there.

He smiled down on me. "Now it's my turn, baby. I hope you're ready."

Oh, I was definitely ready.

When I shifted, I felt the full effect of those damn weights dragging down my balls. I groaned but somehow managed to lift one foot up onto the table so Brax and I could trade places.

"Do you think you can come with those things weighing you down?" Zeke taunted.

"Yes, Zeke."

"I'm looking forward to seeing it." He placed his phone back on the table. "Time starts now."

Brax's mouth—hot and eager—wrapped around the head of my cock and I hissed in a breath. Pleasure and pain assaulted me, coalescing into the perfect storm. He worked me in the way only Brax knew how, using his teeth to scrape along my shaft. The man knew exactly what I needed and he wasn't gentle. There were times he would suck me so sweetly I thought I would lose my mind. He wasn't doing that now and I knew he was racing against time. He wasn't into pain the way I was, so he wasn't looking forward to having the weight added to his balls.

Still, I held out even when Zeke had added four weights to Brax's chains. The way he moaned against me, the vibrations racing up my shaft sent wave after wave of pleasure crashing through me. Between Brax's mouth, Zeke's hands, and the pleasant burn from the ball stretcher, I was in heaven. In fact, it overwhelmed my senses, driving me closer to the edge before I was ready.

"Brax ... baby ... damn it. Don't make me come. Fuck. Don't ..." I couldn't stop it and the pain blinded me as my balls drew up against my body, fighting the weights. Zeke's hands gripped my hips firmly as I thrust my pelvis forward, driving deeper into Brax's mouth. "I'm coming ... oh, fuck ... coming. Don't stop, Brax."

By the time Brax released me, my body was wrung out. A fine sheen of sweat coated my skin. That was something I would likely never forget for as long as I lived. I was so caught off guard I didn't realize Zeke was removing the weights from both of us before unhooking the rods.

I found myself staring back at him, completely awestruck that he'd done that. Not once in the weeks we'd been here had Zeke cared for us after the fact. He'd left us to do that for each other because, unlike at the club, there was no one else to tend to us.

It took everything in me to act normal, to pretend it wasn't a big deal. But it was. To the point I felt a strange pressure in my chest. This hard-core Sadist was handling our aftercare and I wasn't sure he even realized he was doing it.

"My turn, fuck toys," he said, his gaze never landing on either one of us when he rid himself of his jeans and took a seat on the sofa. "You're gonna both suck me off. And you better make it good."

If Zeke wanted good, I was going to make it the best he'd ever had.

TWENTY-NINE

ZEKE

Wednesday, October 31

HALLOWEEN WAS ALWAYS INTERESTING WHEN it came to kink clubs, and Dichotomy was no exception. This year, since Trent was in town, it appeared the man was going all out with the theme. Thankfully, he hadn't insisted on costumes, but he did enforce a strict dress code. Masters and Mistresses were to wear black slacks or a skirt and a white button-down dress shirt. Submissives were to wear black or white lingerie only.

Of course, masks were provided, and no matter how much I argued, I was told I had to wear one just like everyone else who was permitted to enter.

When I arrived and noticed all the black lights, the dress code made sense. While the Doms' masks were black, the submissives' masks were white, which glowed beneath the purple light, easily showing who was who.

My fuck toys were wearing leather thongs, leather harnesses, their collars, and the mask. Nothing else. Of course, they were drawing all sorts of attention because men and women both were checking them out. Honestly, I was proud to have them with me and not merely because they were hot enough to draw all eyes to them. The cowboy and the pretty boy had been inching their way deeper beneath my skin with every passing day. At this point, I wasn't sure how I'd feel if I had to sleep without them in my bedroom.

"Nice party," Mistress Jane said when she approached me outside of the main-floor Doms' lounge. "I have to say, your arm candy is rather delicious."

"Good thing for me they're not into females."

She smiled, her eyes and her mouth the only part of her face visible because of the mask. "Yes, that is good for you."

"Did you bring any pets tonight?" I inquired, simply to make conversation.

"No. I'm here solo this evening." Her head turned as she surveyed the room. "However, I'm fairly certain I'll find one or two I can play with."

"I doubt that'll be difficult for you."

"Especially since Trent opened the club tonight to a few extra submissives."

I frowned. "Really? Why's that?"

"Edge approved some of the backlog. And he couldn't have done it at a better time either. The options were slimming."

"I didn't realize there was a backlog."

"Yep. Apparently quite a bit. My understanding is he's added almost two dozen fresh faces. Mostly submissives."

Great. Just what we needed. An overabundance of newbies slinking through the building. I hated when Edge did that because it took time to train them to do as they were supposed to. And to think, I had pretty much punished nearly all of them at this point. Who would do that now that I had my own—

Nope. Not going there. The fuck toys did not belong to me. They were temporary and I had to remember that. It was getting harder to do the more time I spent with them. However, I couldn't let myself get carried away.

"Well, I'll let you get back to it," Jane said as one of the male submissives caught her attention.

I chuckled. "Have fun."

"Oh, I fully intend to."

Those five-inch heels of hers carried her away from me as she stalked the submissive heading for the dungeon. Without the lights on, it was a wonder she could tell one from another. I certainly couldn't.

Then again, there were only two I cared about and I knew exactly where they were.

"I figured for sure you would skip tonight when Ramsey said a dress code was required," Ransom said as he approached.

"And why would I do that?"

"Oh, I don't know. Because you've done it before."

True. I had.

"Did you hear there's fresh meat here tonight?" I prompted in an effort to change the subject.

"What? Where?" His head snapped around in all directions as though he would be able to tell.

"No idea, but they're supposedly here. Jane said Edge approved a new batch of submissives."

"Finally."

Well, apparently everyone seemed pleased with this new turn of events.

"Now that I know that, perhaps I'll see what I can scrounge up." Ransom's head turned my way. "Are you planning a scene tonight?"

"Nope. Not tonight." I figured I could let my fuck toys wander around for the evening. A little free time since they'd done so well lately.

"Hmm." Ransom's head cocked to the side, the whites of his eyes glowing in the black light.

"What the hell does *hmm* mean?"

Ransom held up his hands. "Nothing. I'm just surprised. I figured you'd be getting the miles out of those toys while you had them." He put his hands on his hips. "Unless, of course, you're planning to keep them. In that case, there's no rush to wear them out."

"I'm not gonna keep them," I countered, although the words were bitter in my mouth.

"Right. Okay. Well, I guess if you're not going to entertain the masses tonight, perhaps I should." He scanned the area. "In order to do that, I'm gonna have to find some tough hide I can beat on. I'll check in with you later."

"Yeah. Later."

I watched as Ransom headed over to the section where he would be able to see the submissive selection for the evening. From my vantage point, I could see at least a dozen scantily clad submissives kneeling on pillows, waiting patiently for someone to acknowledge them.

Rarely did I ever have to seek out the kneeling population for entertainment purposes, but I certainly didn't miss having to find someone who might hold my interest for even a few minutes.

My gaze swung over to the pretty boy and the cowboy. They were standing by the bar talking to two other male submissives. I didn't recognize them so I figured they were new. Not that I would be able to tell either way because the masks were obscuring everyone's faces.

No, now that I'd found exactly what I'd been missing, I wondered if it was possible they'd be willing to keep me if I did decide to make this more than temporary. Could I? Would they want me for more than some interesting scenes?

That empty space in my chest ached at the thought. The last thing I wanted was to go through the hell of watching them walk away when they found out I was merely human.

Making that known seemed to be the fastest way for me to let someone down.

Brax
(The cowboy)

I HAD NO IDEA WHO this one guy was—aside from his name being Matt—or why he was following me and Case around like a lost puppy, but no matter how hard we tried to shake him, he wasn't getting the hint.

The other submissive with him—Gary—was a regular here. He seemed quite content to give Matt the lowdown on what was going on.

"That girl over there, she's a masochist," Gary explained. "Not hard-core like Case, though."

Case didn't look at either of them, but his eyes cut to me briefly. I knew he was getting tired of having an entourage.

"Hard-core, huh?" Matt prompted.

Case didn't respond.

"So, how long have you been members here?" Matt asked.

"I've been here a year," Gary informed him. "But I just recently was collared by my Mistress."

Matt nodded, then cast a quick look my way.

"A while," I replied, aiming for casual, uninterested. I was hoping he would take the hint.

"Interesting."

Why? Why was that interesting? He'd said that after nearly every answer we'd given him. If I didn't know better, I would think this was some sort of interrogation. And it was getting old quickly.

Unfortunately, Gary took that opportunity to excuse himself. That left me and Case with Matt and I knew the questions were going to keep coming.

Matt touched his neck. "I see you're both collared. By the same Dom? Male or female?"

"Yeah. And he's a Sadist," I answered, leaving the *what's it to you?* unspoken.

Matt turned his attention to Case. "So, you're a masochist, huh?"

Case didn't respond, simply glared back at the man through his mask. It was clear he was as sick of playing this game as I was.

"I think Zeke's tryin' to get our attention," I told Case. "It was nice to meet you, Matt."

"Zeke?" he asked, the whites of his eyes glowing through the mask. "Zeke Lautner? I'd heard a rumor he was a member here, but I didn't believe it."

Okay, this was going too far. I nudged Case away before Matt could launch another question at us. I knew Zeke wasn't trying to get our attention, but the least we could do was seek him out. It seemed a logical way to get away from the guy who had latched himself to our sides.

Zeke must've seen something that bothered him, because as soon as we approached, his mouth turned down in a grimace. "Something wrong?"

"No," I said quickly. "Just thought we'd check in. See if you needed anything."

"Well, I'll be damned."

Son of a bitch. I spun around to see Matt had followed us. "Look, man, I—"

"Long time no see, Zeke," Matt said, his voice deeper than before, his tone holding a condescending edge to it.

Zeke didn't say a word and I turned back to see him staring. In an instant, his mask was off and he was glaring at Matt.

"What the fuck are you doing here, Matt?"

Holy shit.

That wasn't a *hi, how are ya?* greeting. In fact, I was pretty sure there was steam coming out of Zeke's ears. Apparently they knew each other, and if that was the case, I didn't think it had ended well. And I suspected this wasn't one of those one-and-done scenarios where Zeke had beat on him, then dismissed him for someone else to take care of.

"Of all the kink clubs in all the world…" Matt stared at Zeke, leaving the sentence hanging.

I couldn't breathe for the amount of animosity pouring off Zeke. His back was rigid, his hands fisted at his sides

Matt glanced over at Case. "For a masochist, you sure don't have high standards, do you?"

Case spun to face Matt, his chest puffing up as he took a step closer to Matt. "*Excuse* me?"

I put my hand on Case's arm to hold him back. The last thing we needed was to throw down in the middle of Dichotomy. That was the fastest way to get booted out of the club. Forever.

Matt glared back at Case, going toe to toe with him. "With a reputation as a hard-core masochist, I'm surprised. That's all."

Case's mask came off and he inched closer to Matt. "Choose your words carefully," Case warned. "Because offending my—*Zeke*—is not somethin' I'll tolerate."

"Your Zeke?" Matt laughed. "Sounds about right. You seem more of the alpha in this relationship. Makes sense considering *your Zeke* loses that hard outer layer when he falls in love. Has he done that yet? Told you he loves you? Asked you to sleep in his bed? Because that's where I ended up. All I wanted was a Dom who could stay the course and be true to himself. Turns out, Zeke wasn't capable of that." Matt laughed and it had a sickening tone to it. "He ended up wanting more. Love and shit. I mean, *come on*. What real Sadist says I love you? That shit's for pussies."

Holy shit. This dude was delusional. What the fuck was he even talking about?

I turned to ask Zeke that very question only he wasn't there. I glanced around the crowded room but I didn't see him.

Suddenly Trent appeared and Case backed up.

"What's going on here?" the famous Dom asked. "Why aren't you wearing a mask?"

Case didn't respond, simply continued shooting daggers at Matt with his eyes.

"We're sorry, Master Ramsey," I said politely. "Case and I were just … going to the locker room."

Without waiting for Case to argue, I shoved him forward away from Matt.

"Don't you dare turn around," I hissed. "Keep moving."

"Who the fuck does he think he is?" Case snapped. "And who the hell let him in here?"

Those were good questions. Questions I didn't have answers for.

"Where's Zeke?" Case asked when we were heading up the stairs.

"When I turned around, he was gone."

"What the fuck? Did he leave?"

I didn't know for sure, but I suspected that to be the case. Whoever Matt was, he had a history with Zeke. And based on Matt's patronizing attitude, it hadn't ended on a good note.

Case stopped on the stairs as though he was going to turn back around.

"Come on, Case. Let's get changed. No way can we stay here and let that asshole start shit. I am not losin' my membership to this club."

Although, that was the least of my worries at the moment.

Case and I had to go to Zeke. We had to figure out what was going on and why he had bolted. That was very unlike him and I didn't like the thought of him being by himself.

Especially if he was hurting.

The man might've been hard-core and standoffish in most things he did, but he was as human as the rest of us. It was possible he didn't want people to know they had the power to hurt him, but he wasn't a superhero.

And Matt was a fucking moron if he seriously believed there was a single person out there who could shut himself down indefinitely.

Certainly not Zeke.

THIRTY

ZEKE

NOT ONLY WAS I A shitty Sadist, I was a shitty Dom in general.

The instant I had recognized Matt, I left my fuck toys at the club. Up and left them without a word.

Did I regret it?

No.

I was sure they'd gotten enough from Matt to know that I could never live up to their ridiculously high expectations. I could never be the man they believed me to be. Yes, I was fucking human. Yes, I had fallen in love with Matt and thought for some stupid fucking reason that I could spend the rest of my life with him.

I still remembered the day it had all gone to shit. It was forever etched in my memory.

"What's going on here?" Matt asked when he walked in my front door.

Finally. It felt as though I'd waited forever for him to get here. I couldn't explain the reasons for my nervous anticipation, but I was practically vibrating with energy. For the first time in a long time, excitement fueled me.

I had cooked dinner for the two of us, hoping for some quiet time at home. It was Friday and we generally went to the club, but I wanted something different, something more intimate. Although I knew he enjoyed it, I wasn't up to beating on him in front of dozens of people.

"I cooked," I told him with a smile.

He frowned, his body rigid as though he wasn't sure if he should stay or go. "What do you mean you cooked? Why aren't you ready for the club?"

"We're not going to the club." I figured that was enough of an explanation. Matt was the type who liked for me to be dominant in every aspect of our lives, including when I spoke to him. So, I would put my foot down this time.

"Why not?" His normally cool tone sounded slightly petulant, as though he was gearing up to argue like a teenager who'd been banned from going out.

He looked around as though I couldn't possibly find something to entertain us at my place. It was true, we rarely came here. Matt preferred to go to the club whenever it was open. Sometimes I felt as though I spent more time there than I did anywhere else.

Although I'd asked him to stay the night with me a few times, Matt had always turned me down, insisting that he liked the space we had because it made our encounters that much hotter. And he wasn't wrong. However, I'd started to want more than just the wild, rough sex we had. We'd been together for a year and a half to the day and I was ready to move things to the next level. Tonight, over the dinner I had worked hard to make, I was going to ask Matt to move in.

"Because I have other plans," I said simply. "Now, if you don't mind, I'd like to eat."

"If I don't mind?" He sounded horrified. "Are you asking me what I want?"

After placing the full plates on the table, I turned my attention to him. "I was being polite, Matt. If you want me to insist, I can certainly do that."

"Polite? You?"

All right. Something was up. "What does that mean?"

"You're the Dom, right? I didn't think I had a say."

"Of course you have a say," I explained. "If I led you to believe otherwise, I'm sorry."

His eyes widened. "You're sorry? *What the hell is going on, Zeke?"*

Now I was confused.

His voice rose an octave or two. "You made me dinner, you're asking me my preference and *you're apologizing. What the fuck is wrong with you?"*

"What do you mean what's wrong with me? I thought we'd have dinner at home tonight and forego the club."

"But that's not how this works."

He couldn't have punched me harder if he'd used his fists. Why was he arguing? And what the hell was the big deal? So I wanted to stay in tonight.

I knew my confusion was written all over my face. "How what works?"

"You. Me. This. I thought you were a Sadist, Zeke? I thought you were the Dom in this relationship."

"So, what? Because I'm a Sadist, I'm not supposed to want to have dinner with my boyfriend?"

Matt's eyes bugged out and he took a step back. "Your boyfriend? *I'm not your boyfriend. I'm your submissive, Zeke. Our relationship is Master and slave, remember?"*

"So you want me to tell you to sit your fucking ass down?" I shouted. "Is that what you want from me? I can't make you dinner or want to spend a night in with you?"

"For starters, yes. You're supposed to command me to do things. Not ask. And you damn sure don't apologize. What the fuck is wrong with you? Where's the hard-core man I've spent the past year and a half bowing to?"

"What do you mean where is he? I'm right here."

"And you're cooking and apologizing. That's not ... you, Zeke. You're the guy who flogs me because you need it. Because I need it. You don't make me dinner and you damn sure don't say you're sorry. Why? Why are you acting weird?"

"Because I'm human, Matt. I don't spend every minute of my day thinking about all the ways I want to torture you. I'm still a man, and I was looking forward to your company tonight. Without

having you strip in front of a club full of people while I hit you. Is that okay?"

"No!"

He took another step back, horror glinting in his eyes. As though he couldn't believe I would want something so normal.

"That's not how this works, Zeke."

"Then how does it work, Matt? Explain it to me. I've spent all this time falling in love with you and you're telling me that's not acceptable?"

If he could look more shocked, I would be surprised.

"You love me?" He said it like it was a bad word, as though he would be struck down for even thinking it.

I lowered my voice, wanting to reason with him. I wasn't sure why he was acting like me being normal was somehow blasphemous. Sure, our relationship hadn't been all that normal to begin with. We met at a kink club and we spent a lot of time there, but surely he didn't think that was all this was.

"Yes, Matt. I love you." I took a step closer, but he held up his hands.

"No, don't. I'm... I need to go."

Damn, my chest ached as though he'd wrapped his hand around my heart and squeezed. "Matt...?"

He held my gaze. "Obviously, this isn't working because ... you're not who I thought you were." He motioned toward the table. "You, me, dinner. We don't do things like that."

"We've had dinner plenty of times," I argued.

"Sure. But only when you command me to cook. I thought you wanted that. For me to serve you." He shook his head again. "This isn't what I signed on for, Zeke."

"Signed on for?"

"Yeah. You know. The contract I signed. That's why I'm here, right? Because I'm obligated to serve you. That's what I agreed to. Why you're claiming you love me when I know you're not capable of love... It doesn't make sense."

"Why would I not be capable of love?"

Matt's face fell and I could practically read his thoughts, so I filled in for him.

"Because I'm a monster, right? That's why I can't love you? Because I get off on hitting you. That makes me less than human?"

"You're not who I thought you were, Zeke. I'm sorry, but ... I can't do this. It's not what I agreed to."

That night, Matt walked out of my house and completely out of my life. Eighteen months I had spent with him and he never looked back. A couple of days later, I went to the club we were members of at the time only to find out he had cancelled his membership.

That was four years ago.

I had learned my lesson that night. While the masochists wanted the Sadist, they didn't want me. And no matter how hard I tried not to be, I was still human. I had feelings and Matt had crushed them with his insanity.

I never attempted to find him after that, choosing to lock it all up. Matt was the reason the monster was born. He was the reason I chose not to allow myself to get close.

Tonight was a reminder of that and his timing was impeccable.

Just when I thought I might open myself up again, he showed up and reminded me why that would be the biggest mistake of my life. Because losing Matt was hard, but losing Brax and Case...

Damn it. And now I was thinking about them by name?

I wasn't sure I would survive them turning their backs on me when they figured out I wasn't some fucking show horse. I couldn't always be on display, acting the role they'd cast me in.

Which meant I had to be the one to put an end to this.

It was the only way.

Case

(The pretty boy)

AFTER WE CHANGED BACK INTO street clothes, Brax called for an Uber. The drive back to Zeke's was weird. Brax didn't want to talk, and for some reason, the driver didn't want to turn on music, so we sat in the eerie silence as each mile crept by.

Finally, we arrived back at Zeke's, but from the driveway, it looked as though no one was home. Since Zeke's truck was out front, I knew he was there. I'd learned over the past four weeks that Zeke was rather predictable. If he wasn't home, he was at work or at the club. He had breakfast with Jamie every Friday, and aside from having lunch out, he ate every meal at the house. He spent his extra time working out or playing with his dog.

"Maybe we should give him some space," I told Brax when I climbed out of the car. "It's obvious he's upset about something."

"And we're gonna find out what it is," Brax insisted. "We're not turnin' our backs on him now, Case. He deserves more than that from us."

Maybe, but that didn't mean the man would welcome our interference. He was a very private man and he didn't open up to many people.

I knew Brax was right, but that didn't mean I was eager to go inside and confront Zeke. He wasn't the sort to run from anything, so clearly Matt had meant something to him. At some point, anyway.

The thought didn't sit well with me. I didn't like the idea of Matt and Zeke together. No, I had no claim on Zeke, but ... well, to be honest, I cared about the surly man. A lot. A lot more than I was willing to admit, even. I wanted more time with him. I wasn't ready for this to end.

The Uber driver pulled away and Brax and I had no choice but to confront this situation head on. When we stepped inside the house, I found myself fingering the collar around my neck.

"I've got a bad feeling about this, Brax," I whispered, my eyes taking a moment to adjust to the darkness.

"Zeke?" Brax called out. "Where are you?"

All the lights were off but I could hear the music coming from the basement.

I closed and locked the door behind me, then motioned Brax toward the stairs. With a nod, Brax led the way.

Every step felt like I was trudging through quicksand. I wasn't sure what we'd find when we reached the bottom and I wasn't sure I wanted to know.

We found Zeke pacing the floor, a fifty-pound dumbbell in each hand. He had removed his shirt and his shoes, his muscles flexing, sweat coating his skin, as though he'd been working out for hours. Since it hadn't been that long since his confrontation with Matt, it meant Zeke was doubling his efforts. I knew that was his way of dealing with stress. He didn't drink or smoke like some people. Instead, he abused his muscles with endless hours of working out.

"Zeke?" Brax repeated. "Can we talk?"

Those black eyes shot over toward us but there was absolutely no emotion in them. The light was completely gone. It wasn't until that moment that I realized how much Zeke had changed over the past month we'd spent with him. While he'd never struck me as the angry type, there had always been something missing. A lack of interest, maybe. But the more time we were with him, the more he seemed to change.

I wanted that man back.

"Nothing to talk about," he grumbled as he placed the weights back on the rack.

Brax moved over to the radio and turned it down.

"Why'd you leave?" Brax questioned.

Zeke frowned as he glared back at him. "Why're you asking so many damn questions?"

"Because I'm worried," Brax replied, sounding as though he expected a perfectly rational conversation to result from this.

Zeke didn't look rational right now. He looked ... hurt.

"About what?" Zeke barked a laugh, but it was laced with venom, not humor. "Did you get an earful from Matt? Did he tell you how the big, bad Sadist was actually a pussy because he'd gone and fallen in love with him four years ago? Did he tell you he walked out on me because I wanted something more? Because I'd been a fool and I told him I fucking loved him?"

Actually, no. Matt hadn't shared that much because I'd taken offense to his comments.

"No," Brax explained, "but Trent and I managed to keep Case from killing him if that makes you feel better."

Zeke's hands were vibrating, his eyes cold. "It doesn't make me feel better."

"How long were you with him?" the brave man at my side questioned.

I couldn't believe Brax was interrogating Zeke. In all the time we'd been here, never had either one of us asked as many questions as he had in the past three minutes.

"Does it matter? Is there a certain amount of time before I'm allowed to—" Zeke waved his hand. "It doesn't fucking matter and it's none of your damn business," Zeke shouted as he gripped his head and turned away. "I think it's time the two of you left. Tonight you can stay in one of the guest rooms, but I'll need you both gone tomorrow."

I felt a strange ache in my chest. It was similar to the way I felt when Brax had doubts about our relationship. The thought of not seeing Zeke again, not spending time with him in any capacity made my stomach churn. Why were we being punished because Matt was a dickhead?

"No," Brax snapped. "We're not leaving."

Zeke spun around and stalked toward us, his hands fisted at his sides. "You care to repeat that, fuck toy?"

"I said no." Brax's words were as rigid as his body. "We're not leaving you, Zeke. You can push us away, but it's not gonna work."

Zeke reached for Brax first, his hand coming around his throat. I thought for a second he was going to strangle him, but he wasn't. His other hand was reaching for the key on the chain around his neck, which meant Zeke was trying to release the latch on the collar.

Brax jerked out of his hold, knocking his hand away. "You're not taking my collar."

In all the time I'd known him, never had I seen Brax as serious as he was right then. When Zeke's eyes darted my way, I shook my head. "You're not taking mine, either."

"Fine. Keep the damn things." Zeke grabbed the silver chain on his neck—the one he kept the collar keys on—and ripped it off before throwing it at Brax. "But I still want you gone. The contract's void from this moment forward."

"No, it's not," Brax stated, his voice rising. "I'm not lettin' you out of it that easily. Just because some little shithead comes into a club and thinks he knows every goddamn thing. No way, Zeke. I don't give a fuck who he was to you. I don't care about your past, the same way you don't care about mine. That doesn't mean I'm willin' to walk away. That's not how this works."

"That's *exactly* how it works!" Zeke bellowed. "I don't have time for your shit anymore, Brax!"

My heart slammed into my ribs the second Brax's name was out of Zeke's mouth. Not once in the entire time we'd known Zeke had he ever called either of us by name. I'd picked up on that a long time ago. He had no issues referring to the people close to him by name, but everyone else wasn't allowed that privilege.

A noise from upstairs caught my attention and I realized it was Tank. He was whining, a pleading sound that I'd never heard before.

Zeke's eyes widened and I swore that was fear I saw on his face.

The next thing I knew, Zeke was racing up the stairs while Brax and I ran after him.

Tank was standing by the front door. Another whine followed by a low woof. Then another. Within seconds, Tank was growling and barking ferociously.

When the doorbell rang, I damn near came out of my skin. With all the lights off and the dog going crazy, it scared the shit out of me.

"Tank, heel," Zeke commanded.

Tank's ass hit the floor but he remained where he was, continuing to growl, his eyes forward, tail straight. The dog looked as fierce as his owner.

I prayed there wasn't some unsuspecting trick-or-treaters on the other side of that door. If there was, they were going to get a surprise. Then again, I wasn't sure which was worse. The growling dog or the growling man.

Zeke jerked the front door open and you would never fucking guess who was darkening Zeke's front door.

The very man who obviously was looking for me to kick his ass. After all, why else would he be here?

THIRTY-ONE

ZEKE

SON OF A FUCKING BITCH.

"What the fuck do you want, Matt?" I snapped when my eyes registered who was standing on my front porch.

Matt smiled. "Trick or treat?"

I glared back at him, not amused by his childish antics. I wasn't in the mood for his shit. In fact, I wasn't in the mood for him, period. I could've spent the rest of my life happy never seeing him again.

He must've realized I wasn't in the joking mood because he followed with, "Can we talk?"

"No. I have nothing to say to you."

"But I have a lot to say to you, Zeke." His tone softened, his amusement gone. "Please. Let me come in."

Knowing I would never get him to leave otherwise, I took a step back and motioned him inside. "You've got three minutes. Then your ass needs to be gone."

Matt moved past me, his eyes instantly going to the pretty boy and the cowboy, who were still there, completely ignoring every command I'd made tonight.

"Would you mind giving us some privacy?" Matt asked them in that haughty tone that irritated me.

"No," Brax snapped. The man had shocked me with his backbone tonight. He wasn't backing down from me and he clearly wasn't backing down from Matt.

"No, they can't," I stated firmly. "Whatever you have to say, they can hear it."

Matt's wary gaze turned toward me, and I flipped on the living room light.

His eyes scanned the room as though he was looking to see what was different from the last time he was here. He wouldn't find anything because I'd left it exactly the way it had been. Since he'd rarely been to my house, I had never associated it with him.

Matt turned back to me, his gaze darting to them briefly before finally coming to rest on me again. "Is this thing with them serious?"

"They're of no concern to you. Now tell me what you came here to tell me."

He was silent for a moment, his eyes never leaving my face. Like all those years ago, I saw the man behind that front, the man I thought had given a shit about me. But he was the same man who had walked out on me, taking my heart and smashing it into pieces on his way out the door.

"I didn't know you were a member of Dichotomy, Zeke. I honestly was just looking for a new place to play."

"Funny," the cowboy snarled. "You said you'd heard a rumor he was there."

Matt glared at him, then shot a pleading look to me. "I didn't believe it. And I don't want you to think I've been stalking you or anything."

"Never crossed my mind," I answered truthfully. "You're the one who left me, remember?"

He nodded, his eyes softening. "And I've regretted that every single second since that night, Zeke."

"I didn't get the feeling you gave a shit," the pretty boy said. "Based on the bullshit coming out of your mouth at the club."

Matt rolled his eyes at the pretty boy. "I was caught off guard. It was a knee-jerk reaction."

"Not buyin' it," the cowboy stated.

Matt turned back to me and motioned around him, a small smile forming on his lips. "We were standing right here that night. Remember, Zeke? You made me dinner, told me you loved me, and I ... I ruined it."

"That you did," I confirmed.

My chest constricted as those fucking feelings ghosted through me. I had long ago gotten over Matt, but the memories still hurt. I certainly didn't feel an ounce of love for him now.

"I love you, Zeke," Matt said, his tone so soft, so irritating. It was a lie. I knew because I could read him like a fucking book. "I should've told you that night but I didn't. You scared me and I ... I wanted to tell you I loved you back, but I panicked."

I laughed, a sound I imagined the devil made. "You have a fucking strange way of showing it."

"I've wanted to find you—"

"You knew where I lived," I said, cutting him off.

"I know. But I knew you were mad. I thought maybe—"

"You thought that waiting *four years* and accidentally bumping into me was the perfect time for you to come over here and spout this bullshit?"

"It's not bullshit, Zeke!" Matt's temper flared. "I saw you tonight and it all came back."

I watched him, noticing the way his eyes continued to dart over to the cowboy and the pretty boy. It was as though he was enjoying the fact that they were here.

And then it hit me.

They were the reason he was here. Matt didn't want me because I couldn't live up to his standards, but he didn't want anyone else to have me, either.

He confirmed my suspicion when he said, "They shouldn't be wearing your collar, Zeke. I should. That's my right, my privilege. Not theirs."

I glanced down at his neck. "Looks to me like you discarded it long ago."

Matt started to open his mouth but quickly closed it.

I was beginning to think Matt had some psychological issues. I'd thought so the night he left. The way he had turned on me so quickly. It wasn't normal. This wasn't either. I hadn't seen or heard from him in four years and he just drove over here to confess his true feelings. Nope. Like the cowboy said, I wasn't buying it.

"You need to go," the pretty boy said, his tone far more rigid than it'd been before.

"This isn't your house," Matt countered.

The cowboy stepped forward, that same temper he'd lashed me with shining through. "No, but Zeke is our Dom and we have every right to protect him from those who want to hurt him."

I swallowed hard, floored by how ballsy the cowboy was. He'd confronted me in the basement and he was standing up for me here. Not that I needed him to, but I was so shocked by his words I couldn't speak. I'd seen a couple of different sides to him over the past few weeks, but this was new.

Matt's voice lowered. "I'm not here to hurt him. I'm here to get him back. I never should've left."

The pretty boy was the one who stepped forward this time. "But you did. And that dumb-ass move is something you have to live with for the rest of your life. It's time for you to go."

Matt's pleading eyes shot to me, but I shrugged as I turned and headed toward the back door. I needed some air.

"Come on, Tank," I commanded and my best friend fell into step with me.

Once on the back porch, I dropped onto the top step and stared into the inky darkness. It was cold, but I ignored the chill. Adrenaline was still racing in my veins. Anger, disappointment, frustration. It churned inside me, making me feel sick. But it wasn't directed at my fuck toys or even Matt. I was disappointed with myself. How I'd reacted tonight. I shouldn't have left them but I didn't know what else to do. Seeing Matt again had fucked me up, caught me off guard.

Who the fuck was I kidding? I hadn't even thought of them in that moment. I was completely selfish. I didn't want to deal with Matt's shit, so I had worried about only myself.

Just another thing that made me human. Something else that would have the fuck toys turning away because I couldn't give them what they needed all the time.

Tank returned to my side, placing his head on my chest as he stared up at me.

"What's up, boy?" I asked. "Too much disruption for one night? I doubt you'll have to worry about it for long. They'll all be gone soon."

"No, we won't," a voice said from behind me. "Matt's gone and he's not coming back, but we're not leaving."

I peered back at the cowboy over my shoulder. "You don't know when to quit, do you?"

"Actually, no. That's not in my repertoire of skills. I do make a mean *pasta e fagioli* though."

I didn't have the energy to fight with them anymore tonight. I needed to sleep and perhaps everything would look different in the morning.

Pushing to my feet, I turned to face the two men standing there. "Look. I know you don't have anywhere to go right this minute, so you're welcome to stay here. I've got guest rooms. One or two, your preference. When you find something, just let me know."

I started to walk into the house, but they blocked my path.

"We're not sleepin' in the guest room," the pretty boy stated.

"Whatever." I didn't care if they slept outside. That was their prerogative.

"You have two choices," the cowboy said.

I glared back at him. "Do I?"

"Yes." He squared his shoulders. "Either we continue our nightly routine and we sleep *under* your bed where you want us"—he paused, his eyes scanning my face—"or we're sleepin' *in* your bed. Those are your choices."

I barked a laugh because this was fucking ridiculous. "My bed?"

"Yes," they both said at the same time.

"You'd risk my punishment to defy me?"

"Yes," the cowboy stated. "If you want to dress me up like a dog or a fucking pony, I don't care. But we're not leaving. Not like this. If you truly want us gone, we'll go. However, that won't be until you're acting civilized and under different circumstances. We won't let you push us away because some dickhead was stupid enough to walk out on you years ago. That's on him. Not you."

Rage fizzed in my veins. They were standing up to me and it pissed me off. I preferred the fuck toys who took instruction, not the ones who thought they knew me.

"You feel the same?" I asked the pretty boy.

"I do. I've always believed things happen for a reason. We're here because we were meant to be in your path and you in ours."

I was too tired to argue about this anymore. Shrugging, I motioned them back into the house. "Whatever you feel you need to do. I don't give a shit anymore."

While I wanted that to be true, I knew it wasn't.

And I suspected they knew it, too.

Brax
(The cowboy)

WHILE I WANTED TO PUSH Zeke to his breaking point, I knew it was best to back off. But only a little. And only for tonight.

However, I still wasn't allowing him to push us away.

When Zeke went upstairs, I followed him. When he went into his bedroom, I was there, too. I waited until he had gone into his closet to change. When he returned, I was standing beside his bed with the chastity device in my hand. He cast a quick look at it, but then ignored me, walking around to the other side of the bed.

I was serious when I told him we weren't sleeping in the guest room.

So, to prove my point, I got into the bed when he did.

"What the fuck are you doing?" he growled, his black eyes slamming into me.

"Going to sleep."

Case didn't seem quite as eager to earn Zeke's wrath, but he finally complied, climbing into the bed behind me.

Zeke flopped back on the mattress, pretending to ignore us. I knew he couldn't, because for the four weeks we'd been with him, not once had we slept in his bed. Not like this, anyway. The time he dressed me up like a dog didn't count as far as I was concerned.

"Get out of my bed," he said, but there was no conviction in his tone.

"No." I didn't care what he did to me at that point, I wasn't backing down. I knew Zeke would toss us out at the first opportunity and I wasn't going to let him do it. Not without a fight. He needed to know we wanted more from him than to simply be his playthings when he wanted to entertain himself.

"Fuck toys don't argue," Zeke stated, his tone harder.

"We're not your fuck toys right now," I clarified.

He bolted upright, then shot out of the bed. "The hell you're not."

This was the Zeke I could work with. The man behind the mask. The man who needed more than to beat on people. Beneath that crusty outer later was a man whose heart beat the same as mine did. A man very much like me and Case. A man with feelings. One who needed to know we were there for him. Not because he commanded us to be but because we wanted to be.

Knowing this could backfire on me in a big way, I inched out of the bed on Zeke's side and came to stand toe to toe with him. I had to look up into his face to do it, but I didn't care.

"Right now, I'm not your fuck toy," I told him. "And you're not my Dom."

His eyes searched my face as though he was looking for the lie.

"We're here because we want to be here, Zeke," I stated, lowering my voice. I reached up and placed my hand on his wrist. "I'm sorry Matt hurt you. And I'm sorry he showed up tonight. But I'm not gonna let him ruin this."

"There's nothing for him to ruin," Zeke said, but his tone had softened. "We all knew this was going to end at some point."

"No," I argued. "We didn't. Perhaps you did, but Case and I … we don't want this to end."

I knew I was assuming Case felt the same way I did, but I didn't care about that, either. I knew Case on a primal level and I knew how he felt about Zeke without him having to tell me.

"What do you want from me?" Zeke asked, his words softer than I'd ever heard them.

At some point between seeing Matt at the club and right this minute, Zeke's armor had been stripped away. He wasn't the Sadist and we weren't his fuck toys.

"We want all of you, Zeke," I told him. "Not just the man who forces us to wear chastity devices because he owns our dicks. Not just the man who comes up with creative ways to get us to come."

I moved my hand up Zeke's arm, surprised when he didn't pull away.

"Believe it or not, we're not submissives all the time, either. Right now, I'm just a man, Zeke. Just like you. And I…" I swallowed back the emotion. "I don't like the idea of not having you in my life."

"I didn't agree to this," he said, his eyes still searching my face as though he was seeking the truth.

"That's fair. You didn't. You warned us up front that you weren't in it for a relationship or for commitment." My hand moved higher and I gripped his bicep. "We agreed to your terms, Zeke. But somewhere along the way, it changed."

"Not for me," he countered.

Case appeared beside me. "Liar."

Zeke's eyes shot over to him. I couldn't read his expression but I could tell he was trying to figure out what the point was. Why we were being persistent about this.

"We didn't abide by your rules, Zeke," I admitted. "We couldn't. It's not possible when we had the opportunity to get to know you."

"You don't know me," he snapped.

I kept a firm grip on his arm and closed the space between us. We were so close he couldn't keep his eyes on my face. His beard was brushing against my lips.

"Look at me," I demanded.

He shifted his head down, and when he did, I kissed him.

At first, I thought he would shove me away, but he didn't. Zeke merely stood there, his lips firm, his hands still hanging down to his sides.

"Tell me you didn't feel anything," I whispered when I pulled back.

I felt Case shift, his hand sliding over mine when he moved to stand behind Zeke.

"I didn't," Zeke said, but there wasn't any truth in his words.

Case's hands slid between my chest and Zeke's. He was wrapping his arms around Zeke, holding him in place. Not because he thought he would bolt but because he wanted to be as close to Zeke as I was. I couldn't blame him. This thing between us might've started out as a game, but it wasn't a game anymore.

Now came the hard part.

Convincing Zeke to take a chance when I could still see in his eyes that he wasn't going to give an inch.

THIRTY-TWO

ZEKE

DESPITE THAT INNER DESIRE TO want more than I knew they could give, giving in would only end up hurting the three of us in the long run.

I wasn't an idiot. I knew the cowboy and the pretty boy wanted something more from me. Perhaps one night would slake the lust, give them the rush of having conquered the big, bad Sadist, but it wouldn't last.

I placed my hand on the cowboy's where he was clutching my arm. For a moment, I let the warmth of him seep in. I felt the pretty boy's arms wrapping around me. I felt safe with them for the first time in a long time. However, I couldn't bank on that for eternity.

Which meant I had to do the three of us the favor of ending it now.

I easily pried the cowboy's hand from my bicep.

"This is nonnegotiable," I told him, my eyes locked with his once more. "I'm not willing to give more than I agreed to. It's best we end it now."

With that, I worked my way out from between them and whistled for Tank to follow. They could sleep in my bed for all I cared. I had plenty of other beds in this house. And worst case, I could always sleep on the couch.

"If you follow me," I warned, "I will make you leave tonight. So, for your own sakes, just leave me alone."

To reiterate my point, I closed my bedroom door, effectively shutting them completely out.

That was the only way this could go.

I was sure they would see that by morning.

Friday, November 2

As I sat at my desk, I stared down at my cell phone.

It had been buzzing endlessly since six o'clock this morning. My sister was evidently pissed at me for not being home when she came by for breakfast. I couldn't blame her. However, I also couldn't stand the idea of listening to her interrogate me about all the shit going on in my life. No doubt she was aware of the issues I was having with the cowboy and the pretty boy. Based on her texts, they'd filled her in on the situation with Matt, too.

Jamie: *I'm on my way to your office. You better be there when I get there, Zeke.*

Son of a bitch. I didn't think she'd actually come after me. She should be getting ready for her class right about now.

Zeke: *I'm not in the office. I'll check in with you later tonight.*

Not even a minute later, my cell phone buzzed again.

Jamie: *Too late for lies, big brother. I called Dale. He confirmed you're in. Do not move.*

Damn it. The kid was too smart for her own good.

A body appeared in my doorway and I looked up to see Greg standing there.

"What's up?" I asked, going for nonchalant.

"That's supposed to be *my* question." Without waiting for an invitation, he stepped into the office. "Need to talk?"

"About?"

"For starters, what went down at the club on Wednesday."

"Nothing went down," I assured him. "I had some things to take care of."

"Yeah?" He dropped into the chair across from me. "That's why Trent informed me I'd made a serious mistake by approving a certain submissive's membership."

I shrugged. "I don't know what you're talking about."

"Matt Steinberg. Name ring a bell?"

I didn't move, didn't so much as blink. "Actually, no."

"Shit, Zeke," he said in a rush as he leaned forward. "I had no idea who he was."

I sighed because it was clear Edge wasn't going to let this go. "It's not your fault. Not like I'm big on sharing details of my past."

"Well, if it's any consolation, I've revoked his membership because of the incident on Wednesday."

I couldn't deny I felt better knowing that. The last thing I wanted was to have to stop going to Dichotomy because he was going to be there. I didn't have a stake in the club, but it had become my safe haven, the one place I could go and not worry about anyone trying to get up in my business.

"Trent had a conversation with him before he left. From what I gathered, it wasn't good."

I nodded. "Matt showed up at my house that night."

"Damn it." Edge looked sincerely distraught. "I'm sorry, man."

"No need to apologize. It's been taken care of."

"How about Brax and Case? They cool?"

I shrugged again. I honestly didn't know how they were because I was avoiding them. The only thing I knew was that they were still sleeping beneath my bed although I refused to go back into the room. With the weekend coming, I knew keeping my distance would be more difficult to do, but I had no choice.

Edge leaned back in his chair. "Don't tell me you booted them because of Matt."

"Not because of Matt, no."

Edge sighed and rolled his eyes. "Where are they now?"

They were at my house. I knew that because I'd heard them talking this morning. They had nothing on their agenda, so they were sticking close. I didn't tell Edge that. "Who knows."

"Have you talked to them?"

I sat up, feeling the stirrings of irritation. I didn't like all the questions. "Nothing to talk about. They've run their course. I'm ready to move on. I warned them already so it's not a surprise."

Edge laughed, a hard, unamused sound. "You honestly think I'm buying this bullshit?"

My eyebrows shot downward, anger replacing the irritation. "I don't give a shit what you're buying, Edge."

Before he could blast me with whatever was about to come out of his mouth, a knock sounded and I turned to see Jamie standing in the doorway. Her eyes darted from me to Edge, then back.

"I don't mean to interrupt," she said softly, her eyes once again swinging over to Edge.

There was something on her face I'd never seen before. Something I wasn't fond of seeing now.

Edge pushed to his feet. "He's all yours, Jamie. Maybe you can talk some sense into him."

I watched their interaction, the way Edge moved toward her, the simple touch he offered as his fingers brushed her arm. My eyes narrowed and I wanted to beat him to a bloody pulp for touching her so intimately.

"Come find me when you're finished with him," Edge said softly.

"Bullshit!" I shot to my feet. "She's not gonna come find you, Edge."

Electric-blue eyes shot to my face. "I wasn't asking your permission, Zeke."

"Stop. Please," Jamie pleaded, placing her hand on Edge's arm. "I'll come find you when I'm done."

That seemed to placate Edge because he shot me a quick glare before disappearing down the hall.

Jamie stepped into the room and closed the door behind her. When she turned back to me, she pointed toward my chair. "Sit down. We need to talk."

For fuck's sake. Why the hell did everyone insist on telling me what to do?

Hesitating briefly, I finally sat when she positioned herself in the chair Edge had vacated.

"I stopped by your house this morning," she said. "The boys said you left early."

"They should be gone by now," I muttered, then glanced down at the desk.

"They're not leaving," she replied.

"When I give them no choice, they will," I assured her, meeting her determined gaze.

She sighed, then settled into the chair. "I heard what happened with Matt. I'm sorry you had to run into him again, Zeke."

"It's no big deal."

"The hell it's not." She pointed at me. "Look at yourself, Zeke. You're a mess. Last Friday, you were actually happy. And now, you look like shit."

"Tell me how you really feel," I snapped.

"Fine. I will." Jamie sat up straight. "I think you've found something that completes you, Zeke. Was I surprised when I found out you'd taken two submissives? Absolutely. But it made so much sense. You're a difficult man to deal with, so I get how it would take two men to handle you. And those men … Brax and Case … they're the real deal."

"You don't know a damn thing about them," I countered.

"Oh, but I do. For one, I spent the morning with them. When you weren't there to take me to breakfast, I took them. And we talked. They're good guys and"—Jamie smiled—"they think you hung the moon."

"The hell they do."

"Okay, fine. Maybe they didn't say as much, but I see it when they talk about you."

"They shouldn't be talking about me."

Jamie sighed heavily. "Will you quit being hardheaded and just listen?"

"I don't like what you have to say," I said truthfully.

"That's never stopped me before, Zeke." Her eyes narrowed. "And yes, I'm sure you'll tell me it's not my place to interfere, but that's exactly what I'm about to do, so you can shut up and listen to me."

This bossy shit was starting to get on my nerves. First the cowboy, now my sister. They were both overstepping in a big way.

However, I didn't say a word.

Case
(The pretty boy)

THIS THING WITH ZEKE WAS bothering Brax more than he was letting on. Or rather, more than he was saying, anyway. I'd known the man long enough I could read every one of his expressions, and the one he'd been sporting the past couple of days was filled with hurt.

After breakfast, I proceeded to clean Zeke's kitchen, feeling slightly out of place. I knew the man wanted us to leave. For the past two nights, he had slept in one of the guest rooms, avoiding us at all costs. This morning, I had intended to corner him during his workout, but by the time I woke up, he was gone.

And no, Brax and I hadn't slept in Zeke's bed. That had been a challenge, and since Zeke hadn't fallen for it, we had opted not to push our luck. However, we had slept in the cage beneath it. Perhaps that made us far more warped and twisted than I'd originally thought, but it was what it was. I wouldn't apologize for it.

Only now, I knew we had to do something. And by something, I meant we needed to find a place to live. Intruding on Zeke's personal space wasn't right. He'd insisted that we leave and I knew it was best for all of us if we did.

"I'm gonna take a shower," Brax announced after he'd placed the last of the dirty dishes on the counter.

I nodded, then worked double time to get everything cleaned up. I had every intention of joining Brax.

A few minutes later, after I'd stuffed everything into the dishwasher, I wiped my hands, tossed the towel, then jogged up the stairs. I heard the water running in the guest bathroom in the hall, so I went that direction.

I found Brax already in the shower, his head down between his shoulders as he stood beneath the spray. As quietly as I could, I stripped, then stepped inside with him. He didn't so much as lift his head, although I knew he heard me.

Stepping up behind him, I wrapped my arms around his waist and pulled him into me.

"You okay?" I whispered.

"No. Not even a little bit."

I released him, then turned him to face me. "Look at me, Brax."

Emerald eyes lifted to my face. "Remember how you felt when we stepped into that apartment?"

Oh, I remembered all right. It wasn't a feeling I would likely forget. "As though the walls were closing in," I said.

"Exactly." A wave of sadness clouded his eyes. "That's how I feel right now."

"Because of Zeke."

He nodded. "I didn't see this coming."

I did, but I wasn't going to tell him that. I had known from the very beginning that Zeke Lautner was temporary. And not only because he said as much. I knew it because that was how they all worked. Ever since I was seventeen and unwillingly sucked into a world I hadn't known existed, it had all been the same for me. The very first man to hit me never should've been touching me in the first place. But that hadn't stopped him. He'd taken what he needed and I had suffered only to come out the other side needing things I couldn't explain. Despite the inappropriateness of it all, it hadn't stopped me, either.

Since then, I'd searched for something to ease the constant pain that filled me. Unfortunately, the only thing that ever worked was more pain. It obliterated my mind, allowed me to forget a time in my life that had forever changed me.

The Doms I'd played with since found me to be a challenge. They were always gung-ho in the beginning, trying to find a way to break the man who couldn't be broken. The sad part was, they never realized I already was broken. Apparently, I was good at hiding the fact that I was shattered in a way no one could fix. The only person who'd come close was Brax.

But the Doms I ended up with were always temporary. They stuck around until they didn't. While none of them could give me quite what Zeke could, some of them had tried. A couple had even attempted to break me. But they were all the same. The glitter always wore off and they moved on to someone else.

So, I had expected as much from Zeke, because in the end, they were all the same.

Cupping Brax's face, I leaned in closer. "We have to respect what Zeke wants. This is his house. He invited us here and now he's asked us to leave."

"I don't want to leave him," Brax whispered. "I don't know that I can."

I swallowed hard because the emotion I saw in his eyes tore me up from the inside out. I knew Brax had feelings for Zeke, but thinking it and hearing it were two very different things.

"I know, babe," I told him.

"Do you? Are you ready to wash your hands of him?"

"No." That much was true. "But it's not up to me."

"I fell for him, Case." That admission threatened to choke me. "I wasn't supposed to, but I did."

Not knowing what to do, I released Brax and took a step back. "You love him?"

"I don't know." Brax looked sincerely torn.

I should've seen this coming. It was all my fault. I pushed us in this direction and now Brax wanted far more than I could ever give him. It was bad enough when it was merely about the kink.

Now, I felt as though I was being pushed out of his heart. That was the one place I'd always felt as though I belonged.

I nodded. "I ... uh ... I need..." I couldn't finish the statement, so I simply stepped out of the shower and grabbed a towel.

The water didn't turn off and Brax didn't come after me. He didn't so much as call my name.

My chest constricted, a tight band coiling inside, threatening to send me to my knees. Of all the ways I saw this playing out, this certainly wasn't one of them. Sure, I'd feared something would come between Brax and me eventually, but I never thought it would be my own darkness that would steal him away.

And that was what happened. I'd found something in Zeke that I couldn't find anywhere else and I had pushed Brax to explore it. I'd felt things for Zeke I hadn't wanted to feel. And yes, I'd fallen for him, too, but I knew those feelings were better left alone. He was never going to be permanent in my life.

And now it appeared Brax wasn't going to be, either.

THIRTY-THREE

ZEKE

"YOU CAN'T TURN YOUR BACK on them, Zeke," Jamie pleaded.

She had spent the past twenty minutes attempting to make me see reason. The only thing I saw was a kid sister sticking her nose where it didn't belong.

"They've got each other," I told her. "They don't need me."

Even as I said it, the words hurt.

Jamie's eyes widened. "Is that what you think? That you're the third wheel here?"

"It's not what I think, Jamie. It's what I know. They'll find another Dom who can give them what they need. I'm done."

My sister's cheeks darkened and I could feel the anger inside her. I rarely saw her pissed off, but it appeared I'd pushed her to her breaking point.

Her voice lowered. "You're an asshole, Zeke."

"Yes, I am." That wasn't news to me.

"Have you talked to them *at all?*"

"No." And that was the whole point. I wasn't supposed to get close to them.

"Do you honestly not see that all *three of you* are the third wheel?"

That made absolutely no sense.

"That's what happens when three people are in a relationship, Zeke. There's no longer a couple. It's now a triad. It's hard enough for two people to form a bond. When there's three … it requires more work."

Jamie sounded oddly as though she knew from experience. I kept my eyes pinned on her. "How do you know that?"

For a moment, she broke the staring contest, her gaze dropping to her lap.

"Just trust me, Zeke. You have to put effort into any relationship."

"See, that's where you're confused," I stated hotly. "There's not a relationship here."

Her anger was back. "*Bullshit!* I've seen the way they look at you. And I've seen the way you look at them. You might want to pretend you don't care, but you're full of shit."

We were back to that again. Jamie had ensured she told me as much several times throughout this ridiculous conversation.

"I have work to do," I told her as I sat up in my chair. "I get that you're pissed at me, but you're not gonna change my mind."

"Have you ever asked Case why he needs you to hit him?" she asked, her tone suddenly changing.

I frowned. "Why would I?"

Her eyes softened. "There's something you don't know about him, Zeke."

I tried to hide my curiosity as best I could, but my sister saw through it. Still, I kept my mouth shut.

"After the first time I came over and I found out they were living with you, I decided to do some digging. I know how you are. I know you don't refer to them by name because you want to keep your distance. Which meant I had to be the one to protect you in the event they weren't on the up and up."

"You watch too much television," I told her. "I'm capable of taking care of myself."

"Oh, I know. And what I found out certainly doesn't put you at risk. However, I get the feeling Brax doesn't even know."

I kept my expression neutral. I wanted her to tell me, but I wasn't about to ask.

"Because if he did," Jamie continued, "he wouldn't expect Case to sleep in a cage beneath your bed."

I frowned.

"Yes, I know about that, Zeke." She rolled her eyes. "You might think I'm some sweet, innocent kid, but I've got as much darkness in me as you do. Only mine doesn't involve me wanting to hit someone or have them hit me. Why do you think I pursued psychology?"

"Because it interests you."

"It does. The human brain is fascinating. The way people respond to their surroundings, how they deal with the things that happen to them … I find it riveting. But it was my own desires that drove me to pursue it, Zeke. I've never once wondered why you want to beat on a submissive. I never questioned it. That says as much about me as it does about you. However, I think some have reasons. Not everyone is simply born with those desires. I don't think I was. And I think Case's experiences have made him the way he is, too."

Fucking hell. This was a conversation I could've lived my entire life without having. It wasn't so much what Jamie said about Case that bothered me. More so what she was admitting about herself. I'd always seen her as the kid with the pigtails and the sassy mouth, the girl who looked up to me because I was her big brother. This woman sitting in front of me looked older, wiser, and far more in tune with herself than I thought possible.

"You might be able to blow them off, but I don't think they deserve it. You owe them an explanation. You can't change your past, Zeke. You can't go back and change the fact that Matt hurt you. But you can move forward. You can find the happiness you've always sought." Jamie pushed to her feet, her eyes glassy. "In fact, I think you've already found it, but you're too damn stubborn to see what's right in front of you."

Ah, damn. I wasn't sure I could handle my baby sister crying. *Please don't cry. Please don't fucking cry.*

Jamie straightened her spine. "It's fine if you want to be selfish. But remember, you're no longer the only person who'll get hurt. Those two have feelings for you, and if you're not careful, you might push them to do the one thing you claim you want them to do." She turned toward the door. "And when they walk away, they won't be coming back, Zeke."

Jamie slipped out the door, closing it behind her. I stared at it for several minutes, her words sinking in. I glanced over at my computer. I considered pulling up a search on Case. I knew it wouldn't be hard to find out the details Jamie had evidently unearthed.

However, that wasn't my style. I didn't like when people snooped into my business. And that meant if I was going to assuage this curiosity, I was going to have to address the situation directly.

I yanked open the desk drawer and grabbed my keys.

The least I could do was stop running. That wasn't the way I was programmed. I faced issues head on, so why would I stop now?

Brax
(The cowboy)

I WAS SITTING AT ZEKE'S kitchen table, scanning the Internet for houses. While I didn't want to leave Zeke, I knew Case was right. The man had asked us to go and it was rude to stay when it was evident he didn't want us here. I had held my ground for the past two days, but I knew it would come to an end eventually. I wasn't strong enough to power through those thick walls Zeke had built around himself.

Going back to the apartment wasn't an option. While Ben had assured me it was still available when I called him earlier, I couldn't possibly put Case through that one more time, let alone many. I'd never seen him react to anything like that before and I wasn't sure I could bear to witness it again.

So the only option I had was to find a place for us to go. Buying a place was ideal, but that meant finding somewhere to stay in the meantime. We could stay in a hotel for a few weeks if we had to, but I was hoping to avoid that at all costs.

The sound of a vehicle pulling up caught my attention and I pushed to my feet to see who it was. Case had insisted he had to go for a training session with Trent, although he'd told me this morning he didn't have one scheduled. Figuring he needed some time to himself, I hadn't tried to stop him.

However, Case's truck wasn't the one that had pulled into the driveway.

A minute later, the front door opened and Tank came charging into the room, making a beeline for me. I squatted down to pet him as I usually did.

"Hey," I greeted Zeke, eyeing him in an effort to gauge his mood.

"Where's the pretty boy?"

"With Trent. Had a session."

He looked skeptical. I couldn't blame him. I'd had the same reaction.

"Can I get you anything?" I asked when I stood to my full height. "Are you hungry?"

He watched me for what felt like an eternity before he moved closer. My breath lodged somewhere in my chest as he neared. The man was imposing whether he was wearing a pair of jeans or that damn suit he was sporting now. However, I'd long ago learned it wasn't the clothes that gave him the air of danger. Nor was it the bald head or the tattoos. Zeke's intimidation factor was all in his black eyes, the way they took in everything around him, assessing.

My first instinct was to drop my gaze to the floor, gearing up to submit to him in any way that he wanted.

"I only want one thing right now," Zeke stated, his tone as dark and rich as his eyes.

"What's that?" I found myself asking.

Zeke took another step closer until there was only a breath between us. I wouldn't back down no matter what. Not this time.

The next thing I knew, Zeke's hand went around my head and he jerked me to him. I thought for a second he was going to remove the collar again, but his hand didn't move once it cupped the back of my head.

"I don't know what you and your boyfriend have done to me," Zeke whispered. "Whatever it is, I don't much care for it."

His actions said otherwise. The way he tilted his head down, his gaze never straying from mine.

"I wasn't supposed to want you," he whispered, the dark tenor of his voice sending shockwaves rippling down my spine. "That wasn't our deal."

I couldn't speak. He was too close, too warm, and he smelled so fucking good. Like musky man and erotic promises.

"Fuck it all," Zeke rumbled before he jerked me close and slammed his mouth to mine.

I whimpered as I gave in to him, his embrace securing me to him as our lips met in an eager attempt to get closer. My arms went around him, my hands sliding beneath his suit jacket. I couldn't resist him even if I'd wanted to. And I didn't. The only thing that mattered was that he wasn't pushing me away.

"Christ Almighty. You make me want things, Brax. Things I'm not supposed to want," Zeke growled before changing the angle of the kiss and thrusting his tongue back into my mouth.

He said my name. It was the second time in as many days and it felt the same as before. My entire world tipped on its axis, and I was completely overwhelmed by how good it felt to hear him say it.

Unable to speak, I simply kissed him back, although there wasn't anything simple about this kiss. It was rough and brutal, everything I'd come to know Zeke to be. But there was something deeper, an underlying hunger that belied all the kink I'd ever experienced.

His kiss was intoxicating. Pure, raw lust fueled us both. It had me hanging on for dear life as he ripped my T-shirt up over my head before he tossed it somewhere behind me. Somehow I managed to maintain my balance as he backed me toward the wall. My shoulders slammed up against it, but he didn't stop. Zeke was on a mission, his hunger sharper than I'd ever seen it. Even the other night when he'd taken me bare in his bed. That had been as raw as it got, but there was something more here. A deeper, darker hunger. It made me feel powerful even as I felt overpowered by him.

When his fingers dipped into the waistband of my jeans, I inhaled sharply. He didn't fumble with the button. Instead, he jerked it open, then practically ripped the zipper down before his big, rough hands slid inside the denim at my hips. He shoved hard, forcing my jeans and boxers down my legs.

Zeke's black gaze lifted to mine but he wasn't looking at me. He was… It was as though he was trying to peer into my soul, drawing every emotion I'd ever had to the forefront. I fought for air, my chest heaving when he went to his knees before me.

I wasn't sure what I expected. Perhaps for him to jerk me roughly, or maybe for him to use his teeth because that was his sadistic nature. Instead, Zeke's lips wrapped around the head of my dick and I groaned long and loud, the sensation far more intense than I expected.

I drew air into my lungs as my hand suddenly curled around the back of his head, smooth skin gliding over my palm. I held him there and he didn't try to move away.

"Fuck, Zeke," I said around a moan. "Ah, fuck, that feels good."

Every second he sucked me, I expected him to jerk away, to throw me to the floor, to pin me to the wall. Anything except for him to continue. The man sucked me like he was starving, as though I was the sustenance he needed to survive. My hand slid over his head, my skin soaking up the feel of him. He had rarely allowed me to touch him, but I'd dreamed about it plenty.

His tongue glided over the underside of my shaft and I hissed, my head falling back as the sensations overwhelmed me. It was more than I ever thought I'd get from this man, and every second felt like an eternity, but still not enough. I wanted more of him. I wanted *all* of him.

And I prayed like hell he wasn't going to discard me, because, although he'd tried to break me physically, I wasn't sure the man was aware that he had all the power to break me in so many other ways.

Ways I feared I would never recover from.

THIRTY-FOUR

ZEKE

WHEN I LEFT THE OFFICE to come home, I'd had good intentions. I had mapped it out in my head, how I wanted to sit down and talk to them. My sister was right, that was the one thing we hadn't done in the month we'd been together. I knew very little about them and vice versa.

However, the second I opened the front door, I had no idea what came over me. The moment I saw Brax, something clicked inside me. An emotion, a feeling, an urge, maybe? I was overwhelmed by a strange need to take care of him in any way that I could.

And yes, at some point this afternoon, I'd started thinking of them both by name. They were no longer just my fuck toys. They were so much more.

While it would've been easy to force my dominance on Brax, I didn't. I was testing him, attempting to see just how human he would allow me to be. As I swallowed his dick, groaning as his salty taste coated my tongue, I felt a surge of power. More so than I did when I was hurting him. Oddly enough, it didn't make me feel weak as I'd expected. It made me feel invincible.

"Fuck ..." Brax thrust his hips forward, driving his cock deeper into my throat. "You're gonna make me come, Zeke. I need permission to come. Fuck ... it feels too good."

I pulled my lips off his cock and stared up at him. Brax's eyes jerked down to my face and I saw the real concern. He was trying to please me and he wasn't sure he had. What he didn't realize was that everything he did pleased me, even when it didn't. The two of them had become part of me in the short time I'd known them. The thought of coming home to an empty house, not having them with me didn't sit well.

"Come in my mouth, Brax," I insisted, my eyes locked with his. The taste of his name was odd, but not in a bad way.

He cried out when I wrapped my lips around him again. Both hands curled around my head, holding me in place as I took him to the root. I growled and groaned, wanting him to feel the vibrations through his entire body.

"Zeke! Oh, fuck … oh, fuck… It's too much. Ah, shit!"

Brax's hips bucked as he forced his cock deeper into my mouth. Seconds later, he roared his release, his cock pulsing against my tongue. I drank him down, relishing his taste, his warmth. Pleasure coursed through my veins.

His body relaxed against the wall, his chest heaving. I pushed to my feet but didn't move away. Instead, I pressed my lips to his, wanting him to taste himself on my tongue. This wasn't my usual style. I was a planner, even when it came to sexual experiences. I had an end goal and a means to get there. With Brax, I was following my instinct, doing what felt right. In this moment, I wanted to please *him*.

I'd never done this before. Never given in to my baser urges like this. Not even with Matt.

Then again, what I felt for Matt paled in comparison to what I felt for the cowboy and the pretty boy. Brax and Case. It would take some time for me to get used to calling them that, but I would. If they would have me.

The question was, would they be able to handle me? Not only the Sadist but also the man?

I managed to pull away, staring into Brax's eyes, looking for … something. I wasn't sure what, but that insecurity waging war on my mind was undeniable. I needed some sort of confirmation that I wasn't setting myself up for failure.

That was my biggest fear, what had held me back all these years. Until Brax and Case appeared in my world, tipping everything off its perfectly balanced axis. Somehow, they had changed me. They had given me the safety and security I needed to open myself up to them. Maybe not verbally, but in all the ways that counted.

The sound of the front door opening had both our heads turning. Case stepped inside, his attention on the floor as he closed the door behind him. When he finally turned around and looked up, his eyes locked on the two of us. We were still standing against the wall, Brax's jeans around his ankles.

"What's … uh…?" Case looked confused, but that was quickly masked by something deeper, something darker. Something that looked a hell of a lot like pain.

Unable to resist, I stood tall and stalked toward him. Case's eyes locked on my face as I neared. He appeared to be searching for something but I had no idea what. I wanted to ask him questions, to find out about his past, but I needed something else from him. A confirmation. I didn't necessarily care about what experiences had formed him, more so about how he felt now. Today.

Without warning, I stepped right into his personal space, close enough that only a breath passed between us when I cupped his head. I wasn't rough, but I wasn't gentle, either. This man didn't want gentle. He wanted the dark side of me, he wanted the Sadist. However, I was pushing that part back. For now.

Angling my head, I watched him as I moved in to kiss him. He didn't budge. Didn't try to move away. Case remained perfectly still even when I pressed my lips to his. At first, I thought he would reject me, push me away and make the decision for all three of us. That lasted all of two seconds and then his hands were on me and he was crushed up against my chest as I kissed him rough and hard, my desperation to have him near me winning out.

I forced myself to speak between kisses. "Can you taste Brax on my tongue?" I could still taste him and I knew Case could, too. It was an erotic intimacy I didn't expect, but it soothed something in my soul. "Do you want to know what we did before you walked in?"

"Yes," he whispered, holding my head and forcing my lips back to his.

"I sucked him," I told him, holding his head still and whispering over his lips. "I sucked him until he came in my mouth. That's why you can taste him."

Case groaned, his hands jerking me closer as though that was the hottest thing he'd ever heard. For whatever reason, it was far more intense than I'd anticipated.

When I finally released him, I was breathing hard. We both were. I held his stare and weighed my options for what came next. Talking seemed overrated right now, so I went with my instincts.

"I want you and Brax upstairs in my bed. Naked." I didn't look away. "No questions, Case. Just do what I say."

He nodded, then peered around me. I knew Brax was still there, watching us, probably trying to determine what my next steps would be.

For the first time in a long time, I didn't have a plan. I wasn't mapping out a scene in my head, nor was I trying to decide which reaction I hoped to coax out of them. There was only one thing I wanted.

The two of them.

Laid bare.

The same way I was.

Case
(The pretty boy)

I HADN'T EXPECTED TO FIND Zeke and Brax when I came home. I certainly hadn't anticipated finding Brax with his pants around his ankles while the two of them made out like teenagers.

Then Zeke was kissing me, calling me by my name. When he had pulled back to look at me, I'd noticed the light had returned in his eyes. I hadn't been kissing the Sadist, I'd been kissing the man.

So, what had happened? Why had Zeke come home from work? And what prompted him to react like this?

I was still processing what he'd said. How he'd sucked Brax, made him come in his mouth. When Zeke said it, it seemed more like a revelation than a simple fact. And he'd been sharing Brax with me afterward.

Was I in some sort of alternate universe? Or maybe I was asleep. This could've been a dream or even a fantasy. God knew I'd been thinking about the two of them all damn day. Ever since I slipped out of the house seeking solitude so I could think. However, none of my thoughts had prepared me to find them like that.

While I was still in a daze from Zeke's kiss, I managed to stumble up the stairs with Brax following close behind.

Once I was in Zeke's room, I paused, staring around, wondering what would come next. Brax appeared in front of me and then he was kissing me. His chest slammed against mine, knocking me backward a few steps. Raw, unbridled passion poured off him in waves. Warmth infused me and not only lust. Emotions churned in my chest as I fought to catch up with what was happening.

"I love you, Case," Brax whispered. "I need you to know that. I need you to know that'll never change. No matter how much … I love Zeke, too."

That twinge in my chest reappeared, but it wasn't painful like this morning. It felt more like hope.

There were only two points in my life when I'd felt like this. The first had been after John's death, when his dad had invited me over to his new apartment for dinner. I'd been so fucked up back then, completely shattered by losing John. I had needed something, someone who could keep his memory alive. That night had changed my entire universe, but not in a good way.

The second time was when I met Brax. From the first moment I met him, there had been something that drew me in, kept me tethered. I fell in love with him almost instantly.

Zeke had never given me that hopeful feeling because he'd always been up front with me. Not that I hadn't done quite a bit of wishful thinking these past few weeks. And this morning, when Brax said it aloud, I'd realized that everything really had changed. Although it hurt to know Brax's love was now divided between us, it was something I could accept. Provided we could have Zeke.

Was it possible to have everything I'd ever wanted? Because I could admit I needed what Zeke offered on a sadistic level, but I needed more than that. I didn't want Zeke to fill one aspect of my life and Brax the other. My feelings for them weren't separate, distinguishable. They had morphed into one. I wanted all of them, not just parts.

"I don't know how this works," I admitted.

I'd never been in a relationship like this one. Never fallen for two men before. Yet that was exactly where I found myself. I was a different person when I was with them. I didn't hold myself responsible for the sins of my past, because everything that had ever happened had led me to this moment. To these men.

Footsteps sounded from behind me and I released Brax so I could turn and face Zeke. His eyes were roaming over us, probably taking in the scene. Uncertainty filled his gaze, and for a moment, I thought he would flee.

But he didn't.

Zeke remained motionless, as though he wasn't sure how to approach us or even what he wanted.

I decided to tell him. "If you're coming into this room, we want Zeke. The man, not the Sadist."

"How do you know they're not one and the same?" he countered, but I could see the relief in his gaze.

"Because that sadistic side is only part of who you are. And we've spent plenty of time with him. But not with you."

I had no desire to dominate him in any way, but I did want to be his equal for a little while.

Brax and I moved at the same time, inching closer to Zeke. He was still motionless, staring as though he couldn't quite wrap his head around what was happening.

Without thought, I reached him first and slid my hand behind his head, pulling him down so that our lips brushed, lightly at first, but I didn't linger, leaning in for a kiss and holding him to me.

Within seconds, his arms were around me, jerking me tightly against him, the heat from his body melding with mine. He walked me back toward the bed and I reached for Brax, wanting him there, needing him with us.

I broke the kiss and Brax picked up where I left off, his lips sealing to Zeke's while I worked the buttons free from Zeke's shirt. He shifted and moved, allowing me access to every part of him. His muscles were tense, but so were mine.

Minutes passed as the three of us alternated, finally managing to shed all the clothing that was keeping us apart. Vertical became horizontal as we spread out on Zeke's big bed, limbs twining, mouths melding. Skin to skin had never felt this good.

I wasn't looking for permission to touch or taste, I simply did what felt right. Brax and I managed to get Zeke onto his back before we kissed and licked every inch of his body. He started out rigid, but quickly relaxed. I wasn't sure if it was the sensations overwhelming him or he actually trusted us, but I didn't question it.

This was where we were meant to be. The three of us.

And I had every intention of taking full advantage of this situation. Because no one knew how long it would last.

THIRTY-FIVE

ZEKE

FUCKING HELL.

I had never felt anything as intense as this. Having both Brax and Case focused on me was more than I expected. My brain was trying to keep up, rioting against the new experience.

Admittedly, I was used to being in control. Here, with them, I felt anything but. It wasn't necessarily a bad thing, not commanding and ordering them to be at my beck and call. Simply different. They were overwhelming my senses, forcing me to ignore that dominant part of myself. But I wasn't sure what to do next. I couldn't decide who to pull closer. I wanted them both at the same time, something I knew wasn't even possible.

Or was it?

"Don't you dare make me come," I warned Brax when he took my cock in his mouth, sucking me roughly, as though he couldn't get enough.

Christ. The cowboy had thrown me for a loop over the past few days. I'd seen a side of him I didn't know existed. I had always suspected he was the strong, silent type, but it was his underlying need to take care of others that pulled me in, sucking me under, making me want so much more than I'd allowed myself to have.

Then there was the pretty boy. And to be fair, there wasn't anything pretty about him. He was ridiculously handsome, his face chiseled and lean, his body stacked with muscle. But underneath all that was a man who needed to be needed. Case was after something, but I wasn't sure what.

Brax lifted his head, those deep green eyes locking on my face. "I don't recall you being in charge right now."

In an instant, I had him flipped onto his back, my bigger body pinning him down.

"For the record, I'm always in control. Even when I'm not."

He smiled and I had no choice but to kiss him. Warm hands were suddenly on my back as he held me to him. I could've easily broken the hold, but I didn't want to. Not yet.

When his knees cradled my hips, I broke the kiss. "You want me inside you? You want my cock?"

His head turned toward Case.

"Or do you want his?" I asked, chuckling. "Because it seems you've got choices now. But you don't have a lot of time to pick."

Brax laughed. "I don't care," he said, gritting his teeth when I dragged my dick against his. "Just someone fuck me, please."

"I do like to hear you beg." Leaning down, I kissed him again, but then I pushed myself up, kneeling between his legs.

Without warning, I grabbed Case's head and dragged him closer, slamming my mouth to his. He moaned, inching toward me on his knees when I refused to let him go. His arm banded around my neck and he held me there.

Unlike Brax, Case hadn't completely opened up. He'd certainly told me in no uncertain terms that he wasn't giving his collar back and he refused to leave, but I got the feeling he would go where Brax went. I wanted that same loyalty. In fact, I wanted that for all three of us.

The room had warmed several degrees since we entered and with every passing second, the intensity was increasing.

Rather than making a verbal command, I broke the kiss with Case and pushed him so that he fell over Brax. I smacked his ass before launching off the bed to grab the lube from the nightstand.

When I returned, Case was sprawled on top of Brax, their mouths fused together, eager, desperate moans coming from both of them.

"Stay just like that," I ordered before joining them.

I positioned myself behind Case, my eyes scanning the dragon tattoo briefly before I brought my attention back to the task at hand. With hurried movements, I squeezed a generous amount of lube in my hand and greased my cock. After tossing it up near Brax's head, I used those slick fingers to penetrate Case's ass.

Their lips broke apart when Case groaned, his knees widening to allow my fingers to sink in deeper.

"I suggest you two figure out how you want this to go, because in three seconds, I'll be fucking one of you. You decide which."

Case didn't move but Brax reached for the lube.

"Oh, fuck," Case groaned. "Oh, shit. Zeke … Brax …"

Yeah. With Brax now stroking Case's cock and me finger-fucking his ass, I could see why he was getting all worked up.

"Looks like you'll be sandwiched between us," I told him as I pulled my fingers out and quickly pressed the head of my cock against his ass.

"Wait!" Case pleaded with a chuckle.

He sat up on his knees and it was then I realized he was getting in position to fuck Brax, who would be beneath both of us in the very near future. I hoped like hell Case could hold out, otherwise, Brax would bear the full impact of five hundred plus pounds of horny male.

"Okay," Case said on a moan. "Fuck, you feel good."

I knew he was talking to Brax as his ass clenched and he pushed his hips forward, sinking all the way into Brax.

Too worked up to wait, I shifted my weight, forcing Case forward before I lined up again. Exquisite pleasure shot through me when I pushed inside him, burying myself balls deep in his ass.

"Fuck," I groaned. "So fucking tight."

When Case tried to move between us, I planted my hand in the center of his back. "Don't you dare move."

He stilled.

"Let me do all the work."

Gripping his hips to hold him in place, I retreated before slamming my pelvis forward. I drove into him, rocking him forward, causing Brax to moan.

"Fuck me," Brax pleaded.

I gave them everything they asked for. Their grunts and groans never went unanswered as I plowed into Case, driving him forward before pulling his hips back as I retreated. My pace increased until my breaths were racing in and out of my lungs, my heart thundering in my ears. I'd done plenty of things in my lifetime, probably would do plenty more, but never had I fucked two men at the same time.

Granted, it wasn't my dick buried in Brax, but I was the one in complete control. Their pleasure belonged to me and only me right now. I owned them in every way.

And strangely enough, they owned me right back.

Never in my life had I imagined this would be where I ended up. Having one submissive all to myself had been the ultimate goal. Someone to love me, someone I could love in return.

But with two ... it was more than I had ever thought possible. More than I felt I deserved.

However, I wasn't about to fight it. Not when I had the opportunity to experience twice as much as I wanted.

"Zeke ... oh, fuck..." Brax cried out from beneath Case. "I'm gonna come. Please make me come."

Case wasn't talking, but he was moaning in earnest, his arm muscles bulging as he held himself up. I drove into him over and over, my balls drawing up as the urge to come hit me like a Mack truck.

I dug my fingers into Case's hips. "Both of you better come right fucking now!"

I tried to hold out, but it was a wasted effort. It felt too damn good, especially when Brax's hand came around and landed on my thigh. He pulled me closer, as though trying to get more of me through Case. I pumped my hips furiously until the rumble in my chest broke free, every nerve in my body firing as the sensations won out.

My release triggered theirs and the room erupted in deep rumbles. Unable to hold myself up, I collapsed forward, crushing Brax beneath Case. When he choked out a laugh, I fell over to my back. Case dropped to Brax's other side as we all three fought for air.

I glanced over to look at them and I couldn't help but smile.

"So…" Brax prompted as he gasped for air. "Can I assume we don't have to leave now?"

I smiled up at the ceiling. "I would prefer you didn't."

I glanced over to see them both staring at me.

"What?"

Case smirked. "Okay, we'll stay." He laughed. "You drive a hard bargain, though."

This time, I felt my smile deep in my soul. So far down, I knew for a fact that these two would be a part of me for as long as I lived.

God only knew how this would play out, but I knew this was what I wanted. *They* were what I wanted.

And I'd be damned if I allowed myself to get in the way any longer.

It was time for something real.

I only hoped they could handle me. The beast they'd unleashed… Yeah, I doubted they would know what hit them when it was all said and done because my love wasn't wrapped in batting and encased in silk. No, they would get everything that I was.

The man *and* the ruthless Sadist.

Brax
(The cowboy)

Wednesday, November 7

THE FOLLOWING WEDNESDAY AFTERNOON, I received a text from Zeke in the middle of the day. I had gone over to Trent's to prepare a few meals for the rest of the week so they would have something on hand should they need it. I'd spent a couple of hours laughing it up with Troy and Clarissa while Trent was off taking care of business for the new talent agency.

The text had been short and simple: *Be home when I get there. Dinner ready. Something light. It's gonna be a long night for you two. I'll be there by six.*

I had absolutely no idea what Zeke had in store for me, but I didn't care. I'd been too caught up on the fact that he continued to refer to his house as home when we spoke. It was an interesting twist that I was still trying to wrap my head around.

Although the three of us had come to a firm understanding that this thing between us wasn't temporary and we weren't willing to do the short-term, no-commitment thing any longer, not much had changed. We were still living with him, still sleeping under his bed when he commanded it.

Not that I was disappointed in any of that. Zeke was still the ruthless Sadist. He was still barking orders and tying us up or chaining us down. Whatever suited him for the moment. And we were willing participants.

However, I got the sense there was something on his mind. I couldn't even begin to guess what it could be, but I had the sneaking suspicion it had to do with Case. Why I thought that, I wasn't sure. Maybe it was the way Zeke looked at him from time to time. As though he was a cryptic picture he was trying to figure out.

Regardless, I was still looking forward to the time the three of us spent together. Even if a lot of that involved me being naked. Zeke was on a kick with that. He was constantly insisting that I walk around the house without any clothes. I feared that Jamie was going to stop by unannounced and get more than she bargained for. Thankfully, that hadn't happened yet.

So, here I was, finishing up the prosciutto-wrapped chicken with garlic and herb cheese, something I'd been making for several years. Since Zeke wasn't fond of rice or noodles, I added roasted corn as a side. Fast, simple. Hopefully it was as light as he'd requested.

Before I had started cooking, I'd shot Case a text, letting him know the plan although I figured Zeke had messaged him, too. He'd been doing that, little messages to get us to open up to him. I found this side of Zeke extremely appealing. Granted, I had a thing for the Sadist, too.

Case arrived a few minutes before Zeke. He had a smile on his face, the same as he'd had every day for the past week. He seemed happier now. But something was different about him, too. I couldn't pinpoint it, and when I'd asked if he had something on his mind, he continued to tell me that he was free and clear for the first time in years. I didn't know what that meant, but I hoped it was a good thing.

When Zeke got home, the three of us sat down to eat. Case told us about his day, how he'd walked the two floors with Ben and Justin, mapping out the floor plan for the new gym. It was apparently going to be impressive.

Zeke didn't say much; however, he chowed down, finishing his meal before either one of us. As he sipped his tea, his attention finally turned to us.

"We're going to be spending some time in the basement tonight."

This caught my interest, because for the past two days, Zeke had kept us out of the basement. He hadn't even allowed Case to go down to work out. I wasn't sure what he'd been up to, but I was certainly curious.

"It's time we had a talk," he added, his eyes serious.

I frowned, concern stirring in my gut, threatening to overpower the garlic and herbs.

"Is something wrong?" Case asked, his fork halfway to his mouth.

"Depends on how you decide to handle the questions I have."

I tried to gauge his mood. He seemed relatively laid-back. Not on edge, for sure.

I glanced at Case, wondering if he knew what this was about.

"But don't worry." Zeke smirked. "For every question you do answer, I'll give you something you want."

"I'm done!" Case shot to his feet with a grin on his face. Obviously he was eager to see what Zeke had in store.

I, on the other hand, wanted more details. "And who determines what we want?"

Zeke's grin widened. "How did I know you'd be the one to ask that?" He leaned back. "I'm gonna let you choose."

"What if we want to ask a question in return?"

"Then I'll answer it honestly."

I studied his face, trying to determine if there was a catch. But there were no shadows or any hint of deceit on his part.

"Well, y'all can talk till your hearts' content. I'll be the one asking for more of that whip."

Zeke's eyes shot to Case. "I can handle that."

Now that we had that laid out, I had to wonder whether or not we could handle the questions.

Something told me this was going to be a turning point.

For who, I didn't know yet.

THIRTY-SIX

ZEKE

ONCE BRAX AND CASE FINISHED eating, I sent them down to the basement while I cleaned up the kitchen. I wasn't sure why I was compelled to pitch in around the house, but I was. Since they were more to me than merely my fuck toys, it seemed only fair.

However, I also wanted to send them down together so they could contemplate what it was I would do when I arrived. I had a few things in mind, but one clear objective. I decided today was the day I would get Case to open up. In return, I would do the same.

While I wasn't the type to snoop in other people's business, my conversation with Jamie had plagued my mind all week. To the point I had decided to do a little research of my own.

What I found had shocked me. More so than ever before.

Case Rhinehart, the man who craved pain unlike anyone I'd ever met, had a dark secret. A very, very dark secret. And, like Jamie, I didn't think Brax was privy to it. I agreed with my sister. Brax was far too protective of Case. If he knew what he'd lived through, I wasn't sure they would even be here right now.

After finishing up the dishes, I headed upstairs to change into jeans. I figured that would be the proper attire for tonight's activities. I had no doubt Case would require something from me. And while I would give it to him because that was what I was promising, I wasn't doing it for me.

The fact of the matter was, this secret needed to come out. It was time we all got a few things off our chest.

That was, if Case didn't decide to bolt.

370

Considering what I'd learned, I had to take the risk. The darkness that man was holding back threatened his happiness. And in turn, mine and Brax's as well.

Once I changed, I made my way down to the basement. Brax and Case were sitting on one of the benches, talking softly. When I appeared, they went silent.

"Get naked. And do it quickly." I kept my tone firm, letting them know I wasn't playing.

They both jumped up, watching me even as they started to undress.

While they got naked, I moved one of the St. Andrew's crosses away from the wall. They were new additions as of this week. Solid steel and strong enough to hold the weight of either one of them. And I'd purchased two so neither of them would feel left out. They were on opposite walls and across the room from each other, so when I felt like it, I could chain them up and they could watch each other. However, tonight, that wasn't my plan. And because I intended to have Case facing the wall, I needed to be able to walk around the one I tied him to.

"Over here, pretty boy." I motioned to the one that I'd moved. "You over there, cowboy."

While I did refer to them by name, I still enjoyed watching the way their eyes glazed over when I spoke to them as though they were merely my fuck toys. It was keeping things interesting, which was key.

Case ambled over, his eyes lacking the confidence he'd had at the table a little while ago. He probably had an idea of what was coming. Since this was a secret he'd been keeping, surely that was a question in his mind. He was likely wondering if I had figured it out and whether or not I wanted the details.

Yes and yes. In fact, I wanted to know everything about both of them, and oddly enough, I was looking forward to sharing more of myself with them.

I spent the next few minutes getting them situated. I restrained Case first, putting him facing the wall, his back to the room. If he was going to request that I beat on him—which he had already admitted he would—then I would need his back to me. I restrained Brax on the other side of the room, with him facing us so he could watch what was going on.

With their arms up and their legs spread, they formed the perfect X's. Their rapid breaths sounded around me and I relished the concern, the anticipation. Neither knew what I would do, but they were willingly submitting.

That was a good start.

"I'm gonna ask you a question," I explained. "You'll answer. Before I ask the question, you're gonna tell me what it is you'll want me to do. It can be anything. However, if it's physical, it will be less than a minute. I'm not here to make you come after your first revelation."

Brax chuckled.

I doubted he would be doing so in a few minutes.

"All right, cowboy. You get to go first. You pick."

"A question," he answered quickly.

"Very well." I picked up a chain flogger and walked around the space. "At what age did you lose your virginity?"

He grinned, obviously pleased by the easy question. "Nineteen."

"Late bloomer," I retorted.

Brax chuckled. "Tell me about it."

I nodded. "Now your question."

"What was your favorite subject in high school?"

"Math. It came easy to me," I admitted, unable to hide the smile. I liked that he was curious about me. "Your turn, pretty boy. What's your pleasure?"

"Three strikes with the whip," Case replied, his tone cool.

"All right. Same question. How old were you when you lost your virginity?"

"Fifteen," he said easily.

After setting the chain flogger down, I picked up the braided whip that he preferred. This one was my favorite. Red and black leather, long tails, and just enough bite to show him who was boss.

Walking behind him, I struck him once. Not too hard. Like a first date, I wasn't going to give it up too soon. The next two followed quickly. He sucked in air but didn't make a sound.

"Your turn, cowboy. Still want a question in return?" He nodded, so I said, "What was the name of your first boyfriend?"

"Timothy. He was the one who took my virginity and I his."

I was glad to see he was going to elaborate. "How sweet."

He laughed, but then blurted out his question. "How old were you when you went to your first BDSM club?"

"Twenty-three," I admitted. "Ransom took me. He and I have been friends since we were teenagers."

Brax looked as though he hadn't expected that answer.

"Pretty boy?"

"Three strikes," he said quickly.

"Same question as the cowboy. What was the name of your first boyfriend?"

"John," he said, his voice soft.

"The one who died?" Brax asked.

"Yes."

I gave him the three licks he requested, watching him closely. When I was finished, I walked around in front of him. He didn't look at me as I passed.

"Okay, cowboy. What's your pleasure?"

"Your mouth on my cock," he said.

I smirked his way, allowing my eyes to trail over him slowly. His cock was hard, as though he'd been thinking about it.

"Very well. Did you ask Case out the first time or did he ask you?"

Brax grinned. "He asked me. But that's only because I was a chickenshit. I met him when I went to work for Trent."

I set the whip on the table and walked over to him. I eased down onto my knees in front of him. "Count to sixty."

"Yes, Zeke."

He drew in a long breath when I wrapped my lips around his cock.

"One one-thousand, two one-thousand..."

I chuckled as I sucked him. Of course he'd make sure he got every second he wanted. I sucked and licked while he continued to count. I wasn't rushing. He wasn't going to come for a while.

When I was finished, I got to my feet, then leaned in and kissed him. Pulling back, I stared into his eyes. "Now what do you say?"

"Thank you, Zeke." His voice was raspy, his lust apparent.

"Okay, pretty boy. Your turn."

"Three strikes," he stated.

We went a few more rounds of mundane questions. Such as favorite movie, in which Brax said the first *Avengers*, Case answered with *John Wick*, and I gave up *Top Gun*. Come to find out, Brax and Case had never seen it. Favorite type of music was next. Brax and Case said country. No surprise there. I answered Brax's return question with hard rock.

I ensured I kept things light, giving Case the necessary strikes that he asked for. By the time he appeared to relax somewhat, I knew it was time to drop the bomb on him.

I was pretty sure he suspected what was coming.

Case
(The pretty boy)

I KNEW FROM THE MOMENT Zeke came down those steps that the man was up to something. He wasn't the type to ask random questions, so he had to have an end game. However, I didn't mind getting to know him on a deeper level. Perhaps that was the only reason I agreed to this. Especially since I'd known all along what he was getting at.

Brax had questioned me a couple of times this past week, obviously seeing the darkness lurking inside me. For whatever reason, my past had come to the forefront as soon as things smoothed out with Zeke.

That was how it worked for me though. When things were going well, I tended to dwell on the past, fighting my own demons. When there was chaos in my life, I could focus on the here and now. The past month had been easy since the interactions with Zeke had kept me fully focused on the three of us.

Now, it appeared my past was coming back with a vengeance and I wasn't the only one who was about to deal with it.

"Pretty boy, it's your turn again. What's your pleasure?" Zeke prompted.

I took a deep breath and swallowed hard. It was now or never.

"First, I need something from you," I told him.

Zeke appeared in front of me, his eyes narrowed. I could tell he was searching my face for a clue.

"If it's in my power, I'll give it to you," he whispered.

I swallowed hard. "I'll reveal my pain if you reveal yours."

He stared at me for what felt like an eternity before he finally nodded. "Deal."

"And what's your request for now?" he asked.

"Subspace, Zeke."

That seemed to surprise him because he didn't respond immediately.

"In return, I'll tell you what you want to know."

Zeke remained where he was, directly in front of me, and I forced my eyes to lock on his face. I didn't want him to see the pain that coursed through me but there was no way to fight it.

He stepped close enough to touch my face. I leaned into his hand. "But you have to agree not to judge me."

"Never, Case," he said, his tone ripe with conviction. "I will never judge you."

I nodded, hoping he meant that, because what he wanted to know wasn't a memory I enjoyed reliving. On the other hand, I knew it was the reason for so many things in my life.

"Brax has to promise, too," I whispered.

"I love you, Case," Brax said from behind me. "I would never judge you."

I held Zeke's stare. "Can I have a minute?"

"Of course."

He disappeared and I heard him moving around. I got the feeling he was releasing Brax from the St. Andrew's Cross. Considering this entire charade had been set up for this moment, it made sense.

"Subspace, Zeke," I said as a reminder.

"You have my word, pretty boy. I'll let you fly."

His words choked me up. I never thought I'd be in this place where I had the opportunity to have all I'd ever wanted. Zeke would be able to give me what Brax couldn't. In return, I could love them both and know that I was complete.

Closing my eyes, I tried to relax. I swallowed past the lump in my throat and forced the words out. "My parents moved to Texas when I was fourteen. I left all my friends behind. People who'd become important to me, some I'd known all my life.

"When we got to Dallas, I knew no one. The school I enrolled in was overpopulated, far bigger than the small town I'd lived in. I met John on my first day there. He was in my World History class. It was ninth grade. We became friends immediately.

"I recognized something in him that I connected with. Although I suspected, I hadn't yet put a label on myself when it came to my sexuality. I was popular with the girls, and I'd had a few girlfriends in junior high, but I had never quite connected with any of them. It wasn't until John that I realized who I really was. With every passing day, we became closer."

I swallowed as the memories consumed me.

"By the time tenth grade rolled around, John and I had already started to experiment. We both knew what we wanted, but we were nervous about what it meant. He was the first guy I kissed and I was his first as well. Like I said, we experimented and things progressed from there. It started out with kissing, groping, then hand jobs.

"That went on for a good six months. We were both nervous, not sure where to go from there. Then one day, while we were making out, things progressed to the point of no return. I ended up fucking him that day. In his bedroom while his parents were at work.

"I knew by then that I loved him. I wanted to spend every minute with him, so we did. Not only had we given each other our virginity, we were best friends. At the time, I couldn't see spending my life without him in it."

I took a moment, breathing through the familiar pain that still slammed me when I thought about all the things we'd done together, all the things we had planned to do after high school.

"Spring break of our junior year, John got sick. Really sick. His dad took him to the doctor, and shortly thereafter, he was diagnosed with leukemia. Evidently, it was advanced. The prognosis hadn't been good, but his parents were determined to find him the best doctors in the world to make him better."

Tears threatened as I remembered the day he came home from the doctor.

"Less than two weeks later, John was hospitalized and it all went downhill from there. I spent every minute I could at the hospital with him and his parents. It was brutal for all of us, watching him slip away day after day. It seemed to take him so quickly. Too quickly. I thought for sure any minute someone would find a cure and he would be back home and we would be watching movies, playing video games, and sneaking kisses when no one was looking."

A warm hand landed on my back, then another. I drew air into my lungs, grateful that I was still restrained. I wasn't sure I could continue otherwise.

"John lived until two days after his seventeenth birthday. July sixteenth. It was the worst day of my life. I fell apart. Completely shredded by the loss. My parents tried to help, but there was nothing they could do to console me. I went over to see John's parents a few times before they moved. According to Lee, John's dad, they couldn't bear to be in the house anymore, so they sold it and moved into an apartment in the city.

"I tried to move on with my life, but it wasn't easy. And strangely, I missed spending time with his dad. Lee had been a connection to John that I hadn't realized I needed."

This was the hard part, so I took a moment, wanting to get through this without completely breaking down.

"Take your time," Brax said softly, his hand sliding over my arm. "We're here, baby."

His sweet words nearly broke me but I held back the sob and forced myself to continue.

"I think I was that for Lee, too. A connection to John. Someone who reminded him of his son. About three months after they moved, Lee called and asked me to come over to the apartment. I told him I would since I had a car at that point."

I felt the warmth of Brax and Zeke behind me, so I kept going. I had never told anyone this story and I needed to get it out.

"Lee seemed different when I showed up. Angrier than the man I remembered. When I got to his apartment, he admitted that his wife had left. Said she couldn't come to terms with what had happened so she thought it would be best if they separate. I felt bad for him, hating that he was alone. So, we started spending some time together. Nothing weird happened. We would watch television and talk. Mostly about John.

"That went on for about a month. I went to his apartment at least three times a week until one day he called and asked if he could pick me up and I thought nothing of it. When we got back to his apartment, he was acting strange. I didn't know what to make of it. That was the day my entire world changed."

The memory rushed up on me, making me shake. I relayed the story as best I could even as I relived it.

"I want to show you something," Lee said when we entered the apartment.

I glanced around, noticing all the blinds were closed. It was odd. Lee always kept the blinds open. Being that he was on the eighteenth floor, there was no one who could see in anyway.

I followed Lee down the narrow hall. The apartment had two bedrooms, but one had been set up as Lee's office. When he opened the door, I noticed that the desk and the computer were gone. In their place ... the room was decorated exactly as John's had been. Right down to the same comforter and the posters on the wall. It took me by surprise.

"Come in here," Lee insisted. "I wanted you to be the first person to see it."

"Why?" I asked. "Why'd you do this?"

The pain I'd seen so many times in Lee's eyes was still there. "I need to feel close to John. I thought this would help."

It felt the opposite to me. As though he wasn't allowing himself time to grieve. I knew we would never forget John, but with every passing day, it got a little easier to breathe. Not anymore. The second I stepped into the room, it took me back to the last time I'd been in John's room with him.

"I need your help, Case. I need you to do something for me."

I looked at him, noticing the pain in his face. He looked so much older than he had before. His face had aged a decade in the short time John had been gone.

Wanting to do whatever I could to help ease him, I said, "Sure. Anything."

"I want you to lie down on the bed."

"What?" I shook my head. "I... That's... I don't think that's a good idea."

"Just this one time. I want to feel like I'm with him again." His eyes, so much like John's, were pleading.

I found myself giving in.

Lee seemed pleased by my response, so he pulled back the blanket and fluffed the pillow.

"Lie down. On your stomach." He smiled sadly. "I just want to remember the days when I would come in and wake him up for school."

It felt weird, but my grieving mind understood his pain. I figured it couldn't hurt anything, so I did.

"The next thing I knew," I told Brax and Zeke, "Lee had overpowered me and I found myself restrained to the bed, facedown." I swallowed the lump in my throat. "I hadn't realized it right then, but John's father had abducted me that day."

THIRTY-SEVEN

ZEKE

I COULD FEEL THE PAIN radiating from Case with every word he spoke. He was reliving the memory.

"What happened after that, baby?" Brax prompted, his hand sliding over Case's back.

"Lee kept me locked in that room for two straight weeks. At first, he acted normal. Well, as normal as he could for a man who had abducted me and tied me to a bed. Each morning, John's alarm would go off the same way it had when he was in school. Lee would come into the room and make sure I was awake. He would talk for a few minutes and I would beg him to let me go. He said he would eventually, but he had to see it through first.

"He brought food into the room three times a day. He cooked a meal, delivered it to the room, and literally fed me because he kept me tied up. The only time I was allowed out of the bed was to use the bathroom and to shower. Lee remained with me at all times, including watching me in the shower.

"On the fourth day from when he'd first tied me up, Lee came into the bedroom and he was angry. Not at me. At the situation. At losing John. That was the first time I'd felt the pain of a belt. Wearing only a pair of boxer shorts, I was strapped facedown on the mattress, my wrists cuffed to the headboard, my ankles to the footboard. I couldn't move, so when he began hitting me with that belt, the only thing I could do was cry. It hurt more than anything I'd ever felt. And he didn't let up.

"While he did it, he cried and yelled, cursing God for taking his son away. I begged him to stop, but he didn't listen to me. After that, he came in and whipped me at least three times a day. I think it helped him in some way. He even said it was therapeutic. I thought he was crazy.

"I begged him to let me go home, pleaded for him to untie me. I promised never to tell anyone. That would only make him angrier. He began using other things to hit me with. He had a whip, a crop, a flogger. I don't know if those were things he had before or if he bought them because he wanted to hit me with them."

Case's words were coming out in a rush, his anguish apparent. My heart fucking ached for him. I wanted to go back in time and strangle that bastard with my bare hands.

Knowing what I did of Case, I could see how that situation had changed him. It was likely the reason he was as big as he was, as strong. He ensured no one was capable of hurting him ever again. Unless he allowed it.

"For nearly two weeks, Lee beat on me," Case continued. "The pain was brutal and it stuck with me even after the session was over. I began figuring out when he would come in. When I was allowed to shower, I could see the bruises and marks on my skin. He would clean the wounds and focus on a different area of my body the next time."

Case sucked in a harsh breath and I put my hand on his shoulder, wanting him to know I was there.

"Until he didn't." Case shuddered. "At one point, he took every bit of his pain out on me, hitting me all over. The back of my head, all the way down to the soles of my feet. He didn't stop until I passed out from the pain."

For fuck's sake. Case had been abused by a man who never should've touched him. A man he should've been able to trust.

"It was never sexual with Lee. He didn't touch me or try to fuck me. He simply beat on me, wearing himself out as he cried and begged God to bring John back. Nearly three long, painful weeks I'd spent like that until finally, the police showed up. I wasn't sure who told them I was there, but I was grateful all the same."

That was the article I'd read. It had mentioned how his parents began a search, asking anyone and everyone for help. By the grace of God, someone had figured out where he was.

"I didn't press charges against Lee and I convinced my parents not to, either. While I didn't approve of how he handled it, I had understood his pain. I even forgave him, but it's not something I will ever forget."

"And now you need pain to deal with that," I stated, gripping the back of his neck gently.

"And that's the reason you panicked at the apartment," Brax noted.

"Yeah," Case said on a rush of air. "I hadn't realized it at the time. Didn't put two and two together, because for the most part, I've blocked out the memory."

But not the pain.

"Zeke?" Case's voice was hoarse, need threading through the single word.

I stepped around in front of him again.

"*Please?*"

"Of course." I leaned in and kissed him before stepping back.

My eyes met Brax's and I could see his pain. He hadn't heard this story before and it was enough to bring a man to his knees. What Case had gone through was intense. The fact that he'd forgiven the man who had done it was a testament to his strength.

I picked up the whip and pulled the strands through my hands. I would get no pleasure from this session, but a promise was a promise and I would always give Case what he needed.

"I want you to fly, pretty boy."

And I proceeded to make him do exactly that.

383

Two hours later, after I had sent Brax and Case to bed, I finally headed up to join them. I thought for sure Case would be asleep, having worn himself out with his confession.

Instead, I found Brax snoring softly while Case laid in the middle of my bed, his eyes open as he stared up at the ceiling.

I quickly shed my clothes and climbed in beside him.

"Come here," I whispered. "Let me hold you."

I knew the marks on his back were still there, still sensitive. I also knew that if I spooned him, they would burn from my touch. For whatever reason, Case relished the pain both during and after a scene. Honestly, I didn't want to hurt him anymore tonight, but I wanted to ensure he knew I was there, that I would protect him in every way possible.

Case turned onto his side and I moved up against him, tossing one arm over him, the other beneath the pillow under his head. We stayed like that for long minutes. I would press kisses on his shoulder, tightening my grip around him because it felt good to have him in my arms.

"Thank you for telling me," I said softly, wanting him to know what it meant to me that he had.

"I feel better. Now that I talked about it. It was a long time ago, but sometimes it feels like yesterday." He shifted, his head turning slightly as though he was trying to look back at me. When he moved again, I let him roll over onto his back.

I peered over to see Brax was now awake, his sleepy gaze pinned on us.

"And you?" Case asked. "What happened with Matt?"

I knew he would be asking, and I had promised to tell him, so I resigned myself to doing just that. I sighed, then dropped onto my back and stared up at the ceiling.

"I met Matt at a kink club. He was a masochist who'd run through nearly every Dom in the place at the time. No one seemed to be able to give him what he needed, or so he had told me. There were a few rumors about him. About how he wanted intense scenes and he preferred to be in public. For a few weeks, I would watch him, see how he interacted with other subs and Doms. He was polite but a little uptight. I thought it was because he was looking for something he couldn't find.

"So, one night, I offered to scene with him when he asked and it went from there. We spent the majority of our time together at the club. Every single Friday and most Saturdays. We never went out anywhere else together. I didn't think anything of it. Things progressed and a couple of months in, I suggested we draw up a contract. He wanted to be owned and he'd told me as much. I figured a contract would keep him from looking elsewhere, perhaps give him the security I thought he was looking for.

"It was a standard contract. Nothing too horrible, but I'd been playing the part of the big, mean Sadist because he wanted me to. So I added a few things in such as he would cook me dinner two nights a week at his place and he would be available for sex whenever I wanted. He seemed to like that.

"After we'd been together about a year, I asked him to stay the night with me a couple of times. He turned me down. Said he liked the distance because it kept things more intense. I didn't argue. It was true. So, I would meet him at the club. It didn't take me long to figure out he was an attention whore. He wanted to be seen, wanted people to watch me beat on him. Over time, I'd garnered a fan club. People who wanted to watch me. Matt ate that shit up, thought he was the star of the show.

"Needless to say, I thought I had fallen in love with him. We talked, we laughed. I opened up to him and I thought he was doing the same. Turned out, he was only there for the scene. He wanted me to be the man who hurt him all the time. He wanted my domination. One night, I decided to change the script. I made him dinner, invited him over. I wanted something more. A real date, some time away from the audience. When I told him I loved him, he freaked. Told me I wasn't allowed to love because I was a Sadist. He walked out and never looked back."

"So, he didn't want you, he wanted the part you were playing?" Case asked softly.

"Yeah. He wanted me to play the part. He didn't like the fact that I was human after all, that I had needs that he hadn't fulfilled because he expected me to be the Sadist at all times. After he left, it was easier for me to be who everyone thought I was. I could keep people at a distance if they thought I was unapproachable."

"I'm sorry he did that," Brax said softly.

I glanced over at them. "I'm not. If I'd stayed with him, I never would've met the two of you."

I turned my head away because what I had to say would leave me more vulnerable than I could bear. While I trusted them more than I'd trusted anyone in a really long time, I was still scared of their rejection.

"As far as I'm concerned, it worked out the way it was supposed to." I took a deep breath and blurted out what was on my mind. "If I'd stayed with Matt, I never would've fallen in love for real. With the two of you."

"Fuck," Case groaned.

I didn't get a chance to look over before he was on top of me. His mouth fused to mine and I felt a warm body move up beside us. I only broke the kiss so I could look at Brax. He put his hand on my face and kissed me. It was far gentler than Case had been and it made me laugh, that uncertainty that I'd lived with for so long finally shattering.

These two were perfect for me. They were the best of everything in two unique packages.

"Well, personally, I think Matt's a dick and you deserve much better," Brax whispered when he pulled back.

Case chuckled. "Yeah. Which is why you've got us. We're so much better than that douchebag."

I grabbed Case's arms and pushed him up before tossing him back to his spot in the middle of the bed. I rose and stared down at him. "So we're even now?"

Case pursed his lips. "Your story pales in comparison to mine, so it might require you to bare your soul a little more in the future."

I couldn't help but laugh again. This was the side of Case I'd seen from time to time and I was grateful it was back. After he'd relived his trauma, I hadn't been sure he would make it all the way back to us, but I was glad to see that he had.

"So, how'd you know, anyway?" Case asked. "About what happened to me."

"Jamie's nosy," I told him. "She told me something had happened, but not what. I gave in and did a search."

"And now that you know?"

"It helps me to understand what you need."

"Will you continue to give it to me?"

"I'll give you both what you need. In every way," I admitted. "For as long as you'll have me."

"Forever?" Brax asked.

"Forever what?"

"Can we have you forever?"

I swallowed hard and nodded. "If that's what you want."

"We do," Brax said, his tone so matter-of-fact my heart skipped.

"I have a request," Case said softly, a smile turning up the corners of his mouth. He reached for Brax and tugged his arm until he moved closer.

"What's that?" My gaze darted back and forth between the two of them.

"You let us give you what you need," he said simply.

"And what do you think I need?"

"Everything," Brax stated.

"What he said." Case smirked again. "But I was thinking we could start with a blow job."

Yeah, well. Who was I to argue with that?

Brax
(The cowboy)

THEIR RUTHLESS SADIST

Friday, November 16

THIS WAS THE FIRST TIME we'd been back to the club since the Halloween debacle with Matt. I was happy to say, that stupid fucker was no longer a member of the club. Had he been, I would've found a way to get his ass tossed out myself. Thankfully, he also hadn't shown up at Zeke's house again. For his own sake, I hope he didn't. I wasn't sure I'd be able to hold Case back if he did. That man had no right to darken Zeke's doorstep. He'd given up the best thing that had ever happened to him, and lucky for us, Zeke now belonged to us.

"So, I hear you've got a scene planned for tonight," Ransom told Zeke as we sat in the Dom lounge.

We had arrived at the club right about nine after I'd made them dinner. From the moment we stepped in the door, Zeke had insisted we remain close. We hadn't argued. And now, Case and I were kneeling on the floor at Zeke's feet while the two Sadists talked with Mistress Jane and Mistress D. The place was relatively busy tonight. I'd already noticed almost all of the club's Masters were in attendance, as well as quite a few submissives and a bunch of new faces I hadn't met yet.

"I do," Zeke said. "But I've kept it a secret seeing as you like to spoil the surprise for my toys."

Ransom chuckled. "Who me? I don't know what you're talking about."

"He's always been that way," Zeke told the Mistresses. "Even back in high school, he gossiped like a girl."

"Hey," Mistress D said firmly. "Just because we're girls doesn't mean we gossip." She glanced at Mistress Jane and laughed. "Okay. I couldn't even keep a straight face when I said it."

"I remember when we were in the twelfth grade," Zeke said. "Ransom had a huge crush on this jock. The guy wasn't gay and he wouldn't give Ransom the time of day. So, to get back at him, Ransom spread a rumor that the guy got crabs from a hooker."

Ransom laughed. "Chlamydia. I said he got chlamydia. Get your story straight, Lautner."

"Whatever. The girls ate that shit up and the guy spent the rest of that year getting the stink eye from every chick in the school. But Ransom ensured that rumor festered throughout the year. Every so often, he would bring it up again and the school would erupt with chaos all over again."

"Teach him to rebuff me," Ransom said in a haughty tone.

As I sat there listening to the stories, I tried to pretend I wasn't as stunned as everyone else that Zeke was opening up so much. Mistress Jane couldn't hide her surprise nearly as well as the rest of us though. She'd been watching Zeke intensely for the past hour, as though she was trying to figure him out. I could've told her that wasn't possible. Every day was a new day with Zeke and I fucking loved that about him.

"So, what's the plan really?" Ransom asked Zeke. "Maybe a flogging? You did the cane not too long ago."

"You'll find out when they do," Zeke said as he inched toward the edge of his seat. "Come on, fuck toys. We might as well get everything ready."

"You need us for aftercare?" Mistress Jane asked as Zeke got to his feet.

"No, ma'am," he said firmly. "These two are mine. From here on out, no one takes care of them except me."

If someone had asked me to speak right then, I would've been at a loss for words. The only thing I could do was look up at Zeke. He could probably see my heart right there in my eyes because aside from hearing him say he was in love with us, that was the single greatest thing he'd ever said as far as I was concerned.

I peered over at Case, who was smiling ear to ear.

"Wipe the smile off, pretty boy," Zeke scolded. "You've gotta make it through what I have in store for you first."

"Yes, Zeke," he said, although there was definite humor in his words.

Zeke led the way down to the dungeon and we followed him. Several people stopped to say hello—both Doms and submissives—

and he greeted them in kind but never slowed his pace. I wasn't sure if he was excited about what he had in store for us or if he was merely trying to get away from all the wide-eyed submissives who were hoping for a chance to scene with him.

Little did they know, but Zeke would never be available to them again. We belonged to him, yes. But he also belonged to us and there was no way in hell I was going to let another sub get near him. I was a very possessive man.

By the time we arrived at the far end of the dungeon, I'd completely forgotten the fact that we were about to scene with Zeke. I'd learned to expect the unexpected when it came to him, but that still didn't prepare me for what I saw in the area he'd obviously commandeered as his for this evening.

"Holy shit," Case muttered, his eyes glued to the items in front of us.

Zeke chuckled. "I'd hoped you'd say that." He motioned us forward. "Come on, fuck toys. This is going to be fun."

Yeah. His version of fun and mine were obviously very different.

"Go stand over there," Zeke ordered, pointing to a spot in front of the row of items before he walked over and set his bag on the table on the outer edge of the sectioned-off area.

Doing my best not to think about what he was going to do to us, I walked over. I was partially grateful that he hadn't asked us to strip. As it was, we were only allowed to wear jeans and our collars tonight, so we were semi-naked at this point. Not that I was going to get too attached to my pants. From what I could tell, they wouldn't be on for long.

"I thought I'd do something different tonight," Zeke said when he stepped up behind us.

His hand tucked into my collar at the back of my neck and he tugged gently, pulling me back against him.

"I'm going to let you choose how you want to be tortured."

"Choose?" I glanced from one thing to the next. "From *those* things?"

Surely he wasn't serious.

Zeke chuckled. "Well, technically, you get to pick from those three things," he said as he motioned toward the right. "And the pretty boy gets to pick from those three."

Oh, shit.

As I stood there in front of the gathering crowd, I stared at the *things* Zeke said I could pick from. Technically, there really were three things. However, each one sat on top of something else that was hidden beneath big black blankets. I suspected the good stuff was hidden beneath. And by good, I mean the real torture devices.

"You can move closer," Zeke urged. "Just don't move the blanket. We'll do that once you decide."

With his hand on my back, I took a couple of steps closer and surveyed the items I had to pick from. The ones I could see, that was.

On the first blanket, there was the parachute ball stretcher that Zeke had used on me the first time I scened with him here in the club. The second had the silicone paddle he'd used on me in his basement the first time I went down there. And the third one had the dog mask that I'd worn for my punishment.

My first instinct was to pick the paddle, except I could tell that underneath the blanket was the largest item of the three that were hidden. I had no idea what they could possibly be. I didn't have the faintest idea what Zeke had in mind here. Knowing him, it would be devious.

Glancing over at Case's choices, I saw the crown of thorns cock ring Zeke had used on him in the basement that first time, the U-shaped ball stretcher on the next one, and the last held the rattan cane Zeke had used on him here in the club. I figured Case was going to pick the cane above everything else, regardless of what might be underneath it.

"Have you made your choices, fuck toys?" Zeke asked, his voice low as he stepped in behind us.

"Maybe another minute?" I suggested.

"Sure, cowboy," Zeke said with a chuckle. "Take your time."

Now, why did that sound more threatening than any of those items laid out before me?

THIRTY-EIGHT

ZEKE

I DID LIKE A GOOD mind fuck. Proven by the way I'd set up tonight's scene. My fuck toys seemed quite baffled about making a selection for themselves, and in a minute, I was going to take that option away.

Granted, they didn't know that yet.

I kept my eye on the cowboy because I knew he was trying to figure out what was beneath the blankets. Little did he know, but two of them didn't have anything beneath them but a large empty box. Like I'd said. Mind fuck.

I had purposely picked items they could associate with. The ones I'd used on them specifically.

"All right," I finally said after another couple of minutes. "Let's change it up a bit."

I grabbed the cowboy's shoulders and shifted him over so that he stood behind the pretty boy. I then did the same with the pretty boy until they'd traded places.

"To make it easier, I want you to pick out the one you'd like to be used on the other. You have one minute to decide."

The cowboy huffed as though this was the hardest thing in the world to do. It was easy. I already knew which ones they would pick. It was the exact same one they would've picked had they selected for themselves.

And yes, perhaps my ego was driving this little excursion. I knew what my toys liked, and I knew what they would select. In the same regard, they knew each other well. It was why things were working so well for us. We had come into our own over the past month and a half since we met. There was no other way to explain it.

"Five seconds left," I warned.

"Number two," the pretty boy blurted.

I glanced over at the silicone paddle. "Nice choice. I think it's perfect."

"Number three," the cowboy stated.

"That was an easy one," I told him. The cane would've definitely been the pretty boy's first choice. "Now go remove the blanket from beneath the item that was chosen for you."

They switched places again and walked over to their selected item.

I watched them both, waiting to see their reaction when they lifted up the blankets to reveal the hidden item beneath.

The cowboy dropped down on one knee and slowly lifted the box he'd uncovered as though a snake might jump out and bite him. He frowned when he picked up the two silver keys that were lying underneath. I turned my attention to the pretty boy as he was lifting up a single silver chain.

"Bring the items to me," I commanded.

They swapped concerned glances before turning and walking back toward me.

I held out my hand for the cowboy to hand over the two keys. "Now turn around. Both of you."

The cowboy's hand instantly went to his collar. "Zeke, I don't want—"

"Trust me, Brax," I whispered.

His eyes widened, but he finally pivoted around, his hand dropping to his side.

I took one key and unlocked the padlock that was connecting the cowboy's collar. I then did the same with the pretty boy. Once they were unlocked, I took the collars off, held on to the padlocks, and tossed the leather bands to the far side of the space.

"Now turn around and face me," I ordered.

When they did, I handed each of them their key and their padlock. I could see the concern in their eyes, knew they were likely thinking the worst.

I stepped up to the pretty boy first, then retrieved one of the thick silver chains from my pocket. I held it up for him to see.

"The dog collar was a reflection of my ownership," I told him. "This collar is a reflection of my ownership as well as my love for you. If you accept my collar, pass over the lock."

The pretty boy swallowed hard and handed me the lock. I wrapped the chain around his neck and secured it in place with the lock. I then moved to the cowboy and repeated my statement. His response was the same as he handed me the padlock. I situated his new collar and secured it in place.

"Stand side by side," I instructed.

When they did and I could look at them both at the same time, I then reached for their jaws and held them firmly in my hands, forcing them to look at me.

"By accepting my collar, you understand that you belong to me. As my fuck toys, you will cook for me, clean for me, do any depraved thing I want. Outside the confines of this club, you will have no safe word, no limits. You belong to me. If I choose to make you sleep in a cage, you will. If I want you to jack off ten times a day, you will. If I tell you to bend over so I can shove my dick in your ass, you will. You're a fuck toy for me to use and abuse. Is that what you want?"

I was sure they remembered this because it was the exact same thing I'd said to them the first night I scened with them here. Almost verbatim.

Almost was the key word.

They answered at the same time. "Yes, Zeke."

"In return, I will hurt you, humiliate you. It will be my sole desire to break you. Is that what you want from me?"

Again in unison. "Yes, Zeke."

"You will be bound to me by an iron-clad contract with no expiration date. You will wear my collar day and night, never taking it off for any reason. Is that what you want from me?"

"Yes, Zeke."

"The only time you will be out of my sight is to live your life and do your job. You will come home to me willingly each and every night. And you will always be at my mercy. *Day* and *night.* Wherever I want you. Can you handle that?"

"Yes, Zeke." Their eyes were still locked on mine.

"If you whine, you will be punished. If you disobey, you will be punished. And if you try to top from the bottom, you will be punished. Do you understand me?"

"Yes, Zeke."

"Ask anyone here, I don't play games. When I tell you that I want to be your friend, your confidant, and your lover, I mean every word. I will fuck you when it suits me. I will deny your orgasm when it suits me. I will beat you when it suits me. And I will love you for every second of every single day. Always."

I felt the emotion swell in my chest. While I had prepared for this, repeated it over and over again in my head, it still didn't get any easier to lay myself out for them. Although I could've done this in the privacy of my own home, I had opted to do it here.

In my safe haven.

With the two men I trusted to love me and protect me for the rest of our lives.

Now, there was just one more step.

Case
(The pretty boy)

YEAH, I WAS PRETTY SURE my heart was in my throat right about now.

My head was spinning. Every single word Zeke spoke hit me right in the chest. Not only his words but the look in his eyes as he said them. The man was stating the same thing he'd said to us that first night, only he'd modified his speech. While he made it clear we were still his fuck toys—something I was more than thrilled about—he was clarifying that we were more to him than that. He had just admitted his love for us in front of every person who was in this club. And there were a lot of fucking people watching.

"Will you accept me as your Dom? As your lover? As your friend?"

"Yes, Zeke," I said with the same croak in my voice that Brax had in his.

"If you do, then please put your key on the chain and place it around my neck."

I lifted the chain that I'd retrieved a moment ago and added my key onto it. Zeke had ripped the original chain off his neck in a moment of anger, so I was happy to see he had replaced it. And this one, although thinner, matched the collars he had placed on our necks.

I held it out so Brax could do the same. It wasn't until he was adding his key that I noticed each key had been engraved with our names on one side and *my cowboy* and *my pretty boy* on the other side.

I allowed Brax to take the chain and hook it around Zeke's neck. I fixed the keys in place on his chest as Brax came to stand beside me once again.

"Thank you," Zeke said softly. "I swear to you I will never let you down."

For fuck's sake. Was he trying to make me cry? Because that would be seriously emasculating right about now. It was one thing to be naked while a giant Sadist beat on me, something else entirely to fucking cry.

"I love you, Zeke," Brax said, his voice ringing with pride.

"I love you, too, cowboy."

"I love you, Zeke," I told him.

"I love you, too, pretty boy."

He smiled. "Now that we've got that out of the way, shall we have some fun? After all, I do have a cane and a paddle to use."

Oh, hell yeah. The night was only getting better. And the good news was, there would be no fucking crying. A little moaning, maybe. But that was to be expected.

Turned out, at the club, Zeke had more in store for us than merely some ass beatings. Not much more, though. Although he had delivered those in the most intriguing way, I'd been hoping for something a little more ... hands on. Unfortunately, that didn't happen.

Granted, I wasn't complaining, because it had been quite the eventful evening. After we'd declared our love for one another in an impromptu collaring ceremony, Zeke had made us strip, then restrained us. Of course, he had opted to take advantage of the stray ball stretchers that were, according to him, *just lying around.* Once that was taken care of and our balls were being thoroughly tortured, he had proceeded to use the paddle and the cane until Brax and I were both flying high.

After the scene, as he'd promised, Zeke had taken us into a private aftercare room and tended to us himself. While he was kind enough to put oil on the welts and ensure we were hydrated, he hadn't offered up anything else. Including himself.

Which explained why I was craving him so badly.

When we stepped into the house, Zeke flipped on the lights while I headed to the back door to let Tank outside.

"Go on upstairs," Zeke instructed. "I want you both in the shower but you are not to do anything until I get up there."

I smiled to myself and headed for the stairs. Brax was right behind me.

Once we were in the oversized master bathroom, I turned on the shower while Brax started stripping his clothes off. My eyes caught on the collar around his neck. I couldn't help reaching for it when he started to move past me.

His emerald-green eyes lifted to meet mine. "I love you, Case."

His admission caught me by surprise. Not that I hadn't expected it or hadn't heard it before. It was more that it sounded so sincere, as though he wanted to ensure I knew.

"I love you, too." I gripped his hips and pulled him closer. "So fucking much."

Brax leaned in and kissed me quickly. Before we could break apart, Zeke stepped into the room and cleared his throat.

Busted.

I looked over at the sexy Sadist, waiting for a reprimand. Since we weren't doing what he'd instructed, I figured punishment was in order. I kind of hoped it was. Although, without the dog mask for either of us.

"Hmm." He took a step closer. "It looks to me like you've got too much time on your hands. Maybe I should put those hands to good use."

Brax and I turned to face him.

"What'd you have in mind?" I asked.

"Let's start with both of you stripping me. Then you can wash me and yourselves. After that, I want you on my bed. I think some mouth action is in order. I'll watch you suck each other for a bit."

His words alone had my cock rock hard in an instant.

Brax was the first to move over to him. He reached for the hem of his shirt and lifted it. With Zeke's help, we got him stripped down to nothing and then followed him into the shower.

We took our time cleaning him. Of course, there was some groping involved. I might've teased him a little more than I should. It had earned me a hard smack on my ass, which had only turned me on more. Once we were cleaned, rinsed, and dried, I took Brax's hand and led him into the bedroom. Perhaps with a little more enthusiasm than was necessary.

"I want to feel your mouth on my dick," I told Brax when he positioned himself over me, his cock above my face.

"Likewise," he groaned when I reached for him, wrapping my lips around the swollen head.

Zeke joined us a few minutes later, openly ogling us as he walked around the bed. His hands moved over us as though he couldn't resist touching.

I had no idea how much time passed while Brax and I sixty-nined one another, but it was a while. During that time, I tried to focus, but it wasn't easy. Not when Brax's wicked mouth was doing wonderful things to my dick. It didn't help when Zeke began finger-fucking my ass, either. I knew he was doing the same to Brax, alternating between us until we were doing more moaning than sucking.

"Pretty boy, I want you on your hands and knees."

Brax's cock retreated from my mouth as he moved off of me. I quickly flipped over, tempted to grind my cock against the mattress to find a modicum of relief. I was so fucking hard I hurt and I needed to be fucked.

"Cowboy, it's your turn to be sandwiched between us."

Brax moaned as though that was the best news ever.

I glanced over my shoulder to see Brax retrieving the lube and coating his dick before quickly kneeling behind me. When his cock brushed against my anus, I pushed back against him, urging him to fuck me.

"Patience, baby," Brax crooned. "I promise, you'll get what you need."

"Yeah, but not soon enough," I groaned. "I need you both now."

Zeke's voice sounded from behind me. "Let me watch you enter him."

I knew he was talking to Brax and I could feel at least three hands on me, which meant Zeke was close enough to touch.

I dropped my chest to the mattress and offered myself up to Brax when I felt the head of his cock push against my asshole. I held my breath, willing him to hurry. I didn't want gentle and I didn't want easy. I wanted to be fucked. Hard. Rough.

Now.

"Oh, fuck," Brax moaned as he pushed in slowly. "So fucking tight."

"Keep going," Zeke urged. "Deeper. He needs more of you."

Brax followed Zeke's command, pushing in all the way.

"Now pull out, slowly."

Damn it.

Brax did as Zeke instructed.

"Again."

"More," I pleaded. "Harder."

"Relax, pretty boy. A little torment never hurt anyone."

I huffed a laugh. "Said the Sadist."

The next few minutes passed just like that. Zeke instructing Brax to fuck me slow and easy. It was exquisite hell. Never enough.

I was just about to beg again when Zeke's words sounded, his tone rough with what I assumed was lust. "Now fuck him, cowboy. Fuck him hard."

Brax retreated, then slammed forward, burying himself in my ass. It felt so damn good. I held myself still, wanting to take the full brunt of every punishing thrust. He started out slow, but quickened his pace, driving in deep and hard, again and again.

I heard Brax's rough breathing and I peered back to see Zeke was kissing him, Brax's head turned to the side as Zeke thrust his tongue into his mouth.

"Fuck him, Brax," Zeke whispered. "Give him what he needs and then I'll give you what you need."

Brax moaned, as did I when he began pounding into me. He wasn't gentle, his fingertips biting into my hips. I rocked back against him, meeting every thrust until I was panting and gasping for air.

"Stop," Zeke ordered. "But don't pull out."

Brax slammed into me, his cock lodged all the way to the hilt.

"My turn," Zeke bellowed.

I turned my head again and noticed the mirror across the room. I could see the three of us perfectly. Me on my knees, Brax behind me, his pelvis against my ass, and Zeke behind him as he guided his cock into Brax.

It was an erotic sight and I suddenly wished Zeke would record it so we could watch it later.

"Fuck, yeah," Zeke moaned. "Your ass is strangling my dick."

Brax whimpered and I felt his cock pulse inside me. "Please, Zeke. Fuck me. Please fuck me."

"Damn, but I like when you beg."

I began to wiggle, trying to get the friction where I needed it most, but a big hand landed on my ass, effectively stilling me.

"My turn," Zeke snarled.

I was happy to say, Zeke took his turn. He began fucking Brax hard, his body jarring with every thrust. I watched in the mirror again, loving the way that we looked, all three of us together.

"Come on, pretty boy," Zeke said. "Fuck him."

I realized what Zeke wanted, so I began to rock forward and back, impaling myself on Brax's cock while he remained crushed between us. The room erupted with Brax's harsh breaths and his frequent moans and pleas.

"Fuck me," Brax urged. "Christ. I've never felt anything this fucking good."

I knew the feeling because I'd been there. Sex was exquisite, but being fucked by one man you loved while your dick was lodged inside another man you loved was likely the best feeling in the world.

"Oh, fuck ... Zeke ... I'm gonna come. I can't stop it. Oh ... shit. Please let me come."

I increased my pace, chasing my own release as I fucked myself on Brax's dick. It wasn't the easiest thing to do, but it worked.

"Zeke!" I growled his name again and again.

"Are you ready to come, pretty boy?" His words were strangled, as though he was barely hanging on.

"Fuck yes. Zeke..." My gaze was locked on the mirror again and I was so close. "Zeke, please ... permission ... oh, fuck."

"Come for me," Zeke shouted. "Oh ... fuck ... yes."

Brax cried out, his cock pulsing in my ass as I continued to rock on him. A big hand fisted my cock and I exploded instantly, not giving a shit that the sheets would have to be changed.

A few seconds later, the three of us fell onto the mattress, breaths exploding from our lungs as we lay there.

"So, I was thinking," I said as my lungs fought for oxygen. "What do you say we record this sometime?"

Zeke chuckled. "Are you a porn star now?"

"No, but I could be." I laughed and turned my head to look at them. "But only for the two of you."

Brax smiled but turned his head back up to the ceiling. "Please don't give the big guy any ideas."

"No," Zeke said. "I like it. Perhaps a live-action camera." He laughed. "I can tie you both up in the basement and watch you while I'm at work."

"Okay," I said quickly. "Never mind. Bad idea. No cameras. Brax is right. Your torture ideas are already wicked enough."

Zeke choked out a laugh. "Baby, you ain't seen nothing yet. I'm just getting started."

The demonic laugh that followed told me he wasn't lying, yet I found myself grinning from ear to ear.

I would take these two men any way I could have them as long as they loved me.

"Do your worst, Zeke," I taunted.

"Trust me, pretty boy. I will. Over and over again."

Brax groaned. "Damn it, Case. You know better than to taunt the beast."

True. I did.

Didn't mean I would ever stop.

Because this was right where the three of us were meant to be.

EPILOGUE

ZEKE

Eight months later, July

"DID YOU SEE THE LINE out front?" Case asked when we snuck into the kitchen to see Brax.

"Gonna be a packed house for a while," I told him. I knew because I'd seen the early reviews for the restaurant. Brax had already made a big name for himself here in Chicago and the restaurant hadn't officially opened yet.

I stopped when I saw Brax shuffling back and forth between the various cooking appliances. He had a handful of people helping him out, every one of them eager to assist in any way they could.

The expression on his face was serious, which made sense. He was in his element. Then again, maybe he was simply thinking about earlier, when I'd met him back here before anyone arrived and commanded him to go to his knees and suck me off right here. His big green eyes had widened, but he hadn't balked, dropping to his knees before giving me one of the best blow jobs of my life. I'd told him it was to help him get his mind off tonight. Which was true. Partly. I'd also done it because I loved his fucking mouth on me.

"I'm so fuckin' proud of him," Case said softly.

I was proud of both of them. In the past eight months, things had … well, let's just say, there was no slowing down this thing we had going together. I woke up every fucking morning thankful that I had them in my world. It had taken a couple of months to level out all the rocky spots, but it had been smooth sailing from there.

Shortly after I had officially collared them, the three of us had gotten them moved in completely, all their shit cleared out of storage. And with Jamie's help, they had redecorated most of my house in an effort to make it more our space than simply mine. The only thing I insisted was that they left the basement and the master bedroom alone.

The basement hadn't changed, aside from me acquiring a few new pieces to complete the play area. However, the master bedroom had received a complete overhaul. I had a bed custom made for the three of us. It was now bigger than a king, and more than enough space for the three of us and Tank to sleep on every night. Since I found I preferred them at my mercy, I no longer needed the cage—that one anyway—so I had left that part out of the design in lieu of some additional ironwork that allowed for more … options. I could now do wicked things to them right there where we slept. Of course, I'd had another cage installed in the basement because, hey, I still enjoyed seeing them locked up.

I'd had a dresser built that would accommodate the three of us. And with the help of a construction company, I'd had my closet expanded to encompass one of the guest bedrooms so that we had plenty of space for all the shit they owned.

A few pieces of their furniture had remained, as well as a lot of mine. Surprisingly, Brax hadn't made any changes to the kitchen, insisting he was more than happy with the way it was. Since that had become his domain, there was no way I could argue with that.

I could admit, I put a lot of demands on their time. Both together and individually. I couldn't seem to get enough of them and it didn't matter where we were. I'd summoned them to my office a few times and I'd come home early plenty as well. With new employees in place—Heather, Lance, and Chris Cavanaugh, the guy Edge had referred—I found I could split my focus between work and home appropriately. The company was growing exponentially, and as it turned out, I did have a great team in place.

Was there still some jealousy on the home front? Yeah. A little. There were times when one of them would sulk because they felt as though I was giving the other more attention. I'd learned to handle that with swift punishment. Needless to say, it was getting better. I continued to assure them there was plenty of me to go around and I backed up my words every chance I got.

Brax's gaze shot over to us and a wide grin split his face. "Hey," he said as he rushed over. "I didn't know you were comin'."

"Wouldn't miss it," I told him.

He glanced back over his shoulder. "I wish I had more time."

"We get it. Just wanted to stop in, let you know we're here."

Brax glanced between me and Case. "Thanks."

I leaned in and kissed him, not giving a shit that half the people in the kitchen were already eyeing us speculatively. "I love you."

"I love you, too," he whispered back.

"What am I? Chopped liver?" Case chuckled. "I love you, too. And good luck. Not that you need it."

Brax leaned over and kissed Case quickly, which definitely caused some stir with the people behind him. Not that he seemed to care.

"Get back to work," I commanded, lowering my voice. "We'll see you at home tonight."

He nodded, smiled, then shuffled back over. A second later, he was barking orders like a chef who'd been doing this all his life.

I grabbed Case's arm and steered him out of the kitchen, but rather than go into the dining room, which was already filling up quickly, I slipped down the hall to one of the offices in the back. I knew everyone who worked there was front and center tonight, so we'd have a little privacy.

Once I had closed us inside, I pushed Case against the door and plastered myself to him. I let him bear my full weight as I kissed him roughly, loving the way he moaned in response.

I liked that he didn't ask questions. He seemed to know exactly when I needed his submission. And right now was one of those times.

"I want you on your knees, pretty boy," I growled. "I've been thinking about your mouth on my dick all damn day."

His light green eyes were glassy with lust when I pulled back and planted my hand on his head, forcing him down. Although the darkness Case had once hidden was out in the open, he still craved what I could give him. And I ensured I gave it to him as often as possible.

Stepping back, I unhooked the button on my slacks before lowering the zipper.

"Open wide, pretty boy," I mumbled darkly. "I'm gonna feed you my cock. You've got five minutes to make me come. If you do, you'll earn a special session tonight. Otherwise, you'll be sleeping with a chastity device on your dick."

"Yes, Zeke." His mouth fell open and his eyes remained locked on my face.

I roughly shoved my cock into his mouth, hissing when the warmth enveloped me. With our gazes locked, I took my pleasure from him, fucking his throat rough, deep, not giving an inch. He moaned softly, his hands at his sides while I held his head in place.

"I love your fucking mouth," I told him, as I always did. "Love the way you swallow my dick."

I could see the way my words worked for him. His face was flushed, his breaths raspy when I pulled out enough for him to breathe.

Damn, his mouth was exquisite. He worked me over for long minutes, his soft moans vibrating straight to my balls. While I wanted to draw this out forever, I knew I couldn't.

"You ready for me to come, pretty boy?"

He tried to nod, but I held his head firm.

I gave him everything I had, fucking his face brutally until I couldn't hold back any longer. With a muted roar, I came hard, holding my cock deep in his throat. When I pulled out of his mouth, I took a step back, giving him room to move.

"On your feet," I commanded as I tucked my cock back into my pants.

Case was immediately on his feet.

"Now what do you say, pretty boy?"

He smiled. "I love you, Zeke. And I love your cock."

I chuckled. The guy was a smartass sometimes.

"I love you, too, but that's not what I wanted to hear."

He grinned, his eyes crinkling. "Thank you, Zeke."

Unable to resist, I leaned in and kissed him again. He relaxed against me, his hand curling around the back of my neck in a possessive gesture I'd come to love. These two had a way of making me feel vulnerable even when I was in control. I no longer allowed it to bother me, I simply accepted it for what it was. Love.

"When the gym opens, are you gonna do the same thing to Brax in my office?"

"You're damn right. It's all about keeping it interesting." I motioned toward the door. "But I've got a few things in store for you, too."

"Such as?" His eyes were bright with intrigue.

"Tying you down to one of the benches," I told him. "Fucking your ass until you're begging me to let you come."

He groaned, a sexy sound that told me he approved.

While I could've told him all the dirty details of everything I wanted to do to him and Brax, that would have to wait until later.

"Now come on. Let's eat, then we'll go home so I can chain you up and torment you for a couple of hours."

"In that case, I don't care to stay for dessert."

Yeah, me, either. In fact, the only dessert I ever needed was in the form of two sexy fucking masochists who had made me the luckiest man in the whole fucking world.

***

Want to see some fun stuff related to my books, you can find extras on my website. Or how about what's coming next? Find more at: www.NicoleEdwardsAuthor.com

If you're interested in keeping up to date on any new releases and preorders, you can sign up for my notification newsletter on my website under "Subscribe". This only goes out when I've got a book coming up.

Want a simple, fast way to get updates on new releases? You can also sign up for text messaging. If you are in the U.S. simply text NICOLE to 64600 or sign up on my website. I promise not to spam your phone. This is just my way of letting you know what's happening because I know you're busy, but if you're anything like me, you always have your phone on you.

And last but certainly not least, if you want to see what's going on with me each week, sign up for my weekly Hot Sheet! It's a short, entertaining weekly update of things going on in my life and that of the team that supports me. We're a little crazy at times and this is a firsthand account of our antics.

You can also find me here:

Twitter: @NicoleEAuthor

Facebook: /Author.Nicole.Edwards

Instagram: NicoleEdwardsAuthor

Acknowledgments

First and always, I have to thank my wonderfully patient husband who puts up with me every single day. If it wasn't for him and his belief that I could (and can) do this, I wouldn't be writing this today. He has been my backbone, my rock, the very reason I continue to believe in myself. I love you for that, babe.

Chancy Powley – Your notes on Zeke's book made me laugh. I fell in love with this man immediately, and I'm glad you did, too.

Allison Holzapfel – Thank you!

Tug James and Justin Cox - While I knew Tug was going to grace the cover of this book, I never expected to actually "meet" you both, much less be able to call you friends. You two make me smile and laugh and your positivity is as charming as it is refreshing. It's a true honor to call you both friends and I'm greatly looking forward to the day I get to meet you in person!

Wander Aguiar and Andrey Bahia - You two are the greatest! Seriously. The. Greatest. You found Tug for my cover and I'm pretty sure this is my favorite one. Thank you for going above and beyond in everything you do!

Thank you to my proofreaders. Jenna Underwood, Annette Elens, Theresa Martin, and Sara Gross. Not only do you catch my blunders, you are my friends and it is an honor to call you that.

I also have to thank my street team – Naughty (and nice) Girls – Your unwavering support is something I will never take for granted. So, thank you Traci Hyland, Maureen Ames, Erin Lewis, Jackie Wright, Chris Geier, Kara Hildebrand, Shannon Thompson, Tracy Barbour, and Toni Thompson.

I can't forget my copyeditor, Amy at Blue Otter Editing. Thank goodness I've got you to catch all my punctuation, grammar, and tense errors.

Nicole Nation 2.0 for the constant support and love. You've been there for me from almost the beginning. This group of ladies has kept me going for so long, I'm not sure I'd know what to do without them.

And, of course, YOU, the reader. Your emails, messages, posts, comments, tweets… they mean more to me than you can imagine. I thrive on hearing from you, knowing that my characters and my stories have touched you in some way keeps me going. I've been known to shed a tear or two when reading an email because you simply bring so much joy to my life with your support. I thank you for that.

About Nicole Edwards

New York Times and *USA Today* bestselling author Nicole Edwards is a hybrid author who has published over 50 books since 2012. Nicole lives in Pflugerville, Texas with her husband and their youngest of three children. Her oldest two have left the nest, but Nicole does her best to keep them close by. Nicole also keeps busy with three rambunctious dogs of her own. When she's not writing about sexy alpha males, she can often be found with a book in hand, spending time with her kids and her granddaughter, or making an attempt to keep the dogs happy. You can find her hanging out on Facebook and interacting with her readers—even when she's supposed to be writing.

By Nicole Edwards

The Alluring Indulgence Series

Kaleb
Zane
Travis
Holidays with the Walker Brothers
Ethan
Braydon
Sawyer
Brendon

The Walkers of Coyote Ridge Series

Curtis
Jared
Hard to Hold
Hard to Handle
Beau

The Austin Arrows Series

Rush
Kaufman

The Club Destiny Series

Conviction
Temptation
Addicted
Seduction
Infatuation
Captivated
Devotion
Perception
Entrusted
Adored
Distraction

The Dead Heat Ranch Series

Boots Optional
Betting on Grace
Overnight Love
Jared

The Devil's Bend Series

Chasing Dreams
Vanishing Dreams

The Office Intrigue Series

Office Intrigue
Intrigued Out of the Office
Their Rebellious Submissive
Their Famous Dominant
Their Ruthless Sadist

The Pier 70 Series

Reckless
Fearless
Speechless
Harmless
Clueless

The Sniper 1 Security Series

Wait for Morning
Never Say Never
Tomorrow's Too Late

The Southern Boy Mafia Series

Beautifully Brutal
Without Regret
Beautifully Loyal
Without Restraint

Standalone Novels

Unhinged Trilogy
A Million Tiny Pieces
Inked on Paper
Bad Reputation
Bad Business

Naughty Holiday Editions

2015
2016

Made in the USA
Middletown, DE
27 September 2018